I'll Be Your Everything

J. J. Murray

KENSINGTON BOOKS
www.kensingtonbooks.com

KENSINGTON BOOKS are published by

Kensington Publishing Corp.
119 West 40th Street
New York, NY 10018

All Kensington titles, imprints, and distributed lines are available at special quantity discounts for bulk purchases for sales promotion, premiums, fund-raising, educational, or institutional use.

Special book excerpts or customized printings can also be created to fit specific needs. For details, write or phone the office of the Kensington Special Sales Manager: Attn. Special Sales Department. Kensington Publishing Corp., 119 West 40th Street, New York, NY 10018. Phone: 1-800-221-2647.

Kensington and the K logo Reg. U.S. Pat. & TM Off.

ISBN-13: 978-0-7582-5897-7
ISBN-10: 0-7582-5897-6

First Kensington Trade Paperback Printing: March 2012
10 9 8 7 6 5 4 3 2 1

Printed in the United States of America

For Amy

Chapter 1

An elderly white woman with a fancy camera around her neck waits alone at Tillary and Jay in downtown Brooklyn. I wish I had a digital zoom camera like that. At first, I think she's a lost bird feeder from one of the nearby parks because she wears a brown wool jacket, matching frumpy hat, and brown corduroys. But she's out here at 7:30 a.m. in this gross, misty, dirty, frigid weather that screams, "Brooklyn is too cold for people to function in November."

Tourists are getting as hardy as the trees in Whitman Park.

She steps in front of me and asks, "Will this bus take me to Times Square?"

I want to tell her that any bus will take you anywhere eventually, but she seems so needy. I squint through my misted glasses at the oversized blue sign. B51. I rode that bus once and hated it. A bus is no way to see the world unless you have a window seat and the person next to you isn't big-boned. I didn't have a window seat that day, decided to save my money and the hassle of feeling like a sardine, and haven't ridden a bus since.

"It might take you to Times Square eventually," I say to the tourist, wiping mist from my lenses and returning my glasses to my face. "But don't take my word for it. I don't ride the bus enough to know."

"You ride the subway instead?" she asks.

Also once. Not a good time. Though I'm five feet tall, slim, and can squeeze into just about any tight space, that trip on the subway gave me major claustrophobia. The fumes, men in suits oozing thick, cloying cologne, little bruises on my booty from slamming into the poles as more people crowded my little body, the intermittent darkness—not my idea of a good time. I kind of miss the booty bumps caused by some random briefcases held by some of the men supposedly reading the *Times*. I never knew briefcases could get so fresh.

"No, ma'am," I tell the tourist. "I walk."

She cocks her head to the side. Maybe she's hard of hearing. Either that or she has to move her head occasionally to focus a wandering eye. "You walk?"

"It's only a few miles."

To MultiCorp, America's number-one multicultural ad agency fifteen years running, and that's why I'm walking. I can *afford* to walk. I've been an administrative assistant at Multi-Corp for *five* years. I *know*. Five years is a long time to be kissing anyone's booty. I've had a couple of bumps in pay, and I even earned a bonus last year, an IKEA gift card that I redeemed for a storage combination with three bright pink buckets that hold whatever comes out of my pockets: keys, receipts, Post-its, and change. But mostly, I survive the daily grind. Walking keeps me in my $1,500-a-month apartment that has a "window office" (a cherry desk and my laptop), a narrow kitchen with a skinny oak table and two skinnier oak chairs, and a view of the Statue of Liberty if I put my face flush to the window and squint just right after the sun goes down.

"Well, thank you anyway," she says, stepping back.

"Anytime." I turn to leave then remember my Virginia-born manners. "Um, enjoy your visit to Brooklyn."

The woman leaps in front of me. "I'm in Brooklyn? I thought *this* was Manhattan." She points in a westerly direction. "Isn't that Central Park over there?"

Manhattan was my favorite Woody Allen movie. I can afford to *rent* that. I work in lower Manhattan, and I even like eating Manhattan clam chowder, but I could never afford to live in Manhattan or anywhere near the big ad agencies on Madison

Avenue like Young & Rubicam, Doyle Dane Bernbach, and Harrison Hersey and Boulder.

"No, ma'am. That's Whitman Park. This is, um . . ."

How do I make her feel better without confusing her and ruining her vacation? Wait. She's touring Brooklyn, which she has mistaken for Manhattan, in November. What kind of a vacation is that? At any rate, she seems lost enough as it is. Nothing I say is going to make her feel any better.

"This is Brooklyn *Heights*," I say. Sort of, but not really. It's complicated. You have to live here. "Tell the bus driver you want to go to Times Square, and he'll hook you up." Again, eventually. I don't tell her that she'll probably have to switch buses during the craziest time of the morning in Manhattan.

"I was so sure *that* was Central Park." She still points over toward Whitman Park. "It looked just like it does in the movies. I got some wonderful pictures that look *just* like they came from that *Law & Order* show. Is Manhattan far from here?"

There's a loaded question. I want to tell her that it takes forever to get to Manhattan and stick around. "It's only a few miles," I say. It's only a few miles as the crow flies, but there are few straight lines around here.

I check out her shoes. Comfortable black Brooks walkers. I love her corduroys. Her whole outfit is a statement. What that statement is, exactly, I don't know.

"We *could* walk together," I tell her. "It will only take half an hour or so, and it may even be faster than taking the bus."

She squints.

Ah.

The lack of trust inherent in out-of-town people whenever someone from Brooklyn stops to give them assistance. I was the same way when I first arrived and spoke good, southern English to people who sometimes spoke English. I now speak Brooklynese with a slight southern twang. I squinted a lot back then, too.

Hmm.

The Good Samaritan in the Bible just went on and did his thing. I should just grab her arm and get her some exercise. But

I had home training, and I don't twist anybody's arm—not even my own.

"I work on William Street in lower Manhattan." Seventeen floors up. "A few blocks from where they're building the Freedom Tower."

No bells. She blinks.

"Um, near where the World Trade Center used to be."

A bell. She nods.

"William Street is about . . ." Again, how do I make her feel better for mistaking Brooklyn for Manhattan? Can it be done? This situation is why people write online blogs. "It's about a cab ride from Times Square."

"That close?" she says.

Wow. And I thought I was naïve and spatially challenged. "Yes. That close."

"Well, I think I'll wait for this bus anyway. Thank you for your help." She steps back.

I continue walking.

At least she said thank you. So many people don't. Especially ignorant people, but ignorance is bliss, and she sure seemed quite happy to wait in her version of Manhattan on a rainy Friday morning in Brooklyn.

What people *don't* know about the world or where they're going keeps them happy.

Bliss is being lost in America.

I doubt anyone will ever quote me on that one.

Chapter 2

All this brings me to my job again. Why do I think so much about my job? Oh yeah. I have to pay $1,500 a month for a four-hundred-square-foot "space" in downtown Brooklyn in a skinny silver rectangle made of glass, metal, and concrete that rises fifty stories into the gloom. On a clear day, you can even see the ocean from the Beach, an outdoor space on the fifty-first floor. The Brooklyner—they brainstormed about half a second when they named the place—is kind of like a shiny graduation pen stuck into a big brown and black asphalt pencil holder. I still have my silver graduation pen from high school. It worked for about two years before the ink ran out seven years ago. Crazy, but I have a graduation pen on my desk at MultiCorp that reminds me that I'm twenty-seven. It does look good on my desk, though. It reminds me to stand tall and shine brightly every day.

Even if *I'm* out of ink.

All the leaves have given up and jumped to their collective deaths over at Whitman Park. I wish it wasn't raining. Those piles of leaves would be fun to kick around with old Walt Whitman himself. But I'm walking late because I helped Miss "Isn't This Manhattan?" take the bus she was going to take *anyway* before I tried to help her.

Some people just need full confirmation of their foolishness.

That quote is going up on my fridge.

What was I thinking about before? Oh yeah. Ignorance being bliss. What people don't know about the products they buy won't hurt them—until the recalls and the lawsuits, I suppose. That happens way too much these days. The only things recalled when I was a kid were cars and cribs, and now car companies are becoming extinct and cribs are houses and penthouses of the rich and infamous. I'm sure there's something ironic about that. "Cribs" cost more than cars these days—at least on MTV.

What a conflicted job I have. I help advertise products that people don't really need or want—at first. "We create the need and the want" is MultiCorp's grandiose and overexaggerated slogan. If we were doing ad campaigns for milk, flour, eggs, hand sanitizer, toilet paper, Vaseline Intensive Care Lotion, Blended Beauty Curly Frizz Pudding for my BB3 spiral curls, hiking boots, and used paperback books, I could see the point of advertising, but . . . no. Most of the products MultiCorp represents aren't necessary for anyone. No one *really* needs the products we promote, and in a way, all advertising does is confirm the American public's foolishness.

Maybe I'll put that quote up at work. I doubt anyone will notice.

All this foolishness does give me a job, though, and for that I'm thankful to almighty God, especially in this economy. Working at MultiCorp is like stepping onto the stage of a wonderfully absurd comedy most days. No. It's an absurd comedy *every* day because the ad account executives take everything so seriously. "We have to sell this overpriced, shoddily built, ozone-killing, ice cap-melting, and lawsuit-begging whatever-it-is if it's *the last thing we do!*"

I trip a lot at work. It seems we do "the last thing" daily while promoting the "next big thing" that, again, no one really needs.

I'm finally hiking up to the somewhat level part of the Brooklyn Bridge, about two miles to go. Whenever it snows, I try not to follow in the footsteps of others. A few years ago, sixteen inches of snow fell, and I was the first person on the bridge. I wonder if anyone followed in *my* footsteps. I wouldn't recommend it because I have small feet. During that snowstorm, the wind blew so much that I experienced complete whiteout for the first time in my life. It was as if I were floating in a sea of cotton.

It was kind of peaceful, actually.

Man, I am running a few minutes behind. I better start power walking.

Today the air smells like a cross between cat litter and cheap wine with a hint of seagull poo and a trace of old pennies. How many times has this bridge been bought and sold? I think this just about every time I walk across, and I still don't have an answer. Foot traffic is light at 8 a.m. today. It must be the rain. Thank God for Gore-Tex and my blue North Face waterproof jacket. I once used umbrellas on rainy and snowy days until I lost or forgot about five of those umbrellas at work when cloudy, wet mornings turned into clear, starry evenings. I wonder where lost umbrellas go. Not *inside* somewhere, obviously. I hope they're not out wandering aimlessly in the street. Maybe the black ones show up at movie funerals and the red ones show up on insurance ads.

But back to ignorance. If ignorance is bliss, does that make the opposite true, that knowledge is pain? It has to be. It has—

"Hey! Stay to the left!" I yell at the bicyclist who veers into and out of my "lane" and speeds past. The nerve! Man, that's got to be the same guy who has buzzed me a few times before. Jerk!

Nice booty, though.

Where was I? Oh. It has been a royal pain for me to take classes online to get my MBA through Long Island University *and* to hold a full-time job—and live in downtown Brooklyn. And to walk twice across the Brooklyn Bridge every day. And to take time out to help clueless tourists who think Whitman Park is Central Park because it looks *just* like it does in the movies. And in just three years—man, that's a long time—I'll have that MBA, and I'll use it to do *exactly* what I've been doing, probably. If MultiCorp wasn't paying for half of the tuition, I wouldn't be trying to get my MBA at all because there are so many people who have MBAs out there who are still looking for jobs. And even if I get the chance to interview for something better, I can hear the interviewer say, "And where did you get your MBA, Miss Nance?" Um, LIU. "Next!" No, I would beg, I was on the *Brooklyn* campus of LIU! That's the nicer campus!

Knowledge *is* pain.

I'm halfway across the bridge now, and I'm catching up to a bottleneck of people. Five years ago, there was only a smattering of people walking. Now, there are literal human traffic jams, because of the economy, I suspect. It's getting windy, not that I have much hair to muss or that I care if it gets mussed. I've gone completely natural since coming to Brooklyn, and my hair is finally growing out.

There's a whiff of the ocean in the air today. Might be the Long Island Sound. Or a fish market. Not much boat traffic today either. Where's the sun? Not that it matters to me. I'm shady enough as it is. I could just use a little golden sunlight today, you know? That would make me happy.

Now, what do *I* believe about happiness and bliss? I believe that bliss is an uncluttered heart and an open mind. So far I've maintained both. I'm kind of lonely about the heart part, though there is a guy down in Virginia named Bryan who has been after me since we were kids, but Bryan's there, I'm here, he's somewhat happy there, I'm somewhat happy here, case closed.

Until he comes to visit again. I used to like it when he came to visit. We're friends first and lovers every once in a blue moon, but his last few visits weren't much fun. We had spent the day at Coney Island, and there he was on his knees on the hardwood floor in my bedroom later that night. I thought he was going to propose and effectively ruin our friendship, so as soon as he said, "Shari Nance," I tackled him and started kissing on him. I didn't give him a chance to finish. That was the only time the neighbors complained about the noise. I may be small, but I can shout. Bryan might have been asking me to turn off the light or to help him find his shoes. He might have been asking me to fix him a sandwich, I don't know. But he was on his knees in my bedroom, you know? Not many men ask for a freaking sandwich when they're on their knees and vulnerable like that in a woman's bedroom.

That was three months ago. Since then Bryan has been pestering me in e-mails and during phone conversations to "come home where you belong." I blame my parents for that. They used to say that to me, too. And he keeps saying "home" as in, "Shari, it's time for you to come *home* before that place makes you crazy" and "The folks back *home* miss you so much" and "Girl, you need you some *home* cooking." *This* is my home now, I told him, and if you really want me, you will come to *my* new home. Home is where the heart is, right? So if Bryan's heart is with me, then he should come up here and stay here with me in my home.

I might have confused him with all that because he hung up on me.

And I wasn't mad.

At all.

I'll bet he felt me shrugging my shoulders all the way from Brooklyn.

He didn't call me for a week, and when he finally did call, he told me that he was planning to visit me for the Thanksgiving holiday. To do what? I asked. "To be with you, Share." He calls me "Share," as if we're still in middle school. Having a visitor would be nice to break the monotony that is my life, but the holidays are such a romantic time of year, and I'm worried he'll drop to his knees, say, "Shari Nance" again, and I'll be too far away from him to knock him down before he pops the question. Not that I would accept. It's just that I don't want to give him an answer that would ruin our friendship.

Always keep men ignorant of your intentions. It makes them crazy, and they pay so much more attention to you, as if they're trying to earn something.

Speaking of ignorance . . .

If ignorance is indeed bliss, then using my earlier definition, *ignorance* is an uncluttered heart and an open mind. That's kind of edgy. So that means the opposite of ignorance—knowledge— is a *cluttered* heart and a *closed* mind.

That is so true!

And *that's* the wench I work for.

Chapter 3

Corrine Ross, my boss, is knowledge personified, only her knowledge comes from management seminars, hardback books, Harvard, an upper-middle-class upbringing in New Haven, Connecticut, and other out-of-touch places. "It *should* work," she tells me whenever we're working on a new ad campaign. "I have a hunch, Shari dear."

Her hunches are butt ugly, gristly, snaggletoothed, and always dead wrong. I *gently* correct her with a well-placed newspaper story or magazine article placed *gently* on her desk, bring her *gently* back to reality with the rest of us in the real world, or I simply ask her straight up, "Have you thought about doing *this?*"

And then she un-gently uses my ideas as her own.

Oh sure, *we* get accounts, but only her bank account prospers. She gets the glory and the ridiculous five-figure yearly bonuses, and I get little shoulder squeezes and the phrase, "Go team!"

Life as I know it goes on slowly, like the drain in my tub that finally *glug-glugs* in about half an hour and ends with an audible burp and a sigh.

I am finally off the bridge. I can't wait till it ices up or snows so I can see if these new Chippewa boots can hack my morning commute. Look at that! I can see my breath. At least I keep my eyes up when I walk to work. The "movers and shakers" around me only look at their shoes. Wait a minute. They can't be movers and shakers if they're walking alongside me into lower Manhattan, lower Manhattan where people aren't Park Avenue old money and actually have to work for a living. While this city can be so cold and while faces of every slice of the American rainbow can often look icy, most folks I've met in this city are survivors like me with warm, multicolored hearts.

I stand in front of my building on William Street, looking up like a tourist. Man, this job sucks so hard. How hard? Imagine you've dropped your keys into the toilet. Okay, maybe not your keys. They'd fan out and get stuck in the hole, especially if you have a lot of keys. You'd probably flush a few times until the water was completely clear, and then you'd reach in and rescue them. Okay, imagine your cell phone or BlackBerry plummeting into the toilet as soon as you push or pull the lever. You want to reach into that nasty water immediately to rescue what is essentially your life, I mean, your cell phone, but you shake your head and watch as it gets sucked away in the swirl.

That's how bad this job sucks.

Dreams are only one flush away.

I may post that saying in the ladies' room where my boss spends an inordinate amount of time primping.

Hmm. I have to face it. I don't just hate my boss. I loathe her. I abhor her. I abominate her. I detest her.

One day, Corrine Ross, the honeymoon's over. *Pow.* Right in the kisser.

Just not today. Today is payday. I'd like to eat for the next two weeks. I'll have to play nice today, and since she's returning from a three-day business trip to LA, I'll have to play even nicer since I have a hunch it didn't go too well, and *my* hunches are usually right.

It's hard being nice when you're seventeen floors up and surrounded by food you have to *fetch* for your boss. Bennie's Thai Cafe is in smelling distance. Corrine usually has me get her dumplings stuffed with ground chicken and shrimp, bamboo shoots, dried mushrooms, and shallots. I get an egg roll because only chicken should be involved when it comes to dumplings. Corrine gets a burger and sweet potato fries at Zaitzeff, but I get nothing but a burger because sweet potatoes should become pies, not fries. I sometimes go to Les Halles to get Corrine eggs Benedict, which, in my humble opinion, is the luxury version of the Egg McMuffin. John Street Bar & Grill provides me with my quesadillas. I *must* have them. Corrine won't touch them because they're "too ethnic." Sometimes I go to Pound & Pence and splurge on their baked mozzarella and onion soup with these cool ale bread croutons on top. Yoro Restaurant on Fulton Street, though, is Corrine's brilliant idea of nutrition. It isn't mine. Fish should be breaded, cooked, and have bones you pick out with your teeth. Sushi and I do not mix. Corrine, however, loves Yoro's designer maki series, which includes avocado, shrimp, crab, and vegetables in sticky black rice. I don't call that lunch. I call that a night in the bathroom. The Libertine Restaurant is where Corrine takes us for caramel cheesecake whenever we've "sealed the deal." We haven't gone there lately. Hmm. She's on a cold streak as long as her extensions, mainly because I've been keeping my mouth shut and not giving her any ideas to steal lately.

All this food is within my grasp, and it's why I need those twice-daily power walks. The folks at MultiCorp eat a lot, at odd hours, late at night, all day, in fact. I know I would put away three thousand calories a day at least if I ate like some of them do. Instead, I sip my Honesty Tea from Soma by Nature, the nicest oasis in the building far away from the seventeenth floor, and I use no sugar or cream, just the straight stuff, because I am the antioxidant queen.

Because I'm running late, I step into the elevator instead of taking the stairs, all two hundred and thirty-eight of them. I have toned, tight calves, thighs, and booty from climbing and descending over one *million* steps in the last five years. This elevator is still stank. I look around at people trying not to touch each other but most likely secretly wanting to. I used to have a crush on a tall Hispanic guy who used the stairs a lot. I called him "Tool Hombre." He had this huge toolbox and hands as big as my head. I'd smile, and he'd grunt. I'd smile some more, and he'd grunt some more.

We were regular conversationalists.

I smile all the time on any elevator, and these real New Yorkers around me think I'm crazy. While they give careful nods at people they *think* they know or that they think know *them*, I just smile. No winking at any time, though. That could lead to a sexual harassment lawsuit in the wink of an eye these days. Hands at sides, feet together, eyes front—I'm a good little Multi-Corp soldier.

The elevator doors open and . . . "Welcome to MultiCorp."

I smile at our main receptionist, Tia Fernandez, sixty-five, widowed, fiercely Cuban, and who still salsa dances every Friday night at Cuba on Thompson Street. She thinks I'm a shorter version of Lauryn Hill, and I think she's a *younger* version of Eva Mendes. Other than me, she is the nicest person here, and like me, Tia trips every day here at MultiCorp.

"Hi, Tia," I say. "Don't you look sexy today."

Tia rolls her eyes and smiles. She has to be the prettiest woman I have ever known. I hope I look half as good as her when I'm her age. She has the smoothest brown skin, always smells of sage for some reason, and other than me, wears the loudest clothes, preferring bold oranges, vibrant yellows, and electric greens. Today, though, she's business casual with a pair of tan slacks, old-fashioned earth shoes, and an oversized white sweater.

"It is Friday, Shari," she says. "Payday."

I smile. "You're making me look bad with that outfit."

"I am not dancing later," she says, adding a few dance steps anyway. "But you will be dancing soon, because Miss Ross is back from Los Angeles."

My heart falls to my stomach and instantly biodegrades. "Miss Ross is here, as in here early?" I whisper.

Tia shakes her head. "She is due back from LA this morning." She points behind her at a master calendar the size of Wyoming. "Her plane should have already landed, but knowing Lady Di as we do, we should not expect her anytime soon."

I smile. Everyone in the office has a different nickname for Corrine. Some call her "Diana Ross." Others call her "Die,

Anna." The latest nickname floating around is "Corrine-cula" because one of her front teeth is kind of, well, pointier than the other. I secretly call her "Miss Cross" since I bear her all day and sometimes bear with her even on weekends.

I walk behind Tia's "edifice," which isn't a desk so much as a building partition the shape of a flying vee with a rolling chair behind it. I check Corrine's mail slot and find yet another catalog from Neiman Marcus.

Corrine and her Cinderella dresses. "It's a Tahari," she told me once about a brown outfit she modeled for me. As I nodded and showed my false approval by forming a little O with my mouth, I wondered why an old game-system maker would diversify into dresses. "You like my Kay Unger?" she asked one day. I'll bet it looked better on Kay. "Paisley is the new black," she once told me while wearing a jade-green dress. Why can't the new black *be* black? Before a date with her longtime boyfriend, Tom "Terrific" Sexton, an account executive at Harrison Hersey and Boulder, Corrine changed at work from a hoochie-kootchy Gucci to a Michael Kors sheath dress, which, I found out later, cost as much as my monthly rent. The rip up the side of that dress was, to be blunt, a rip-off. They must have used the fabric they cut out at the bottom to make the rest of the dress. And Corrine routinely drops five hundred bucks for scary-looking stilettos. I'd like to see her get those spiky heels stuck in a pile of pigeon poo on the Brooklyn Bridge.

I would pay to see that. I'd even film it and upload it to YouTube.

But back to MultiCorp. There are wide-open spaces on this floor and no cubicles anywhere. Only our founder and CEO, Mr. Dunn, has an actual office because "we are a family with no secrets." Thus, we have no privacy, and our phones don't buzz or ring and only light up. As a result, everyone whispers around here, and at first it drove me crazy. I'm used to it now. Except when people have gas. I will never get used to that.

Because of all the glass and lack of walls, I get decent views of Brooklyn and the Brooklyner, which is nice most days, but sad on cold, rainy days. It just shows me how far I have to go after I tidy up Corrine's career, I mean, accounts and affairs by, oh, seven o'clock. I haven't left at five since I started here five years ago. If I ever billed MultiCorp for all those extra hours, they'd owe me over $50,000.

Hmm. Why don't I bill them for those hours? Oh yeah. I'm on salary. Still . . .

MultiCorp is the largest minority-owned, full-service multicultural advertising agency on the planet. We do TV, web, print, radio, billboards, and whatever else you can advertise on, including T-shirts, kids' meal toys, mugs, pens, and boxer's backs. We reach out to the dispossessed, the tired, the hungry, and the poor. Okay, technically we reach out to clients who want to *take* money from African-American, Hispanic, and Asian American urban consumers.

Thus we try to convince Grandma Millie to shop for her eggs, bread, and butter at Kmart instead of Walmart. We want Hector and Juan to join the exciting U.S. Army instead of the boring U.S. Air Force. We urge the New Dons and OYG street gangs to buy their throwaway cell phones from AT&T Wireless instead of Verizon. We want America to shed tears and act indignant about our public service announcements concerning teen pregnancy and spouse abuse. Those are always so uplifting. We want people with no disposable incomes to frequent casinos as often as they can. The U.S. Census Bureau is one of our major clients, and it makes so much sense to use MultiCorp the more multicultural this country becomes.

We also represent Jamaica. No kidding. We represent an entire country. "Come to de islands, mon." That's about all we need to say because folks *go* to the islands. You really can't screw up advertising paradise. Okay, hurricanes sometimes turn Jamaica into a giant mass of windblown palm trees and knee-deep mud, but essentially, keeping the Jamaica account has been a no-brainer and therefore perfect for my boss.

Yeah, um, perfect. When Corrine and I first heard we'd be working on the Jamaica account, I said, "Come to de islands, mon." She didn't make the connection. I had to explain it to her *five* times. Corrine then told me it was a silly idea, that good advertising ideas take time to develop, and that no one would take "Come to de islands, mon" seriously. She said she would think of something "much more upscale and erudite," yet *my* slogan is out there on billboards, in magazines, on the radio, on every bus in the city, and all over the TV. The Jamaican man who did the TV ad and who has lived in New Jersey his entire life (so much for realism) has even been on a few talk shows. Naturally, Corrine took full credit for my idea and got the big bonus and the free vacation to Jamaica. Mr. Dunn has been calling her his "rising star" ever since.

I can't afford to go to Jamaica or to live too long in my disappointing past, so I go to my desk, which is within whispering distance of Corrine's "space," as she calls it. I have vowed to stop whispering because I'm making her too much money. Luckily, Corrine is gloriously late this morning because of her trip. I do a happy dance, my boots spraying water on the plastic carpet protector under my rolling chair. Now I can get so much more work done because the boss isn't around.

Somebody has to work around here.

Chapter 4

And having fulfilling work was one of the reasons I left Salem, Virginia, a little over five years ago.

I was just going through the motions after earning a business management degree from Old Dominion University in Norfolk. I was wasting my life working two jobs in nearby Roanoke, taking extra classes at Virginia Western Community College, and living in my parents' house—and paying *half* of the house note and utilities because I had two "good" jobs. Mama didn't work, and my daddy was cutting back on his hours at General Electric to concentrate on a frozen meat company that never panned out. I basically only slept in my parents' house, but I paid half the bills. I worked as a cashier/"go get it"/stocker at Lowe's Home Improvement from six until twelve, was off for afternoon classes in art history and communications at Virginia Western, and then rushed to Sir Speedy Printing to run copies and prints until midnight. Though I worked sixty hours a week, I had no benefits and no desire to become an assistant manager or manager-in-training at an overgrown hardware store or a glorified copy center.

I was nothing but a robot chasing paper.

In my spare time, I surfed the Internet for jobs, none of which I was qualified for, but it let me dream. When I read the job description for administrative assistant at MultiCorp, it sounded exciting and exotic, I felt qualified, and I jumped, immediately submitting an online résumé. Somebody must have liked my customer service and somewhat artlike background from that one art history class I took, because they asked me to come to New York and interview.

They hired me on the spot—sort of. "We need to give you a sort of tryout, see how you'll do under our demanding, fast-paced working conditions," they said. I asked, "For how long?" They shrugged. "Until we can hire you full-time."

MultiCorp dragged me four hundred miles north to become a glorified temp.

They put me up in the Murray Hill Inn on East Thirtieth Street in Midtown. I had a double bed but had to share a bathroom with another potential administrative assistant from Chicago, Sylvia something. She didn't survive the "tryout" because all she wanted to do was shop and go to shows. I had to walk three miles to and from work every day, me, the girl from Virginia, from Third Avenue to Lafayette Street to William Street.

I loved *every* minute of it.

And I even looked up at all the tall buildings like a tourist because the tallest building in Salem is the Roanoke College library, all *four* stories of it. I looked in every store window, hung out in Times Square, and just generally soaked up the neon and the noise.

At the time, MultiCorp was allegedly having "explosive growth" in its workforce. A lot of people had quit MultiCorp when many clients' advertising revenues fell 10 percent the year before. That's where the explosive growth was coming from. They were expecting "natural account growth," which at that time was as slow as watching moss form on a tree. They needed someone like me to be the right-hand gofer and general masochistic suck-up, as it turned out, to the most underhanded advertising account executive in the company.

They "matched me up" with Corrine, who had a reputation for putting her assistants into therapy, and that first day was rough. I couldn't do anything right. I answered the phone wrong. I dropped some of her calls. I directed some of her calls to the wrong people. I even brought her the wrong food order. I fought with Microsoft Excel all afternoon. However, I stayed not one but *fifty* steps ahead of Corrine the next day and for the rest of that week, kept *her* on track and in her "space" for more than a few hours at a time (she likes to takes long lunches), and was hired full-time only two weeks later.

I should have been more suspicious when they hired me so quickly. Piper, the personnel director, asked me "Are you sure?" at least a dozen times.

I should have gotten the hint.

My mama and daddy were not pleased, but they have never really ever understood me. I was their only child, their "baby," their "blessing from heaven." I believed that they wanted to keep me around for as long as they could so that they could continue to stunt my growth and I could keep paying on the house note. They tried to tag-team me by stressing "home" and "not your home," as in "*this* is your home" and "*that* is not your home." They loved Salem, where they had lived their entire lives. I don't fault them for that, but their minds were so closed because of it. I got tired of the same thing day after day, year after year: Olde Salem Days, Salem High School football, and dusty softball tournaments at the Moyer Sports Complex. I didn't want any of that. When I told them I had a full-time job with benefits in the greatest city in the world and an apartment of my very own in Brooklyn, they begged me to come home immediately. "You belong here, Shari," Mama said. "All your friends are here," Daddy said. "You know that sinful city will chew you up and spit you out," Mama said. "Don't you love us anymore?" Daddy asked. "Girl, I didn't raise you to live in no Brooklyn!" Mama shouted.

And yet Brooklyn suits me just fine.

Mama stopped calling me to come home three years ago.

Daddy hasn't called since last Christmas.

I was always a daddy's girl.

Do I miss them? Sure. Am I afraid to visit them? No. I just don't want all the drama they will throw at me. Do I appreciate them? *Oh yes*. They made me what I am today: strong, self-sufficient, determined, and spiritual. One day I hope they'll understand why I had to leave, but until then, I'm staying. The benefits far outweigh the costs.

And the benefits MultiCorp gives me are outstanding. I get medical benefits I rarely use since I'm so healthy. All that walking, you know. I use my dental benefits religiously to keep my pearly whites pearly. My vision benefits cover my glasses every two years. I don't wear granny glasses, though. Mine are kind of like librarian's reading glasses, and they're the same shade of brown as the color of my skin. MultiCorp even gives me life insurance (my beneficiaries are my parents), LTD ("Long-Term Disability," which I will earn after a few more years of this "Long-Term Depression"), three weeks of vacation or personal days (which I am accumulating instead of using), a *matching* 401k plan (which means I can never *ever* retire), and an IBP—an Itty Bitty Paycheck.

When Corrine isn't here, I usually float among the other account execs, but their assistants don't like me hanging around them at all. They think I'm trying to steal their bosses. I would never do that. Though I know that Corrine is the devil's stepsister, I would never leave her for another executive. Better the devil's stepsister you know, right? I've also heard rumors that the other administrative assistants don't want me to rub off on them. All of them have their MBAs already, and none of them want to *be* me after they work here for five years. Whatever.

So, what do I do all day when Corrine *is* here? First of all, I *own* Corrine's calendar. She can't fart, tinkle, or burp if it's not on the calendar. MS Outlook and I are one. I have trained Corrine to obey MS Outlook. Until lunchtime. I can't control her then because her stomach has a mind of its own. I also own Corrine's travel schedule. She travels nowhere without me, except that she, um, travels *everywhere* without me. What I mean to say is that Corrine could go nowhere without my expert planning and itineraries that are accurate to within five minutes. I order her plane tickets ("first-class window seats only, Shari dear") and book "four-star or better *or else*" hotels, but I don't have to set up rental cars anymore because she expects car services or limousines to drive her everywhere. I also do her expense reports, and I have to be more and more creative every time I do them. Corrine has never seen a spreadsheet or a purchase order, nor does she know what they are for. She buys things or spends the company's money in shady ways, I creatively write the POs and the spreadsheets, Ted in accounting rubber-stamps them with a wink, and the MultiCorp universe continues to spin wildly into debt, I mean, into space.

I read all her e-mails and answer most of them as quickly as she does. She types the letter *K* in reply to nearly all of them. That's it. Just *K*. And she's a Harvard graduate. I'm not allowed to read the e-mails from Tom "Terrific," her LTD (long, tall Dexter), who has yet to commit to her, and who happens to be (shock and awe!) white. And in the twenty-first century, no less. Corrine acts as if this is an earth-shattering thing. It isn't, especially in New York City. It wasn't even that earth-shattering in Virginia since Bryan is also white, though he sometimes tries to act black—and my daddy probably still doesn't like either version of Bryan. I know I didn't mention Bryan's color before. It's no big deal. I've been knowing Bryan since we were in middle school, and like I said, he's more of a friend than anything else.

But what irks me most about Corrine and Tom is what she once told me: "If I want to make it to the next level in my career, I *have* to have a white man on my arm. You need a white man on your arm, too, Shari."

She actually said that to me out loud and in complete sincerity. I didn't want to remind her that she worked for Mr. Dunn, a black Hispanic who started the company from scratch, nor did I share with her that my "one and only male friend"—wow, that is so depressing—is also white. I don't tell Corrine my business because, as the phrase "my business" implies, *my* business is *my* business.

Nevertheless, I do happy dances for Tom all the time, even though I've never met the man and there are, eerily, no pictures of Tom in Corrine's "space." You'd think she'd have at least one picture of him somewhere after five years of dating. Maybe she's afraid of what folks at MultiCorp might think, I don't know. But no pictures after five years of dating? That's odd. I hope

Tom never loses his mind and commits what has to be an unforgivable sin by marrying Corrine-cula. Unless, of course, he can tame her in some way. . . .

Nah. That only happens in the movies or in really old English plays.

Not everything I do is as glamorous as keeping Corrine's schedule. I also do freakishly long, dull, and boring spreadsheets. Excel and I do not get along. Too many columns. Too many straight lines. Too many freaking formulas, and I always forget to type the stupid equals sign at the top. I also get to deal with our current clients when Corrine would rather go out to eat or leave early for the day. Most of our clients are understanding and easy to pacify, but some days they light up my phones all day asking questions about future changes and tweaks that I don't have the answers for. I'm worried that some of our clients will eventually take their business to another agency, and I just know that Corrine will blame me. I'm the dog she kicks.

I also have to clean up her presentations so they sound intelligent, elegant, and feasible. Most of what she gives me is insane, cheesy, and impossible. Each time she gives me her version of a PowerPoint, I want to nod, make my little *O*, and let her go make a fool of herself in the conference room. She'd get laughed out of there for sure, because I am the PowerPoint Queen, and as long as she has had *my* script and graphics, she hasn't gone wrong.

But only if they don't ask her any questions about her (our) proposals and pitches. She's pretty evasive during Q&A and often calls me for help. One time she even texted me right from the meeting *while* she was being grilled by the client. I don't know why they don't let me sit behind her during those meetings. She'll sit on my knee, and I'll be her ventriloquist. That's what it all amounts to anyway.

In between photocopying, faxing, mailing, filing, getting her Toffee Nut Lattes, and, well, generally doing *her* job, I handle all incoming telephone calls. I'm supposed to screen out the unwanted and the desperate, and I usually do a pretty good job without ticking them off. "Hold all calls," Corrine sometimes says, "but put Philip Golden Fat Cow of Make Me Rich So I Can Afford Thousand-Dollar Shoes through right away"—and I do, eyes rolling. "Only the upty-ups," she tells me on other days, and only the *higher* (and I mean that word in all its negative definitions) MultiCorp executives get through to her. "Only Tom Terrific," she says, and, well, I sometimes whisper to him a long time before putting him through to her.

Tom and I have been talking to each other for five years, and I consider him to be a good friend. Tom has a very sexy voice and is so easy to talk to. He's kind of rough, not too refined, and I imagine he wears hiking boots while he travels. Tom travels a lot because he works for Harrison Hersey and Boulder, "the agency God Himself would use if the Almighty ever needed a bigger market share," Corrine once told me. Harrison Hersey and Boulder has offices in many of the places I've always wanted to visit: London, Hong Kong, Tokyo, Sao Paulo, and Paris.

Just last Monday Tom called the second I sat down at nine, and I never put him through to Corrine because he never asked to speak to her. She wasn't in the office, of course, but I might have whispered to him for a while anyway.

"Hi, Shari," he said.

"Hi, Tom. Where are you today?"

"Tokyo. It is an amazing city, Shari, especially when it's all lit up like it is now. It's a little too crowded for my tastes, but I bet you'd love it."

"Yeah," I said. "I'd love it because I'd be almost as tall as everyone else for a change. What account are you working on?"

"Panasonic. They have some fancy new digital zoom cameras. Very cutting edge stuff."

"Expensive?"

He laughed. "Yeah. I'd wait a few years for the price to drop if I were you. I could recommend a few cheaper brands that do much the same thing if you like. How's your weather?"

"Cloudy, crappy, and raw with a one hundred percent chance of gray," I said. "What time is it over there now?"

"Seven p.m. Just settling in for the night."

"So early?" Tom rarely stays out later than ten no matter where he is.

"I'm bushed. They work thirty-hour days over here."

"You work too hard, Tom." He does. He's rarely in New York.

"Hey, it's a living. Did you read any good books over the weekend?"

I laughed. "Is that all you think I do on my weekends, Tom?" It kind of, um, is.

"You read more than anyone I know, Shari. And your recommendations have always been accurate. You have another recommendation for me? I just finished *The Girl Who Played with Fire*, and I need another good read."

I recommended Alice Munro's *Too Much Happiness*, a wonderful collection of short stories.

"You can never have too much happiness," he said.

"As long as they don't start taxing it," I said. "When are you coming home?"

"Shari, I wish I could just stay home for a change," he said.

"But you love to travel."

"Yeah, but my next stop is Detroit, and that won't be any fun . . ."

I have *no* idea what Tom sees in Corrine, but like the rest of us, he has to see a lot of her whenever he does see her. She's just out there, as in busting out there. She never leaves her Upper West Side penthouse without a plunging neckline that shows off all her stretch marks, I mean, cleavage. She sometimes wears so-called custom-made skirts that I think belong to a woman swiveling down a pole. Corrine definitely has the legs for it. She wears so-called designer spiked heels that I think also belong to women swiveling down poles. She has long relaxed hair that, well, glistens so much I wish I could wear sunglasses. Think Black Beauty (the horse) at noon on a cloudless day a few feet from the *sun*. I didn't know black hair could blind someone, but it does. I sometimes have little spots floating in front of my eyes after one of our "storm sessions," as she calls them. "Tom just *loves* my hair this way," she says.

Tom must squint a lot. I'll bet Tom, who's thirty-four, looks older than he really is. Corrine can age a person a lot in just one day, and all she has to do is, well, do her hair.

Now here's the ultimate question: Why am I still here at MultiCorp if I loathe this job and my boss so much? It pays the bills. Period. I know, I don't have a whole lot of fulfillment here, but it does keep me under a roof, in clothes, and fairly well fed. If I get to the end of my month with enough money to splurge on a dozen glazed at Dunkin' Donuts, I *am* fulfilled.

I also stick around because I'm good at what I do. Yeah, it's infuriating to see someone else getting credit for my intelligent ideas, but at least my words are out there. I also have power, and I sometimes even let Corrine think that she has it. I get to walk eight miles a day in all sorts of weather, I get to take initiative daily and even hourly, and I get to keep trade secrets. I get to be creative. Remember "Buy this, by George"? That was me. Yeah, I let that one slip, too. Corrine sold the idea to Kmart. It's still cool to see that phrase out there harassing Kmart shoppers this holiday season.

Corrine is the most fickle boss I've ever had. She says she likes my "strong work ethic" (at least one of us works) and my "positive and productive attitude" (at least one of us is productive), but she usually finds something petty to put in my "Yipe," my YPE or Yearly Performance Evaluation. "Shari needs to brush up on her Spanish," she wrote four years ago. Corrine has never had a Spanish client and pronounces the *J* in frijoles. "Shari might advance with proper, intensive training," she wrote three years ago. The woman has barely trained me.

I take classes to help me with advertising and business lingo and practices, but I still use a commonsense approach to any product thrown our, I mean, *her* way. I simply ask myself, "Why would I *ever* buy this?" My mama used to say that to me whenever we'd shop. It works. The more you think that question, the less likely you're going to buy anything. In other words, I *think* for a while about any product we're trying to sell, and then I come up with possibilities. Corrine? She just spews the first thing that comes into her pointy, horse's hair head and expects this single thought to be the junk.

The dig she gave me last year on my YPE—"Shari must learn to dress more professionally"—is kind of true. I schlep around in my clothes. I've learned a lot of Brooklyn-ese in the last five years, and I certainly schlep around fashionably unfashionable every day. I have a decent body, somewhat ample cleavage for my size, and a definitely toned booty, but I like to hide it. I wear boots. Waterproof. Warm. Sensible. Rugged. Able to leap long puddles and potholes—or walk right into and out of them if I have to. I live in jeans, preferably faded and frayed, no designs, a little baggy, held up by braided rope or twisted leather belts. Flannel shirts and earth tone, oversized fisherman's sweaters hide me in warmth in the fall and winter, garishly bright and loose tank tops keep me cool in the spring and summer. I wear my waterproof North Face Windbreaker and long johns under my jeans on really cold days. I like wearing multicolored knit or wool caps and hats that match nothing I'm wearing. I even have multicolored mittens with little finger holes. I call my fashion style "Y'all Don't Pay Me Enough to Dress Professionally" chic.

And my whole ensemble doesn't cost as much as *one* pair of Corrine's shoes.

My phone lights up, and my caller ID tells me it's Ted from accounting, and he's one minute late. Ted is slipping. "Corrine Ross's office," I say. It is just so stupid to say "office" when there is no office! "This is Shari Nance. Hi, Ted."

"Shari, uh, is Corrine in yet?" Ted asks.

I look at Corrine's creepy space. She uses this huge, clear piece of Plexiglas to cover her mahogany desk while my standard-issue wood-grain and metal desk overflows with files. Most sane people put pictures or mementos under their Plexiglas. Corrine places nothing. The Plexiglas magnifies the wood nicely, though. Other than a port for her laptop, there's only a green banker's lamp and a phone on her desk—and not a single fingerprint.

It's nauseating.

"No, Ted, Corrine isn't here yet." I wave at Ted, who sits in his "office" forty feet away and with a direct view of Corrine's desk. "What's up, Ted?"

"Have you seen Miss Ross's expense account from last month?" he asks.

I wrote the stupid thing, Ted. "Yes."

"What does 'various and sundry client incentives' mean again?"

I made up that frivolous phrase five years ago, and now all the administrative assistants are using it. "Alcohol, Ted. Booze. Cigars. Gifts. Anything that makes it easier to sell the client."

"Oh right, right."

But Ted already knows that. Ted just likes to flirt with me. He could just take a few seconds to walk to my desk and say, "Hi," but Ted's super shy, and I know he doesn't like to talk to or even spend time with anyone face-to-face. Five years ago he asked me out to see *City Lights,* an old Charlie Chaplin silent film. What a date that would have been. Silent Ted, silent movie, silent me. I turned him down gently, but he still calls me every morning. It's not as creepy as it sounds. It kind of jump-starts my day, you know? I even rented *City Lights* once, and I cried at the end— not because I didn't go out on a date with Ted. That was *such* a romantic movie! The little blind flower girl regained her sight, and a grown man didn't speak for almost two hours!

It was beautiful.

"Um, Shari, are you doing anything interesting this weekend?" Ted asks.

Ted is white and divorced, chain-smokes seventeen floors down on William Street every three hours, and roots for the Mets. The Mets bobblehead doll on his desk is cuter than he is, though it has far fewer freckles than Ted does. He asks me the same thing just about every Friday. If he would just drop the word *interesting,* I might think he's trying to ask me out again. I'd turn him down gently again, I'd probably rent another silent movie again, and I'd probably cry again.

"Everything I do is interesting, Ted," I say. Not really. What exciting thing will I do (but not *really* do) this weekend to impress Ted? Last weekend I "attended" an all-day novel writing contest, and Ted was fascinated. Who would ever go to one of those? "I'm in a Skee Ball championship tournament this week-end," I tell him. I love that game. The Brooklyner actually has a Skee Ball machine in the Lounge, and while the other cool, hip, and generally drunk singles and couples play pool and snuggle up to an imminent hangover in the Lounge, I shake my booty and rack up the points.

To the excitement of no one, apparently, but me.

"Yeah?" Ted says. "A championship Skee Ball tournament? I didn't know they had those."

They don't, Ted. Only I have them. I am always the champ because I'm the only one who plays.

"So you're pretty good, huh?" he asks.

"Good" is such a relative term. I'm good at managing my boss. I'm good at flossing. I'm good at singing and praising at Brooklyn Tabernacle, my church. I'm good at walking. I'm good at cleaning my glasses with my sleeve. I'm good about paying my bills. I'm good at eating. I'm good at giving massages.

"I'm the reigning champ, Ted. No one has ever beaten my high score." Mainly because no one else ever plays. "Anything else you need to ask me, Ted?"

"Um, no. Bye, Shari."

"Bye, Ted."

I loosen my boots under my desk and attack Corrine's e-mails, most of them memos from the upty-ups. None are par-ticularly interesting or well written. They all want to know how it "went" out in LA. I'm sure it didn't "go," since Corrine de-cided to "go it alone" this time without one of our usually pro-ductive "storm sessions" because the client had an upscale and ridiculously unaffordable designer clothing label. "What could be more perfect for me?" she had asked.

I so much wanted to answer her. In my mind, I saw a blade from a guillotine dropping onto and through her neck. That would have been "more perfect" for her.

And yet . . . and yet . . . we work together.

I know, I know. It makes *no* sense.

We're kind of like Fluff and Mutt. She's *Ebony*, and I'm *Jet*. She's Toni Morrison (although I *do* love Toni's writing), and I'm graffiti on the wall. She's *Stormy Weather,* and I'm *Uptown Saturday Night.* She's haute couture, and I'm greasy spoon, pass the ketchup and the salt. She's Whitney Houston when she wasn't strung out, and I'm Tracy Chapman, only without the deep voice or the dreads. Corrine is steak tartare, and I'm "Burn me one!" She's—

Here.

Well, isn't this a fine how-do-you-do.

Chapter 5

A nd she's not happy.
   She must have sucked up in LA.

And how do I feel about this? Do I feel happy? Do I feel angry that she didn't consult me before going on this little jaunt all by herself? Do I want to say, "I told you so"? Yeah, I do. Will I?

No. It is payday, and I want to eat for the next two weeks.

I usually have something to hand her, some slips of paper or some Post-its that really mean nothing at all to her since she only flips through them once and throws most of them away. Memos. Phone numbers from clients who need a callback. Reminders for meetings and events. Today, I have nothing to hand her but the Neiman Marcus catalog and a compliment.

"You look no worse for wear, Miss Ross," I say. Okay, so it's not much of a compliment. *You* work tirelessly for the wench for five years with absolutely no recognition and see if you can come up with something better.

"We need to talk privately," Corrine whispers. She wears something neutral for a change, a crème pantsuit that still accents her cleavage, two evil prongs springing out at me from behind the silky fabric. Is it that cold in here? Back off, evil prongs!

"It didn't go so well, Miss Ross?" I whisper back, rolling my chair around to the right side of her desk. This is our "private space" where we're not supposed to be heard. She used to call me from all of six feet away to have these talks, but then she worried that our conversations were being monitored and her (my) ideas were being stolen by other account executives.

Corrine drapes her Fugli (or whatever) "throw scarf" over the back of her Corinthian leather chair and sits, her dark brown eyes drifting over to Brooklyn. "It didn't even begin, Shari dear," she says in her clipped Connecticut Yankee accent. "And I wore my Jason Wu."

I blink. I know no one by this name. He is not in my (our) files.

"The *green* dress, Shari. The one you said you liked."

Ah, the green one. Too high up on the thigh for Corrine. That dress makes her look like a Christmas tree with a brown face on top instead of a star.

"I walk in to talk to . . . what's his name."

"Carlo Pietro." I memorize all client names so Corrine doesn't have to. One day I will memorize the names of her dresses, too. Not.

"Yes, him," she says. "He was a dreadful, frightful man. He was also bald as an eagle."

I want to tell her that eagles aren't really bald, but why spoil her inaccurate metaphor? She went to Harvard, not me.

"That dreadful, frightful man smoked like a chimney the entire time I was there. I had to take my Fendi jumpsuit immediately for dry-cleaning. The silk was actually bruised."

The horror. The shame. The pain of it all.

"I pitched my ideas . . ." She sighs. "And he shrugged. The dreadful, frightful man actually had the nerve to shrug at me."

I almost shrug. It's a Brooklyn thing. "Fuggedaboutit," I want to say, but I don't. It's payday.

"What, um, what were your ideas, Miss Ross?" I ask, pinching my thigh out of her sight. I hate being so polite to her, and my thigh pays the price.

"I only had one excellent idea, Shari dear."

This should be good.

"A glamorous black woman sweeps into a room wearing a

whatever-his-name-is original. A handsome white man in a tux, tails, and white gloves takes her hand."

So far so stupid.

"He says, 'You look absolutely ravishing in that dress, my dear.' And she says, 'This old thing? I only put it on when I don't care how I look.'"

No. *This* is about as far as stupid goes. Only Mae West herself could have pulled that off, and while Corrine has the cleavage, she sure doesn't have the chutzpah.

"You understand my concept, don't you, Shari dear?"

No. I don't get stupid, and I am not and never will be your dear. "Um, you were going for a little . . ." If I say "humor" and I'm wrong, I'll regret it. "It's, um, it's edgy, Miss Ross." I like that word. "Edgy" is just vague enough to sound like a compliment, especially when it isn't.

"It was edgy, wasn't it? He just didn't comprehend it. I took him to the precipice, to the very edge, and he just shrugged and lit up another cigarette."

I respect Carlo Pietro. He didn't like stupid either. "Did you, um, did you have a backup plan, Miss Ross?"

She stares at me. "You agree that my concept was sound."

I agree that your concept was butt. "It has possibilities." I know how to suck up like the rest of the people here. "Possibilities" is another compliment that's not really a compliment at MultiCorp.

"I didn't think that I needed a backup plan, Shari dear. Brilliance is not always perfection. You know that. I've been telling you that for years."

And you've been *wrong* for years. "The principal mark of genius," so the saying goes, "is not perfection, but *originality*." I doubt Corrine has ever had an original thought that *I* didn't give to her.

"So there I was, stunned, staggered, and bewildered, as you might imagine," she says. "*Me,* and with how many active, thriving accounts?"

Us . . . with fifteen accounts. "Fifteen so far, Miss Ross." But no more if I don't help you anymore, wench.

"I was aghast, I was flabbergasted, and I was appalled."

And wearing Jason Wu, too. How *wounded* you must have felt.

She leans in. "Have any of the upty-ups called?"

I shake my head. Not yet. "No, Miss Ross."

"Mr. Dunn hasn't called today?"

Yesterday, yes. Today, no. "No, Miss Ross." I'll spring Mr. Dunn's earlier call on her in a minute. I just want to prove to her that I listen to everything she says.

She leans in closer, and I smell her perfume. It's something almost musky. "Well, if Mr. Dunn calls, I'm not here."

She talks to her boss less than the president talks to Congress. "Yes, Miss Ross. And if anyone else calls, I'll handle them."

She sits back, throwing one part of her mane to the side.

I see spots, lots of little white spots.

"He was a beastly, horrid, revolting, hairy man," she says. "And you know what?"

I know nothing. I just do most of the work here, and right now I can't see. Wave your hair somewhere else.

"He was wearing an Armani sports jacket with Lee jeans and one of those . . . those . . ." She points to her shoulders.

I see a blur of motion through the spots. "Wife-beaters?"

"Yes. A common T-shirt. And he was barefoot. He had these little wooly worms squirming out from under his frayed jeans."

I have to meet this guy. He's just the kind of fashion misfit the world needs.

She hands me an envelope. "Here are my receipts. Do your magic as you always do."

It's too thick for only three days of normal travel. I'll have to do a lot of magic.

"Did Tom Terrific call while I was away?" she asks.

This means that Tom, her alleged boyfriend, didn't call her for three whole days. But why would Tom call here this morning if he knew Corrine was in LA? "No, Miss Ross."

She shakes her mane, I mean, her head, little streaks shooting off her like lights beaming off a disco ball. I'm sure Ted and Tia are blind by now, too.

"We've, um, we've been missing each other lately, Tom and I," Corrine says. "He's such a workaholic that it's often so hard for us to keep in touch."

In touch? You're out of touch, wench. It's most likely Tom is sending you a message by *not* sending you *any* messages. The man obviously doesn't want to talk to you. He'd rather talk to me.

"I think he's supposed to be in Detroit this week or next," she says. "Can you imagine? Detroit, and this time of year. It must be awful for him."

Tom's a survivor. He'll be fine. I mean, Detroit is kind of like Brooklyn only farther west and hopefully with smarter tourists.

"Any other calls?" she asks.

I nod.

She looks around her spotless desk. "Where is the memo then?"

"I didn't write it down, Miss Ross." Mainly because of who the caller is. "Um, Mr. Dunn called *yesterday* and said to send you to his office as soon as you returned."

Corrine blinks her false eyelashes. They have to be false. She looks like one of the Marvelettes. "Shari, I distinctly asked you if Mr. Dunn called."

"Today. You asked if Mr. Dunn called *today*, and I said no, Miss Ross." I love messing with her like that.

She breathes heavily. "Well, when did Dunn call yesterday?"

"About two o'clock, which would have been eleven a.m. out in LA."

Corrine fans her face with both hands, a nervous habit that never fails to amuse me. One day I'm hoping that she'll actually achieve liftoff. "I had my meeting with . . . What's his name?"

"Carlo Pietro," I say.

"Yes, him, at ten. Do you think . . ."

"Carlo Pietro," I say again.

"Yes, him, do you think he called Mr. Dunn immediately after I left?"

After hearing your stupid idea, I would have called Mr. Dunn the *second* you left. "I don't know, Miss Ross." Of course he did. Duh. "Um, we're getting near the end of the year, you know. Bonuses. The year-end party. Parties are your forte, Miss Ross." I hate bucking up a crumbling diva, but whatyagonnado? It's payday.

Corrine smiles, her lips tight, her dimples visible, even her eyebrows blinding me. "You're probably right. I'll bet that's it."

Yeah, and there's this bridge I'd like to sell you in Brooklyn. It's on the other side of that window you keep staring through over there.

"But, Shari dear, what if it isn't?" she asks. "What if, heaven forbid, what if it's about LA?"

Then I might be working for someone else very soon. I'd even return any IKEA gift card they might give me this year. I wouldn't need *another* bonus if Corrine is gone. I do a happy dance in my mind. "But what if it *is* about the party, Miss Ross . . . or your bonus?" Always buck up snobs with bucks.

"The timing, Shari dear, is obvious."

Against my better judgment, I decide to do damage control. This is what she's been waiting for me to do anyway, and I do it well. "Well, if Mr. Dunn says something about your not getting this account, simply say something like . . ." Start up some Mamadou Diop music. "We Are the World" might also suffice. "The Carlo Pietro clothing line does not represent the aims or thrusts of MultiCorp's vision statement."

Corrine's eyes widen slightly. "Yes. Go on."

I know she'll make me type this up for her to memorize in a few moments, so I begin jotting down notes as I talk. "We are a multicultural ad agency specializing in Latina, African, and Asian demographics. As lucrative as this account might have been, it flies in the face of everything MultiCorp stands for." It ought to work. We, I mean, Corrine has brought in many millions to MultiCorp. Mr. Dunn wouldn't fire her because of her Mae West fiasco.

"Yes," she says. "Go on."

Shoot. I was done. "Um, do Latina, African, and Asian people really need to wear Carlo Pietro?" Or Jason Wu. Shoot,

Carlo Pietro wears Lee. I wear Levi's. I guess we all wear *some-body* daily.

"But weren't, um, doesn't . . ." Corrine's eyes glaze over.

"Carlo Pietro," I say. I will hear this name in my dreams tonight.

"Yes, but doesn't he produce his clothing primarily in African and Latin American countries?"

Oh yeah. There's that. "But Carlo Pietro's very workers cannot afford the clothes they make." It's time to wrap it up. "If we had gotten this account, we'd be sending the wrong message to the multicultural world." End music. Hit the lights. I'm done. Applause all around.

"Yes. Go on." Corrine's voice gets all dreamy sometimes, and it makes me want to earl all over her nice clean Plexiglas.

Cue music. Something with a marching band to speed this up. "What would it look like to, say, the typical Kmart shopper—"

"Buy George, by George," she interrupts.

She has to rub it in. "What would it look like if we simultaneously represented Kmart's George line *and* Carlo Pietro? We are not hypocrites here at MultiCorp, are we?" That ought to do it. Tell the band to go home.

Corrine smiles, her jagged tooth spiking her lower lip. "Type that up for me."

"I will." I push my chair away and stop. "Miss Ross, you *did* raise some objections about going to LA before you went, didn't you?"

Corrine looks away. Of course she didn't. She never misses a chance to travel and spend the company's money.

"Don't worry," I say. "I can send a memo that voices those concerns, and these concerns will arrive in Mr. Dunn's inbox a week ago."

Corrine stares at me.

I am chilled to the bone. Look away! Look away!

"You can do that, Shari?" she asks.

My boss is Harvard-educated and doesn't know how to type

up a memo, back date it, stuff it in an envelope, and hand it to Tia with a wink so she can suddenly "find it" and bring it to Mr. Dunn. "Yes, Miss Ross." I've done it plenty of times before, and all it takes is an extra order of quesadillas for Tia from John Street Bar & Grill.

She points at my notes. "Make a note of my objections in your notes."

Duly noted. "I will, Miss Ross."

Corrine rises. "I'm going to . . . lunch."

It's barely ten a.m., wench. "Should I reroute any calls to your cell?"

"Not today," she says. "*Only* transfer Tom's calls."

Gee, thanks. I'll have to lie like a dog to everyone all day. "I will, Miss Ross."

"Have that . . ." She points at my notes. "*That* ready for me by . . . two."

This means she's taking a four-hour lunch. Geez. I hate asking the next question. "Should I type up these notes on three-by-five cards as I've done before, Miss Ross?"

She picks up her "throw," shawl, blanket, whatever the heck that is. "Of course. Could you make the type bigger this time? I could barely read it the last time."

Of course. "And if Mr. Dunn should call, Miss Ross?"

Her voice catches, probably on that stupid Afghan-looking thing she's holding. "Tell him I'm on—" She stops. "Just . . . divert him as you usually do."

"I will." Flight delayed, traffic jam, or illness? Decisions, decisions.

Corrine flips the overgrown *carpet runner—that's* what it is—around her neck and shoulders, and the "tail" hangs almost to the ground.

I hope that carpet gets caught in the elevator door, and it goes up while she goes down.

"Um, I'll be gone until . . ." She checks her watch. "I may be back."

Do I remind her that I have to have this "cheat sheet" ready for her by two? No. It's best not to confuse her with her own words. "Yes, Miss Ross." And the world will go on without you whether you come back or not.

She leaves looking very much like an unraveling Egyptian mummy with long, black, sparkly hair, and I look at the clock on my computer. Gee. It's a few minutes past ten. What more could this day have in store for me?

At least I'll get paid today.

Chapter 6

My phone lights up. Ted again. "Yes, Ted?"
"Did Miss Cross just leave?"

I wave at Ted again. "Yes, Ted. But that was Miss *Ross*." And stop using *my* nickname for her. She's not your cross to bear.

"Did I call her Miss Cross? Oh, I did."

"Anything I can help you with, Ted?"

"Um, I'll need Miss Ross's most recent receipts."

I roll to my desk and pull Corrine's receipts from the envelope. Hair, nails done. I'll file this one under "business attire." Hey, she wears her nails and hair, right? A receipt for an Art Deco diamond snowflake brooch. Who wears brooches these days? And why a snowflake? I'll have to file this one under "business attire," too. *Eight* receipts for food and "various and sundry client incentives" at Grace, Koi, and The Ivy in LA, but she would only have had time to eat five meals. A receipt for a facial, too? More "business attire." She wears that face all right. A few extras on the Chateau Marmont bill, too. The honor bar tab is higher than usual. She called room service to get a bottle of 2007 Beringer Private Reserve Chardonnay? I file these under "meals." Oh my! Her hotel bill lists an "In-Room Movie" with no movie title listed. A little adult entertainment, Miss Ross? The things I know about my boss that I wish I didn't know. So this is how she deals with failure. She pampers herself, eats expensively, gets drunk, and watches soft porn. Gee, when I don't win the lottery, I deny myself some glazed donuts for a few days.

"Ted, I'll try to get these to you as soon as I can."

"Thanks, Shari."

I wave again. "Anytime, Ted."

My phone lights up again. Ah, there's my man.

"Hi, Tom."

"Hi, Shari."

We're way past "Mr. Sexton" and "Miss Nance" now. We are too cute. It is such a dreadful, frightful shame that Tom just missed Corrine. Transfer his call to her cell? Nah. I'll just have to talk to him for her. Again. Oh, the perils of this abysmal job.

"You're in Detroit, right?" I ask.

"Um, well, I'm on my way."

This is new. "You're calling me from the plane?"

"Something like that. I'm at JFK."

"So you're in the city," I say. This, too, is rare.

He sighs. "Yeah, but I'm only here long enough to get off one plane and get on another. I didn't even get a chance to go home for a change of clothes."

"Poor baby," I say.

"Thanks, Shari," he says. "You're the only one who seems to understand what it's like out here. I'm looking through their business plans right now." He sighs, and it's a sexy, breathy sigh. "These guys are living in a dream world, Shari. They want us to shine up their crap and pronounce it gold."

Tom is so colorful. And real. He doesn't sugarcoat anything. I bet his lips taste salty. Where'd that thought come from?

"But," he continues, "that's what we do at Harrison Hersey and Boulder. We shine up crap for a living."

"I hear you." And I shine despite the crap I take from Corrine.

"Their crash tests are first-rate for a change," he says, "but they keep making European knockoffs, you know? Yet they'll probably win some 'car of the year' awards."

From the American press. Never fails. I swear it's a conspiracy.

"They don't have a creative, innovative bone in their bodies," he says.

Unlike me. "Everything driving by looks the same out there when I'm walking to work."

"Yeah. Um, if you did ever buy a car, Shari, what would you buy?"

He is always asking for my opinions, and unlike Corrine, he's actually interested in hearing them. "I'm a country girl, Tom. I'd probably buy me a truck, a four-wheel drive with high ground clearance."

"Like a Jeep?"

"I would *love* to drive a Jeep." I would. Those are *bad*. "Wind in my hair, sunshine on my face, heading for the mountains every chance I could get."

"The mountains, huh?"

"I like to climb, Tom." And I'd really like to climb into, well, just about any situation with this man. Where are these thoughts coming from today?

"When would you head for the mountains?" he asks.

I look out on Brooklyn, so flat when you remove all the buildings, so urban, so unnatural from this or any distance. "Man, I would just . . . go."

"Just . . . go, huh?"

"Yep."

"That's good," he says. "I like that."

After ten seconds of silence, I say, "Tom?"

"Oh, I was just writing that down."

I smile. "Did I just help you out again?" I just give away ideas all day!

"You always do, Shari. Just . . . go. Simple. Direct. Powerful. Real." He laughs. "Shari, you're a genius."

The only compliments I get are from a man I've never met who works at a rival agency and supposedly sleeps with my boss. Life is a beautiful mess sometimes. "Just keeping it real, Tom. You'll send me my cut when Detroit eats up my idea, right?"

"How much do I owe you now?" he asks.

I don't want to put a price tag on our friendship. "Twice as much as you owed me before."

"I owe you so much," he says. "And I *will* repay you one day."

And for some strange reason, I believe him. "Just glad I could help."

"Corrine doesn't know what she has in you, Shari Nance."

I'm blushing hard now. He said my whole name.

"I, uh, I guess I should be talking to Corrine now," he says. "Um, is she there?"

That was a buzzkill. "Um, no. Do you have a message you would like me to convey to Miss Ross?" And now I'm acting professional all of a sudden.

"No, uh, it really just concerns Corrine. Something big."

And there's another buzzkill. "Big, huh?"

"Huge. Hey, how did LA go for her? I've heard some disturbing rumors."

And that's where I have to keep the wench's confidence. Ad people talk. Her Mae West mess will be watercooler talk by the end of the week as far north as Madison Avenue. "You'll have to call and ask her about that yourself, Tom. You know that." Though I doubt she'd ever tell him. There *is* a way I can tell him without telling him. "Should I have her call you *if* she returns to the office sometime this afternoon?"

"Ah." He laughs. "*If*. Hmm. I understand. Well. Um, no. That's not necessary, Shari. Oh, there's my flight. Thank you once again for an illuminating conversation."

See, I told you I could shine. "Stay warm out there, Tom."

"I'll try. You stay warm, too, Shari Nance. Bye."

I do a little happy dance and stop. I have to keep reminding myself that he's the wench's boyfriend. I wish to God that I knew why.

I turn to my computer to work on making Corrine's receipts acceptable to accounting, when the phone lights up again.

"Shari, Dunn. Where's Corrine?"

Since Mr. Dunn is the only person at MultiCorp with a door he can close, he couldn't have seen Corrine arrive or vanish. "She's, um, she's been delayed from JFK. Must be those extra security precautions again." How would I know? I've never even been to JFK.

"Peterson Bicycles," he barks. "Ever heard of them?"

That was abrupt. "No, sir." Why should I? I walk.

"High end bikes. Nearly fifty million in sales last year. I need her to get on it immediately. I need to get my star back into the game after what happened in LA. You did hear about that, right?"

I smile. "Oh, yes sir. She called me from the plane." Not.

"A new client is the best thing for her right now," he says. "And this time we're in competition for the first time ever with HHB."

Mr. Dunn never says "Harrison Hersey and Boulder." I guess he thinks saying "HHB" diminishes them somehow, as if that could ever happen.

"And who knows?" Mr. Dunn says. "She may be slugging it out with Tom Sexton."

Whoa. Is *that* why Tom called to talk to Corrine? Oh my goodness! He called to tell her that—

"Woody Peterson will be calling Corrine at eleven sharp, so if she's not here, you'll have to forward the call to her wherever she is. This is very important, Shari. Think you could do that for us?"

For *us*. Go team. "Yes, sir." I do it all the freaking time. "Um, Mr. Dunn, is there a chance I can get into the JAE"—Junior Account Executive—"program *before* I have my MBA?" I bug him about this every chance I get, which isn't that often. "I'm halfway through my MBA, and you know I have five years of on-the-job experience." I already know his answer. I just like to keep my name in Mr. Dunn's head.

"You work for a talented woman, Shari. Learn all you can from her, and once you have your MBA, we'll look into getting you your chance with JAE."

How nice for him to "look into" giving me a "chance." I wish I had proof in my own handwriting of the George or Jamaica accounts, and then maybe he'd take me more seriously. "You will keep me in mind, won't you, Mr. Dunn?"

"You're on the top of my list, Shari. The top of my list."

And then he hangs up. I shake my head. It's the same exact thing he said last year and the year before that. At least he's consistent.

I punch up Corrine's cell phone.

"I'm just sitting down to eat, Shari dear," she says. "What is *so* important that you have to interrupt my lunch?"

She's always a little testy when she's hungry. Why should I spoil her day with important news? It's not as if she will do anything about it immediately. She'll only set me to work on it, and I just want to have a quiet day that ends at five. "I'm just, um, checking in with you, Miss Ross. Where are you eating today?"

"Delmonico's."

Geez. Home of the ninety-dollar porterhouse steak. She must be *really* depressed. "Will you be back in the office, say, by eleven, Miss Ross?" Please say no! I need some more blissful silence.

"Shari dear, I already told you I wouldn't be in until two at the earliest. Besides, there is no chance of me getting back by eleven, not when you eat at Delmonico's."

As if I would ever know that. "So, you'll be back in the office around two then."

"Shari dear, I thought you knew me better than that after all these years. I am not returning to the office today. I am going straight home to sleep off my jet lag as I do after every long trip, and you will not disturb me in any way, shape, or form."

A whole blissful Friday afternoon without her. Yes! "Yes, Miss Ross." She won't be here, and Mr. Peterson is calling. She doesn't want me to disturb her. Hmm. Therefore, I'm in a familiar pickle. "So, I guess I'll see you Monday morning, Miss Ross."

"No," she says.

No?

"I am taking next week and Thanksgiving week off to spend some time with Tom scuba diving and snorkeling in Australia. We're going to the Great Barrier Reef."

Or is *this* why Tom was calling? He said it was huge. I guess the Great Barrier Reef is huge. But, eww. Scuba diving with my whale of a boss? She'll need extra weights to keep her cleavage from floating to the surface and being mistaken for buoys. But if Tom is working the Peterson thing, why would he be going to Australia? Maybe he isn't working that account. Harrison Hersey and Boulder wouldn't send Tom, a senior account executive, to win such a small account.

"I want you to start working on my year-end reports," Corrine says.

"Yes, Miss Ross." I'd love to work on those crappy—wait a minute. I'll have the rest of today *plus* two weeks without her? This is an early Christmas present. This might not be so bad.

"File the necessary vacation forms for me with personnel."

But something just isn't clicking. If Australia is the huge thing Tom is talking about and Tom is *possibly* competing for this account, they wouldn't be working together on the account on their vacation, would they? Maybe she already knows about the Peterson account. I'll have to test her. "Um, Miss Ross, will you be conducting any business on this trip?"

"Of course not, Shari. It's a vacation. I just *told* you to file vacation forms with personnel, didn't I? I wish you'd listen to me."

Oh yeah. If Corrine were working, she wouldn't want me to file those forms, and she'd charge MultiCorp for the entire trip. "And, um, Tom will be joining you, Miss Ross?"

"Yes," she whispers. More eww. She sounds like a snake. "But not for a few days. He promised to meet me there after he finishes in Detroit. He just called me a few minutes ago, and I can't wait to see him."

A few minutes ago? I just talked to him a few minutes ago. And he was supposed to be getting on his plane! Tom is really joining her after Detroit? Why? Oh yeah, something huge. Oh no! He isn't going to propose to her in Australia. I mean, after five years, I suppose they should make it legal. That's kind of romantic, but the Great Barrier Reef? Aren't there sharks there? I wonder if any of them are wench-eaters.

Always the good MultiCorp soldier, I have to ruin her vacation somehow. "Miss Ross, there's something really important that I need to tell you."

"Oh, can't it wait?" she says.

Not really. "You see, Miss Ross, there's a—"

"Shari dear, don't worry about a thing," she interrupts.

"But a client—"

"If any of our clients call," she interrupts again, "you take care of them as you always do. Unless there is an absolute crisis, do *not* call me, not when I'm with Tom Terrific."

Should I ask her to define the word *crisis?* No. A chipped nail or a hair out of place is a crisis to her.

"Don't even text or e-mail me, Shari. I do not wish to be disturbed while Tom and I reacquaint ourselves. I haven't seen him in so long that I've almost forgotten what he looks like! Oh, I must go. My lobster Newburg is here."

Click.

Hmm. I guess I won't be transferring Mr. Peterson's call to her anytime soon. Her lobster Newburg is *there.* Oh, we *must* eat the overgrown crustacean before it crawls back to Newburg.

Chapter 7

I take off my glasses and rub my eyes.

I am so tired of this!

All of it.

Corrine.

Covering Corrine's absences.

Making *her* shine.

Lying to clients all day.

Lying to Mr. Dunn.

Taking MBA classes one at a time.

Mr. Dunn and his condescending "maybe next year" tone.

The elusive JAE program.

What am I doing here? All I'm doing is chasing the freaking pavement, eight miles a day to and from anonymity, futility, and misery.

I look at the phone.

Mr. Peterson is going to call in twenty minutes, I can't transfer his call to Corrine, and I don't know . . . what . . . to . . . do.

Hmm.

Yeah. That's what I'll do.

I am going to take the call.

As Corrine Ross.

I did it once before when she was in "vanish mode." It wasn't hard at all to mimic her accent and use her high-end vocabulary. I know the lingo. That client never knew, and Corrine never suspected a thing.

Yes.

No one will be the wiser. Corrine is going out of the country and will be incommunicado. It shouldn't be too hard to field phone calls for her *as her* for two weeks. And when she gets back, we'll go to work as we normally do on the account, and she'll probably be just as ungrateful as always.

Grr.

I take a deep breath. I'll just have to look at this as practice. Yes. This is only practice. Mr. Dunn won't let me into the JAE program, but if I can pull off this account on my own—and make sure he knows about it this time with lots of written proof—I'll be the only person on that list when I finally get my MBA.

It's game time.

If I'm going to do this, I'm going to do it right. I log off MultiCorp's network and hit the Internet to research Peterson Bicycles, taking rapid notes. Geez, the prices for these bikes are outrageous. Two thousand bucks for the *standard* model. I like the idea of getting and staying fit, but I also like eating. They're called "the Rolls-Royce of bicycles"? That's so elitist and snobby. I'm surprised their sales are so steady. And they don't look that special. They look more like longer versions of BMX bikes.

My phone lights up again. Ted. Again. This is a record.

"About those receipts, Shari."

Shoot! "Just a sec, Ted."

God, I hate Excel. I quickly list Corrine's three extra meals as "client incentives," lump the facial, nails, hair, and brooch as "business attire," and call the bar tab and adult movie "meals and entertainment." I save it and send Ted a copy. "I'm sending the spreadsheet to you now, Ted."

"I'll, um, also need the actual receipts for our records."

I slide the receipts back into the envelope and walk all of forty feet to Ted's desk. Whoa. Ted has some new black hair plugs. They look so fake! The man has jet-black hair and orange freckles, and only a few weeks late for Halloween. I place the envelope on his desk. "Here they are, Ted."

"How'd you get so good at Skee Ball?"

I don't have time for this! "I practice every night, Ted. Bye."

Geez, it's 10:45. I only have fifteen minutes to prepare. Clients don't usually just drop out of the sky like this. There are rules to this sort of thing. Clients call in and ask for an appointment with Corrine, I crank up MS Outlook, and I "pencil" them in for whenever it's convenient for her. This . . . this is tantamount to treason!

I heard that line in a movie once, I forget which. It's a very cool line.

But I have so little written down. I mean, it's a nice bike, but would I ever buy one of these? I sigh. No.

Okay, think like an ordinary ad executive who isn't named Corrine Ross and has more than a dozen brain cells. Forget the product and how useless it is to you—just sell the stupid thing. Focus!

There are bike paths all over New York, mostly in the parks, one on the Brooklyn Bridge. A bike can be a commuter vehicle like those courier guys flying around. It's an eco-friendly commute. I could tie the bike into breast cancer—you can tie anything into breast cancer if you paint it pink. Pink bikes? That might work. It's a fashion statement. A bike saves gas, energy, the planet, the universe, the whales, and the Democratic Party. A bike helps prevent traffic jams. Riding is healthy for you, great for your booty, thighs, calves, and cardio. Oh sure, you'll arrive sweaty to work, but you'll probably beat the bus. Peterson Bicycles have all the accessories New Yorkers could ever want: outfits, gloves, briefcase carriers, lights, bells, horns, rearview mirrors, speedometers, turn signals, even a cool cell phone/MP3 holder. The helmets Peterson recommends are pretty bland. Maybe we can get them to market specific helmet models for the Knicks, Nets, Mets, Jets, Yankees, Giants, Islanders, and Rangers—

The phone lights up again! And it's not even Monday. Oh man, it's Bryan.

"I bought my plane ticket today, Share," he says. "I'll be arriving at five thirty next Friday night."

This is such a bad time for me. "Five thirty next Friday."

"You don't sound too excited about it."

Because I'm not. "Um, yeah, I'm excited, Bryan." But I'm more excited about this campaign. I think a moment. Hmm. This campaign isn't likely to kick off till the spring when the weather changes. That's when you ride bikes, right? I'll have time.

"I'm excited, too," Bryan says. "Anything I can bring?"

Oh no! What if the client wants a Christmas sales boost now? But Christmas ads started assaulting the airwaves after Labor Day two months ago. This client is way behind. "Uh, no, Bryan, just, um, just bring yourself. But I'll be really busy. I, *we* have a new project, and I'll, *we'll* be working on it. I might have to pull a few late nights here at the office."

"And I'll be waiting for you back at your place. I'll even cook for you."

That is never a good idea. The man burns water and thinks black toast tastes good if you scrape it off just right. "Um, how long are you planning to stay, Bryan?"

"Through Thanksgiving Day if that's all right."

I like the guy, and we usually have some fun, but that's . . . five days! I don't know if I can tolerate him for five days. And I have this *golden* opportunity now. "You won't be at your mama's for Thanksgiving dinner?"

"Oh right," he says. "I'll be leaving Thanksgiving morning so I can get back home in time."

Something about his mama's cranberry sauce, mashed potatoes, and dressing has always been more important than I am.

"And I was hoping you could come back with me, Share," he says. "You have that Thursday and Friday off, don't you?"

That's not going to happen. For one, I can't afford the plane ticket. Two, Daddy might open the door for me, but Mama wouldn't, all because I chose to live my dream in this "nasty city." And three, I get so few days off! I need that "me" time.

How do I calm him down? "We'll see, Bryan." It's how Mr. Dunn calmed me down, right? "We'll see."

"So I'll see you next Friday, Share. I can't wait. Later."

Oh, *can't* it wait?

I organize what few notes I have into some sort of plan that lacks a slogan. I jot one down: "For the urban commuter who's not a polluter." That would tick off everyone who drives, though. Um . . . songs! "You Spin Me Round"? No. Too monotonous. "Proud Mary" has something about wheels, but you don't go rollin' on the river on a bicycle. Didn't John Lennon have a song about spinning? "Ezekiel Saw the Wheel"? Geez, *I'm* spinning. I hum "The Wheels on the Bus" and envision a scene of a biker passing the bus, the bus not seeing him—ouch. I need something vibrant, um, something alive. "Live dangerously"? No. There aren't any air bags on those things. "Live by the seat of your pants." Yeah. Like I'm doing now. "Live . . . something something."

I check the clock. Eleven on the dot.

My phone lights up.

"Corrine Ross's office. This is Shari Nance. How may I help you?" That's *not* what I wanted to say! I am such a creature of habit.

"This is Woody Peterson. Miss Ross is expecting my call."

"One moment."

I take the deepest breath I've ever taken. Corrine said not to bug her, so it's her fault I have to do this. I exhale. Okay, Shari, you're ready for this. This moment has been five years in the making. This moment has been your whole life in the making. You can do this. And stop tripping. You've done this before, and you didn't get caught.

"Sorry to keep you waiting, Mr. Peterson," I say in a southern version of Corrine's voice. I can't help it! "This is Corrine Ross. How are you?"

"Did Mr. Dunn give you the skinny?" he asks.

I smile. Mr. Peterson is country. I can deal with a country man. This may just work out. "Yes sir."

"Did he tell you how soon we wanted this thing turned around?" he asks.

"No sir, but I am confident that we'll meet your deadline. Sometime in the spring perhaps?"

"Nope. The deadline's the day before Thanksgiving."

No . . . *freaking* . . . way! That's . . . twelve days from now! He has to be kidding! And if Corrine is going to be gone for two weeks—

"Miss Ross, I'd like to meet with you today at . . . what's the name of this place? Thank you, honey. That was my waitress. I'm at the Church & Dey restaurant, third floor of the Millennium Hilton."

He's not kidding. He wants to meet with Corrine Ross at the famous misspelled hotel across the street from the World Trade Center rebuild. That's just three blocks away from me! And he wants to meet with me today! No Friday should be this stressful.

"You know where it is, Miss Ross?" he asks.

My heart is threatening to leave my chest and bounce over to Ted and his bobblehead. "I'm only three blocks from you, Mr. Peterson." And my legs won't stop shaking. "When would you like to meet?"

"I'm already here," he says. "How soon can you get here?"

This is happening *way* too fast! He wants to meet with me now! "Um, I can meet with you in about fifteen minutes, Mr. Peterson. I have just one more task that requires my attention." And that task is screaming and then pulling myself together! "I'll be there directly."

"I'll be waiting. See you soon."

Click.

The receiver falls out of my hand, bounces on my desk, and rattles a little.

The whispers at MultiCorp stop.

I replace the receiver.

The whispers continue.

All is well in their self-satisfied, silent worlds, while my world has just gotten very interesting.

I can't do this. I just can't. It's payday. I want to get paid. I want to eat. I've never even thought of impersonating Corrine further than a few phone calls. What if I get caught? I could lose my job. I don't want to go back to Virginia a failure. I just . . . I have to let Corrine know what's going on. That's what I have to do. I have to keep being the good little MultiCorp soldier. I'll tell her that a client wishes to meet with her, and Corrine will leave Delmonico's and go to the meeting, and all will be blissfully crappy ever after.

I call Corrine's cell, and it doesn't even ring, sending me straight to her voice mail. I hang up before leaving a message. She told me not to call her unless there was a crisis. This . . . this is a crisis. This is important.

I call Delmonico's and have her paged. "She must have just left," they tell me. Heifer! She ate a lobster in less than half an hour? So that means . . . she's on her way home—or on her way to the airport. Is she leaving for Australia already? I'm sure she has to go home to change and pack fifty suitcases. I don't have time to check flights to the Great Barrier Reef. I wonder if her plane could land on the reef. Nah. Sharks would spit her up, and there would be a nasty international incident.

So if her phone's off and she's en route somewhere, and I'm the only one who can do this . . .

I have no choice, right? Corrine is obviously gone, not that she's ever truly here when she is here.

I *have* to be her now.

Eww. Rephrase.

I have to be her *position* now. I have to represent her *as* her.

I stand, willing my legs to stop shaking.

We can do this. Right foot, you lead, and the left one will follow.

I grab my jacket and put it on, looking out the window. Yo, Brooklyn, I'm about to do something as crazy as you are. What would Walt Whitman think? He said that freedom was to "walk free and own no superior." He also said that the "future is no more uncertain than the present." If Walt were still in Brooklyn today, he'd be asking, "So, whatchagonnado, Shari?"

I am oh so tired of sleepwalking through this job. I've already logged ten *thousand* miles walking to and from this place. I've taken enough steps. I've walked enough miles.

"Keep your face always toward the sunshine," Walt said, "and shadows will fall behind you."

Let's do this, and let the shadows fall where they may.

Chapter 8

I walk somewhat steadily to Tia, waiting till Candi, a new administrative assistant with big teeth, clogs, and a green denim dress, rushes away, clogs clomping on the carpet. And *that* already has her MBA.

"Corrine-cula is going on vacation," I whisper to Tia.

"Why are we whispering?" Tia whispers back. She nods her head at the scurrying MultiCorp robots. "We are not like them. We *talk* to each other."

"This time we're whispering, okay?"

She nods. "But this is cause for celebration. Lady Di is gone for a while."

"Tia, um, a client wants to meet with Corrine at the Millennium Hotel right now," I whisper, "and I can't get her on the phone. She expressly told me not to call her for *any* reason." Well, except for a crisis, but I'm handling it. "I, um, already answered the phone as her."

Tia's eyes bulge. "As her."

"Yes," I whisper. "I told you that I've done it before, but never like this."

"It sounds dangerous," she whispers.

"Yeah. I'm, um, I want this, Tia. I want to get this client all by myself to prove to the upty-ups that you don't need an MBA to do this job right."

Tia smiles. "And this is your chance."

"Yeah. They won't let me into the JAE program, and I'm ten

times more qualified than the Ivy League garbage they're bringing in. Can you help a sister out?"

She nods. "Miss *Ross,* we must do *something* about your
outfit for this important meeting." She pulls out a drawer and
holds up a handful of colorful scarves, putting several up to my
sweater. "What kind of man is the client?"

"He's country. He's from Georgia."

She looks at my boots. "The boots are okay then. Do you
plan on wearing that raincoat?"

"It's not a raincoat, Tia. It's a North Face jacket."

"It is a raincoat to me." She takes her coat from her chair.
"Use my jacket."

"Why?" That jacket is as old as I am.

"It has fur on it, and it will make you look older. And you
must switch shoes with me."

"I am not wearing your shoes." I'll wear the coat. I will not
wear another person's shoes. I pose. "How do I look?"

She sighs. "You look . . ."

"What?"

"Confused."

I try to smile. "It's my style, Tia." And yes, I am confused.
And hyperventilating.

She touches my arm. "You will be fine. You are my rock. You
have something worked out in your head to say to this client?"

"Sort of. It's probably just a meet and greet." I hope. "I'm
sure he just wants to measure me up, see if I can jump when he
says jump."

"And how do you feel, Miss Ross?" Tia asks.

I blow out a shaky breath. "Ready. Powerful." And scared to
death!

"I will pray for you," she says.

I give her a little hug. "Thank you, Tia."

As the sun sneaks through a few gray clouds, I sprint three
blocks down Fulton till I get to St. Paul's. I'm not Catholic, but
I cross myself just the same. I zip in through the Millennium's
front entrance, taking the elevator to the third floor and the
Church & Dey restaurant. Considering how I'm dressed, I'm re-

lieved that the restaurant is not that fancy. It's actually kind of ordinary, not intimidating at all. No good china, not too much silverware or too many glasses, lots of wood, paper not linen napkins. I look through the window at the World Trade Center site. We seem always to be rebuilding in this city, and now I'm rebuilding my life. I say a quick prayer—"Help me, Jesus!"—to the cross made of steel beams that survived 9-11. That cross is a survivor, too.

"I have a meeting with Mr. Peterson," I say to the hostess, and I get goose bumps. I have a *meeting*. Whoo.

The hostess takes me to Mr. Peterson's table, and I see kind of what I envisioned as I talked to him on the phone. He's a good ol' southern boy, about sixty, tall and wide and jowly. He has to be hating that light-blue pinstriped suit that billows out around him and that very seventies wide blue tie. I sneak a peek at his shoes and see cowboy boots.

I like this guy.

He stands and offers his hand. I've never done the shaking hands part before. Corrine just leaves her hand out there, expecting the client to take it, and they usually do because they probably want to see her breasts bounce.

I decide to shake his hand. I may be using her name, but I'm not her. "Mr. Peterson. It's a pleasure to meet you."

He sits, I sit across from him, and I continue shaking in my boots. "You're not what I expected, Miss Ross."

"Oh?"

He waves a knife with his right hand while holding a biscuit in his other. A rib-eye steak oozing blood and a baked potato oozing butter fill his plate. He's a meat-and-potatoes man. I can deal with that.

"Your getup," he says. "Not what I expected."

He has noticed my "new" outfit. I should have stuck to my North Face jacket. "It's, um, it's dress-down day. Friday, you know. We have a relaxed atmosphere at MultiCorp." I just wish that I could relax.

"Well, I hope I don't un-relax you," he says. "You know my bikes?"

I've only seen pictures. "Yes sir. The Rolls-Royce of bicycles."

He laughs. "That is a horrible slogan."

I don't disagree.

"I have a lot of iron and rubber to move quick, Miss Ross," he says while buttering his biscuit. "You up to it?"

"Yes sir. What's our time line?"

"I'll need the works out the day before Thanksgiving."

This just isn't done! The works! He's out of his mind! But I'm not going to tell him that. Why am I not breathing? Oh yeah. That will only give me twelve days, including weekends and Bryan, who is not going to be a happy camper, to *produce* all this. Dear Jesus, I know I'm wrong for impersonating Corrine, but could You maybe ease off a little? What Mr. Peterson's asking is, well, tantamount to treason!

"Will y'all have enough time?" he asks.

"More than enough time, Mr. Peterson," I say confidently while thinking *no freaking way!*

"I've also given Harrison Hersey and Boulder the go-ahead to see what they can come up with. Just met with Tom Sexton not ten minutes ago. You just missed him."

I blink. He just met with . . . Tom. How could I have just missed Tom when he's supposedly on a plane to Detroit? Or did I just pass him while I was coming here? Was he ever even going to get on a plane? He's obviously still in the city. What is he up to? I stealthily look around the restaurant just in case, which is stupid because I don't even know what Tom looks like!

"So it's kind of like a competition," Mr. Peterson says. "You like competition, Miss Ross?"

"Yes sir." Just not competitions with no chance of winning. Harrison Hersey and Boulder is Goliath and I'm David. And now that Tom is involved, geez, I'm compromised! He's my friend! Who *lied* to me today. What's up with that?

"I don't normally do business this way, you understand," he says, "but the missus thinks that with our retirements coming up, we need to protect ourselves, capitalize a little more on our investments before we hand over the company to our sons."

"I couldn't agree more, Mr. Peterson. It's always wise to keep your options open."

He takes a bite of his steak and chews for a moment. "I'm kind of taking bids for service," he says *while* he's chewing.

Corrine would have a cow and call Mr. Peterson "a dreadful, nasty man."

"I'm not afraid to spend money to make money, you know," Mr. Peterson continues, "but if MultiCorp can sell my bikes better than Harrison Hersey and Boulder and cheaper—and on time—why, I'll be very happy, you understand?"

"I understand completely." He wants bang for his buck.

A waitress comes over. "May I get you anything, ma'am?"

"No, thank you," I say. I couldn't eat a thing right now!

"It's on me, Miss Ross."

I shake my head. "I've already eaten." On a whim, I say, "So I'll be fussing with Tom Sexton." I can't believe I just said "fussing"! It has to be Mr. Peterson's accent. I always let my hair down in the presence of good, southern English.

"Where are you from?" he asks.

"Salem, Virginia." Oh shoot. If he checks up on Corrine's background, I'll be sunk!

"Thought I heard a little twang in your voice." He takes a sip of iced tea. "Yep, you'll be going up against Tom Sexton. Ever hear of him?"

I blink. "Um, yes sir." But Tom's supposed to be on a plane to Detroit and then he's supposed to get on another plane to Australia to go scuba diving with Corrine. Wait a minute. Tom was just here, maybe in this very chair, so he obviously has no intention of going to Detroit. Or he *is* going to Detroit only later today. What was he calling to tell Corrine? And why didn't he tell her about this?

"Miss Ross?"

Oh yeah. I have a meeting. I look up. "I know him well, Mr. Peterson." Okay, not as well as I'd like to know him. I mean, we've only been talking together on the phone for five years! "He's very good at what he does." And I sometimes unwittingly help him because I let my ideas just . . . go. And what about that? I just helped him with something he needed for Detroit, so maybe he doesn't have to go to Detroit? What is going on?

"They say he's a tough nut, a real sharpie," Mr. Peterson says. "I hope you're sharper than he is."

I just hope I don't run into him! "I won't let you down, Mr. Peterson. How should we proceed?"

"Well, I'll be back up here two days before Thanksgiving." He smiles. "Freda, that's my wife, she'll be accompanying me. She's always wanted to visit here. Never got around to taking her. And then, you and Mr. Sexton will put on a show for us. Mr. Sexton has already graciously offered one of the conference rooms at Harrison Hersey and Boulder for the meeting. Is that acceptable?"

That isn't fair! But you just can't shout something like "That isn't fair!" to a potential client. "I could also make the same offer, Mr. Peterson." Which isn't going to happen because I don't have that kind of power. Think! "Why don't we meet at a neutral location, a hotel conference room, perhaps . . . here." Corrine and I pitched Jamaica and Kmart, *my* two wins, right here at the Millennium! "I've used the presidential suite here at the Millennium before. It's on the fifty-fifth floor, and it has an amazing view of the city."

He narrows his eyes. "You know I'm staying here, right?"

"No, I didn't know that." Lucky guess?

He points at his steak with his fork. "This is the best rib eye I've had in years. My wife would like it here, too. Not too fancy. Great views, like you said. Sure. I'd agree to a meeting here. Why don't you set that up? I'll let Harrison Hersey and Boulder know."

Because I can't! Corrine had to set up the meetings we had here before. "Perhaps you could set up the meeting for us, Mr. Peterson."

He squints. "You want my business, right?"

Oops. What did I say? "Yes sir."

"And yet you want me to do a little legwork for you?"

Oh. That's what I said without saying it. Never put the client to work. Hmm. "Yes. If you set up the meeting, this will show both parties your impartiality before we go to war."

Mr. Peterson smiles, and it's a genuine smile. I haven't seen many of those around here lately. "I like your style, Miss Ross. But what if that other outfit doesn't like it?"

Then I've already won a small battle in the war, Mr. Peterson. "A neutral location evens the odds a little." I smile. "I, um, I don't wear a suit or drive an expensive car."

He laughs. "I see your point."

He's warming up to me. What does Corrine do next? Oh yeah. She travels. My legs start shaking again. I am about to go a lot further than I've ever gone before. "I will also be touring your plant in Georgia early next week. What day suits you?"

"You're coming down my way. What for?"

"I want to immerse myself in your product, Mr. Peterson." Wow. I've just used one of Corrine's standard lines. "If I'm going to sell it, I have to know it from the tires up to the handlebars. Would Monday be acceptable?"

He smiles. "Sure. Monday's just fine. In fact, I think Monday would be the best possible day for you to visit."

I stand. "I don't want to take up any more of your time, Mr. Peterson. I need to get further along on this project." Hey, my legs are sturdier than they were before. I'm doing this! "How can I reach you should I need to know more of the particulars?"

"You want me to remain impartial till the show?"

I nod.

"Then you're on your own, Miss Ross, from this point on."

Just where I like to be. "Will you be in Georgia on Monday?"

He nods.

"Perhaps we'll see each other there and I can meet your wife." I get another idea. "No offense, Mr. Peterson, but I could really use some home cookin'." Did I just drop a G? I did. My hair is falling *way* down. "I'll be looking you up for a recommendation."

"Fine, fine." He stands and offers his hand, and this time he shakes my hand.

"Let the competition begin, Mr. Peterson."

He lets go of my hand. "And what an interesting competition it will be, Miss Ross."

On my way back to MultiCorp, my sturdy legs turn into marmalade. What have I just gotten myself into? Not only have I successfully impersonated my boss, but I've also just invited myself to Georgia! I rest against the base of the Millennium, staring out at that cross. "Thank You, Jesus, for getting me through that, and if it's not too much trouble, keep Your eye on me for the next twelve days."

Okay. Breathe. My stomach is grumbling! I need quesadillas! Take stock, take stock. Corrine is out of the picture for two weeks. My heart is slowing already. Tom, who may be watching me right now, is my competition. Hmm. A worthy adversary. He has to be handsome. I look around and don't see any remotely handsome men. For all of Corrine's ways, she would not be seen with an ugly man of any race. And I'm going on a trip! My first! But *as* her! I really don't know enough about these bikes to sell them. The key to the whole campaign has to be down there. One day in Georgia, then eight days to get the presentation going.

Wait. Mr. Peterson wants the *finished* copy of everything to run the day before Thanksgiving! I don't have that kind of time! I don't have the technical support to produce all that and somehow keep it a secret from Mr. Dunn! Wow. Harrison Hersey and Boulder is going to kick my tail.

I look to my right and squint. Is that the woman whom I helped without helping this morning? What are the chances? I approach her. "Hi again."

She turns and smiles. "Hello there. I made it to Manhattan."

"Yes, you have." I wish I had her camera for what I have to do. I wonder if I can borrow one from production. No, because then they'd ask why, I'd say "never mind," they'd start some rumor or other, the whispers would travel to Mr. Dunn . . .

"You've changed clothes," she says.

I look at my furry coat. "Yes. I had lunch with a client." Sort of. He ate, I watched. Such a . . . homespun guy. I have to run a homespun campaign. What could be more American than the pulled-up-by-his-own-bootstraps story? Mr. Peterson has made the best bicycle money can buy, the highest quality, American-made, good for you, good for the environment . . . too expensive for normal people to actually own.

"May I take your picture?" she asks.

I blink. "You want to take a picture of me?"

"Yes. With that cross in the background."

Oh, the ironies here. Well, Miss Cross *is* in the background now. I pose. "How's this?"

She takes the picture. "Marvelous. What's your name?"

I am not nor will ever be Corrine Ross. "Shari with an I, Nance no Y."

She actually writes it down! "Thank you."

"Enjoy your visit to Manhattan," I say.

"I will," she says. "You, too."

I don't exactly know how to take that. I hope I've made it.

And even if it's just a short visit, at least I hope I make it in Manhattan for a few days.

Chapter 9

"How did it go?" Tia asks as we exchange jackets.

"It went," I whisper. "I have twelve days to get a fully produced ad campaign going and *without* a production team for some high-end bicycles that I would never buy."

Tia clasps her hands together. "This is so exciting!"

I blink. "Did you hear what I said? Fully produced, as in ready for air, ready for print." Geez, all this is going to be too late to get into any December magazines. Blow-ins to newspapers are an option, but most people throw them away because they're so annoying. The Internet! Geez, I almost forgot the Internet! I am severely losing it.

"If there is anyone I know on God's good earth that can do it, it is you." She places me in her comfortable chair. "Shari, you must relax."

Relax. Right. "I may need your help. I mean, what if Mr. Peterson calls? I can't keep answering my own phone twice, right?"

"I have you covered. I will route all your calls through me. I will be you, you will be her, and Corrine will be gone."

I almost laugh. "I may not be in the office as much."

Tia nods. "Just like *her*."

"And, Tia," I whisper, "I need to go to Georgia on Monday, and I have to make them think Corrine is going. Can it be done?"

She exhales. "Putting Corrine in two places at the same time is kind of tricky. She is barely in one place at any time. I know, we can make her sick for a day. I would really like to do that. I would like to make her vomit all over one of her fancy dresses. Make your reservations, Shari. I will just delay Miss Ross's vacation for a day."

Will one day be enough? I have to fly out, tour the plant, and fly back, and I will be stressing the entire time. "Um, I'll need two days." Corrine would take *three*.

"She will be sick for two days then." She winks. "No problem. Now, shoo! Go. Win this account."

Back at my desk, I start to stress, and when I stress, I make notes. I write "What could go wrong" on the top of a page.

(1) Get fired or lose my job (or get prosecuted!) for impersonating my boss, misusing MultiCorp funds, and lying to a client

That's a stopper. Not much more needs to be written than that. My career could end in less than two weeks, and I could be back in Virginia—or in prison?—with my tail between my legs. It has its allure, but . . .

No. I can't let that happen. Okay, let's get practical.

(2) Can't meet deadline

Oh, I'll meet that deadline if it's the last thing I do. And it *might* be the last thing I do here. How am I going to produce all this? Geez! I mean, I know people in production, but I don't really know them well enough to get them to hook me up. And mainly, they don't know *me*. All those geeks ever did was stare at Corrine's cleavage, and they bent over backward for her. I don't have her cleavage. The fewer people who know about this, the better anyway. So who can I use who will keep it all on the down low? I may have to hire someone using my own money, and with the amount I have in savings, I'd have to hire someone as desperate as I am.

(3) Can't create decent ads

Corrine just runs my PowerPoint presentations with a script, and the production staff, which understands art, film, and print, does the rest. They're the real geniuses and geeks who really do all the work. We're just the idea people. A single PowerPoint won't cut it this time, especially if Mr. Peterson wants the campaign going national the very next day. I need to design billboards, magazine ads, T-shirts, and web banners, and I also need to produce radio and TV commercials of fifteen and thirty seconds. I know nothing about editing, and I can't draw a lick.

I can doodle. Hmm. A doodled commercial? How hard can it be to doodle a bike? I could doodle a cartoon. But then it wouldn't show the actual product.

I have to get one of those bikes. Mr. Peterson might let me borrow one. I'd have to have it shipped up here on Monday, or maybe I could fly one back with me. If I had a camera, I could film while riding to work. That's what I can do. I can tape a camera to a bike helmet or attach it in some way to the handlebars. I'll have to take a day off and ride around. That would require a lot of editing, and once again, I don't have any way of doing that.

I shake it off. I'll just cross that bridge when I come to it.

I get out a calculator. If I go, say, fifteen miles per hour across the Brooklyn Bridge and it's about six thousand feet across—I'll never make it all the way across in time. I hit a few more buttons. At fifteen miles per hour, I can only go three hundred and thirty feet in fifteen seconds, six hundred and sixty feet in thirty seconds. That might be enough time to capture the Manhattan skyline ahead and to the left of me. But where can you go three hundred and thirty feet on a bicycle in New York City in fifteen seconds and not get hit by a bus or a taxi? I'll . . . I'll figure something out.

Geez. I have to figure *something* out.

(4) Can't think of memorable slogans or taglines

I have never had trouble being creative in the past. Those "hooks" just came to me. But when I think about this expensive bike . . . nothing. Nada. Zip.

Use what you've learned from your classes, Shari. Personalize this product. What do you know firsthand about bicycles? Well, I rode a bike back in Salem when I was a kid. It was red and had plastic red and white ribbons dangling from the handgrips, reflectors everywhere, a little "Sherry" license plate (Mama couldn't find a "Shari"), and knobby tires. I felt free on that bike. Freedom. That might be a good theme. No. I can't say "feel free again" while riding a bike that costs two thousand bucks. "Free your mind"? No, that sounds like an ad for anti-depression medication. "Land of the free"? Ain't nothin' free in this country anymore.

Okay, relax. Get on the bike. You're riding to work. You're flying by pedestrians, zipping around taxis and buses, and getting to work on time. Then you have to find a place for it, maybe chain it somewhere to a lamppost or a bike rack. I can't remember the last time I even saw a bike rack. Hmm. Or you carry the entire bike into your office. Riding the elevator while holding a bike? That would annoy people in the elevator, maybe mud, slush, or pigeon poo on the tires. Your bike will stink up the office.

Such nice images.

Hey—"Get to work on time for a change" might work. No. This is where I'd put newspaper clippings of local "bike versus vehicle" accidents onto Corrine's desk. I'll think of something. It will come to me.

Random thought: a bumper sticker that reads, "My other vehicle is a Peterson bike"?

Too random. And too snobby.

All I have to do is whisper something to *myself* this time.

(5) In over my head, competition too stiff, out of my league with Harrison Hersey and Boulder and Tom Terrific

Tom and his team will be slick. Perfect, probably. But brilliance isn't always perfection, or so Corrine tells me. I'll just have to be more creative than they are. Maybe they'll miss the boat entirely. Maybe they'll go snooty when Mr. Peterson wants homespun. Maybe they'll hype the environmental end too much. Mr. Peterson is a businessman, old school. He wants to make money. He seems old-fashioned, conservative, full of American values, and he might even be a Republican. I'll have to research him along with his company. Maybe his company is an extension of his personality.

I look around and see administrative assistants scurrying, account execs worrying, no one talking above a whisper, some even doing long-distance sign language to each other. Mr. Dunn is most likely locked in his office. Ted is glued to his computer monitor.

I am effectively alone as usual.

It's time to do some heavy-duty research.

According to the Peterson Bicycles website, Mr. Peterson made his first bike frame in his garage when he was nineteen. I could say he's "the Bill Gates of bicycles." No, that would tick off Apple users, and after Microsoft's last lame operating system, it might tick off PC users as well. Mr. Peterson raced his own homemade bike at the University of Georgia during his freshman year and scorched the brand bikes: Murray, Schwinn, Huffy, and Ross. He dropped out of college after his sophomore year, developed some family land north of Macon, and built his first plant, which looks like a long, low barn. Over the years, it has expanded quite a bit. The first production models rolled off the line in 1969. Sales are impressively steady, only a minor dip in 1980 for some reason. What happened in 1980? I run a search. Hmm. I guess I can blame Reagan, "Just Say No," jelly shoes, mullets, "Word," breakdancing, and spandex. Their mountain bikes sell well, and Mr. Peterson even has a few "name" riders use his bikes for BMX races, triathlons, and long-distance races. He sponsors twelve road races around the country every year. That has to eat into his profits, but I'm not here to judge how a multimillionaire spends his money. I'll bet he gets plenty of orders when his riders win those races. Hey now. He has a contract with the U.S. Olympic cycling team through 2016 and is bidding for an extension. "Peterson Bicycles: Bring home the gold."

No. I know I'm biting off somebody. Relax. It'll come to you, Shari.

I finally find out why these bikes are so expensive. Every single nut, bolt, wire, spoke, rim, seat, accessory, and brake assembly is made down in Georgia at his plant. Only the tires come from elsewhere. Mr. Peterson is such a throwback. He doesn't even order accessories from other suppliers to ease his workload. He cuts out the middle man—like I'm cutting out Corrine—and he profits nicely.

I hope I do, too.

I run a quick check for bicycle recalls. Wow. I didn't think there would be so many. Bad frames, forks, handlebar stems, brakes, U-joints, and seat posts. But not a single recall for Peterson Bicycles for the last twenty years. None. Okay, that's a major selling point. These things are built like tanks. They last. They survive. "Peterson Bicycles: built for the *next* millennium."

No. That's too much of an exaggeration.

I click on a button marked "quality control." According to the website, Peterson Bicycles are tested more than any other bicycle on the planet, and they even do crash tests. Crash tests for bikes? With or without riders? I watch little videos starring Mr. Peterson, who wears coveralls, an orange vest, hard hat, goggles, and boots. I knew he hated wearing that suit. Then I watch bike after bike running into walls, poles, and trees at various speeds. The tires pop occasionally, but the frames and wheels stay intact. I also see some frightening videos of cars crashing into the bikes, and the bike frames survive these often-explosive collisions. "Space-age technology" is a phrase they use often on this site. That's a little dated—and strange. You don't ride a bike in space.

I write down several other ideas:

Peterson Bicycles: They take a poling and keep on rolling.
Peterson Bicycles: They take a drilling and keep on thrilling.
Peterson Bicycles: They take a crashing and keep on dashing.
Peterson Bicycles: They take a beating and keep on speeding.

Okay, they all suck and bite off the old Timex ads, but at least my mind is warming up. I must be at "lukewarm."

Peterson Bicycles utilize the same brake pads used on the bikes that race down Haleakala, a 10,000-foot volcano in Maui. Geez, these brakes go for fifty bucks a pair, a hundred bucks a bike. That's more than I paid for the last brake job on my Mazda ten years ago.

This is serious stuff here. I thought bikes were supposed to be for fun, discovery, and expanding a kid's boundaries. There is nothing kidlike about these bikes. There's more second-childhood stuff here than first childhood. They're so expensive that a buyer probably needs to get bike insurance. Is there such a thing? Would I *ever* buy one of these bicycles?

Well . . . no.

I look outside. It's dark already? Where is everyone? Even Tia has left, and without even waving at me. Geez, I'm hungry. I forgot to eat lunch. I better get going.

I collect my stack of notes and wish I had a briefcase. I go behind Tia's space and look at the cardboard box that serves as MultiCorp's lost and found. Would you look at all those umbrellas? Half of them are mine. I pick up a fairly clean, white L.L.Bean tote bag and drop in my notes. It'll have to do.

On my walk back to Brooklyn, I feel different. I can't explain it. I stayed late and actually wanted to stay late. I also did something meaningful for a change. I feel like a real person, like someone who actually *does* something for a living. People ask me, "What do you do?" I usually say, "I'm an administrative assistant at MultiCorp." But that's not what I *do*. If someone asked me *now* what I do, I'd tell them: "I develop advertising campaigns."

And that makes me feel taller.

Halfway across the Brooklyn Bridge, I look back at lower

Manhattan, at all those lights, at all those American dreams. And then I look up at a few stars escaping the clouds. I don't make many wishes, but, I just wish, hope, and pray that this works out.

And then I kick myself for not getting quesadillas before I got halfway home!

And all I have handy in the house are . . . Hot Pockets.

Yum.

I can't wait.

Chapter 10

After booking a flight to Macon, I spend most of Saturday sitting at my window desk researching bikes on my laptop. Normally I'd curl up on the couch with a few good books. Today, though, I'm different.

I'm on the job.

I look at how other bikes are marketed and how other bikes compare to Peterson bikes, and most don't do very well head-to-head. Peterson bikes consistently make all the "best" lists, and even ratings at Amazon.com, where buyers are often critical of a product because *Amazon* screwed up the delivery, are four and a half stars or higher for every Peterson bicycle, even some ten and twenty years old. And some of the prices of used Peterson bikes are *higher* than the new ones! "Most Peterson bikes," *Consumer Reports* says, "are still on the road fifteen to twenty years after purchase."

Mr. Peterson needs to go to Detroit to show the automakers how it's done.

It takes me quite a bit of digging to find more information about Mr. Peterson, because unlike other millionaire entrepreneurs, he's a very private man. I had to read through clips I found online in the *Macon Telegraph,* the *Georgia Informer,* and the *Macon Daily.* All I can say is that Mr. Peterson is the proverbial salt of the earth, or as we say in Virginia, "He's good people." He has three kids, who all have his chin, and eight grandkids, who *also* have his chin. Member of the Chamber of

Commerce, Kiwanis Club, the Rotary Club. Member of Highland Hills Baptist Church for forty-five years. His residence, a modest two-story with a wraparound porch, adjoins the plant property. The man lives where he works and works where he lives. He hunts, fishes, rarely takes vacations, and gives away hundreds of kids' bikes every year.

The man is a saint.

On a whim, I navigate the Harrison Hersey and Boulder site looking for any pictures of Tom Sexton. I have, um, been looking for these pictures for about four—no, five—years and have come up completely empty. Yeah, Tom has had a listing, a simple bio ("Mr. Sexton has been with Harrison Hersey and Boulder for twelve years"), but there hasn't been a—

Is that him?

I do a happy dance in my bare feet.

I even fog up my glasses a little.

This man is *hot*. And it's only a head shot. He has thick, wavy dirty-blond hair that brushes his medium-sized ears, devastating dark brown eyes below dirty-blond eyebrows, an aquiline nose, a strong jaw, nice lips, tan skin, and a laughing smile. He had to be laughing when they took that picture because that smile seems to say, "I can do anything I want. Ha! Whatchagonnado about it?"

He has told me he's tall. I wonder what the rest of him looks like.

I type "Tom Sexton" in Google pictures and find the *same* freaking head shot. Shoot. I wish I could see more of him. All I know is that he's terrific. Maybe I could find his high school or his college picture. I check Reunion.com, MySpace, Facebook, and LinkedIn. Nothing. Why doesn't Tom network? I'll bet he doesn't have to. All he has to say is, "Hi, I'm Tom Sexton from Harrison Hersey and Boulder." Yep. That's enough information to give out to impress and network with anyone.

I return to the Harrison Hersey and Boulder site and search for any kind of account information. All Harrison Hersey and Boulder does is list their major clients, and there's a freaking long list. Since each client is hyperlinked, I wear out my index finger clicking till I finally find the executives who maintain each account. This could take all night! But what else do I have to do? No Skee Ball tonight. My high score is safe.

After clicking literally hundreds of accounts, I learn that Tom Sexton, my competitor for the Peterson Bicycle account, has had forty-three "wins." I am so in trouble. I have two unacknowledged wins, three if "Just . . . go" impresses Detroit. If I had only known from the first time I talked to Mr. Peterson that Tom Sexton would be my enemy—

Oh no! Mr. Peterson told *me* about Tom, and I'm sure Mr. Peterson has told Tom that Corrine is his competition! Was that why Tom was calling to talk to Corrine on Friday? Was he calling to tip her off? Oh no! What if Tom has already told Corrine about it? And if he did tell her—

I'm basically wasting my time.

I pull away from my laptop, wave at a full moon, and call Corrine. Her phone rings seven times, doesn't shoot me to voice mail, and then she answers.

"Hello, Shari dear," she says. "How's the world treating you?"

She sounds drunk. "Um, you sound funny, Miss Ross."

"I'm on medication, Shari dear. Heavy, wonderful, magnificent, astounding medication."

She's not drunk. She's high. "Are you all right?" As if I care. "Have you, um, arrived in Australia, Miss Ross?"

"Yes. I took an early flight, and ooh, I'm still flying."

Yes! She's ten thousand miles away where she can do no harm. And, strangely, I almost like her soft, spaced-out voice. "Have you done any scuba diving yet, Miss Ross?"

"I smell like vinegar."

She is *heavily* medicated. "Um, why do you smell like vinegar, Miss Ross?"

"I went snorkeling as soon as I stepped off the plane. I was only in the water five minutes, and a box jellyfish stung me. They practically bathed me in vinegar. I had tingling in my hands and feet, the worst headache, and terrible back pain." She giggles.

Corrine never giggles. How terrible could it be?

"But I don't feel a thing anymore, Shari dear. I love this stuff. I'm floating on water. I'm flying on air. I am encased in a fluffy marshmallow."

I will never eat another marshmallow as long as I live.

"Has Tom called for me, Shari dear?"

Which means—yes!—that he hasn't called her yet! But . . . why hasn't he called her yet? "He, um, he hasn't called you, Miss Ross?"

"No, and I miss him *so* much." There's the whiny-voiced wench I've come to hate. "I need him here beside me to nurse me back to health."

Why hasn't Tom called her? Hmm. She told him to meet her in Australia, so he knows she's in Australia. He also knows that Corrine is supposed to be competing against him for this account.

The rat! He knows that she *doesn't* know about the account, and he's not letting her know *what* he knows. Or, he knows she knows and thinks that *she* thinks that *he* doesn't know—

My brain hurts. A lot.

Maybe he thinks she's really *not* in Australia and is only trying to sabotage his project by getting him to waste his time flying out there. She's not that devious. She's not even that smart. Or maybe . . .

"He is supposed to be here to take care of me," Corrine whines. "I call and I call. I call just to hear his voice on his message."

Nice. I hope Tom calls me so I can hear his voice, too—and I can ask him what he's up to! "Have you been leaving messages when you call him, Miss Ross?"

"Yes, of course. I never hang up on Tom without leaving a message. Why won't he call me, Shari?"

I wish I knew. I know Harrison Hersey and Boulder folks play cutthroat, but this . . . this is just weird.

"Is vinegar flammable?" she asks. "I want to smoke a cigarette so badly."

I didn't even know she smoked. "So when was the very last time Tom called you, Miss Ross?"

"Um, let's see. . . ." She fades out. "He called me while I was eating at Delmonico's."

And he called *me* Friday morning about the same time she was there. "Did he mention anything about his work, Miss Ross?"

"No. Why would he? We're supposed to be on vacation together. Oh, I miss him so much. I need him to make love to me, Shari. I need him to bathe me in rainbows and whipped cream. You know what I mean, don't you?"

Too much information. Whipped cream? What a waste of an ice cream topping. "Um, Miss Ross, are you in a hospital?"

"Yes, and they all speak Australian. What a dreadful language."

It's your own language, wench. "Which hospital are you in, Miss Ross? I want to send flowers." Not. She only likes bird of paradise flowers, and those are usually expensive.

"It's near the hotel, which is on Dunk Island." Corrine giggles again. "And there are no basketballs anywhere! Get it? Dunk Island? No basketballs? Oh, I kill me."

Oh, please do. "Is it the Dunk Island Hospital?" I ask.

"I don't know. They took me on a boat ride, and I was in too much pain to notice."

I'll have to ask a nurse. "Um, do you know how long you'll be in the hospital, Miss Ross?"

"I don't know, Shari dear. Days, weeks. I could have died, you know."

Really? I run a search for "box jellyfish" on the Internet. Geez. Some species' venom can be fatal in as few as four minutes. "Oh, you poor dear." I may vomit. "Where were you stung, Miss Ross?"

"On my left breast, Shari. It's all swollen and puffy now, and it looks so . . . huge."

How can she tell? How could the doctors tell? And when the swelling goes down, will her stretch marks have stretch marks?

I may vomit for real. "Is there anything I can do for you, Miss Ross?"

"Well, now that you mention it, and I was going to tell you this before I left, but could you air out my penthouse sometime this week?"

Who airs out anything in New York in November? "Um, air it out, Miss Ross?"

"Yes. Just open all the windows, Shari dear. Surely you know how to do that."

Grr. I'll have to find something heavy to "open" them.

"They all have screens," she says. "I just want some fresh air in there."

"Okay." Great. I have to go to Trump Place on the Upper West Side on my day off for a wench who has an overinflated breast. "Um, how do I get in, Miss Ross?"

"I've left a message with the concierge. He'll let you in."

Well if *he* can let me in . . . "Um, why not just have the concierge air out your apartment, Miss Ross?"

"Because I've asked you to do it, Shari dear. But if you really must know, I'm afraid the concierge will steal my shoes. He looks like a transvestite. I know that you won't touch my shoes, will you?"

"Um, no, Miss Ross." I'd only touch them long enough to make a bonfire of her excessive vanity.

"Did Mr. Dunn call me again on Friday?"

Oh yeah. Mr. Dunn. "Yes, but it was like we thought. He only wanted to know about your plans for the Christmas party." The first creative lie you tell your boss is the hardest to tell. "He didn't even mention LA." The second lie is easier to tell. "In fact, he seemed glad that you were taking a vacation and wished you well." Wow. That last lie was like second nature to me. I'm executive material for sure now.

"Ah, the party. I may have to wear a turtleneck this year. It looks like a football, Shari!"

"What does, Miss Ross?"

"My breast! It has laces and everything. They had to shave me."

If the sting was on her breast . . . "They . . . shaved you?"

"Yes. They shaved my poor breast. They put cold shaving cream on it and shaved it. They said they had to get all the stingers out, and my poor nipples were out there for everyone in Australia to see."

There's an image I hope to forget soon. "Um, well, uh, do you want me to . . ." I have to get a hold of Tom . . . I mean, I have to get in contact with—

Geez, I don't know what I'm doing.

"Do you want me to call Tom for you, Miss Ross?" I do, after all, have all his phone numbers memorized. I've just been too chicken to call him myself because I could never think of a valid reason.

"Why on earth would I *ever* want you to do that?" she asks.

Yeah, why would I do that? "Um, you're obviously in no condition to be making phone calls, Miss Ross. You need to rest."

She sighs. "I suppose."

"And you *have* been trying to get through to him, right, Miss Ross?" I ask.

"Every second of every moment I've been in here. I have left him fifty messages at least. I miss him so much. I need him to pleasure me so badly. My happy spot has been so alone, so alone for so long."

Her . . . happy spot. Is that something she learned in anatomy class at Harvard? "Miss Ross, I'll try calling him until I get ahold of him, okay?"

"Would you do that for me, Shari dear?"

Of course not. The less contact I have with this man now, the better. "I will, Miss Ross. And as soon as I've gotten in contact with him, I'll have him call you immediately."

"You are the best, Shari. Go team!"

Yeah, right. Go team. Go into a coma, wench. "You just rest and, um, take all your medication now, Miss Ross."

"Oh, I will. This medicine is almost as good as having Tom deep inside me."

This is the most twisted conversation I've ever had.

"Have I mentioned Tom's tongue?" she says.

I don't want to hear this.

"It can do so many tricks. And it's so long and thick! Oh, I miss him so much!"

This conversation is over. "Rest, Miss Ross. Um, could you hand your phone to a doctor or nurse, please?"

"What on earth for?"

So I can see how long you'll be out of action and so I'll know the chances of my plan's survival. This usually works. "The holidays are coming up, Miss Ross, and perhaps they can buy something there for you that I can't get for you here."

"You want to get me a present?"

Yes, and I hope they have designer straitjackets in your size in Australia. "Give someone the phone, Miss Ross."

"Hello?" a female voice says.

"Is this Miss Ross's nurse?"

"Yes."

"I am Shari Nance, Miss Ross's administrative assistant back in New York. She's not very lucid right now, is she?"

"Hold a minute." Twenty seconds later she says, "I'm outside her room now so I don't have to listen to her."

Well said. "Yes, I know she can be a handful."

"Who's this Tom fellow she keeps crowing about?"

I can't tell her Tom is her boyfriend. If Tom calls, they'll hand the phone to Corrine immediately. I can't just say that Tom is her "friend," mainly because he isn't treating her in a friendly way. If he really cared, he'd at least call her back. "Uh, well, you see, Tom doesn't really exist." And where am I going with this? I'll just go with the flow. "When Miss Ross becomes, um, inebriated, or in this case, heavily medicated, Tom springs to life. He's like her imaginary friend." Which may actually be true. Hmm.

"I knew he was too good to be true," the nurse says.

Might as well go for it, and I can even include Mr. Dunn in this! Yes! "It's really become sort of a joke in the office. In fact, there are even a few men who call and act as if they're Tom or another of her imaginary friends named Mr. Dunn when they *know* she's had a few too many."

"For something like phone sex?" the nurse says.

That wasn't where I was going with that, but whatever floats your boat. "Something like that. It's quite mean. What I'm asking is that you and your staff screen Miss Ross's calls for her. If anyone calls and tells you he's Tom or Mr. Dunn, please don't hand the phone to her. It will only upset her." Hey, that was pretty good.

"I may just talk to this Tom myself," the nurse says.

She must be hard up Down Under. "How long will she be in the hospital? She couldn't tell me."

"No telling. She had a whopper of a sting. It looks like a zipper across her breast. She'll be here at least until all the swelling goes down."

"So at least . . . four, five days?"

"No telling."

Shoot. "I will call to check on her tomorrow. What's the name of the hospital?"

"Tully Hospital in Tully."

Of course it's named Tully Hospital. It's in Tully. "Make sure her phone is near one of your staff at all times."

"Right."

"Bye."

I should immediately add number six to my list of what can go wrong: "I will probably forget and mix up all the lies I've told."

But if I can make it through the next eleven days and win this account, I may only have to remember the biggest *truth* of all— that I *can* do this on my own.

And that will hopefully put me *exactly* where I want to be.

Chapter 11

Sundays I go to Brooklyn Tabernacle, and this Sunday is no exception.

I need all the help I can get.

The Brooklyn Tabernacle is only a block or so from the Brooklyner, and it has to be the most multicultural church on the planet. The United Nations should meet there. I usually only go to the 9 a.m. worship service and get my praise on with the world-famous Brooklyn Tabernacle Choir. Today, I go to the 9 a.m. *and* noon worship services *and* the 3 p.m. Gospel celebration service.

And it isn't five minutes into the first service that I start to feel guilty for what I'm about to do. This church was built on prayer, and I often pray alongside five thousand other folks on Tuesday nights. Today, I do some serious praying.

"Hey, God, um, it's me, Shari Nance. Yeah, You already know what I'm up to and what I'm planning to do, so there's no use explaining. If You could, I don't know, make a way for me, I'd surely appreciate it. You know I have a good heart, and You also know I'm an impatient person. I'm tired of waiting, You know? I know Your Word says for me to stay still and wait quietly for You to work and that You will deliver me. Lord, I haven't been still since I was a baby, and even then I was all arms and legs and energy. And I'm rarely completely quiet, right? I've been waiting patiently, and I know You've heard my cries. I'm trusting You to do what you did for David: Lift me out of this horrible pit, set my feet upon a rock, and establish my goings. I'll try not to let You down. Amen."

It is the most selfish prayer I have ever prayed, and instead of feeling renewed and uplifted, I drag tail the rest of the evening, barely sleep, and roll out of bed at 4 a.m. on Monday morning.

Yawning, I stand outside my clothes closet and realize that I have no business attire, nothing that says "advertising account executive."

I do have a lot of clothes that say "mountain climber" and "lumber woman."

The last time I wore a dress was Becka Short's wedding ten years ago. I had to wear a long frilly dress the color of green olives, white hose, and shiny red flats. And it wasn't even Christmas. I looked jacked up, but I guess that's the way weddings are supposed to be. The bridesmaids have to look like butt so the bride can look more fabulous.

I wouldn't wear a dress while touring a plant anyway, and since Mr. Peterson said that I wasn't what he expected, I'll just stay with the unexpected. Jeans, boots, sweater—done.

I could have gone to Corrine's apartment yesterday to air it out and raid her closets. She tells me she has two closets—one for clothes and one for shoes. Her clothes and shoes would all be way too big for me, but I bet she'd have a spare briefcase or an attaché case. Having something more professional like an attaché might help my cause today. I like the L.L.Bean tote bag, though. It's so uncomplicated. Open, dump, close. No locks, no combinations. Simple. And although I really wanted to see what a transvestite concierge looked like . . . no. I'll bet the concierge is a nice man who once ticked off Corrine, and reducing him to a transvestite makes her feel superior.

But I really should be dressing up a little. I am a professional now.

No! I can't wear a dress or a business suit.

This Cinderella isn't going to put on a new gown.

She's just going to be her uncomplicated, uncluttered self. I pick out some steel-toed Chippewa boots. Waterproof. Made in the USA. They have little American flags attached to the laces. A blue and black flannel shirt to go with my jeans. I'm sure they'll give me a hard hat for my tour of the plant. I put it all on and look rugged. This is a look that says . . . construction worker. Hmm. I still want Mr. Peterson to see me as self-sufficient and ready for anything and everything, so I take off the flannel shirt and put on a red, white, and blue wool sweater. There I am. The all-American girl.

I drop a few toiletries and a change of clothes into the tote bag. They barely ruffle my notes. I am certainly traveling light.

Now, how to get to JFK. I've never had to do this myself before. Corrine always had me call some car service to take her. I suppose I could do the same. I call Arecibo Car Services, and they promise to pick me up in five minutes for thirty-five bucks. Hmm. A bit pricy for eleven total miles, but I won't have to ride over an hour on two subways and on two buses. I tell them to come on.

Twelve minutes later (even time is subject to inflation these days), a black Mitsubishi Lancer shows up. Very nice. The driver motions me to the back door, I get in, and twenty minutes later, I'm short thirty-five bucks but standing in front of the Delta terminal at JFK.

This travel stuff is easy. Maybe God is making a way for me?

Though the search procedure is tedious, mind-numbing, and wearisome, and taking off my Chippewa boots is such a pain, I survive the march of the zombies and wait for my flight. The Delta flight leaves on time at 6 a.m., I get on, get a window seat, we fly, I look at the tops of clouds for the first time in my life, we land in Atlanta, I rent a GMC Acadia, and I'm zipping down I-75 to Macon, Georgia, by 9:30 a.m.

There's nothing to this! God *has* to be making a way for me. I hope.

I did little research on Macon over the weekend. Population 93,000. Home of Otis Redding, Lena Horne, Little Richard, the Allman Brothers, and Alabama Vest, African-American inventor of the kazoo. Well, somebody had to invent it. I'm sure there's much more to Macon than what I found online. I'll just have to see Macon firsthand.

As I'm driving on I-75, I soak up the scenery, and it reminds me so much of Virginia. Forests, mountains, hills, views, a kaleidoscope of colors—it reminds me of home.

I drive straight to the plant in a section of Macon known as Cross Keys. I'm amazed at how much Macon reminds me of Salem. Lots of trees, hills, open spaces, flat areas, and parks. And I am also amazed at how non-industrial the bicycle plant looks. It's a long and low green prefab aluminum barn maybe fifty feet high and three hundred feet long that blends into the surrounding pine trees perfectly. It has two small garage doors in front, few windows down its sides, and a loading dock way at the other end. An Office sign hangs over the entrance to a small gray trailer to my right, so I park near the trailer, get out, and walk through the door.

Sitting behind a simple L-shaped desk is a hefty woman in coveralls who is busily playing solitaire. "Hello," I say.

She turns from her game. "Hello."

I look at some pictures on her desk and see Mr. Peterson with her in several of them. This is Mrs. Peterson? She's the secretary? This is a mom-and-pop operation, all right.

"I'm, um, I'm Corrine Ross." I almost forgot who I was. "From MultiCorp."

She smiles. "I'm Freda Peterson, and you're here to tour the plant. Splendid. How was your trip?"

"Decent," I say. "The scenery was breathtaking."

She nods. "Always is this time of year. I've just sent out the gentleman from Harrison Hersey and Boulder with Woody."

Tom Sexton is *here? Now? He's here now?!* "Tom, I mean, Mr. Sexton . . . is here already?"

"You just missed him," she says in a honeyed drawl. "Perhaps I can delay Woody enough for you to catch up with them, and you can both get the full tour with Woody."

That can't happen! What am I going to do? I can't let Tom see me. While I want to rub elbows with Mr. Peterson, I have to stay as far away from Tom as I can. I shouldn't have come today, but Mr. Peterson said today would be the best day!

"You know," I say, "I'd much prefer a woman's perspective of this facility."

Mrs. Peterson stands. Whoa, she's a healthy woman. She has girth, but it's in all the right places. Those coveralls, though. They're screaming at the seams. "Then I'm your gal. We're usually slow on Mondays anyway. Where do you want to begin?"

"At the beginning?"

She sweeps around the desk. "I like how you're dressed. You're prepared. That other fellow's wearing a suit, and it's a might bit dusty in there."

Chalk one up for me.

"If I know Woody," she says, "he'll take Mr. Sexton straight to the machines. Men."

"Yeah. Men." Yes, Mr. Sexton is a man who should be in Australia or Detroit or anywhere on earth instead of *here* today! What is he up to?

Mrs. Peterson takes me inside the plant to a little holding area surrounded by large plastic strips hanging from the ceiling, and the noise isn't as bad as I expected. Some clanging and a steady humming.

She hands me a hard hat. "Regulations."

I put it on.

She hands me some goggles. "You never know what might be flying around in here."

I put them on over my glasses. The goggles are a little scratched up, but I can see fairly well.

She hands me some heavy leather gloves. "Keeps your hands clean."

I put them on.

She helps me into an orange vest. "Gives our workers the impression that you're on an inspection tour. Usually keeps 'em on their toes."

I look as far as I can down what looks like an assembly line, bike frames and wheels hanging on moving chains, noise assaulting my ears the closer we get to the machines I desperately want to avoid. I wish she had given me earplugs. I don't see Mr.

Peterson or Tom, and I almost feel safe because of my disguise and the fifteen thousand square feet of plant in front of me.

And then, I immerse myself in Peterson Bicycles. I learn they make one hundred bicycles a day, two hundred and fifty days a year, giving them slightly more than one million bicycles "on the road" since 1969. I learn how the wheels are made, how the frame is made, why the frame is shaped the way it is, how many safety checks they make, and how many African-American workers they employ.

"We're up to thirty-five percent," Mrs. Peterson says. "We're getting there."

I stand beside men and even women grinding, drilling, pressing, folding, extruding, attaching, clamping, tightening, painting, and testing. The tour takes a little over an hour, and I still don't see Mr. Peterson or Tom by the time we get back to the holding area. Maybe they went out to lunch. Which reminds me . . .

"I told Mr. Peterson that I was expecting some home cookin'," I say, purposely dropping my G this time.

"You did?" She whips out a walkie-talkie. "I'll give him a call."

Oh no!

"Woody, this is your better half, come in." She waits a few seconds. "Woody, this is your wife calling." She waits a bit more then puts the walkie-talkie in her front pocket. "He isn't here. He *always* answers me, or else. Guess he and Mr. Sexton have already left for lunch."

Whew. I try to look disappointed, but I'm sure I'm not very convincing. "Where's the best place to go?"

"You'll want H&H," Mrs. Peterson says. "Where Oprah came one day to visit. Big news around here. Made all the papers."

I leave the holding area and step outside into the sunshine and see a tall man with dirty-blond hair wearing an expensive blue suit getting into a Chevy Suburban only fifty feet away from me.

I turn quickly and nearly collide with Mrs. Peterson. "Um, I'll need directions."

Mrs. Peterson looks past me. "There's Woody and Mr. Sexton leaving right now. Let me call him." She pulls out a cell phone.

No! "Um, that's okay. Maybe it's better that the three of us don't sit down together. It's kind of a conflict of interest." And it will get me caught!

She stares at me for a moment. "All right. I can take you."

"Oh, don't go to any trouble." *Please* go to some trouble!

"Nonsense," she says. "I want to go. Mondays H&H has fried chicken potato pie. You have never tasted anything like it. Heaven."

I step outside again. Tom and Mr. Peterson are gone, and my heart stops battering my chest. I should probably escape to my hotel after lunch and then escape to New York. "I can drive us," I say, digging for my keys.

"No, my treat," she says, pointing at another Suburban.

But I can't make my escape if you drive!

"And you can leave that gear inside the plant," she says. "You have to be hot."

I can't take off my disguise! "I'll, um, I'll want to wander around the plant after lunch, so if I keep this stuff with me, I can just get to wandering when we get back." Wandering right on out of here.

"Suit yourself."

I remove the goggles, gloves, and hard hat in Mrs. Peterson's Suburban, but I keep on the orange vest. I have no idea why. Maybe I like the color.

We ride down to Forsyth Street, park, and enter a simple all-brick building on the corner. I notice a mushroom on the only window and another mushroom on the sign hanging over the entrance. Inside I see fresh flowers resting on multicolored vinyl tablecloths. Four chairs, only a few of them matching, surround each table, and every table seems full of people chowing down. Even the four stools at the counter are occupied with a mostly African-American crowd.

The smell *is* heaven. I do not *ever* want to leave. I will eat myself to death here.

"They're not that busy today," Mrs. Peterson says. "We won't have to wait long."

Not that busy? There's nowhere to sit, is there?

Mrs. Peterson nods at an older black woman moving among the tables. "That's Mama Louise Hudson. She's been here for nearly fifty years. Best cook I ever knew. Better than my granny."

I see motion from my right and smile at an ancient black woman waving us over. "There are two chairs at that table in the corner," I say.

"Told you we wouldn't have to wait long," Mrs. Peterson says, and I follow her to the table.

"Y'all can sure join us if you like," the waving woman says. "I'm Tillie, and this is my sister Millie."

Twins. They have to be. Both have the same toothy grin and wear the exact same Carolina-blue sweat suit. "Thank you. I'm, um, Corrine." I've got to stop saying "um"! I sit opposite Millie.

Mrs. Peterson sits opposite Tillie and to my right. "And y'all already know me."

"Good to see you, Freda," Millie says. "I said to myself, 'Isn't that Freda Peterson?' And I turned to Tillie here and said, 'Tillie, it must be Monday if Freda's here.'"

"That's right," Mrs. Peterson says. "I try not to miss the fried chicken potato pie."

"You look powerful hungry," Tillie says to me. "You don't look like you've eaten in days."

"I am pretty hungry," I say, taking and scanning the orange paper menu.

"Everything's good here, child," Millie says.

The menu tells me I'm in heaven. Collards, macaroni and cheese, lima beans, okra and tomato, rice and gravy, squash, roast beef, barbecue ribs, fried chicken potato pie, bread pudding, and peach cobbler. "I'll have . . ." I smile at Millie. "You think they'd let me have a sample of everything?"

Mille nods. "I told you she was powerful hungry."

Mama Louise appears out of nowhere beside Mrs. Peterson. "Welcome, welcome. Good to see you again, Freda. Who's this?"

"Hello," I say. "I'm Corrine Ross." Better. I even included my last name this time.

"Where you from?" Mama Louise asks.

"Macon," Mrs. Peterson says before I can answer.

"I know that, Freda," Mama Louise says with a smiling scowl. She looks at me. "That one ain't from around here."

I nod. "I'm from Brooklyn by way of Virginia."

Mama Louise looks at Millie and Tillie. "We don't get many folks from Brooklyn by way of anywhere around here. Did I hear you want a little of everything?"

Mama Louise has amazing powers of hearing. "Yes ma'am."

"Bet you're more Virginia than Brooklyn, am I right?" Mama Louise asks.

"Yes ma'am," I say. "Twenty-two years in Virginia."

Mama Louise nods. "You put it away, and I'll keep bringin' it."

And then . . . I eat. Everything, and I mean, everything tastes of home. *Everything.* I haven't had okra or collards or even a decent cobbler in years. Home. I nearly mist up over the rice and gravy while Millie and Tillie keep up a running commentary about Oprah, Capricorn Records, and the Allman Brothers, who used to "borrow" food when they were just starting out and paying Mama Louise later. They also fuss about the cold snap they're having.

It had to be at least sixty-five outside.

Home. Not that I'd go back to Virginia, but this place just gives me the feeling of home. Those were craftspeople I saw making an American product at that plant. The woman behind that counter doesn't even use recipes, Millie tells me. She cooks by feel, cooks by heart, cooks by touch. *This* is what home is about. Nothing fancy. Just . . . home. No matter where you go in Macon, Georgia, you're home. If MultiCorp ever represents a city like Macon, they can use that slogan. No matter where you go . . .

I gulp some lemonade.

No matter where you . . . *ride* . . . you're home.

Home. That has to be the centerpiece of anything we do for Peterson Bicycles. I wish I could write it down on a napkin. I won't forget. Home. There's no place like home.

"Where do you think Mr. Peterson took Mr. Sexton?" I ask Mrs. Peterson.

Mrs. Peterson sighs and shakes her head. "They'll be at Between the Bread Café. Woody can't go two days without his grilled rib-eye sandwich. It's only about half a mile from here. We can drop by there on our way back if you like."

"That's okay," I say quickly. "Um, you see . . ."

Millie and Tillie lean in.

I have a captive audience. "I think it's best, Mrs. Peterson, that my competition and I stay separated, you know, for impartiality."

"Not much is impartial when your competition is hogging the boss, and it's the boss who makes most of the decisions," Mrs. Peterson says.

"True," I say.

Millie and Tillie are still staring at me. I hope I don't have some okra stuck in my teeth.

"You, um, you know Mr. Sexton well?" Mrs. Peterson asks.

Define "well." There are so many variations. "I guess so. Pretty well."

"Was he your sweetie?" Mrs. Peterson asks.

Millie and Tillie smile.

My mouth drops a few inches. "No. Um, actually he's a . . . he's the, um, he's the boyfriend of a friend of mine." Whom I'm impersonating. Please don't press me for more.

Tillie shakes her head. "You are the worst little liar I think I've ever met."

"I'm . . . not lying, Miss Tillie." *This* time.

Millie drums the table with her wrinkled fingers. "He's a

boyfriend of a friend of mine. Girl, either he *was* your boyfriend or you want him to *be* your boyfriend. Admit it."

"I really don't even know him," I say. "I've had some conversations with him a few times, that's all." Okay, more than a few. More like . . . sixty a year times five. Three hundred conversations? Maybe I *do* know Tom.

"A few conversations," Tillie repeats. "That's all it would take."

"He sure is handsome," Mrs. Peterson says. "Right successful, too."

I nod and wish I had left something on my plate to eat. "Yes, he's . . . he's very good at his job. He's . . ." I look up.

Lord Jesus, he's in the window!

Lord, I asked You to make a way, and You have—sort of. Can You maybe make a way out the back door right now?

Tom is here!

Chapter 12

Millie and Tillie follow my eyes to the window where Tom, all six-feet-two at least, is peering through the glass.

"That him?" Tillie asks.

I can only nod. C'mon, feet, let's go to the ladies' room. My feet won't budge. They want me to look at the right handsome man.

Millie squints. "Either my eyes are worse than they were yesterday, or that is one very big man. He must lift weights."

Why is my heart stopping? Beat, please. Stop staring at the right handsome man standing under the Allman Brothers magic mushroom with Mr. Peterson! Now they're both looking in, and now . . .

I am so busted.

Millie and Tillie get up. "We'll leave y'all to talk," Millie says.

Don't leave! Have some more cobbler! I'll pay!

"It was nice chattin' with you," Tillie says. "See you next Monday, Freda."

Mr. Peterson and Tom weave their way to our table, and I try to hide my face with my tiny little hand.

Mr. Peterson says, "Tom, you already know Miss Ross, don't you?"

I wave my other hand but don't look up. Lord Jesus, I'm *begging* You, *please* don't—

"Yes," Tom says. "Yes, I do. Hello, Corrine. It's so nice to see you again."

I am so busted, I am so—What did he say? He said . . . Corrine? I look up and see Tom grinning at me. Why didn't he bust me out? "Hi, Tom," I say in a wee, tiny, minuscule, microscopic voice.

Mr. Peterson squeezes Mrs. Peterson's shoulder and gives her a peck on the cheek. "If we're here, who's mindin' the store?"

She takes Mr. Peterson's hand and smiles. "It runs itself, you know that."

Mr. Peterson waves at Mama Louise. "A round of lemonade, if you please."

Don't sit, please don't . . .

They sit, Tom on my left, Mr. Peterson across from me. Mama Louise brings us the lemonade.

"So, Miss Ross," Mr. Peterson says, "what'd you think of the plant?"

I sneak a peek at Tom, and he's still grinning at me. "To be honest"—oh, the irony—"it was the first plant I have ever toured. It was fascinating. Efficient. Busy."

Mr. Peterson laughs. "You lookin' to buy the place, invest, or hawk my product?"

I try to look away from Tom, but his grin is blinding. "This project is an investment, Mr. Peterson," I say. "As you prosper, MultiCorp prospers."

"Mr. Sexton here seems to think we could do some expanding into foreign markets." Mr. Peterson shifts his weight in his chair. "What do you think, Miss Ross?"

This . . . this is a trap. "I'll let you know what I think in a few days."

"Fair enough," Mr. Peterson says. "So, Tom, how long have you known this firecracker here?"

This firecracker is about to go off. Why isn't Tom busting me out?

Tom loosens his tie. "Oh, about . . . five years now. Isn't that so, Corrine?"

He knows it's me, Shari, he's not busting me out, he's playing nice, and I don't know why. I guess I had better be politer than polite. "Yes, Tom. We talk on the phone quite frequently, don't we, Tom?" He'll probably wait until I incriminate myself a little more, and then he'll bust me out. Oh, he's *good.*

"Yes, we do, Corrine," Tom says. "Corrine here recommends books to me that are just fantastic."

But *how* does he know it's me, I mean, that I'm Shari? I have never seen him! Is my voice that distinct? Where has he seen me?

"Yes," Tom continues, "Corrine has never led me the wrong way when it comes to books. She gives her honest assessment, and she never lies."

Oh, he's certainly having fun. I have to turn this to my favor somehow. "You remember Shari, don't you, Tom?"

Tom blinks. "Oh yes. Shari Nance. Such a sweet, independent, beautiful woman, and I have noticed that she is so much more beautiful in person. Shari has such a soft voice."

Okay. He's referring to me, which is nice, and I *am* all those things, but . . . "Well, Shari is in Australia right now at the Great Barrier Reef expecting her sweetie to spend some time with her."

Tom's smile doesn't fade a bit. "She is, is she? Imagine that."

Imagine this. "And a box jellyfish attacked her while she was snorkeling. She's laid up in a hospital in Tully in quite a lot of pain."

"A box jellyfish?" Mr. Peterson says. "It attacked her?"

It was probably trying to swim away from her. "Yes sir. They have deadly venom. She's very lucky to be alive, Tom."

Tom nods. "I will have to send my dear *friend* Shari some flowers then."

He said "friend." Hmm. I can't just ask him if she's more than just a friend in front of the Petersons. "I'm sure your *friend* would like that very much. She loves bird-of-paradise arrangements."

Tom won't take his eyes off mine. "So Shari has told me." He raises his eyebrows. "You remember Nance?"

Geez! Why won't he stop dropping my names? I'm glad I

never told him my middle name. "Sure." Lord Jesus, make him stop!

"How is dear, sweet Nance?" Tom says. "I really miss talking to her."

That was sweet, too, but . . . "Nance is fine. Busy as always. Working hard. You know good old Nance."

"I hear she's doing some traveling these days," Tom says. "Did she get a promotion?"

Geez, it's like he's moving in for the kill. "Nance likes to show initiative when others aren't up to the task." Or even in the country! "Nance really takes advantage of her chances, you know?" Now please stop talking about Nance!

"I'm sure she does," Tom says. "It's obvious." He looks under the table at my boots. "Chippewa! I have a pair just like those. Shari recommended them to me."

Oh yeah. I did once. And he actually bought boots based on my recommendation?

"Best boots on the planet bar none," Mr. Peterson says. "I even have a contract with them for my workers. They all get nice discounts."

I stare a hole in Tom's . . . cute, mischievous smile. "You should have worn your boots today, Tom."

"Yep," Tom says, removing his tie and unbuttoning the top button of his shirt. "I surely should have worn my boots."

And now he's referring to my lies again. Yes, I am laying it on thick.

"I came totally unprepared today," Tom says. "I should have expected the unexpected."

I roll my eyes at him. It's the only defense I have.

"I have really misrepresented myself, Mr. Peterson," Tom says.

Oh no! Here it comes. Be brave, Shari! You can just drive the rental back to Virginia.

"The fact is, Mr. Peterson, I don't much like suits," Tom says, unbuttoning another button. "Unfortunately it's a requirement at Harrison Hersey and Boulder." He looks at me. "I'd rather wear jeans, boots, and a sweater any day."

Yes, you'd look good wearing me—Where'd *that* thought come from? Sorry, Lord.

"But aren't you a little hot, Miss, um, Ross?" Tom asks.

Hot *and* bothered. "I am, actually." I take off the orange vest. "So, Tom, weren't you just in Detroit?"

"Yes, I was," Tom says. "Detroit is a wonderful city. So cold, though. I had so much trouble staying warm."

Yeah, and with my help, you got to leave that city quickly so you could warm up down here in Georgia. "How did Detroit, um, *go,* Tom?"

Tom's grin is back. I like it, but I don't know if I can trust it. "It went very well thanks to Shari. She has so many wonderful ideas. Her mind just . . . *goes* in so many interesting directions. I wish I could work with her more often."

But now I want to just *go* back to Brooklyn. "Yeah. That Shari. Always sharing ideas."

Mr. Peterson checks his watch. "I gotta run, y'all. Freda, can you run them back?"

Mrs. Peterson stares me down, and I have to look away. "I'm coming with you, darlin'. Let me finish my lemonade." She hands me a set of keys. "You can find your way back, can't you, Corrine?"

I nod.

Mr. Peterson nods, lays a twenty on the table, and leaves.

Mrs. Peterson doesn't touch her lemonade. "Tom, Corrine, my husband's mind rarely strays very far from that plant, so I'm sure he didn't understand the little show you two just put on."

Oh no! *She's* going to bust me out?

"I sense a great deal of tension between you two," Mrs. Peterson says, "and whatever it is, don't you think you two should work it out?"

Work what out?

She looks at Tom and then at me. "It is obvious to me that you two were once very close, and not too long ago." She reaches out and squeezes my hand. "Don't let a little business come between you two."

Oh . . . my . . . goodness!

She turns to Tom. "And Tom, you do right by her, you hear?"

"Yes ma'am," Tom says. "I certainly will. I've been hoping for the chance to make things right."

Mrs. Peterson drops another twenty on the table, nods at both of us, and leaves.

I stare at the keys in my hand. I bet I could get to the car before Tom could. He's too big to navigate this crowded place. Where's the bathroom? I could go find a window, squeeze out, and strand him here.

"Good lemonade," Tom says. "A little sweet, a little sour. Not too cold. Just right. Very refreshing."

Everything he says has a double meaning. I must be sweet, sour, not too cold, just right, and very refreshing.

"May I ask you something?" he asks.

"No."

"Okay." I hear him finish his lemonade. "Then I'm going to tell you something."

"No."

He leans his head down until it's almost level with the table, only one of his dark brown eyes visible. "Then I'm just going to talk."

"No."

"You don't have to listen."

I look him dead in that eye. "I can't help but hear, Tom. I'm a foot away from you."

"And I'm glad," he says, leaning back. "Really. I'm glad that I finally get to meet you face-to-face, Shari Nance."

He seems sincere, but . . . "Just . . . say your piece."

"Is Corrine, the *other* Corrine, is she really in Australia?" he whispers.

"Yes."

"And the story about the box jellyfish?"

I nod. "That's true, too."

"I thought so. It seemed too specific to be a lie." He leans farther back in his chair, the chair tilting off the ground. "This is all very interesting," he says just like Jimmy Stewart did in *It's a Wonderful Life*. "Very interesting, indeed."

"You think?"

He clasps his hands behind his head, balancing his chair on the back two legs. "I thought Australia was a trick to take me away from my game, a ploy to help Corrine win this thing." He leans forward, returning the chair to four legs, and then he slides his chair closer to mine. "So, did Corrine send you down here to work or what?"

He thinks I'm on a mission for Corrine? "I am doing this entirely on my own."

His eyes light up. "Really, now. Even more interesting. How much does Corrine know about your clandestine activities?"

I stare at the floor. "She, um, she doesn't know anything about this."

He puts his huge hand on the back of my chair. "I see. So you're going solo on this. And without a promotion."

"Yes."

He taps my chair several times. "This is very interesting, indeed."

I wish he'd stop saying that! "You want to know what I find so very interesting, Tom?"

His hand gets dangerously close to my shoulder. "What, Miss Ross?"

I roll my eyes. "I find it very interesting that you're leaving your girlfriend to suffer in a hospital in Tully, Australia."

He pulls his hand from my chair and places it on the table. Both of my hands would fit inside that paw. "Shari, I know this is going to be hard for you to believe, but Corrine is not my girlfriend anymore."

"Yeah, it is hard to believe when you've been seeing her for five years."

"Yes, we've been seeing each other, but it's been more off than on for the past two years," Tom says without a tinge of sadness. "You know how obsessive she gets. She sees much more in us than I do. Understand?"

There's some truth here. Corrine is obsessive and deranged. "So you're just leading her on, then?"

"I guess you could call it that." He nods. "Yeah, I'm leading her on."

An honest jerk? Hmm. Maybe he's still just setting me up. I have to be careful.

"Yes, she invited me to Australia, and yes, I said I'd *try* to get out to see her after Detroit. But when this thing came up, I thought she was trying to scam me with this crazy trip idea of hers."

I try to read his eyes. Hmm. They seem honest, but you never know.

He smiles. "Honestly, Shari, all of this just fell into my lap . . . and your lap." Then he drops his eyes to *stare* at my lap!

What do you say when a man stares at your lap no more than thirty minutes after meeting him for the first time? "Don't . . . don't stare at my lap, Tom."

"Um, you have . . . peach cobbler, I think, there, um . . ."

I look down. Yep. Cobbler crumbs. I whisk them away. I don't know whether to be angry that he *only* saw the crumbs. I have a sexy lap. "The, um, the Petersons shouldn't have had to pay for us, so . . ." I take the two twenties. "I'll return their money later. I'll pay."

He reaches into his suit jacket and pulls out a wallet. "We'll go Dutch."

"No," I say. "This one's on me. You only had a refreshing lemonade." I jump up and go to the counter.

"You need a receipt, honey?" Mama Louise asks.

"Yes, please."

She rings me up. "Twelve-fifty."

She's joking. "You sure?"

Mama Louise nods.

"For all that good food and the round of lemonade?" I ask.

"You could leave a nice tip." She looks past me to Tom. "Oh, your man is leaving the tip."

A twenty? "Um, he's not my man."

Mama Louise rolls her eyes. "Uh-huh."

I hand her one of my own twenties. "Keep the change."

"Y'all come back. *Soon.*"

I go back to the table, collect the orange vest, and walk toward the door. Tom rushes around me and holds the door.

"I'm not thanking you," I say. "I can open my own door."

"I can see that," he says. "And I don't ever expect you to thank me, Shari."

We get into the Suburban, and I start it up, over-revving the engine before I pull away from the curb with a jerk.

"Shari," Tom says, buckling up and holding on to the door handle. "I always thought that was a pretty name, by the way. And it matches its owner."

Oh, tell me anything.

"Of all the people I've talked to in my life," he says, "you have been by far the nicest, most caring, and best listener I've ever known."

Nice, caring, good listener. Hmm. All the things Corrine isn't. I sneak a look at him and continue driving. I have no idea where I'm going, so I turn right for no reason. Okay, I have a reason. If I turn right, I can look at right handsome Tom.

After a few more right turns, I say, "You've been pretty . . . easy to talk to and nice, too, but now that you're my enemy, this conversation is over."

"You're really stepping out on this one, aren't you?" he asks.

On a wing and a selfish prayer.

"I'm glad you are, Shari," he says. "I really am. I've known for years that you're really the power behind the throne. Corrine is as creative as Congress. She's as intuitive as mud. She's as spontaneous as a blueprint."

Correct on all counts.

"Well, she's *your* boss," he says. "You know how shallow and superficial she is. She has no depth. A Hollywood diva has more depth than she'll ever have."

Amen! Preach on!

"Sure, she's brilliant and occasionally witty," he continues, "but her grip on reality is the opposite of the grip you have on that steering wheel. Doesn't that hurt your fingers?"

I look down at my knuckles frozen in the two and ten position. "And yet as psychotic as Corrine is, you've been sleeping with her for five years."

He does not answer. I think I have silenced him. I turn on the radio and crank it up. Shoot, it's a talk radio station. I click over to a country station. Oh well . . .

"Slept!" he shouts. "Past tense! We haven't been together in years!"

I turn off the radio. Hmm. Maybe I'll hear him out.

"Thanks," he says. "Shari, Corrine and I haven't been together like that in almost two years now."

I take a left. I'm sure I'm going in circles. "So you don't like shallow and superficial as much anymore, huh? But you *did*, right? What does that say about you?" And we'll let that hang in the air for a while, shall we?

"I, uh, didn't notice it so much in the beginning."

Typical man. "Cuz you was gettin' some, huh?"

Tom laughs. "True. You got me."

More honesty from this jerk? This man is right refreshing, but he's still a jerk.

He laughs some more. "Yeah, I was gettin' some, and she was more than willin', darlin'. Amazing stamina. Very long legs. Good kisser."

I can't believe. . . . Who does he . . . I have never heard such . . . Eww. And this is my boss he's talking about.

"No more talk about Cringe, okay?" he says. "I'm having a good day. A very good day."

Because he has all the power. "What did you call her?"

"Cringe. That's one of my nicknames for her. She makes me cringe."

And yet he still sees her. "So typical."

"What is?"

I look at a stoplight. I know I've been here before. I turn left this time. "She's nothing but a booty call to you."

He doesn't answer right away.

"I knew it."

He sighs. "She was, but only for the first three years."

So what are they doing now? "And the last two?"

"I like how direct you are. I'll try to be as direct. Corrine sometimes used to share some great information about her projects while she was gettin' some."

He used her! "And I'm sure you just drilled her till she spilled it, huh?" That didn't come out right.

Tom can't stop laughing.

"Okay, okay. It wasn't that funny." A four-way stop? I, pause, spell out *S-T-O-P* in my head, and drive straight ahead.

He's still laughing.

"Which projects has she . . . squealed on?" That didn't come out right either.

"She's not much of a squealer," Tom says. "More of a panter and a scratcher."

I give him a withering stare. "Which projects, Tom?"

"Let's see, um, she told me all about your army spots, and that helped me with the air force spots. Ever notice how similar they are?"

As if the same ad agency did both of them. Geez. I'm up to four accounts that should be mine.

"A couple others. Nothing I ever used to any great extent, though. You, Shari dear, always gave me the best ideas over the phone."

I am so lost. Where's the sun? Directly over us. That's no help. I know I have to go north. "So, Tom, where are you from? All the years we talked, I've never asked you."

"Trying to change the subject?" he says.

Yes. "Just answer the question."

He turns on the radio and scans until he finds "Be Ready," a Jill Scott song. You're telling me, Jill. I thought I was. Now I have to be ready for anything.

"I am from a little town in Oregon called Klamath Falls," Tom says.

"Never heard of it." And I've never been so lost! Wait. Oh, shoot! That's H&H! I've made a complete circle.

"Klamath Falls is not far from northern California. I escaped from there to go to Berkeley, took a bus cross-country to New

York, started a special junior account exec program Hairiest Son, Hershey Squirts, and Older. . . ."

I almost laugh. It was mildly amusing.

"I survived that ridiculous butt-kissing program, got a promotion eight years later from junior to senior account exec, and in about one hundred years when all the old farts die, I'll make partner."

I think I've finally met someone who hates his job almost as much as I hate mine. "So they treat you like crap?"

"Oh, no. At Hairy Ads, Hershey's with Almonds, and Moldier, they treat me like wildebeest dung."

I wish he'd quit doing that. I'm almost glad I'm lost. I took a right here last time. That gas station looks familiar. "Why do they treat you so badly? You've brought millions to them."

"I'm from the worst coast, Shari. I'm the only worst coaster there. I'm the token. The rest are all poison Ivy League." He sighs. "Well, that's my story. What's yours?"

No way. I'm not sharing any more information than I already have with this man. "I am so lost. I know I'm supposed to turn left somewhere. Do you know where we are?"

"Take the next right," he says.

I turn right. "But isn't this taking us south? We need to go north to get to the plant."

"Another right," he says.

I turn. "None of this looks familiar." But that hotel does. The Hilton Garden Inn.

"Turn in here," he says. "I need to change."

That's . . . that's *my* hotel.

Tom is staying at my hotel.

I turn in and park near the entrance.

"I need to look as rugged as you do so I can score more points with Mr. Peterson," he says. "I'll only take a few minutes. You won't drive away on me, will you?"

I really want to. "No." I turn off the Suburban. "And I don't dress like this to score points. I normally dress like this."

He opens his door. "And you've been an administrative assistant for how long?"

I get out and slam my door behind me. "Shut up."

Tom strolls around the front of the Suburban. "Makes one think, doesn't it?"

I sidestep him and go to the door. "The clothes don't make the woman."

He stares at me *that* way. You know what I'm talking about. He's imagining me with fewer clothes.

"Your clothes *hide* the woman," he says.

I don't respond. At least he has an imagination. I continue to the door.

"Where are you going?" he asks.

I bust through the door, Tom trailing behind me, and go directly to the front desk, tapping my short nails on the counter.

"This isn't your hotel, too?" he whispers. "No way. What are the chances?"

Yes. What are the chances, God? There must be fifty hotels or more around here, and I picked this one. Not only don't I know what Tom is up to, but I'm beginning to suspect that God is up to something, too.

"They won't let you check in until three," Tom whispers. "It's only a little after one."

"Hush."

"If you traveled more, you would know that," he whispers.

"Hush!"

A tall stork of a man comes out of the office. "Sorry to keep you waiting."

"Corrine Ross. MultiCorp." It's rolling right off my tongue now.

"One moment," Stork Man says, clicking a few keys on a keyboard.

Isn't he supposed to be wearing a name tag? Where's his name tag? How can you work at a Hilton without a name tag?

"Yes, we have your reservation, Miss Ross," Stork Man says. "But your room isn't ready yet. Check-in is at three."

"Told you," Tom whispers.

"It's okay," I say. "I have some more work to do at the Peterson plant." I stare at Tom, and he gets the hint, heading to the elevator. "Could I get my key now?"

"Sure."

Stork Man makes my card key with several swiping motions and hands it to me. "Room three fifteen."

I take the key, turn, and see Tom step into the elevator, his shirt already unbuttoned, the T-shirt underneath showing off a perfect set of abs. He waves.

I do not.

The doors close.

I slump into a plush chair in the lobby and look out a window. Well, Shari. Well, well, well.

Isn't this *another* how-do-you-do.

Chapter 13

Tired of waiting on Tom and still beyond nervous, I wander out to the Suburban. The Petersons are sure some trusting people. Country people are like that. Mrs. Peterson just handed me the keys.

So I can "work it out" with Tom.

And what are we working out? I have no freaking idea! I am so helpless right now, but I can't let Tom know that.

I'm sure he already knows how helpless I am. There's just something about that grin of his.

Just when I'm about to leave his butt, Tom comes out dressed in well-worn jeans, scuffed-up Chippewa boots, and a long-sleeved Cal sweatshirt. If he weren't my adversary to the death over this account and the man who could bust me out at any moment with the Petersons, I'd say he looked good. I love me a rugged man. But since he's my adversary, I can't say that.

Once we're going in the right direction for a change, I pull into an empty church parking lot and turn off the Suburban. "Okay, let's get to it. Are you going to bust me out for impersonating Corrine or not?"

"No."

No hesitation. What is his game? "Do you mind if I ask why?"

"No," he says with that grin of his.

"Okay," I say, "why won't you bust me out?"

He shifts in his seat to face me. "I have my reasons."

"And they are?"

He smiles. "I'll let you know."

All this mystery. He's just playing mind games. "Well, whatever your reasons are, I suppose I will owe you, right? What will I owe you for your silence? I know I have to 'pay' you somehow."

"You don't owe me anything, Shari," he says softly. "Really. In fact, I'm glad I'm going up against you. This job has gotten just plain boring, grueling, and old for me. It's become stale. This is fun. I know I'm in for the fight of my life."

He's just saying that. . . . "Oh, right. You have the best production team on earth, and I don't have any access to our production team without Corrine there to get permission. I can only do this bare bones, totally old school, and completely on my own."

"And I promise to do the same."

Again, he answers so quickly, almost as if I'm walking into a trap. "Right."

"I actually planned to do this old school," he says. "Mr. Peterson is old school. This town is old school. The product is old school. It makes perfect sense. We think alike, Shari."

It's hard to argue with him there. "How old school are you talking?" He has to be holding something back.

"I will be a man with two cameras, one for stills, and one for video. That's it."

I still don't trust him. "So it's my cameras and ideas against yours."

"Right."

Something is still . . . off. "What if it were you going up against Corrine?"

He props up those long legs on the dashboard. This Suburban is huge! "I hope you don't think I'm patronizing you. I'm not. I'd probably still do the same thing. I think low-tech is the way to go with a low-tech product."

"Old school all the way."

He nods.

I reach out my hand. "Will you shake on it?"

"Gladly."

He takes my hand, and my hand vanishes. Where did it go? I shake his hand once, he lets go, and my hand reappears. That was some magic trick.

"Um, I'm going to hold you to this promise, Tom."

"And I'll hold you to the promise, too," he says, adding, "Shari."

I like how he says my name. And now for a different subject. "Didn't you *promise* to visit Corrine in Australia?"

He sighs and turns away. "That again. I told her I'd *try*. That's not a promise. My exact words were, 'I'll try to get there, but I'm making no promises.'"

That makes sense. Corrine certainly has selective hearing. And now is the perfect time to check on Tom's *friend*. "Why don't you call her, see how she's doing? I mean, after all, she is your *friend*."

Tom smiles. "You caught that."

"I'm a good listener."

"So I'll call her."

This should be good, but only if that nurse does what I asked her to do.

I watch Tom go to his contacts list, scroll down, and hit the OK button. He doesn't even have Corrine on one of his speed dials. Maybe he's telling the truth about him and Corrine. I quickly banish the thought. Tom is in advertising. I can trust very little of what this man says to me.

"Hello, may I speak to Corrine Ross? This is Tom." He listens a minute, his eyebrows rising. He turns to me. "She's heavily sedated and can't talk, but this nurse wants to talk to me for some reason. Excuse me?" He covers the phone, and it, too, disappears. "She just said, and I quote, 'Talk dirty to me, you nasty man.' What do I do?"

Yes! "Um, hmm." I sigh. "I rigged it so anyone named Tom or Mr. Dunn couldn't talk to her."

He frowns. "You better explain."

"Um, I told them that Corrine has an imaginary friend named Tom and an imaginary friend named Mr. Dunn."

He smiles. "There's a lot of truth in the first part."

I was right! "I also told her that anyone who calls himself Tom or Mr. Dunn only calls to, um, have, um those *kinds* of conversations."

"Oh."

I look for the phone and only see his hand. "You don't want to talk nasty to her, do you, Tom?"

He shakes his head. "No. I'm only supposed to be checking up on my friend." He opens his palm and puts the phone to his ear. "Look, I'm her brother, Thomas, not that imaginary friend she supposedly has." He listens for a few moments and covers the phone again. "She won't believe me. She's actually asking me what I'm wearing."

This is fun! "Well, tell her."

He does the phone reappearance trick again. "I'm wearing boots, jeans, and a sweatshirt," he says matter-of-factly. "Uh-huh . . . uh-huh."

He hits a button on the phone, and I hear her panting. Over some boots, jeans, and a sweatshirt? Hmm. I kind of do that, too. I mean, not all the time. I mean, now I am. A little.

"Wait a minute," the nurse says. We hear a door close. "I had to go to a closet. You want to know what I'm wearing?"

Tom shakes his head.

"Go on," I mouth.

"Sure," Tom says. "What are you wearing?"

"I'm wearing some yellow scrubs," the nurse says, "with nothing on underneath."

"Nothing?" Tom says.

"Nothing," the nurse whispers.

Tom looks at me, and I only shake my head. I hope all nurses don't do this.

"Um, don't you, um, chafe down there?" Tom asks.

I choke off a giggle. What a question!

"No," the nurse whispers, and then *she* giggles.

A question about chafing down there makes a woman giggle? Man, this woman is hard up.

"I mean, well, doesn't your skin get raw?" Tom asks.

I bite my lower lip, anticipating another strange response from the nurse.

"Oh yes," the nurse says. "Yes. It does. I have to massage it with lots of lotion. I'm covering my body with lotion right now."

I reach up and press several buttons on the phone until the static disappears. "I didn't think you would really do this, Tom."

"Neither did I," he says. "I seem to have a knack for it, don't you think?"

"And you're hardly even trying."

He shrugs. "What can I say?"

"You think you can sell anything, don't you?"

Tom nods. "I can. She's really, um, into this, and I'm being so dull."

Because she's a bored nurse . . . and you have a sexy voice whether you're trying to be dull or not. "And you aren't into this?"

"No, I'm not," Tom says. "I've never done anything like this before. I've never even wanted to do anything like this." He reaches for the phone. "I have to end this."

I grab his wrist. "Hold on there." Wow, he has a thick wrist. I let go. "I bet you dinner that you can't make her, um, scream and shout." I can't believe I just said that. At least I didn't say something else that rhymes with "spasm."

Tom blinks. "You want me to talk a strange Australian woman into screaming and shouting."

"Well, if you don't want to prove how good a salesman you are, just hang up."

He drums his thighs with a serious set of fists. "This is crazy."

I roll my eyes. "I thought you could sell anything, Tom Terrific."

He purses his . . . soft lips. They didn't look this soft in his picture. "You really want me to?"

I nod. "I want to hear you in action."

He hits another button. "Sorry for the delay. I was unzipping my pants."

The nurse immediately shouts, "Yes!"

Oh . . . my . . . goodness!

He mutes the phone. "Dinner." He shakes his head. "I'll end it now."

"Double or nothing," I say *way* too quickly.

He sighs. "Okay." He hits the mute. "You still there?"

"Yes!" she shouts *again*.

He mutes the phone. "I guess that means . . . breakfast."

If I knew that this wench was the horniest woman in Tully, Australia, I never would have made the bet. "That was an unfair bet."

He shrugs. "I just made a nurse in a closet twelve thousand miles away scream and shout without really trying. Want to bet lunch tomorrow?"

"Leave the poor girl alone."

Tom shakes his head. "I like lunch." He hits the mute button. "What's your name?"

I hear heavy breathing before she says, "Angela."

Tom rolls his eyes. "Oh, Angela."

The freaking wench shouts *again!* Then the nurse actually howls. "Ooh. Someone's coming. Gotta go."

Click.

Tom snaps off his phone, reclines in his seat, and smiles.

No way that just happened. Is it getting a little steamy in here? I restart the Suburban and roll down the window. "Let's get back to work."

"That's it?" Tom says. "I induce a perfect stranger in Australia to do some shouting, and you just say, 'Let's get back to work'?"

I don't want to give him more credit than he's due. He really didn't say anything that erotic at all. "So she was hard up. Big deal."

He only smiles.

"You really didn't do anything amazing," I say. "It wasn't even that kinky. You didn't even mention her happy space."

Tom drums on the dash. "Corrine told you about that?"

I nod and start to laugh.

He laughs, too. "Yeah, Corrine and her 'happy space.'" He puts on his seat belt. "By the way, I like omelets. Lots of ham, onions, and green peppers."

Grr. "I'll call room service for your dinner and for your breakfast, and I didn't bet on your lunch."

"Well, you have to join me for dinner at least."

Which would be very nice, I'm sure. . . . "I bet you dinner and breakfast, and that's all you're going to get. I wasn't part of the bet."

Tom snaps up the phone.

"Who are you calling?" I ask.

"I'm going for four shouts so you'll eat with me."

And he'll easily get it. "I'm not betting you."

"I don't expect you to. Hello? This is Tom."

A male voice says, "Yeah?"

"Um, I'm trying to reach Corrine Ross. She's a patient there."
Click.

"I think," I say, "your little bimbo left Corrine's phone in the closet."

Tom pockets his phone. "I wish he didn't hang up. I was going to hand the phone to you."

No, he wasn't. "To do what?"

"So you could try to win back breakfast."

"Uh-uh. I wouldn't give you the satisfaction."

Tom hums along with a radio jingle. "So you're saying you wouldn't have satisfied me."

Hey now. Watch it, man. "You know what I mean. I don't just . . . get all freaky in the presence of someone I just met."

"But, Shari, we've known each other for five years."

Kind of true. "All of it on the phone."

"Until now."

And that's where I have to draw the line. *Now* is a scary word sometimes. "Right or left?"

"Straight. Up the hill, take a left."

And we're back at the plant. The man has a good sense of direction.

I park in Mrs. Peterson's spot, a simple wooden sign announcing her as "THE REAL BOSS." I get out, and Tom gets out and goes straight to the plant.

"Where are you going?" I ask.

He points to the plant. "To work. You know. Take some notes, get some ideas."

"I'm coming with you," I say, gathering my goggles, gloves, and hard hat.

Tom returns to my side, and his shadow engulfs me. "Why? Don't you trust me?"

"I trust you." A little.

"I thought you were a solo act."

"I am." Shoot, I'd need a stepladder just to kiss his chin. I mean, not that I would ever kiss his chin. I'm just trying to describe how tall he is. Either a stepladder or longer lips. "I want to learn from the master. I want to look at the world through your eyes."

Tom stares into my eyes. "If you could only see what I see now."

I brush past him and head for the door to the plant. "What do you see?"

"The word *beautiful*."

I open the door and look back. "So I'm just a word."

He holds the top of the door. "It's a good word."

I put on my goggles and hard hat. "What if I consider myself to be pure, chaste, and wholesome?" See, God, I haven't forgotten about You.

He puts on some goggles but has trouble with the hard hat. "You would still be beautiful, Shari."

Yep. The man is good. And he's right. I am beautiful, and he's . . . he's the poster boy for the fantasies of horny nurses in Tully, Australia.

Ah, who am I kidding? He'd be a poster boy for fantasies of any woman anywhere.

Including mine.

Sorry, Lord, but the man is *hot*. Well, You made him. I'm just sayin'.

And then *we* wander. I take notes where he takes notes, and he takes notes where I take notes. When I doodle, he doodles, hiding his drawings. He takes more notes. I doodle some more when I see the guys working on the handlebars. I bet I could film over those handlebars while the bike is moving. I could even put the tire just about anywhere since "PETERSON" is visible on the fork. I could use Photoshop and have the bike "go" anywhere, like the Grand Canyon, Niagara Falls, Mount Rushmore—landmarks. Yes. I could make a collage of famous American places the bike could visit. No matter where you ride, you're home. Sweet!

"Yes!" I cry.

Tom blinks at me. "You just shouted, and I didn't even say a word."

I ignore him. "I just nailed my print ad."

"I did that yesterday morning," he says.

"Liar."

"You should talk," he says with a smile.

I put my hand on his chest and push. Nothing happens. I push harder, and he moves maybe an inch. "Get lost, man." I now know what a wall of muscle is.

"You must work out," he says. "I bet you have some nice cuts."

I have plenty of those, and some are of the verbal kind. "I said, get lost."

I go outside to the employee eating area and find a picnic table in the sun. Get lost, I told him. As if my little arm could push him anywhere he'd ever get lost. Hmm. Get lost . . . in America. Fantastic! "No matter where you ride, you're home—Get lost in America." That would make a *great* T-shirt. And it's another tagline! I don't yell this time. I look up and smile at

Tom, who is standing in the doorway. The man can sure fill a doorway.

I know what I'll do. I will ride across the Brooklyn Bridge for the thirty-second shot. Sound? No sounds but the natural sounds of the city, no announcer, just a graphic like . . . "Come home to America." That's good! Silent commercials get my attention more than the talking ones, mainly because they don't say anything stupid. Okay, the print ad is done, and the T-shirt is done. What about the radio ad? I could use the sound from the Brooklyn Bridge crossing again, and an announcer—probably me—will say the tagline. That only leaves the fifteen-second spot.

Shoot.

Those numbers again. Three hundred and thirty feet at fifteen miles per hour. I look up and still see Tom filling the doorway. I look down at the table where someone has drawn a diamond ring with some initials carved inside. It's kind of cornball, but it's not as bad as the one next to it: "I ♥ Billy Sue." I trace the diamond onto my paper and find it's roughly square. Nice diamond. Wait—

A diamond! I draw three bases and home plate. That could be the infield at Yankee Stadium. That's home plate. The left-field foul line is really short at the new Yankee Stadium. I could ride from left field and skid across home plate in a cloud of dust. An umpire's voice yells, *"Safe!"* Ride one home! No. *Drive* one home. Better. No matter where you ride, you're home. . . .

"Wow," I whisper as I write it all down.

"What's wow?"

How did Tom get across from me without shaking the table? I know I have amazing powers of concentration, but he has to weigh at least two-twenty. His shadow should have blocked the sun. Oh yeah. The sun's behind me. "Nothing is wow."

He leans closer to look, and I pull back my notes.

"You like baseball?" he asks.

Shoot! He saw my idea. "I was just tracing a diamond ring I found on the table here."

He folds his hands on the table. "A diamond ring doesn't normally have bases."

"I was just . . . tracing."

He drums his fingers on the top of the table, and it's got a nice rhythm. "You know, Shari Nance, it might be easier if we worked together on this."

He's kidding. "I don't work for you or your company." I smile. "And I never will."

"I happen to know that there's an opening in the junior account executive program," he says.

He can't be serious. "Um, Tom, I'm twenty-seven, I don't have an MBA, the MBA will eventually be from LIU, not Harvard, in three years, and I'm a black female. Oh yes, I'd be perfect for Hairy Ads, Hershey's Syrup, and Moldy."

Tom laughs. "Well, maybe you wouldn't have to work for Hairy Ads."

"Who would I work for?" I ask.

"Me."

Oh sure. Tempt me. "Right."

"Seriously. I've been thinking about doing something like this for a long time. I'll never make partner. That's a given. But with my track record and your brilliance, we'd make a fantastic team. We should open our own agency."

Oh sure. Tempt me some more. What does Corrine say at a time like this? Oh yeah. "Go on."

He sits back. "I mean . . . I manage a bunch of accounts."

"Forty-three," I say. "I checked."

He nods. "And you, I mean, Cringe manages . . ."

I sigh. "Fifteen."

Tom seems genuinely surprised. "That many?"

"Hey, I'm good at what *we* do."

Tom stands and walks around to my side, sitting a few splinters away from me. "Well put. You are good. You get down and dirty with the client. You take an interest in what you're selling. You care. You know how rare that is in this business?"

I know I'm rare, Mr. Sexton. You just haven't convinced me yet. "Go on."

"I know I won't be able to take all those clients from Hairy Ads, but if I retain even a third of my clients, that's a great start for us."

It's an incredible start, actually, especially for two people. "Did you make this offer to Corrine, too?"

He takes a short, quick breath. "Wow, you're sharp."

The sharpest. "And I'm betting it was, oh, two years ago."

He bumps his knee with mine. "Yeah."

"But let me guess," I say. "Corrine wanted to play it safe. She wanted the sure thing. She loved having an assistant like me do all her work for her."

"You're right," Tom says. "Corrine doesn't have an adventurous bone in her body. She only wanted to talk about all the risks involved, and she wanted me to find out if my current accounts would retain me if I left Hairy Ads. She likes the status quo, and I just want to go."

Time to hurt him a little. "So you stopped sleeping with her because she didn't follow your dream?"

He nods. "Something like that."

Which, as it turns out, is similar to my own situation with Bryan. An interesting coincidence. "Are you really serious about this offer?"

"Yes."

Again, no hesitation. It would be so nice to prove my worth to the world, but what can I bring to the table? "So you'll try to bring your clients on board, and I'll bring nothing, Tom. I'm not exactly an asset."

He moves his leg to rub fully against mine. Geez, his thigh is as big as both of my legs. "Nothing? Shari, you will bring realism. You will bring down-to-earth common sense. You'll bring sanity. You'll bring fire. And we wouldn't represent any product we didn't believe in."

"We're going to starve." I said that out loud? I mean, I said the "we" part out loud. "There are a lot of products out there not to believe in."

"True. But we'll find the worthwhile ones together. You're outdoorsy, and so am I. We'll do ads for any product that's good for the environment or helps put people in the great outdoors. We both like to eat healthy, so we can promote health foods."

I look at his chin. "How do you know I like to eat healthy?" I had Hot Pockets all weekend.

"You look very fit," he says, "and you have flawless skin."

I, um, yeah, I do. Flawless.

"You don't strike me as a junk food queen," he says. "Except for maybe . . . donuts. Yeah, you look like a . . . glazed donut eater."

How does he know this?

"And once we're established as an environmentally conscious and outdoorsy agency, the West Coast will come calling, I guarantee it."

And that's his old stomping grounds and a place I've always wanted to visit. "I don't know. It sounds . . . okay." It sounds freaking wonderful, but I have to keep him guessing.

"So, what do you say, Shari Nance? Are you willing to give old Tom a chance?"

And now he rhymes. "That was a cheesy rhyme," I say. I take a deep breath. "I say that you're just trying to A, get into my jeans, and B, get into my notebook. In that order."

"You got it half-right."

Which half? Do I ask him out loud?

"To prove my good intentions," he says, "here are my ideas."

He opens up his little notebook and I see cartoons. Cartoons? Each page has four boxes, and there are little stick riders on simple bikes. No words, just pictures. There's some sort of order in these drawing, but I'm not seeing it. "You can't draw a lick, Tom."

"I've been too busy watching you," he says. "I had to sketch quickly."

"There are no words, no taglines, no hooks."

"They haven't come to me yet." He touches my arm with a single finger, and my whole body shudders. "My mind has been kind of . . . occupied." I watch him trace a heart on my forearm.

My happy dance is about to begin under this table.

"I was all gung-ho this morning, but then I saw you through that window at the restaurant. The light hit you just right." He traces a diamond on the back of my hand. "You make it so hard to concentrate, Shari."

I slide my hand from under his. "How'd you know it was me in that restaurant? Where have you seen me before?"

He puts his hands on his thighs. "I've seen you about, oh, two hundred times over the last two years."

I blink. "Where? At the office?"

"Mostly on the Brooklyn Bridge," he says softly. "I don't always stay in my lane."

Him! "You're the guy who can't read signs!"

He nods.

"You nearly ran me over just last Friday." And he called me just thirty minutes or so later.

"Yep, that was me."

I blink. "So you weren't at JFK."

He shakes his head. "I flew out after I talked to Mr. Peterson at the Millennium. Who was that woman you were talking to after your meeting with Mr. Peterson?"

He has been stalking me! "Um, just a lost tourist." My eyes are so wide that my eyelids hurt. "You saw me while I was talking to her?"

He nods. "And she took your picture. What was that about?"

"I don't know." I've been followed for two years by every woman's fantasy, and I have no idea why. I am so confused!

"I just don't see how you stay so trim," he says. "You get a dozen glazed, mainly on paydays, and yet you stay so svelte."

Oh my goodness. "What are you? A stalker?"

He looks down. "No. I'm just the guy who's too shy to stop and talk to you, um, because . . ." He sighs. "Because you intimidate me with your beauty."

I cannot believe this. "You nearly hit me a dozen times with your bike! What, were you hoping you *would* hit me so you'd have a reason to stop to admire my beauty?"

He shakes his head. "I, um, I didn't know what I was doing.

I mean, if a random white guy on a bike just skidded to a stop in front of you and smiled, what would you do?"

"I'd run!" I say with a laugh. No, I wouldn't. "No, I would have probably . . . kept on walking, I don't know. I might have. . . ." I know I would have talked to him, especially if I knew it *was* him. "I know I would have recognized your voice, but we'll never know now, will we?"

He looks sideways at me. "Whenever I was in town, and it wasn't as often as I would have liked, I used to follow you on your way to and from work. At a distance, okay? I wasn't . . . stalking you. I was, um, shadowing you."

"Why?" I ask, though I think I already know the answer.

He sighs. "I just wanted to make sure you were safe. I didn't want anything bad to happen to you. I know it's crazy."

I had a knight out there when I was walking at night? "I'm a big girl, Tom," I say, which makes no sense because I'm so small. "I can handle myself."

He catches my eyes for a moment. "I can see that, Shari."

Geez, I'm blushing. "So you've just been out there watching over me, huh?"

He nods.

"Right."

"Really." He flattens his hand on the table. "I've always liked talking to you, and if I had any guts, I would have somehow found a way to talk to you face-to-face. In my mind, I saw you dropping something, like your purse or a package, and I would rescue whatever it was and bring it to you. But you don't carry a purse."

"I like to travel light," I say. "What, were you waiting for me to drop my handkerchief or something?"

He looks away. "Something like that."

It's actually kind of sweet. "So you're saying that I was Lady Shari and you were Sir Tom?"

He nods. "Yeah. I know it sounds corny."

It's actually wonderfully, sweetly romantic. "So you pretty much know my schedule."

He nods.

Let's find out. "What do I usually do on Tuesday nights?"

"Prayer meeting at Brooklyn Tabernacle," he says. "I usually sit in the back."

He was there? "You attend regularly?"

He nods. "Whenever I'm in town."

I know I would have noticed him. Unless he was hiding. But how can Tom hide anywhere? He stands out like a sore . . . god. "Where do I go on Sunday?"

"Nine a.m. service, and again, I sit in the back. You sure can dance. I've never been one to go to church, and, well, you have me going. I don't understand everything, but I really like going just so I can see you."

Wow. I have no snappy comeback. He has made me speechless.

I turn several more pages of his notebook and see—*wow.* That's an astounding drawing of *me,* and I'm wearing a hard hat, goggles, and the orange vest. The goggles make my eyes seem fifty times their normal size. "Is this supposed to be me?" Hey, he even drew in my sexy glasses. He has good eyes.

He reaches over and uses a pencil eraser to remove the goggles and the hard hat. He redraws my eyes, my eyebrows, my glasses, and even recreates my natural hair. He is *really* good. He adds one of my dimples. Is that what he sees when he looks at me?

"You can draw," I say, and I wish I could say more. I have to keep reminding myself that this man beside me is the boss's man, friend, man-friend—or something like that.

"I can draw well when I have the right subject, yes." He looks at my face then adds my lips and a sly smile. "And I finally have the right person to draw now." He stares at me then draws my little potato-chip ears. "I'd, um, do more with your body, but . . . I mean, um, well, I meant . . ."

Is he blushing? I think he is.

"You know what I mean," he says.

I know exactly what you mean, Tom, and it feels . . . scary. I've never had anyone protect me, even if from a distance, and

I've never had anyone draw me before. I've never had anyone even draw me a bath. And yet here he is, drawing me in . . .

"If I had the right kind of pencils, I'm sure I could capture you better."

You're doing some capturing of my heart right now. I cannot believe that this sexy hunk of a man is shy!

He drops the pencil and slides a few inches away from me. "I can tell you're not interested in hooking up with me, I mean . . ."

He blushes again! I am tying his big ol' tongue in knots.

"I mean, I can tell you're not interested in working with me."

Where'd his leg go? My leg was just getting acquainted with that tree trunk. "You said earlier that I'd be working *for you,* not with you."

"I like how you hang on my every word."

"No, I don't." Okay, I do.

He slides back. My leg says "howdy" to his. They're becoming old friends.

"We'd be equal partners, Shari," he says. "Fifty-fifty splits all the way. We'll even have a written agreement if you like. A legal partnership, and if either of us should want to walk away, we'll split everything down the middle."

I feel the warmth of his leg seep into my *other* leg. "It, um, it sounds tempting."

He puts his hand lightly on my back.

How can one hand warm an entire body?

"So you'll at least think about it?" he asks.

My back is suddenly hot. "I might think about it." Of course I will! I just don't want him to know how badly I want this— and a back rub from that hot hand. I wiggle a little, and he removes his hand. No! I wanted you to rub my back, man!

"And you don't have to buy me dinner or breakfast, Shari. I just got lucky. That nurse had to be the horniest woman Down Under."

Now there's the title of a good flick for Nicole Kidman to make.

Oh, now my back is cold. And if one of his hands could warm me up like that, what could two of his hot hands do?

"I'm, um, I'll be going back to the hotel now," he says. "I'm sure you'll want some face time with Mr. Peterson."

I'd rather have some more face time with you. Wait. How can I play this off as something other than what it's starting to be? "I need to follow you back to the hotel. I don't want to get lost. Let me say my good-byes to the Petersons."

"Sure." He stands and offers his hand.

"I can get up by myself, thanks."

He leaves his hand there. "Could you hand me my note-book?"

"Oh." I put the notebook in his hand, and he slides it into his back pocket. That poor notebook! It's going to get crushed!

After dropping off my equipment in the holding area, I walk lazily to the office while Tom waits by his rental car, a Ford Mustang. *That* man and *that* car in *any* kind of ad—that car would be a best-seller for sure.

Mrs. Peterson is still at her solitaire game. I guess this business does run itself. "Leaving?" she says.

"Yes. I wanted to thank you for your hospitality." I take out the two twenties and lay them on her desk. "Lunch was my treat."

She nods and collects the bills.

"Is Mr. Peterson around? I'd like to say good-bye to him, too."

"Trouble with one of the machines, don't ask me which one," she says. "He'll be at it till dark. And Mondays used to be so slow around here." She smiles. "We don't normally get visits from outsiders, no offense. And then we get two on the same day."

Hmm. "And Mr. Peterson told me Monday would be the perfect day for me to visit."

Mrs. Peterson wrinkles her lips and looks at the ceiling. "Hmm. Now why would Mr. Peterson say that this particular Monday would be perfect for you?"

I have no idea, unless . . .

She raises her eyebrows.

"He knew Tom would be here," I say. "He knew we'd both be coming."

"That's my Woody," she says. "He likes to make people uncomfortable, put them on the spot, see how they react. While he didn't seem to be paying attention at H&H, he really was."

And Mr. Peterson heard our crazy conversation. "I hope I didn't let him down."

"Just don't let him down next week. You're good people, Miss Ross. Truth be told, I didn't think it was wise for my husband to even use a New York ad agency. That place is so far removed from here in every way. We've been doing just fine without y'all, you know? I said Atlanta has ad agencies. Why not use them? And then you show up. You're not what I expected. You're just a little slice of home, you know that?"

A little slice of home. Another possible tagline. "Thank you for your kindness, Mrs. Peterson."

"Did you and Mr. Sexton settle your differences?" she asks.

She is so perceptive. "Um, there was nothing really to settle." Because we're really not that different. Okay, he's huge and I'm not. He's a real hunk, and I'm just a slice of a home girl. He's shy, and I'm . . . sort of shy.

"Did y'all come to some sort of agreement at least?" she asks.

"Something like that." I just wish I knew exactly what "that" was.

I know I'm forgetting something, something important. Geez. I need the freaking product! I am such a rookie. "Um, I should have run this by Mr. Peterson earlier today, but I'm going to need a representative bicycle to take back with me."

She nods toward the door. "It's already in your truck."

"It is?"

"You left your door unlocked, Corrine," she says. "See, you haven't completely lost your country roots. He didn't want to forget either. He said it was a present."

"A present? I can't accept a present from a client, Mrs. Peterson." Though Corrine does it all the time.

"He likes you," she says. "Say it was for your birthday. Use it however you wish."

"I just wish I could thank him. Does he have his walkie-talkie?"

She whips hers out. "He should." She hands it to me. "First button on the right there."

I press the button. "Mr. Peterson?"

"That's a strange voice," Mr. Peterson says. "You okay, Freda?"

"It's me, um, Corrine." Almost blew it again. "Thank you so much for the bicycle."

"I just figured you'd need it, Miss Ross. Might be a tad tall for you. Didn't have time to measure you. You drive safe."

"Yes sir. Thanks again." I hand the walkie-talkie to Mrs. Peterson. "Well, thanks again to you, too."

"You take care now."

I go to the GMC and look in the back. Wow. It's a red and black bike with all the accessories and attachments, including a really cool digital speedometer.

"Ah. You got the red one."

I turn and look at Tom and only see his chest. "I suppose you have one, too."

"Two, actually." He smiles. "And you've already seen them both on the bridge."

He didn't tell me he already had a Peterson bike! And he has two! He already uses the product and has been using the product to follow me around! How unfair an advantage is that? "Oh." I nod at his car. "You ready?"

"Oh. Yeah."

I follow him to the hotel, and I can't keep my legs still. Why do I feel so much anticipation? Nothing's going to happen. Bryan's coming Friday, and Bryan and I have a long history, even if it's stagnant and dull. Tom's still kind of evasive about Corrine. She may be psychotic, but there has to be *something* going on if she's still pining for him. He hangs around her for two years *without* sleeping with her? That's hard to believe.

And the only reason he's doing her dirty is so he can win this account. But he's been following *me*. He calls *me* all the time.

He's here with *me* instead of in Australia with her. Oh, he didn't know I would be here, but still.

And that offer of a partnership. Man, I wish I knew if it was genuine. Part of me thinks he's probably just trying to get a leg up tonight and an edge up on me tomorrow. He wouldn't work for Harrison Hersey and Boulder for so long without being super slick like that.

I am either a complete sucker . . .

Or it's going to be a very bumpy night.

Chapter 14

At the hotel, we stop in the lobby and stare at each other till my neck starts to hurt. Either I need to wear heels (not), or he needs to wear flats.

"Well," he says.

"Well," I say.

We're so eloquent.

"Shari . . ."

"Tom . . ."

At least we're still on a first-name basis.

"You're not making this easy, Shari."

"I'm not supposed to make this easy, Tom."

At least we can agree on something.

"Well, could I at least take you *out* to eat?" he asks. "A public place with lots of people."

"I'm afraid that would be a conflict of interest." And my heart is right conflicted now. I need an uncluttered heart and an open mind to pull this charade off, not more complications, even if he is so hot!

"Most of this afternoon has been a conflict of interest, Shari."

True. "I just don't think it's a good idea."

"Why not? It's just food and conversation."

After what his fingers, hand, and leg did to me today, it wouldn't just be food and conversation. "That could lead to other things, Tom, and, well, I have . . . I have this guy friend in my life."

He doesn't speak for a full minute. "I've never seen you with anyone, I mean, you've never mentioned . . ."

I nod. "I know. Five years of talking to you, I should have mentioned him, right?"

"Corrine never said anything about it either."

"I never share my business with Corrine," I say. "It's safer that way as much as she runs her mouth."

He looks at the floor, the chairs in the lobby, his suitcase, his shoes. "Well, wow."

My heart! Cut it out. Bryan is going to be in your apartment on Friday. "Sorry. I should have told you."

"Well, of course you have a man in your life. I'm, um, well, just . . . hmm."

I have completely flummoxed this man, and for some strange reason, it makes me like him even more.

He frowns. "Just consider it a compliment then." He almost smiles. "He's . . . he's lucky."

I tap him on the hand. "And you have Corrine."

He sighs. "I *don't* have Corrine. She's my *friend* in Australia, remember?"

Was that anger? I think it was. Wow. "Um, I probably shouldn't tell you this, but the jellyfish stung Corrine on the, um, on the breast."

He winces. "Ouch."

I wince, too. "She says it looks like a football. She's, uh, going to be a lefty for a while."

"That is such an odd image." He shakes his head. "Well. I guess the next time I see you will be at the meeting."

And a part of me thinks that's so wrong. That's eight days from now. "Yeah."

"Don't beat me too badly."

"I intend to." I hold out my hand.

He takes it, but he doesn't shake it. "Good night, Shari Nance."

"Good night, Tom Sexton." Don't think about what that hand can do to you, Shari. Remove your hand now. That's it.

There's your hand. Yes, it's already getting cold, but you can warm it up all by yourself.

Tom gets in the elevator. "Going up?"

Do not, under *any* circumstances, get in that elevator. You might do something incredibly impetuous and regret it in the morning. Besides, that elevator probably has a camera in it. "I'll, um, I'll wait for the next one."

He sighs and throws his head back. "Good night, Shari."

"Good night, Tom."

Now don't stand here looking to see what floor he's on. The stairs are *that* way. Use them.

I roll my eyes at myself and trudge up three flights to my room. My card key works the fourth time I swipe it, and I enter a suite that is almost as big as my apartment! I don't throw myself on the king-sized bed and get all dreamy and stupid like the dumb wenches in the movies. I don't go out and linger in the hallway looking up and down for the man of my dreams.

Because nothing is going to happen.

I set my tote bag in the closet and hit the couch. I check the clock. Five thirty. I should have called Tia to check in. And I should have gotten Tia's cell and home phone numbers before I left. I'm so bad at being sneaky. I guess it will have to wait. I'll see her tomorrow morning.

On a lark, I call Corrine just to see if her cell is still wandering the hospital. When it goes straight to voice mail, I decide not to hang up. "Just checking up on you, Miss Ross. I hope you're feeling better. Give me a call when you can." *If* you can.

I peel off my clothes and step into the shower—that has a bench seat? Cool. Very cool. It has to save cleaning a tub, I guess, not that I would have taken a bath anyway. I didn't bring enough lotion, and this hotel only gives you little bottles good for one elbow anyway. I'm about to sit on the bench but keep my booty from hitting the seat. No telling who or what was on that last. Maybe bench seats aren't so cool. I use up most of a little bar of soap to clean away the day, and when I let the hot water roll over my body, I think immediately about Tom.

I shouldn't be thinking about Tom.

I close my eyes and try to think about Bryan.

I can't.

I see Tom's hand, feel his finger on my hand, feel the warmth of his leg against mine.

I open my eyes.

My skin is ashy. I need to get out of this fantasy before I turn gray.

I turn off the water, towel up, use up all the hotel lotion and some of my own, and put on baggy red flannel pajama pants and a tight white tank top.

Denial. That's the name of the game. I must deny myself and keep my head clear if I am to succeed.

I look over my notes while lounging on a soft, dark brown couch, digging my toes between the cushions to warm them up. I've got some good ideas, but I'm missing billboards. Let's see . . . a picture of a commuter. Definitely a female. Dressed like me with boots. It'll probably have to be me anyway.

Two bikes? Who can *afford* two bikes? What one person *needs* two bikes?

Focus, Shari. Stop thinking about the man with the big hands. He is your enemy.

Where was I? The billboard. I'd have to get someone to take my picture as I . . . as I do what? Leap over a pothole? I can play Superwoman! I could put a briefcase on the back rack, wear one of Corrine's fancy tight pantsuits that might fit me—with my boots on, of course—and soar over a Brooklyn pothole. That reminds me of those Virginia Slims ads that said: "You've come a long way, baby." And I have. I'm here! I'm in a suite at the Hilton. I wish I could call and tell someone that. "Yes, darling, I'm at my suite in the Hilton, and it is *fabulous,* darling."

Okay, should I put any words on the billboard? Maybe the picture and the product name will suffice. If it's good enough, it could double as an Internet banner. I might have to do one with a man and one with a woman, though. It shouldn't be too hard to find some big, tall, rugged man in Brooklyn to help me out.

Mmm. There's one somewhere in this hotel. He has this chest, oh my—

I shake it off. Maybe I should have taken a cold shower.

Um, billboards. Right. New York billboards have to be artsy, though. They have to be thought-provoking, even controversial. A woman flying through the air with the greatest of ease won't even make anyone blink.

His eyes were so penetrating, so intense, yet soft. Intense and soft. The way they danced whenever he laughed. Not so much sexy as . . . genuine. Yeah. He has genuine eyes.

Focus, wench! You do not have eyes for this man. The billboard. Now.

I sigh at myself.

At least whatever I come up with won't get bad press like some of the fashion ads lurking around New York. Some of the billboards I've seen—wow. Some sell the most expensive clothing and fragrances using violence, blood, rape, and bondage. Some only use drug-addicted, bulimic, and plastic models to sell clothing that won't even be available in their sizes. Some models on those billboards are barely wearing the clothes they're trying to sell. I know skin is in. I know sex sells, but in the final analysis, these ads sell sex, not the product. But people do talk about it, and talk is the cheapest form of advertising, so, unfortunately, these controversial billboards can be highly effective.

His voice, soft, husky, juicy at times. And the way he looked when I told him about Bryan! He looked like he needed a big ol' hug, and I could sure use one after the stress I've been through since Friday. Oh, he's so precious and—

Sell the stupid bike, Shari!

I am no fun when I'm alone with myself.

Okay, where would this billboard go? It has to be displayed near a park. Those billboards are hard to get. It would be stupid to plaster it on the subway or on a bus. That would be kind of counterproductive, especially if I add the tag "If you owned this bike, you'd be home by now." Ha!

I write that one down. You never know what might work in

the world of advertising. I mean, "Where's the beef?" sold a butt load of hamburgers.

As much as I ate today, I should not be hungry, but I am. Being creative burns a lot of calories. I look at the room service menu for the Great American Grill. Hmm. It's open till nine. I could just put on some more clothes, go downstairs, get fed, and maybe some random guy from Klamath Falls, Oregon, shows up, we eat, have some conversation, laugh at each other's jokes, rub knees, maybe go somewhere to compare . . . notes. Sounds like a plan—

No. I do not need that complication.

I'm still no fun.

I call room service, order a burger and fries and some bottled water, and then begin doodling T-shirts. I put little stick people on bikes and realize that I really suck at drawing, even if it's only stick figures. I give some riders smiles, others Afros, a few only sideburns and glasses. They sort of look like Elvis. A child could draw better than this with crayons. I am no artist, but at least doodling keeps my hands and my mind occupied.

I should have asked Tom what his major was.

Shari, get back to—

Hush.

Maybe he has an art degree *and* an MBA. That's a logical assumption. And from Cal Berkeley. Ooh, la la. I'm ODU and now LIU. I have more acronyms than he does but none of the prestige. Why aren't people paid according to their skills and not their degrees in this country? Some of the most talented people in this country don't go to Ivy League schools, don't have MBAs, don't have silver spoons up their butts—

A knock at the door, and me without a bra.

I look through the peephole at a teenaged girl. I open the door, and she sweeps in, placing my dinner tray on the worktable in the bedroom. Since MultiCorp is paying, I add 20 percent to the tab.

The girl looks at the receipt. "Thank you so much. You know we already added the tip to the bill."

And she's honest? "I know. I, um, I just . . ."

Don't do this!

"Well, there's a, um . . ."

Are you even thinking? What happened to no complications? Don't start something you can't finish. Leave the man alone.

No.

"There is a man in this hotel who—"

"Two fifteen."

I look at the floor. Tom is right under me? "Um, white guy, six-two . . ." Nice eyes, great big paws . . .

"Gorgeous eyes," she says. "Burger and fries just like you. Some fancy wine."

They're not . . . gorgeous. They're soft. She's so young. "Um, could you . . ."

You're out of your freakin' mind! Stop doing this!

No!

"Yes?"

The girl seems so willing. Why aren't I? "Could you . . . wait." I tear a blank page from my notebook while my heart pounds.

What are you doing?

Nothing.

Then why are your hands shaking?

I'm just . . . sending a message. One simple message.

You're going to send him the wrong message.

No, I won't.

I write: "Why didn't you tell me you had two bikes?" Just a question, that's all. No harm in a question. I hand it to the girl. "Just take this to him, and if he has a reply, bring it straight back to me."

"Sure." She zips out, closing the door behind her.

It's just a note. It's not like I'm asking him up to my room, right? So what if he's right under right now . . . reading my message. I wish the floor was transparent. I wonder if he can hear me.

I tiptoe to and turn on the flat-screen TV, which would take up so much less space than the behemoth I have in my apartment, and I surf commercials while I eat. Yeah, I'm weird. Most folks watch the shows. I surf the commercials.

Oh geez. Charmin and the cartoon bears! So what if your toilet paper doesn't attach to dingleberries? And what are you trying to say about us? That we're all hairy as bears down there? That which is everybody's business is nobody's business. When I purchase toilet paper, I do not think of your stupid bears or dingleberries.

What's this? I have no idea what they're selling. Is it a feeling, an aura, a lifestyle, what? What is the freaking product? And where can I get it? I want to be the first person in my neighborhood to have this, um, emotion.

Family size! Whose family? Not mine. What if your family has twelve people? You'd have to buy four cans. Or what if you're a single lady like me? Aren't you afraid to offend me and lose my business? This commercial only reminds me that I'm alone. Thanks a lot.

Oh, here's a stop smoking aid that sounds like fun. It doesn't contain nicotine? Where's the fun in that? If I experience aggression, anxiety, suicidal feelings, dread, anger, rage, or bewilderment, I should discontinue using it? I live in Brooklyn! I work for MultiCorp! I experience all those things *every freaking day* before lunch! What's this? Rash, puffiness, peeling skin? Dag, this junk gives you diaper rash. Common side effects include unsettled stomach, gas, and vomiting. Sounds like a night on the town gone bad to me. And why would I want to see the doctor who prescribed this junk to me if I have all these problems? Go on. Don't quit smoking. Save yourself the rash and the vomiting. This is yet another product where the cure is worse than the disease.

Improved taste! What's that one about? Does that mean your earlier product tasted like butt and we didn't know it? All those years we thought it tasted just fine were a lie? Thanks for ruining my childhood.

Oh, not this foolishness again: contains *no* fill-in-the-blank. You can say that about any product, right? Milk—contains no alcohol. Cheese—contains no rat poison. Water—contains no MSG. Aspirin—contains no LSD. Like this little nugget of information will make your product seem safer and healthier. Ridiculous.

A knock on my door. At this time of night? And in a strange city? I wonder who it could it be.

I open the door, and the girl shoves the note in my face. "He wrote you back."

Obviously. I smile at the girl. This is fun for you, huh? I read Tom's answer, which is written just under my question "I thought YOU already had a bike. You seem like the type."

I seem . . . like the type. Hmm. Pretty vague. I'll have to have him clarify this.

Don't, Shari.

It's only a clarification.

Now who's leading someone on?

Honestly, it's only a clarification.

Yeah, and this is only a rationalization.

Nothing is going to happen.

"You gonna write him back?" she asks, having the nerve to tap her foot on the carpet.

Are we a tad bit impatient? "Yes." I write: "And what is my type, pray tell?" I fold and hand her the note. I know she's reading these.

"I'm really not supposed to be doing this," she says.

Neither am I. "Will twenty bucks be sufficient?"

She shakes her head. "Oh no, you don't have to pay me. I'm *really* not supposed to be doing this."

Oh. "You're just giving excellent customer service."

"I guess."

I cannot resist asking. . . . "Um, what was Mr. Sexton wearing?"

The girl's eyes practically roll back into her head. "Tight gray sweatpants and a T-shirt. He has incredible abs. And his chest is just . . . you know?" Her eyes dart down the hall.

"Yes." I know you want to see his incredible abs again. "Go."

I seem like the "type." What's that supposed to mean? I am no one's "type." I pride myself on being different, on being my own person, on not being a "type." I hate being pigeonholed into a "type." Let's flip this around, shall we? What "type" of man is Tom? He's obviously into dark skin. Is that a "type"? He's obviously in incredible shape. Is his shape or how he achieved it a "type"? He is very smooth, especially when he talks, except when I tie up his tongue. Is the way he talks a "type"? Is he even my "type"? I'm barely five feet tall and weigh as much as one of his legs. I am petite. I have small feet and tiny toes. Even my teeth are kind of small. He's larger than life, and my neck is sore from looking up at him. He should be massaging my neck. Is he the sensitive, massaging "type"?

A knock on the door. That was quick. I open the door.

"He wrote a longer one this time." She hands it to me. "But he wrote it really fast."

And I read: "Honestly, Shari, when I first saw you in the flesh two years ago, I thought you were a lesbian. Boots, jeans, sweater. Either that or you were from Oregon or Canada. Just thought you'd have a bike, though I never saw you riding one. I bike to work every day twenty-five miles each way from Great Neck. We both get a good workout on our way to work. Coincidence?"

A lesbian? Is he kidding? "Are you reading these?"

The girl looks down.

Yeah. She's reading them. "I am not a lesbian."

The girl nods. "Um, why don't you just go talk to him?"

Because I'm not supposed to be doing even this much. "It's complicated," I tell her. "Just one more note, okay, and then you're done."

The girl looks sad.

So am I. Hmm. Why am I sad?

End this now, Shari.

Oh, do I have to? That must be why I'm so sad. Thank you, Self, but I don't want this to end.

I tear another sheet from my notebook and write in large block letters: "I CANNOT BELIEVE THAT YOU THOUGHT I WAS A LESBIAN! I AM HURT AND WILL NEVER RECOVER! SWEET DREAMS, TOM TERRIFIC."

I don't even fold it this time, and I give the girl a twenty.

"I couldn't take that, really."

"Please take it," I say. "You've been a good sport."

"Okay." She pockets the money. "Thanks for, um, an interesting evening."

I turn off the TV then turn it back on to look at the adult movie offerings because the real Corrine would. They aren't my cup of tea. *Sizzlin' Sistas 6*? "Watch these sexy sistas as they explore each other's sizzling caramel bodies."

I turn off the TV. Caramel? Why not mocha? Or *café au lait*? Or bronze? They all can't be caramel-colored. I have *parts* of me that might be caramel-colored. If Tom ever drew my entire body, he'd need lots of different shades.

I can't believe that Tom thought I was a lesbian. Okay, I fit some of the stereotypes with my clothes, but I am heterosexual to the core. I love men. They have parts that fit naturally into mine. And yes, I'm twenty-seven and unmarried. What of it? That man is just delusional, that's all.

I look outside. I look at the clock. I look at the TV. I collect my notes and put them into my tote bag. I look outside again.

I check the clock. Too early for bedtime. I check my teeth for okra. Nope. Pearly white. I brush my teeth anyway.

I could call Bryan. Nah. I'll see him soon enough.

I look at myself in the mirror. Do I look like a lesbian? I've been hit on by women before. I must have something they like.

I look outside again. I look at the clock. I turn on the TV and watch a free preview for *Sizzlin' Sistas 6* for about ten seconds. It reminds me of health class. I hated health class. And none of y'all are caramel!

I turn off the TV.

I lie on the couch.

I examine my cuticles.

I decide not to trim my toenails.

A knock on my door. Another note? Maybe an apology. I rip open the door.

Tom.

Gulp.

In all his Tom-ness.

Chapter 15

Why aren't I breathing? How can I handle this professionally if I can't breathe? One needs oxygen to form professional thoughts.

He stands there in his boots, no socks, tight sweats, and a tight T-shirt.

And he holds a few pencils, some blank white paper, and a full bottle of wine.

"Yes?" I wheeze. I will never take oxygen for granted again. Maybe it's the altitude. I *am* on the third floor.

"I came to apologize," Tom says.

I make full eye contact with his chest again. "So . . . apologize."

"I apologize."

That's it? My eyes wander up to his.

"To make up for my infraction," he says, "I would like to draw you, free of charge."

Well, he is obviously prepared to draw me. Maybe that's all he wants.

What about the wine, hmm? The cork is already out, Shari.

It's a standard, um, hotel room–warming gift.

Yeah, and there's this bridge in Brooklyn I could sell you. The cork is out! You don't give *used* wine to people.

I swallow and try to get my tongue to work. "Well, um, how'd . . . how'd you know this was my room?"

"How'd you know where my room was?" he asks.

I look back at his chest. I could curl up into a ball right there. "The girl just blurted it out."

He laughs. "I had to pay her forty bucks."

The little tramp! And I just gave her another twenty. Sixty bucks she made off us plus the original gratuity plus 20 percent. An interesting evening for her, indeed.

"So, may I come in?" he asks.

I drop my eyes to his shoelaces. Yes. Shoelaces are safe. Such big feet. "I don't let strangers into my room."

"How about old friends?" he asks.

Good answer. Acceptable. He can come in.

No!

He's an old friend. We've been talking for years. No problem.

Still no!

Well, I'll just step aside slowly, and if he comes in or maybe a gust of wind blows him inside, it's not my fault. I step aside slowly.

You're in trouble, Shari.

Probably.

Tom enters, and I get the strongest whiff of oranges, lemons, and musk. I don't know what cologne that is, but it is intoxicating. I close the door behind me, and I hold my breath again. I have a man in my suite at the Hilton. So many firsts today.

Ask him to leave now.

He just got here!

He stands beside the coffee table. "Where would you like to, um, pose?"

I've been posing as Corrine all day, and I'm tired! Where to do this thing. Me at the window looking back? Nah. I'd look like an early seventies album cover, and that window is in the bedroom. Can't go there. Won't go there.

That's the first sensible thing you've thought tonight.

I'll lounge on the couch, and he'll sit in that chair. Distance. Must keep my distance.

"Sit in that chair," I say. Why don't I have any feeling in my hands? I see them. I just don't feel them.

He holds out the bottle of wine. "I, um, I didn't know if you liked wine. I hear this is pretty good."

I know nothing about wine. "The glasses are in the bathroom."

Are you crazy? You haven't had anything to drink since last New Year's!

I'll be fine. I just ate.

You'll probably get drunk just from the fumes.

Well, I do need to relax. I have been under a great deal of stress.

He returns a minute later with one glass of wine.

"You're not having any?" I ask.

"Oh, um, I don't drink," he says.

And yet you bought a bottle of wine with your meal, and you expect me to drink it. Hmm. Interesting. Presumptuous, but interesting.

He's trying to get you drunk.

No, he isn't.

I take a sip, and it burns so nicely down my throat. I want to chug it and get another so I can relax.

"You can sit," I say.

He sits.

I recline on the couch and look off into the distance trying to look contemplative and vulnerable.

You were vulnerable the second you let him in the room.

Hush.

I can just see him out of the corner of my right eye, and he looks so *good*. Should I take off my glasses? No. Then I won't be able to see him looking so *good*.

Take off your glasses, Shari.

No.

"Oh, I'll need to use the table," he says.

I pick up my glass and take a swig of wine as he pulls the coffee table to him, sets down the paper, and stares at me.

He's not staring at me. He's staring at the glass.

The glass is empty.

"Would you like some more?" he asks.

I am a fish.

Yep. You're going under.

"Sure," I say. What can one more glass do to me?

Twice as much as the first one did!

Hush. I'm on vacation.

He gets up, gets me another glass—this one full to the top—and returns to his pencils and paper. And he still looks *good*.

He filled it to the top. You sure he isn't trying to get you drunk?

He's just being . . . economical. He won't have to get up for a while, right?

You're blind, Shari, with or without your glasses on.

Tom doesn't move for a solid minute.

"I don't hear any scratching or sketching going on," I say.

"Just . . . mapping you out."

Yeah right. He's groping me with his eyes, those soft brown eyes. And he's probably staring at the toenails I should have clipped.

What a creepy thought, Shari!

I know. It's the wine talking already, okay?

Then stop drinking it and speak for yourself!

I hear some sketching and relax a little. I take another sip and begin to relax a lot. This is some *nice* wine.

"You're not smiling," he says.

I suck in my cheeks. "I am a model. I do not smile."

"It's okay," he says. "I have your smile memorized."

That was sweet.

Yeah, it was.

I hear more scratching sounds.

"I used to do this for extra money in college. I'd set up an easel on the sidewalk in San Francisco and just draw. Ten bucks a portrait. Used to bring in a couple hundred a weekend."

I think up a relevant question, which is amazing since I have no oxygen going to my brain right now and the wine is tearing swiftly through my brain cells—and my conscience. "You don't do caricatures, do you?"

"If people want them, I can do them. I prefer doing portraits.

Shows off my skills. Caricatures are too easy. It's not hard to add size to a pair of breasts, length to a nose, height to a forehead, hips to a skinny booty."

Breasts . . . booty. He's pushing my buttons. I wonder what he would add to me? Would he turn my B-cups to C-cups?

You'd tip over.

At least I'd have more cushions for my fall.

I take a peek while he has his head down. Hey, that's my shape. I'm kinda sexy. Why don't I have a face yet? And why can't I still feel my hands? "So you were an art major."

"Nope. MBA all the way."

I peek again. Ten toes. They are so tiny. "How boring."

"Yep. Completely."

"So why'd you stick with it?"

"Money. Opportunity. Possibilities. Adventure."

Opportunity. Possibilities. Adventure. Doesn't he know he's talking dirty to me? I mean, I now have the opportunity and the possibility for some adventure!

And a hangover.

Hush. Let's enjoy our company.

"What would you rather be doing?" I peek.

He catches me peeking.

I look off into the distance.

"You really want to know the answer to that question, Shari?" he asks.

And that gives me my answer. Whoo. Yeah, I know what he'd rather be doing—*me*. These pajamas are certainly warm. Oh, my hands are starting to tingle. Must be the wine. I sip some more. "I mean, career-wise."

"What I'm doing, only I'm not doing it for someone else."

Doing it. He is *merciless!* "You want to be your own boss."

"Yes."

"You want to be the master of your own destiny," I say.

"Yes. Can you hold still?"

No. C'mon, feet. Chill out. "Holding."

I hear him sketching again. "You have the cutest little dimples," he says.

Since birth.

"Um, could you turn your head this way just a touch?" he asks.

Touch! He's killing me! "Define 'touch.'" And now *I'm* killing me.

"A quarter inch."

I turn a "touch" and smile. "Better?"

"Yes."

I peek again. Man, he's good. My body is still disembodied, but my face is definitely my face, and my glasses are sexy glasses. "You plan on giving me a body, Tom?"

He looks straight into my soul, I swear. "I don't need to give you a body, Shari. God gave you a very nice body already."

Yes, He did.

This man is incredible.

Oh, now you agree.

I'm just sayin'.

But now my body is at war with itself! My legs are on fire, but the rest of me is freezing! I should have turned up the heat. That has to be the AC kicking on, and I know he can see my, um, nipples. "When you do get to my body, be kind."

"Are you cold, Shari?"

He noticed! "The thermostat is . . . is in the bedroom." I just said the B-word. I should never drink wine.

I told you, but would you listen?

Hush.

"I already turned the thermostat in my room way down," he says. "I can't sleep unless it's cold. You want me to turn up the heat?"

Too late! This man is *ruthless!* "I want you to turn up the thermostat, yes."

When Tom stands and turns, I let my mouth drop open. That is a booty only God could make.

Lord, You done good.

I smile. I didn't know my conscience could be so naughty.

I suck down the rest of my wine, and it makes my eyes water and my conscience take a nap.

Tom returns, and I try not to stare, but I can't help it. A mountain is moving toward me.

"I bumped it up to seventy-eight," he says.

Bumped! He has to know he's putting a hurting on me with his words! "Thanks."

He sketches a few minutes more then slides the picture across the coffee table. "How's that?"

I'm . . . I'm actually kind of beautiful. I suppose if I had a piercing or two and some tattoos, I could be exotically beautiful. His shading is outstanding. He's drawn my eyes and my glasses. I'm even a little cute. "Um, could you draw me without my glasses on?"

"I think they're sexy."

I'll leave them on then. Anything to fuel my, I mean, *his* passion. "Um, why don't you draw the rest of me? I look like a disembodied Dali angel." I know *some* art.

"I'm not very good at drawing clothes," he says. "I can never get the folds, contours, and shades right."

"But you're good at drawing skin."

"Faces. Yes. Neck up. Shoulders."

Skin. The man likes skin. I have some of that. "Have you ever done any nudes?"

He looks away. "No."

"Not even Miss Cringe?"

"No."

So I'd be his first nude? It's the wine talking, I swear. "Bare shoulders."

"Yeah."

I hold out my glass. I am such a lush! He brings me another glass full to the top. I wonder if there's any left.

I slide out of the straps of my tank top and let the straps dangle to my sides. "At least give me a neck and shoulders." And if you want to massage this neck and these shoulders, you go right on ahead and do it, big boy.

Keep it down, my conscience says. I'm trying to sleep.

Shh . . .

Tom stares at me for a full minute then draws. The heat kicks on, but my shoulders are already getting warm. He turns the drawing toward me. "Better?"

The little devil. He's even given me a little cleavage line. "Yes. But . . ." I'm starting to sweat, and I just told him to turn up the heat. I am so conflicted. "I have a really nice stomach." I pull up the bottom of my tank top, rolling it up to just under my breasts. Hey, I still have some abs. "Can you see everything you need to see, Tom?"

Tom nods and goes back to work while the wine and I have a long chat.

I hear heavy breathing? Is it me? I hold my breath. No. *He's* breathing harder. And that makes me sweat more. Little beads of sweat trickle down my back into my pajamas.

He turns my picture around. "Better?"

Man, he makes me look sexier than I've ever felt. Even my belly button is sexy. "I also . . ." What's left? "I have some nice legs, Mr. Sexton."

"Yes, you do," he says. "But, um, that's really not necessary, Shari."

I can't believe I'm thinking of taking off my pajamas. And *without* his help! I stare at my glass. Bottoms up! Glass number three tasted just like Kool-Aid.

I suck in a breath and slide out of my pajama bottoms, and my legs fill with goose bumps. I am so glad I did a little shaving down there earlier. "Can you, um, work with these, Tom?"

"Yes," he says. "I can work with them."

He takes a *lot* longer drawing my legs. He stares at them, sketches. Stares at them some more, sketches. His eyes drift over my hot skin like . . . like . . . I can't think. Like eyes drifting over hot skin.

"Better?" he asks.

He's made my panties quite small. Well, I am quite small. Duh. It looks as if I'm wearing a string bikini. This is the moment of truth. "You want to draw all of me, don't you, Tom?"

"Yes," he says, and oh yes, he's really panting now. "I want to draw all of you, Shari, but we don't have to, I mean, I don't need to." He blushes and shakes his head. "I think I should be going."

Without thinking, I hold out my empty glass.

"It's almost gone," he says. "Should I get you another bottle?"

No . . . way. I have almost killed an entire bottle of wine by myself. "Only if you join me, I mean, only if you have some with me, I mean, only if you drink some wine." My tongue isn't cooperating at all.

"I'll get you the rest," he says. He takes my glass. "You ate dinner, didn't you?"

I blink up at him. "Yes. Why?"

"Just checking."

He goes into the bathroom and returns with half a glass of wine.

I chug it all down and use my eyes to return him to my drawing.

He sits.

What was I about to do? Oh yeah. I start to remove my tank top when the couch decides to tilt. "Whoa," I say. Man, I drank too much too fast.

"Are you all right?" he asks.

I nod, but I am not all right. I want to feel his hot breath on my skin. I want all those oranges and lemons and musk to seep into my skin. But most of all, I want this couch to sit still! The online description of this hotel did *not* mention tilting couches!

Now where was I? Oh yeah. I was about to have him draw me nude. I'll bet it was some French wine. Yeah. An American wine wouldn't have made me think these things.

"Shari?"

I look up and see a vaguely Tom-shaped, um, shape. "Yes?"

"You don't look so good," he says. "Maybe I should just put you to bed."

I'm not drunk. I'm just not sober at all. "But I want you to finish my picture." And now I'm whining. Wine does that.

He tries to slide my pajamas back on, but my legs go into convulsions.

"I can use my imagination, okay?" he says.

He tries to slide them on again, and I nearly kick him a few times till my pajamas are safely back where they're supposed to be.

I try to sit up, but something slams my head back into the arm of the couch. Am I wearing my glasses? I am. Then why is the room spinning? I close my eyes, and the spinning gets worse.

"Let me help you," I hear him say, and in a few seconds, I am airborne.

"But Tom," I whisper, "I really want to see what you see when you look at me."

"Shh, Shari," he says. "It's okay."

And then he holds me. It's like he folds me into himself, and I am surrounded by hot muscle, citrus, and musk.

I . . . have . . . never . . . felt . . . so . . . safe.

And this isn't the wine talking. This is some primitive part of me that feels completely secure for the first time in my life.

He is so strong. I bet he could curl me fifty times and not break a sweat. I wrap my arms around his neck and stare at his lips.

"Tom?"

"Yes, Shari."

I want to tell him never to let me go. I want to tell him that if I died this second, I would die the happiest woman on earth. I want to tell him I have never felt so safe, so aroused, so—

Hey, I'm on the bed and under the covers, a stack of pillows under my head. He's pretty fast for a big guy.

"Tom?" I'm practically pawing at him. How can I be missing him with my hands? He's huge!

"Just rest, Shari," he says. He takes off my glasses.

He's so fuzzy! "Tom, what cologne do you use?" That was random.

"Jade East."

"I love it." I smell my arm. "I smell like you."

I feel the bed move. "Tom?" Where'd the lights go?

"Yes?"

"You're not leaving, are you?" I say to a moving mountain. How'd that mountain get in here?

"I really should," he says.

Oh, the bed is turning now. Stay still, bed! I will not come back to this Hilton if this bed keeps moving. "Please stay with me, Tom. Protect me. . . ."

And then I dream of marshmallows, Boston cream pies, whipped cream, big fluffy clouds, and even some freaking Charmin toilet paper.

Chapter 16

I wake up at midnight in my bed and under the covers, and I have the worst taste in my mouth. That's pretty normal. What isn't normal is the pajamas that I took off are now on, and Tom is lying fully clothed beside me and snoring softly.

What just happened? I have lost five hours of my life.

I see my glasses lying on the nightstand and put them on. I hear the heater kicking on. I smell alcohol in the air. My tongue tastes like rusty metal.

And I *feel* stupid. Why'd I drink so much? Stress and wine do not mix.

I slip out of the bed and walk on unsteady feet to the bathroom where I drink a glass of water, stare at an empty bottle of wine, and then brush my teeth. I'm just rinsing my mouth when Tom appears in the doorway.

"Are you all right?" he asks.

I was nearly naked on that couch, but I woke up clothed. A man is still here with me and was recently lying beside me on my bed. I vaguely remember the man drawing my picture and me taking off most of my clothes. I have lost five hours of my life. No, I am *not* all right. "Yeah," I say.

"You sure?" he asks. "Oh. Sorry. I put your pants on backwards."

I look. Yep. "It's the new style," I say, shutting the bathroom door and turning my pajama pants around. I take a deep breath, open the door, and see Tom sitting on the couch, that evil couch where this evening began.

I sit on the opposite end, curling my feet under me. "Um, Tom, I have to know."

He narrows his eyes. "Know what?"

Oh, don't play coy with me, Mr. Sexton. "Did anything happen?"

"Oh." He shakes his head. "Nothing happened, Shari. You, um, you passed out. I just put your clothes back on, and, um, put you in the bed. I didn't want you to catch cold. I stayed to make sure you were all right. I never should have brought you that wine." He smiles. "I should have cut you off after the first glass."

I nod. He stayed with drunk me for five hours and didn't try anything? Well. He'd have to be one of the few men on earth not to try. "Did I, um, make a complete fool of myself?"

"No," he says. "You're a cute drunk."

"No, I mean, did I say anything I shouldn't have said?"

He blinks.

"I mean, what did I say?"

He looks at the ceiling briefly. "Nothing you should be ashamed of. Although you said the word *juicy* a couple times just before you passed out."

I am about to blush myself off this couch. Either that or I'm having an entire body hot flash. "I don't drink very often. I'm sorry I was such a fish."

"It's okay," he says. "You're under a lot of stress. It's not easy being two people."

I look at the coffee table and see my picture, only Tom has added a flannel shirt and tight jeans to my formerly almost naked body. "Why'd you change the picture?"

"That's the real you," he says.

Yeah. The real me. "Thanks."

He slides closer to me. "Are you sure you're okay, Shari?"

I nod. "I'm okay. I am such a lightweight. I have no tolerance."

He rubs my shoulder. "You're a sweet drunk, though. And so

quiet while you sleep. I had to keep checking to see if you were breathing."

And how'd he do that? I sniff my shoulder. Oranges? "Um, did we kiss?"

"No," he says. "I, um, I did kiss your cheek. You, um, kind of purred."

It must have been a sweet kiss. I just wish I could remember it. "Well, you must be pretty tired, Tom, so . . ." Please go so I can properly vent my embarrassment on a pillow.

"Before you passed out, you asked me to stay, Shari," he says, "so I stayed."

Because I was drunk and horny.

"And really, nothing happened," he says. "I made sure you were warm enough, I fixed the picture, I watched you for a while, and then I guess I dozed off myself."

I nod. "Well, thank you for, um, for respecting me."

He slides even closer, and I feel his heat. "If we ever did, um . . ."

Yeah. If we ever did, um . . .

"I'd want you to remember everything," he says.

I want so much to snuggle up with him, but I can't send him the wrong message. Wait. I've been sending him the wrong messages all night. I sigh. "Tom, I want you to know that what happened, um, that's not me."

He rubs my back. "I know."

Oh, that's nice. "And it won't happen again," I say. I have to get him out of here. "Um, did anything like this ever happen with Corrine?"

He reaches around me and grips my shoulder gently, pulling me closer. I can't stop him, and I don't want to stop him. "Pretty much for the last two years, yeah."

Corrine gets drunk, passes out, falls asleep, date ends. "Not much of a relationship."

"No," he says, his cheek brushing my hair. "I just lost interest, especially when she started drinking so much. I've been going through the motions. I don't call her, don't return her calls, I make vague or no commitments, I make excuses. I've been hoping she would break it off so I wouldn't have to."

I can't see Corrine ever giving up Tom, not with all he has to offer. "It's not very fair to her."

He nods. "No. It isn't. I should have broken it off immediately after she turned down my offer."

"So why haven't you?" I let my right hand wander to his thigh because, um, my hand is cold. Geez, he's made out of steel. Hot steel?

"I still like her," he says. "But only as a friend. She turns heads, and clients notice. She really knows how to schmooze. She knows how to work a room. She's been good for business." He sighs. "I know that's superficial and jacked up and wrong, but there it is. I use her, and she uses me. . . ." He pulls me even closer. "But nothing in my life has ever felt anything like this, Shari. I am really. . . ." He sighs. "I've never met anyone as special as you. You're not afraid of anything. You're fearless."

Oh, I have plenty of fears, trust me.

"I know this is going to sound cliché, but you make me feel like a man." He moves a stray lock from my forehead.

"And Corrine doesn't?"

"No. She doesn't make me feel anything."

I want to tell him that he makes me *feel*. I want to tell him that I need him to feel every inch of my body. "So if Corrine is good for business, what am I good for?"

"Don't take this the wrong way," he says.

I probably will. I have a horrible headache.

"You're good for business and, um, pleasure, Shari. You're the perfect mix of both." He kisses my forehead. "You make me smile. Just being with you today did my heart some good, even when we were arguing. You are an amazing woman, truly amazing."

I look up at his lips. I want to kiss him so bad for saying such amazing things about me. "You're . . . pretty amazing, too. I have never . . ."

No. Don't tell him anymore. He already knows too much, and he's already seen too much.

"Never what?"

Don't.

"Nothing." I rest my head against his chest.

He stares down at me. "Never what?"

Can I trust him not to laugh? I sigh. "I have never been with anyone but Bryan. He's been my, um, one and only."

Tom doesn't react at all. "Tell me about Bryan."

I'm in a god's arms, and he wants me to talk about Bryan. What is up with this man? "You don't want to hear about him."

"Sure I do," he says. "He's my competition."

Not at this moment. "He's just a very good friend." Whom I occasionally sleep with. Hmm. I am such a beautiful mess. "Bryan wants to drag me back to Virginia to marry me." I snuggle closer to Tom. "And I don't want to be dragged."

"I can't imagine any man dragging you anywhere," he says.

This man knows me. I look up at his face. "He's, um, Bryan's coming to visit me this Friday."

He laughs. "You're having a busy week."

Aren't I? "I'm going to break it off completely with him." This feels right. It has to be done. "I'm going to tell him that I found somebody."

"Who?"

I hide in his chest again. "You. I hope."

He runs his fingers through my hair, and I get goose bumps down to my pinkie toes. "You hope correctly, Shari Nance." He hugs me, kissing my forehead. "I've been hoping for someone like you. If I had known that I was talking to the perfect woman for five years, I wouldn't have wasted so much time."

"I've wasted about twelve years with Bryan," I say.

His body jolts. "Twelve?"

Why'd he say that louder? "Much more off than on," I say quickly.

He shakes his head. "Twelve years?"

Yeah. It does sound jacked up. I slide my booty onto his legs and sit in his lap. "I'm cold."

He surrounds me with great big arms.

I could get used to this. "Yeah, um, since we were kids."

"I've known very few people in my life for twelve years," he says. "Wow."

I am sensing Tom pulling away. I can't let him do that. "I should call Bryan and save him the trip, but . . ." I sigh. "He'll probably come up to New York anyway to hear it from me in person. He's old school like that." And why was I holding on to Bryan again? Oh yeah. I was afraid to be alone, even though I was four hundred miles away from him and really didn't need or miss him. *That's* jacked up, too. "I, um, kept Bryan around while I was waiting for someone better, someone better didn't show up, so I held on to almost as good."

"You have a wonderful way with words."

"Thank you." But they're sad words. Man, I've wasted some serious time here. "I, um, Tom, you're someone better. You're the best."

"I'm not the best."

"Yes, you are. Any other man would have taken advantage of me like I'm sure I wanted you to." Geez, I told him I was juicy! "And you didn't. You respected me." I rub my head on his chest. "You protected me from myself."

"I would always protect you, Shari," he says. "But that doesn't make me the best. I'm really pretty ordinary."

And he's humble. That is so sexy. "If I say you're the best, Mr. Sexton, you're the best. God blessed you with outstanding good looks, charm"—buns, abs, and body of steel—"and the softest brown eyes. . . ." I can't stop smiling. Maybe it's the effect of the alcohol, or maybe it's the alcohol's effect wearing off. Either way, I'm smiling.

He smiles. "I like your eyes, too. How, um, blind are you?"

"Not very."

"I really do think your glasses make you look sexy. Something about the way they make your pretty brown eyes bigger."

I look at my hands. "I wouldn't have pegged you for a romantic."

"You're pretty romantic yourself."

I'm just all out of practice. "What do we do now?" I take his hands and hold them to my stomach, which isn't feeling so hot. "We're obviously compromised on this competition."

He squeezes my hands. "No, we aren't."

I lean back. "How aren't we? We're seeing each other again after tonight, aren't we?"

"Yes."

That's right. This isn't a one-night thing. Man, his hands are so big! I put one on my stomach, and my stomach disappears. "This is kind of like snuggling with the enemy, though, Tom. You can't go to war with the person you're snuggling with. It is just not done." Why do these sound like movie lines? I watch too many movies.

"Ever see Spencer Tracy and Katharine Hepburn in *Adam's Rib*?"

"No." I rub his legs. "I've seen a lot of movies, though, just not that one."

"They're both lawyers, and while he prosecutes a woman who killed her husband, she defends the woman in court *and* at home. And despite their differences and a bunch of verbal fights, they still love each other."

"Good thing we don't have any differences." Inside, where it counts. "So what you're saying is that . . ." I squint. "You're saying we can still snuggle, and maybe more." I give myself goose bumps. "And we can still be competitors?"

He pulls my hips closer to him, my booty firmly planted on a very nice, firm spot. "That's why I wanted you to join me in our own ad agency. Then we can do this . . . and maybe more."

I like that phrase. "Maybe more" has so many possibilities.

"And we'll work late together," he whispers, "and travel together and eat out together."

"We'll never get anything done," I whisper. Why am I whispering? Geez, I want to grind on him so badly! C'mon, God, I'm three years from thirty, my sexual peak.

He moves his hands to my hands, holding them gently. "Is never getting anything done such a bad thing?"

I'm almost panting. "It is when you have a huge monthly rent bill." I want to arch my back and grind on him, but I don't. I want to do so many things with this man.

"Two can live much more cheaply than one." He pulls me even closer.

Doesn't he know that he's driving me crazy? "I like my space." I like this space, too. He surrounds me, but I feel no claustrophobia.

He kisses the top of my head. "I'd give you your space."

"I like my freedom."

He drops his head and looks me in the eyes. "I'd give you all the freedom you needed." He kisses my lips lightly. "I'd even give you an entire bedroom of your own at my house in Great Neck."

We've just kissed. My stomach is fluttering. I hope it's from the kiss and not the wine. "Is it a big house?"

He kisses my cheek, oh so softly. "It's more of a bungalow, and it's only half paid for. The taxes are ridiculous, but . . ."

And then we kiss for real, his hand holding my chin, and it's the kiss you've wished for since you were first hitting puberty and noticed that boys were sort of cute sometimes when they weren't being so stupid, and it's a real, deep, soul-stirring, tears-causing, toe-curling kiss that sends shivers up and down your spine and back again and makes you want to sing "A Whole New World" while soaring on a flying carpet.

So I liked *Aladdin*.

It was *that* kind of a kiss.

I am never leaving this room.

Ever.

I am never leaving this man's arms.

Ever.

Shoot.

I have to pee.

Chapter 17

I break lip-lock and roll out of his lap. I go into the bathroom, do my business for a very long time, wash my hands, and return to the couch, moving as far away from him as I can, squirming my toes under the cushion.

"Why are you way over there, Shari?" Tom asks.

I'm hiding. "I can't think objectively about anything if I'm touching or kissing you, okay?"

He, too, moves farther away from me. "Neither can I."

That didn't turn out the way I wanted it to. He was supposed to come down here to *keep* me from thinking.

I lean into the arm of the couch and catch my breath. "Tom, we barely know each other." Okay, I know I let him see most of me. "I've only been a voice on the phone for five years and a person for you to follow around for the last two. And now you're asking me to change my life completely. You're asking me to jump, and it sounds like you're asking me to jump over to Great Neck." Well, maybe he is. I know I'm jumping to a pretty big conclusion here. "Tom, I love Brooklyn. I don't want to leave it."

"So you'll keep your apartment. We can commute. Weekdays in Brooklyn, weekends in Great Neck."

That sounds . . . doable. And logical. But *way* too fast. Shacking up after truly only knowing each other in the flesh for one day. It's crazy!

Only I don't want to stop him, especially the flesh part. I need my life to start now!

"I've been scouting out locations for an office," he says. "You wouldn't believe how many empty floors there are in Manhattan alone. But we wouldn't need an entire floor. We wouldn't even need a real office. We could work out of your apartment or out of my house."

This is starting to sound less like a spur-of-the-moment proposal. He has really thought a lot of this out. But working out of my tiny apartment? We'd bump into each other every two minutes . . . which does have its advantages, but . . .

"What about a production crew?" I ask.

He smiles. "You're looking at him."

"Right."

"I have many skills."

Whoo. I'll bet he does. Sorry, Lord. He has to. Just look at him! You made him that way.

"As I told you, Shari, I'm doing this project old school. Pen, ink, camera, Photoshop if necessary. I have all the machines in the studio at my house. My gear isn't as high-tech as what the real professionals have, but I know how to use what I have. And we can be old school together."

"I don't know, Tom. I'm . . ." I hesitate. "I don't have any artistic skills or technical skills."

"You have art in your bones, Shari."

This from a man who's seen most of my bones. I'm blushing.

"It's in your blood, Shari. And you have fresh ideas, and they're fresh because you haven't been infected by an ad agency that promotes crap and calls it gold."

"MultiCorp shines up a lot of crap, too," I say. I sigh. "I just don't . . . know. You know?"

"No."

"No more no's!"

"I like your nose."

I like *his* nose. I want it nuzzling me. "Are you this witty all the time or are you only witty after, um . . ." How to put this into one phrase? Hmm. "Are you only witty after drawing a semi-naked drunk woman, putting her to bed, *not* taking advantage of her, telling her you've been protecting her from afar, and then giving her the best kiss she's ever had?"

"Yes."

Good answer. The *only* answer. "Do you mind if I think it all over?"

"I expect you to. No deadline, no pressure."

Man, he is like a fresh, cool breeze on a hot day. "Thank you."

He turns slightly.

I hop up onto my arm of the couch.

He laughs. "I'm not coming down there."

"You, um, startled me." I like this coy part of me. I think I should expand on it.

"Just know, Miss Shari Nance, that I am going to kick your pretty, sexy booty all over that conference room next week."

"You wish," I say, wishing he was kissing on me some more.

"Well, let's put a wager on it."

Another bet? I want to win this one. "Okay. When I win the account, you have to . . . do what we just did, even the drawing. There are other parts of my body I've never seen." I smile. "You can even use a magnifying glass if you want."

"So if you win," he says, "I have to snuggle with you and maybe more."

I nod. I also want to drop the "maybe."

"And I get to draw more of your sexy body."

Hmm. Yeah. It doesn't sound like much of a hardship for him. Or me. "And . . ." Hmm. A bet we both can win? I like it. "No. That's it."

"Okay," he says, his hand sneaking across the couch, which is silly. That hand could never sneak anywhere, as big as it is. "When I win the account, you'll have to quit MultiCorp and join my new ad agency."

He has a one-track mind. "You'd hire a loser?" I ask.

"I'd hire my favorite rival."

"And what would be the name of this new agency? Sexton Nance or Tom and Shari?"

His body follows that hand across the couch, and his hand gets to my right thigh before I can blink. Tall people sure have it easy. It would have taken me another five seconds to cross that distance.

"Nothing as ordinary as Sexton Nance," he says. "Tom and Shari sounds nice."

It does. Kind of just . . . rolls off the tongue I want to use on him.

"I'd let you name it, Shari."

"I'm not very good at naming things." I slide off the arm of the couch and scoot closer to him. "I named my first dog Methuselah. He was a shar-pei. All wrinkly. I named my first car Hiccup because that's about all it did."

"The Methuselah's Hiccup Ad Agency. Trendy."

"The word is *edgy*."

"The sharpest."

"But I wouldn't name it that," I say, sliding up onto his lap again, this time deciding to straddle him because, I'm, um, cold, and it's, um, much more comfortable, for, um, *him*, and it's easier to talk to him, you know, face-to-face.

Okay, I'm tripping. It feels really good down there. My "happy space" is rejoicing.

"I'd probably name it Breezy," I say.

"Breezy?" He holds me closer.

I am definitely warming up. Good thing I, um, straddled him, so I could, well, capture all that warmth. "You had no problems with Methuselah's Hiccup, but you have concerns about Breezy?"

"Not very edgy." He pulls me even closer to him, and I don't fight it. I want to smell like oranges and lemons for days.

"It's family friendly," I say. "It's cool. You know, breezy." I sneak my hands around to his back. Geez, I can barely reach around this guy.

"Not very avant-garde. Sounds like a lot of wind to me."

I begin to massage his lower back. "Hush. It's how I feel right now with you. Breezy." And very juicy. Well, I *am*. His body feels nice to mine.

"Why not . . . Methuselah's Breezy Hiccup?" he says.

I hunch farther up his lap, locking my feet around his back. I am about as close to this man as the law—and God—allows. "We'd be an ancient, windy burp." I dig my fingers lower into his back, and he sighs. "I'm not hurting you, am I?"

"No." He closes his eyes. "We should, um, separate soon."

Not while I'm this close to you. "Separate? Why?" I slide my hands under his shirt and rub his back, his skin so smooth and hot.

"The game's afoot at six a.m. tomorrow."

I stop rubbing. "You're getting up at six?"

"I booked the earliest flight I could get," he says. "I have to get back to the city fast. Otherwise, I won't be able to kick your booty."

I dig my nails into his back. Ow. I think I just bent a few nails. "So you're leaving me . . . now?"

"I really should, Shari. I wouldn't want to wake you in the morning."

No. He can't leave. Not now! "I want you to wake me in the morning. You have to stay."

"I'm afraid we'll, um . . ." He frowns. "I know I might try to . . ." He sighs. "I'm worried that if I stay . . ."

The man just read my mind exactly. I can't finish a sentence in my head either.

"We don't have to do anything but keep each other warm," I say.

He nods. "I think I can manage to do only that, but what if we get too hot?"

Yeah, what if. "I'll turn down the thermostat."

He smiles. "Okay, I'll stay."

He puts those big meat hooks under my shirt, rubbing on my lower back. Yeah, buddy. Tear it up. Nice. "But I must leave at four," he says.

"Why?" I kiss his chin. I kiss just above his chin. I have to strain to kiss his lower lip.

"I turn into a pumpkin."

"This isn't *Cinderella,* Prince Charming." I nuzzle his neck with my nose. "You're not leaving me."

"I don't ever want to leave you, Shari."

No one has *ever* said that to me. I might start crying. I move my hands around to his front and start feeling me a real man's chest. Geez, I'm jealous. Not too much hair, bigger nipples than mine, definite cuts.

"But to get you to work with me for the rest of my life, Shari," he says, "I have to win this competition, and I can't win it if I'm only thinking of you. Or what you're doing to me right now."

He noticed. That spot must be especially tender. I graze his nipples with my nails. I don't play fair.

"Shari," he groans, "it took me five years to get you, and I don't want to lose you."

"You got me, Mr. Sexton." I'd be certifiably insane to let this man go!

He rubs the back of my neck. "I . . . want to kiss you again."

I climb as far up his body as I can, and we kiss, tenderly, soulfully, our eyes open the entire time. And despite all the wonderful things I just know that his body can do to me, these kisses turn my legs to rubber and make me juicier than anything he's done or said to me so far.

I pull back. "Promise not to leave me."

"I promise." He holds me close.

"Don't leave me, Tom," I whisper.

"Never," he whispers.

And as I listen to his heartbeat, I realize that win or lose, I win.

I win. . . .

Winning is the *junk*.

Chapter 18

Since we both decided that the bed would be too great a temp-tation, I awake the next morning on the couch smelling like citrus fruits. I also have a headache, cotton mouth, and a stitch in my side.

And no Tom.

Tom is not in this room.

He broke his promise!

Wait. The shower's running. He's humming? Imagine that. A man is humming in my shower.

He stayed.

I'm not going to cry. He said he would stay. I still might cry. He does what he says he's going to do. I'll have to nominate him for a Nobel Prize.

I search for my glasses and find them on the coffee table. How'd they get there? He must have taken them off when I dozed off. I go to the bed, take off the bedspread, wrap it around me, and shuffle to the bathroom, where I stand there watching a god wash himself. Oh, I can't see much because of the curtain. And the steam billowing above and below the cur-tain steams up my glasses.

And my loins.

I want to join him in there so badly.

"Morning," I say brightly. I start brushing my teeth with cold water.

He sticks his head out of the curtain. "Morning. Hope you don't mind."

Me? No, I do not mind that a god is showering in my bathroom. Heavens no. Feel free to invite me in and wash my back. And the rest of me. "Just leave me some hot water."

He smiles, returns to his shower, and continues humming.

I rinse my mouth and spit. "You stayed."

"You asked." He laughs. "Nice hair."

I look at my natural tresses flying every which way. I am such a wild woman. I shake my head, and my hair doesn't move. And now I know what he's been humming: "Natural Woman"!

So I have to sing the words.

We make a nice duet.

"I'm going to buy you breakfast after all, Mr. Sexton."

He shuts off the water. I watch his arm come out and grab for a towel. I could get the towel for him, but I have to, um, see how far he can reach. A long, wet leg and half a *perfect* booty leaves the shower. I've never seen one of those. I don't even see him take the towel or return his leg and half booty behind the curtain. I'm still blinking at where his leg and booty were when he slides open the curtain and stands there with just the towel around his waist.

"I hope they have omelets," he says.

I drape my arms around him, and the towel stays around his hips. He must know a special towel trick. "You like eggs Benedict?"

"No."

"Good." I kiss him on the chin. "You're gonna have to bend down lower." I keep my eyes down as he does, we kiss, and the towel still stays put. Hotel towels need to be smaller. I bet they'd be easier to dry.

"We need to get a move on," he says. He collects his clothes, gives me a hug and a kiss, and leaves my hotel room only wearing that towel.

I close my door quickly. I hope no one saw. I crack the door and take another peek. I close the door. Only *I* want to see that.

After I dress and do nothing more than shape my hair, I decide to check in on Corrine, even though I have no idea what time it is in Australia. It rings this time, so I wait.

"Shari! It's about time!"

The wench is awake and is obviously off her meds. "I had my phone turned off, Miss Ross. I've, um, been having some trouble with the, um, battery."

"But I got your message, Shari!"

Oh yeah. Hmm. "It was working when I called you *then*, Miss Ross." That was weak.

"Have you been able to contact Tom yet?" she asks. "He called my cell twice while I was heavily sedated, but he didn't leave me a message. I have been leaving him messages for the last four hours!"

Where do I begin to answer her question? Let's see. . . . Yes, I was able to contact Tom, repeatedly in fact, all night if you really want to know. You might even call it some serious contact. "I haven't been able to call him, Miss Ross." Because he's right here! Well, he's walking to his room in only a towel right now. "My phone is so messed up."

"I don't think he's coming to see me, Shari!"

I bite my tongue. I want to say, "Ya think?"

"I must have left him a thousand messages, and I've heard nothing! Not a peep!"

Well, I heard him snoring last night. He kind of growls. It's sexy.

"Where could he be, Shari?"

Well, he's in the room below me. I just watched a very mean towel stay on his perfect booty.

"At any rate, Shari, I am coming home immediately."

Oh no! You can't come back yet! "You're, you're all better, Miss Ross?"

"I may never be completely healed," she says. "There is still so much swelling. I had to buy some bras off the rack here."

Not off the rack! The horror! But you still can't come back!

"And they have the strangest numbers for sizes. I'm not staying here another minute. Did you air out my apartment?"

I never even went there. "Yes, um, you have such a beautiful place, Miss Ross. Do you want me to shut your windows before you return?"

"Of course, Shari."

Then I've already done it. That was an undone task done without me doing anything. Or something like that. But she can't come back now! I need a few more days!

"Didn't you say you were sending me flowers, Shari?" she asks.

Oops. "Miss Ross, they, um, they didn't have the bird-of-paradise flowers at the florist there." I *might* be right about that. "I know you like them, Miss Ross. I only wanted to send you the best."

"It's just as well. I'm about to go into the terminal now."

Already! "Which terminal? The one on, um, Dunk Island?"

"The one in Brisbane. I left Dunk Island hours ago. Why do you ask?"

Why do I ask? "Um, no reason."

"Shari, you sound stressed. Is there anything I need to know?"

"No." I said that *way* too quickly. "Will you, um, be recovering at your apartment then, Miss Ross?" *Please* don't come in to work, not until after Thanksgiving, you wench!

"What day is it there, Tuesday?"

"Yes." She doesn't even know what day it is! Oh yeah. The International Date Line thing.

"Well . . ."

I hold my breath.

"I've already taken the week off."

Sort of. You were in Macon, Georgia, yesterday and today. You ate at H&H, and oh, you even drank a bottle of wine with your, um, friend, who didn't sleep with you but really wanted to, I'm sure. You had a busy night.

"And I need to see my doctor right away," she says. "Set up an appointment."

She has so many doctors! "Which doctor, Miss Ross?" She *needs* a witch doctor.

"Dr. Fine, of course."

Her GP? "But don't you need a specialist, Miss Ross?" One who specializes in box jellyfish stings and blown-up breasts?

"Dr. Fine will decide that, not you, Shari dear."

I reach into my tote bag for some paper. "What day should I set it up for, Miss Ross?"

"Thursday."

I write it down.

"I won't be getting in to JFK until late tomorrow night."

Whew. With her taking the rest of the week off, that gives me today through Friday to nail this thing. I can call in sick next Monday and Tuesday, and Corrine will be none the wiser. This *could* work, but it would stress me out less if . . .

"You could probably take all next week, too, Miss Ross," I say. "Like you said, we've been really slow. All our clients seem to be content." Just not the newest one yet.

"I'll let you know. Keep your phone on at all times from now on, Shari."

"I will, but I don't know if it will work, Miss Ross."

"Get a new phone then."

Click.

Yeah. On my way back to JFK, I'll just pick one up somewhere. What a wench.

I pack what little I brought, check all over the suite for anything incriminating, find nothing, put my picture in the tote bag, grab my tote bag, and open my door. Tom stands there blinking.

"She left me seventy-three messages," he says. "What kind of woman leaves seventy-three *three*-minute messages, all of which essentially say the same exact thing?"

The desperate kind of woman might do that. "I just called her myself. She's on her way back. She'll be in the city on Thursday."

He hums a little. "So soon? Hmm. That scrambles things a bit, doesn't it?"

Like a bunch of eggs. "She's still taking the rest of this week off, though."

He lifts my chin. "That's . . . that's good, isn't it?"

I step into him, feeling his warmth. "It doesn't give me much time, but I'll manage."

"And next week?"

"That . . . that could get tricky. I guess I'll just . . ." Shoot. I haven't thought that far ahead. So many variables. "If she *should* come in this week and Mr. Peterson calls and asks for her, I mean, me, what am I supposed to do?"

He wraps his arms around me. "You'll just have to be her again."

"Our desks are a few feet apart, Tom." Think! "Tia will just have to route everything to my cell."

"A solution."

Sort of. Tia does have duties of her own that don't include being *my* assistant.

He grinds me a little. "Remember to keep your phone charged." Then he hugs me. "Don't worry. We'll figure this out together."

I kiss his chin. "Thank you for the hug."

"You are so welcome. Now where are the omelets?"

Watching Tom eat an omelet is an erotic experience. I may not ever be able to watch him eat again. He slurps, he tears, he sucks. If it weren't for the green peppers, I might think he was working on me. But I'm not yellow. Hmm. What do I eat? Pancakes and link sausages, the three-inch kind. Yep. They're disappointing, and no matter how much I try to annoy him by drizzling syrup on them and eating them end-to-end, he isn't fazed at all.

He looks at his watch. "We need to get a move on if we're going to make our flight."

"*Our* flight?"

"I, um, looked at your ticket," he says. "I wanted us to travel together."

"And we'll be driving together! Thank you!" I really need some more sleep.

"We don't have enough time to drop my car off and make our flight."

I shrug. "I can drop mine off."

"The bike might not fit in the Mustang."

Oh yeah.

"Wanna race?" he asks.

"What does the winner get?" I ask. I love betting with this man.

"A kiss," he says.

Another bet I can't lose. "You're on."

After collecting our statements from the front desk and turning in our card keys, we race out of Macon on I-16. My GMC has some horsepower, but I have difficulty keeping up with Tom's Mustang zipping in and out of traffic.

Traffic thickens when we hit I-75, and Tom slows to a reasonable speed. I take a moment to call Tia.

"How did it go?" she asks.

"Okay," I say. "Anything from Mr. Peterson?"

"All quiet."

"Can you route anything from him to my cell?"

"Will do."

I hesitate to say the next thing. "And if Miss Ross should return, um, early, like maybe Monday, can you still transfer all calls, especially if they're to her, to my cell?"

"She is coming back early?"

"Yes. As early as Monday morning, I think."

"But that means . . ." Tia's voice trails off.

"I know, I know."

"We will think of something. Oh, I am sorry. I should have told you this immediately. Mr. Dunn called this morning and wants an update from Corrine."

No! "I'll have to give him the update."

"But what if he wants to talk directly to Corrine?"

Yeah, what if? Hmm. "I'll just tell him that Corrine has been working on it while on vacation, became temporarily incapacitated, handed the reins to me, I ran with it, here it is."

"Mr. Dunn is no fool. Why would Corrine go on vacation in the middle of a project, especially if she is in Georgia now?"

Oh yeah. That. "I'll figure something out. When did he call?"

"A few minutes ago. At nine sharp."

A nine o'clock call from Mr. Dunn usually means the call is of utmost importance. "Well, if he calls again, route him to my cell. I'll see you in a few hours."

"I will be here. Bye."

I want to share all these new complications with Tom, but they are not his problems. I just have to get back. I think better in New York.

We turn in our rentals, and we meet in the main terminal. I'm not hard to find because I'm pushing a bicycle. He makes me kiss him for losing the bet, but he returns the kiss just fine. Checking the bicycle isn't as tricky as I thought it'd be. They must fly bicycles all the time. Bicycles that fly . . . over potholes. That is still a good idea.

We sit several rows apart on a packed flight to JFK, but that's okay. I'd probably be messing with him instead of thinking all this through. I try to think about all the possible variables, the wild cards, the tragedies that could happen . . . and I fall fast asleep.

And I dream.

It's kind of an ordinary dream at first. I'm walking across the Brooklyn Bridge on a sunny day, only the bridge is completely deserted. Halfway across, I see a man on a bike rolling my way. As he nears, I look down and see my boots. I look up and he makes a beeline for me. I have to jump out of the way, but it's all slow motion like something out of *The Matrix*. He hits the brakes. He smiles. I walk over to him. He takes my hand.

"Shari."

I open my eyes. Tom is holding my hand. "Hi."

"We're here."

I look around at an empty plane. I jump up. "Wow. I was out of it."

I keep holding his hand out of the plane, through the tunnel, and out into the terminal. I like this feeling. It's as if we're returning from a business trip together, which we kind of are. He turns to me in front of all these people, kisses me tenderly, and gives me a hug.

"I guess we can't be seen together till this thing's over," I say, pouting.

"We'll survive." He squeezes my shoulders. "We're survivors."

"Yeah." I stand on tiptoe and lightly brush his lips with mine. "Call me, okay?"

"I will."

And then I stand there with all those people rushing around me and watch Tom walking off ahead of me. He's not hard to see. He walks with purpose, his head up, his eyes straight ahead. I want to run up to him and, I don't know, dip him to the ground and suck the tongue from his head.

But I don't.

Mainly because I'm at JFK.

Without a ride.

Hmm.

Why didn't I put this part in my itinerary?

Taxi?

Why not?

I'm just full of firsts these days.

Chapter 19

As soon as I leave the terminal and turn on my phone, I see voice mails waiting for me. I listen to the newest one first: "Corrine, this is Dunn. Give me a call soonest."

I shudder a little. That was a *recent* transferred call. What if I hadn't had Tia do that? Wait. It would have gone straight to Corrine's office phone, and she never checks her messages on that thing. I have to do that for her. I stop shuddering. Because of my boss's incompetence, the holes in my plan fill themselves.

I listen to the next voice mail: "Oh, this is ridiculous. What kind of a phone do you have? I will reimburse you for whatever phone you get, now, just get one! Oh, for goodness' sake! Call me now, Shari! I need you!"

I sigh. I'll bet the rest of these are from Corrine, too. I listen to the next one: "Shari, this is Tia. Dunn needs an update from Corrine. You better call him."

Okay. I've already gotten this information. I listen to the next one: "Shari, I told you to keep your phone on. Don't you ever listen to me? I leave and you fall *completely* apart. Call me immediately!"

And the next: "Shari, where are you? We need to talk! Call me *now!*"

I erase them all and prioritize. I have to deal with Mr. Dunn first since I will be seeing him in a little while. I call the office and have Tia transfer me to him.

"Mr. Dunn, this is Shari Nance. I understand that you've been trying to reach Corrine."

"Yes, I have."

"Mr. Dunn, Corrine's been in Australia." Please don't ask me any questions!

"But I have an itinerary right here in front of me that says Corrine was in Macon, Georgia, yesterday touring the Peterson Bicycle plant."

Okay now. Get your "facts" straight, Shari. "That's right, Mr. Dunn. She *was* in Australia for a little R and R following the LA fiasco, you know, just to clear her head." And get stung by a box jellyfish, have her breast become a big football, the usual Down Under adventure.

"She went to *Australia* in the middle of an important project?"

Yeah, it does sound suspicious. "Oh, Miss Ross has been working on the Peterson project, I assure you. I have all her notes with me." In my handy tote bag in my own handwriting. "She gave me quite a bit of information from yesterday's tour of the plant."

"I didn't see you at your desk when I came in. Where are you?"

At JFK eyeing taxis. They all look the same. Who decided taxis should be that shade of yellow? How can you tell which ones won't rip you off? "Um, I took a half day, Mr. Dunn. I'm getting over a bad chest cold, but I'm all better now." Yeah, my heart was cluttered, and now it's clearing. "I'll be in after lunch, and I'll bring our ideas straight to you."

"When will Corrine be back from Macon?" he asks.

Never. "Um, well, you see, she did some snorkeling out in Australia and got stung by a box jellyfish."

"Nasty sons of bitches."

I'll have to send that box jellyfish a thank-you note. "Yes. And she needs to see her doctor Thursday, so she's going to take the rest of this week off to recover at home. I will be in constant contact with her, so if you need anything, Mr. Dunn, you just give me a call." And call me first! "Um, she's turned her cell off. You understand. She doesn't want to be disturbed. She wants to rest after her, um, harrowing ordeal."

"And yet in her condition," Mr. Dunn says, "Corrine flew from Australia to Macon to see Peterson anyway? That's dedication. That's determination. That's the kind of leadership we need around here."

Yeah, right. She was in Australia waiting on Tom to pleasure her happy space. "Yes sir. It sure is."

"So what's our timetable on this Peterson thing?"

Our? What's he mean by that? "We have a sit-down in the presidential suite at the Millennium on Tuesday." But I don't know the time! Shoot. I have to call Mr. Peterson to find out.

"That's quick. What time?"

"Um, the time hasn't been confirmed yet. I'll get right on that. I, um, I talked Mr. Peterson out of having the meeting over at Harrison Hersey and Boulder."

"Those nasty sons of bitches. I knew they'd try that. How'd you convince Mr. Peterson to do that?"

Yeah. Um, that's something *Corrine*, not me, would have done. "Corrine was, um, indisposed, you know, with the box jellyfish sting, so she instructed me to call him." Well, I kind of told *myself* to call him, right? "I mentioned fairness and impartiality, and Mr. Peterson agreed wholeheartedly."

"Good thinking, Shari. That's the take-charge attitude you need to have to succeed around here."

Yeah, and here I am taking charge and waving taxis away. "Yes sir." Do I mention that we have to have the *finished* product ready to roll for the day before Thanksgiving? Mr. Dunn probably has high blood pressure as rotund as he is, so . . . no. It will have to be a surprise to him. And to me. I don't have anything finished.

"Are we ready for battle?" he asks.

No. "We'll be ready, Mr. Dunn."

"I don't want to be embarrassed in front of HHB. You better be readier than ready."

Is *readier* a word? "We'll, um, we'll knock 'em dead, Mr. Dunn." If I live through this.

"I can't wait to see those sons of bitches when we smoke 'em."

He'll . . . *see* . . . their faces? "So you'll be, um, joining us at the Millennium, sir?" Please say no! This isn't a huge account! I mean, it's a nice account, don't get me wrong, but it's nothing to brag about in *Advertising Age*.

"I wouldn't miss it for the world," Mr. Dunn says. "See me as soon as you get in the office with those ideas."

"Um, will do, Mr. Dunn."

Click.

He is so rude. Well, hmm. Mr. Dunn will be there. That's okay, isn't it? He'll see *me* in action and . . . I don't have anything to show! I have so much to do! Who do I call next?

A taxi beeps at me. I shake my head.

I call Tia and fill her in on more of the madness. "Can you think of anything I haven't thought of?"

"No," Tia says. "I think you have everything covered, but I am so afraid for you."

That makes two of us. "It's okay. I'm good. Oh, could you call Mr. Peterson as Shari and ask if the time for the meeting has been finalized? All I know is that we're meeting on Tuesday at the Millennium." I give her Mr. Peterson's number.

"Am I your assistant now?" Tia asks.

She kind of is. "I owe you big-time, Tia."

"It is okay," she says. "Of all the people here, I would gladly be your assistant."

Tia is such a good person. "Um, Corrine may call the office looking for me. Shoot her to my cell, too. Oh, and if Tom calls, do the same."

"Tom Sexton?"

How much do I tell her? I have to tell someone about Tom! I want to tell the world about Tom! "Yeah, we're, um . . . we've become better acquainted."

"Why is your voice so soft, Shari? How well acquainted are you with him?"

Pretty darn well. "We're, um, we're . . . close."

"How close?"

I can't tell her that. "Let's just say that I didn't mean for this to happen, but I'm glad it did, Tia."

I hear nothing for several seconds. "What are you saying, Shari?"

"I might have, um, kissed on him. A lot. And he kissed back. A lot." And we cuddled and snuggled and even spooned a little on the couch. It's not such an evil couch anymore.

"But he is your boss's boyfriend," she whispers.

"Not anymore." I sigh. I don't have time to explain all this to her. "He's wonderful, Tia. Amazing, truly amazing."

She says something in Spanish. "Your life, Miss Shari, is one big carnival."

Yes, it is, and I'm caught in the middle of a three-ring circus right now. "I'm going to need all the help you can give me, Tia. I'm going to need your help big-time for the next week or so."

"I will do what I can. And I will pray for you."

I love good New York Catholics. "Light some candles, too. I'll be in this afternoon."

"I am lighting a candle right now. I keep one in my desk for occasions such as these."

"Thanks."

"I hope you know what you are doing."

So do I. "Bye, Tia. See you soon."

I look at yet another taxi driver waving to me. What? Get on! Maybe if I move away from the curb I won't get harassed.

Now how can I totally shut out Corrine until I really need to talk to her? If she's in the air, she won't be able to answer me if I call now, so I call her cell and leave a "technical difficulties" message: "Corrine." I count to three. "Shari." I count to three. "Dropped." I count to three. "Damaged." I count to three. "Broken." I count to three. "Your message." I count to five. "Call me." I count to two. "Office only." I end the call. Now if

Corrine gives up on my cell phone and calls the office, Tia will redirect the call to my cell.

Sometimes I am brilliant.

But brilliance isn't always perfection.

I'm sure I'm forgetting something.

But so far, so good.

Who's next?

Bryan?

Bryan.

I need a clean slate. Okay, it's more like a scorched earth, but I have far too many complications right now to have Bryan show up on Friday—or any day for that matter now that Tom and I are . . . bonding? We've really already bonded. We're connecting. Yeah. I can't have Bryan break that connection even for a second.

If I can just hold Bryan off until after Thanksgiving, if I can keep him away from me for a little while longer, I can . . . I can end our relationship. What sense does that make? I can't just put him on hold and then lower the boom later! I have to end it now.

I zip my North Face jacket to the top. It's getting a little chilly, and here I am about to do the coldest thing to someone who is, despite his small town mind, lack of vision, and inability to accept my choice of a home, my friend. And it's the longest friendship I've ever had. Maybe that's the angle I have to take. Shoot. "Let's be friends" doesn't mean "let's be friends" anymore. It means, "We're through, and I don't want to see you again." I just . . . I just have to put him off for a few days. That's all.

What time is it? A little after twelve. I hope he's still working second shift at Advance Auto. He should be at his apartment. I dial the number.

"Hey, Share. What a nice surprise."

"Hey. Um, this week has been insane, Bryan. Corrine has me busting my tail over this new account, and I'm afraid I won't have any quality time for you until *after* Thanksgiving, so maybe it's best you just hold off on your visit." That should do it. Oh. He probably didn't hear me the first time. "Um, hold off until after Thanksgiving, okay?"

"But I've already got my ticket, Share. I got it real cheap. It's one of those nonrefundable kinds. I gotta drive down to Charlotte to catch the plane, but it'll only cost me about a hundred bucks to fly nonstop to New York."

Oh, Bryan! This was not the time to show some sense. The last time he flew out of Roanoke and had to pay seven hundred bucks to fly to LaGuardia. "I'll pay you back, I promise." I am so warped. I'm promising to pay for a ticket to bring Bryan back to Brooklyn *after* Thanksgiving so I can break it off with him forever. How heartless is that?

"Share, I had my heart set on coming up. I cleared my work schedule and everything. I miss you."

Don't return the sentiment, Shari. Don't do it.

But I have to pacify him. I have to make him see things my way.

"I miss you, too, Bryan," I say. "It's just that this account is so important, you wouldn't believe how important, how *crucial* it is." How much the rest of my life depends on it.

"No. I guess I wouldn't believe it. I've never understood any of what you do."

Which is another reason to dump your shortsighted tail. Why can't I just let him have it now? Because I know him. He'll fly up here Friday and harass the crap out of me. He might even pull a Stanley Kowalski on me and yell, "Shari!" all night long outside the Brooklyner.

"Bryan, I am so stressed right now. I mean, I'm late for work. I am never late for work." And no, fool, I do not want to get in *your* taxi. Fuzzy dice *and* a hula girl on the dash? Are you kidding? You are a driving cliché, man. Scram!

"You sure there isn't something else?" he asks.

"There's nothing else, Bryan." Just everything else. And *someone* else. "I'm just swamped."

"There is something, Share. I can hear it in your voice."

I take a deep breath. "There's nothing wrong, Bryan. Really."

"Girl, I know you. Tell me what's bothering you."

What I used to love about this man I now despise. He could always read me so easily. He was a living, breathing shoulder to cry on. "You really want to know?"

"Well, yeah."

What can I say that will *guarantee* that he stays there? Hmm. A snowstorm might do it. I look at the sky. It's only mid-November. Little chance of that. "I'm, um, I'm thinking of coming home for Thanksgiving." This should jolt him. I haven't been home for Thanksgiving since moving here. "And it scares me, Bryan, you know?"

"You coming home for good?" he asks.

Another thing I don't like about Bryan. He can leap to the wildest conclusions based on little or no information. Okay, I sometimes do it, too, but not all the time like Bryan does.

"I'm coming home for a *visit*, Bryan. You know, turkey, stuffing, seeing my family who still don't speak to me for leaving home in the first place. It's already stressing me out just thinking about it."

"So, what, I was going to come up there and we were gonna travel back together?"

Yet another wrong conclusion. "Um, no. I mean, you can't come up this week, right? Right?"

"I don't know, Share. It sounds like you need me."

Like a hole in the head! "Bryan, I'll need you *next* week more when I come home."

"That doesn't make any sense, Share. Either you need somebody or you don't, and it doesn't matter when."

I never said I needed you, Bryan! Hmm. That taxi looks safe enough. It even looks somewhat clean. "Look, Bryan, I'm about to get into a taxi."

"You never take a taxi, Share."

"I know. That's how crazy it's been. Promise me you won't waste your time and just show up on Friday. I will have no time for you, no time at all."

"But I already paid for the ticket. I might as well use it, right? I'll see you when I can."

I get in the backseat. "William Street, Lower Manhattan."

The driver nods and pulls away from the curb.

"Bryan, you really *can't* come up Friday. I won't be able to see you." Hey—I can escape to Tom's house in Great Neck. Yeah. And if Bryan flies up anyway—no. He'll have no place to stay, and Brooklyn is no place for a country boy to wander around in. "I mean that, Bryan. I can't see you at all. I have told you before that when we work a project, we have *no* time for anyone. I may not even come back to the apartment all weekend or even Monday or Tuesday." I'm really stretching it here. "We are on a serious deadline here."

After a long pause, Bryan says, "You serious about coming home for Thanksgiving?"

No. "Yes."

"You've said that before."

Oh man, as part of an unimportant conversation, not as something I actually meant! "I mean it this time." I really ought to. I need to rebuild a few bridges in my life. Just not next week!

"Well, I don't believe you. You sound like you're falling apart, Share."

I am, but . . . "I'm fine, Bryan. Really. I've never been better."

"You can't fool me, Share. I'm coming up Friday anyway. You need me."

I bang my head against the seat. "Bryan, please don't come up. I'm begging you."

"Now I know I have to come up. You've never begged for nothing as long as I've known you. I told you that place would get to you one day."

He is such a caring, sensitive man, but . . . "Okay, Bryan, you got me." The gloves have to come off. "I have been holding back on you."

Silence on his end.

"I'm, um, I hate to break this to you, but . . ." I hate myself. "I met somebody."

"Somebody . . . else?"

That's what the phrase means, man! "Yes."

"Since we last talked?"

Yes and no. "I've known him for five years." Oh, man. I shouldn't have said that. I've just opened a can of worms for a man who likes to fish.

"You've been seeing him behind my back for *five years*?"

I can't remember the last time Bryan yelled at me. "It's not like that." I look at the driver looking at me in the rearview mirror instead of at the road. "Watch where you're going!"

The driver's eyes return to the road.

"You talking to him *now*?" Bryan asks.

Twice he yells at me. "No, I was talking to the taxi driver." He's looking at me again? "May I help you?"

The driver throws up his right hand and scowls.

"This is not taxicab confessions, mister." Okay, it is. "Sorry about that, Bryan."

"I don't understand, Share. You've known this guy for five years, and now all of a sudden . . ."

"I'm sorry, Bryan, but I am who I am, and, as sad as this is for me to say, I . . . I'm not interested in you anymore." I am the worst person on Planet Earth right now. Sure enough, here come the tears.

"You sure seemed interested in me the last time I came up there."

"And I was—then." Sort of. I was just so lonely, and he was about to pop the question, and I didn't want to answer. "This all happened so fast, Bryan." I wipe away a tear.

"But you just said it was five years in the making."

I am confusing everyone—me, Bryan, and the stupid driver who keeps looking back here! How can I explain this without hurting Bryan's feelings? "You remember the junior prom, when you first asked me out?"

"Yeah, but what does that have to do with this?"

Walk with me a bit, Bryan. You'll see my point. "Remember how long it took you ask me to go?" Forever. Okay, the word *forever* as defined by a junior girl in high school, which is really only a few weeks.

"Cuz we were friends, Share. Since seventh grade."

Since I had braces. "Right. I waited *four* years for you to ask me out." Not really. We went out all the time, just not as boyfriend and girlfriend.

"I didn't know you were waiting," he says.

What an opening! "And I've been waiting. . . ." I really shouldn't go here, but I have to. "I've been waiting *twelve* years for you to ask me to marry you." Man, I am the worst person who ever lived.

"But I tried to ask you the last time I was up there!"

I'm so glad I tackled him. "Did you? I didn't hear you say the words."

"I couldn't. You were all up on me."

Yeah, he remembers. "You were with me after that for two days, Bryan. Did you ask me then? No. Did you have the ring with you?"

"No. I thought we'd go pick one out together. Remember when we used to go look at all the bling at Henebry's?"

I did a lot of dreaming at that jewelry store, and Bryan was right there beside me. "Yes, I remember, but that was when we were kids, Bryan. We aren't kids anymore, and I'm past all that now. Besides, you told me you would never move up here. That sealed it for me."

He's silent for a few moments. "You never should have left home, Share."

"As I've told you many times before, I *am* home."

"You weren't crazy when you were here."

True, but I was bored out of my freaking skull. "Bryan, please understand, you'll always be one of my best friends. Always."

"Right. One of your best friends. I don't get you anymore, Share."

Because I changed and you didn't.

"Well, do you love him?" he asks.

Oh . . . man. "I don't know. Maybe."

"You know the guy five years and you don't love him?"

No matter how I answer this, I am so screwed. If I say I *don't* love Tom, Bryan will hightail it up here to "win" me back. And if I *do* say I love Tom, Bryan will probably do the same thing. "I do love him, Bryan. I didn't want to say it because I didn't want to hurt your feelings." And I never used to lie at all. I hate myself so much.

"My feelings are already hurt, Share. There's nothing more you can do to them now. Just be honest about it."

This seems to be a recurrent theme here lately. "You want honesty?"

"I think I've earned it."

And he has, but I doubt it's the kind of honesty he wants to hear right now. "Okay. You stood by me for a long time, Bryan, but that's all you did. You stood there. You only see your little slice of the world. I see the big picture. I want more out of life than Salem, Virginia, and you've never been able to see that. All you want to do is go play softball with your buddies, drink beer before going to Salem High School football games and reliving your glory days, and then disappear during hunting and fishing season. I have never wanted any part of that. I want something more, and I've found it." Hey, I'm not crying anymore.

"Then why'd you let me believe you loved me?"

Not *this* again! "I don't think I've ever really loved you, Bryan. I was drunk off my tail the only time I ever told you that, and what was that, ten years ago?"

"I thought you meant it. I thought we had something, Share."

We did. It was so ordinary and dull, but the old Shari liked ordinary and dull then. "But that's all in the past now. You have to go on. Find someone who loves you for who you are." What is this foolishness coming out of my mouth? I am so sleep-deprived.

"But Share, I thought that person was you!"

I sigh. "Didn't it occur to you that when I left Salem, that maybe I wasn't satisfied with life? That maybe I wasn't satisfied with you? I left you, too, Bryan."

He's silent for a few more moments. "Remember that poster you got me? The one that said if you truly love someone, set them free?"

Okay, the tears aren't quite finished. "Yes. I remember." The poster had seagulls on it.

"Well, I let you go, didn't I?"

Now both eyes are leaking. "Yes, you did."

"And I still love you." Now *he's* crying. What a mess! "I'll probably love you for a good little while, Share. Just wanted you to know that. I gotta go."

Click.

That was heartbreaking! It shouldn't be, but it is. Tom is the one, not Bryan. Bryan was never the one. He was my fallback plan, that's all. He was always just "almost as good."

Why aren't we moving? Oh. We're here.

I wipe my eyes. "How much?"

"Forty-five," he says. "I need no tip from you."

Wow. I scrape up forty-eight bucks, leaving me three dollars for something to eat until I hit an ATM. I hand him the money.

He counts it and hands back three ones.

"I said, I need no tip from you." He stares hard at me. "Four years, five years, twelve years? It is a long time not to love a man."

Geez, everybody's a critic. "Have a nice day."

"He sounded like a nice boy," he says.

I walk toward the entrance to my building. Yes, Bryan was a nice boy.

But at this time in my life, I need me a nice *man*.

Chapter 20

I rush to Tia. "Any calls? Any messages? Did Corrine call?" I feel like an ad exec already. My pulse is racing, I don't say "hello" to my only friend here, and all I do is ask questions without waiting for an answer.

"No." She hands me a Post-it. "Your meeting is at two p.m. Tuesday."

"Thanks."

She squints. "Have you been crying, Shari?"

I nod. "It's just some stress. I'll be okay."

"Are you sure it is only stress?" she asks.

"There's more to it, but I'll manage."

She points to her phone. "You want me to open up the floodgates?"

"Um, sure."

I go to my desk, unloading and sorting through my notes. What an unholy mess! I can't go in to see Mr. Dunn with these. This isn't very professional at all. I just don't have enough time to type them up. That's how I'll have to roll. I organize them as best as I can, putting the broadcast ads on top. I'm about to bolt for Mr. Dunn's office, when my phone lights up.

Ted. "Hi, Ted."

"Hi, Shari. Is Miss Ross back?"

"No, Ted." Wait, I'm her. I have "her" receipts. "But I have all her receipts. She only has a few this time. Could you be a dear, Teddy, and do the report for me if I bring them to you?"

"Sure, Shari."

So that's how account executives roll. All they have to do is use some sweet talk and call people "Teddy."

I go to Ted's desk and hand him the receipts. "Here they are."

Ted pores over them. "She flew to Atlanta and drove a rental the rest of the way? She never does that."

I *knew* that. I should have flown the whole way to Macon.

"H and H?" he says. "This isn't a fancy restaurant. Only twelve-fifty with tip."

"Um, I hear Oprah visited there once," I say. "I'm sure Miss Ross just wanted to see the place for herself, you know, soak up some of Oprah's, um, presence."

Ted doesn't look up. "Hilton Hotel, okay. Room service? Is she sick?"

Do I mention the box jellyfish and Australia? I can't. The less I have people talking about Corrine, the better, and a box jelly-fish sting on a breast would zing around here in a heartbeat. "Not that I know of."

"Is this all she gave you?" Ted asks.

Did I forget any? I don't think so. "Yes."

Ted squints. "How did she give these to you? I didn't see her come in."

Geez! This guy is MultiCorp's neighborhood watch. "She met me outside, Ted." Now be a good boy, and stop prying, Teddy.

"No waxing, manicures, spa treatments, client incentives." He shrugs. "She's normally over two grand on a trip. This one comes to a little less than a thousand."

"She's hard to figure, huh?" *What?* I could have spent a *thousand* more and no one would have blinked? "I'll see you, Teddy."

The light on my phone is blinking when I return. What does Piper in personnel want?

"Hello?"

"This is Piper in personnel."

I'll bet she spits when she says that. She's a gruff old lady. "Yes?"

"I've been told that you're here today, and yet you put in for a sick day."

"Um, I felt a lot better, so I came in."

"Your sick day is already in the system, so technically you're not here today, Miss Nance, system-wise."

That is so messed up. "I'll, um, just take off tomorrow then, and you can mark me, um, present." This is too much like school to be an ad agency.

"I can't do that, Miss Nance. The system won't allow it."

But you run the system, right? But no. The "system" runs everything around here. "Why can't you just hit a few buttons and make me here today?" This is the stupidest conversation.

"Like I said, your absence is already in the system, and if I tell the system you're here, the system will reject the change. You can't be here and not here at the same time."

Corrine's like that every day. In fact, she's currently here and not here according to the receipts I just turned in. "So what can I do?"

"Nothing. You could take the rest of the day off. The system wouldn't mind."

The system can kiss my tail. "So in essence, I'm not here today even though I am."

"That is correct."

"But Miss Piper, I am obviously physically here. That makes no sense."

"It makes sense to the system," she says. "Have a nice day, Miss Nance."

I hate this place.

I gather my notes again and stand just as the phone lights up again. Corrine!

"Miss Ross's office, this is Shari—"

"Shari," Corrine interrupts, "is your cell turned on?"

"I'm having terrible problems with it, Miss Ross. Didn't you get my message?"

"I couldn't understand it. It was all garbled."

Uh-duh. That was the point. "I was afraid of that. Where are you, Miss Ross?"

"Hawaii. My flight from Brisbane was late getting to Honolulu, and I missed my connection to LA. I have a three-hour wait until the next available flight that has room in first class. Can you believe that?"

Tia's candle is working. "That's so terrible, Miss Ross."

"If Tom were with me, it wouldn't be so bad."

Don't you say a single word, Shari Nance.

"Has he called the office?" she asks.

"No, Miss Ross. He hasn't called you?" I am so mean.

"No. Oh, Shari, I need him now more than ever. He's my rock."

He's *my* man of steel.

"Whenever I've had a setback, he's always been there to pick me up, you know?"

The wench! I've picked her up more than he has! I've been picking up after her for five years!

"I can only assume that he's gone to the mattresses in Detroit. He's stuck hammering it out until he's done."

Gone to the mattresses? I didn't know she knew Mafia slang. I smile. Yeah, Corrine, he went to my mattress and watched over me while I was hammered. I will never listen to "Red, Red Wine" again.

"Those automakers can be so brutal, Shari dear. When they go to the mattresses, they don't allow cell phones or any contact with the outside world. And after all the handouts we've given them. They're keeping me from my Tom! They have their claws in him and won't let him go!"

Um, no. I check my nails. I have to file that one. It bent a little when I tried to gouge the skin off Tom's back.

"What am I going to do, Shari? I miss him so much!"

At least we're in agreement there. I miss him, too. What to do, what to do . . . "Why don't you . . ." Stay away from here! "I know, why don't you find yourself a nice hotel, Miss Ross. A nice hotel on the beach. I think you should continue your vacation and your recovery there in Hawaii."

"Why?"

Why stay in Hawaii and away from New York in mid-

November? Is she nuts? "You need to relax and unwind, Miss Ross." So *I* can relax a little. Stay gone! "And it's really cold and nasty here." Not really. "I hear it might even snow this weekend." It could snow *somewhere,* right? "The city is no place for you to recover, Miss Ross."

"But what if Tom comes back to the city? I won't be there! He'll be all alone without me!"

Me, too. I won't see him till next week. "Well, if you were Tom and you had been hammering it out on the mattresses in Detroit, wouldn't you want to go somewhere warm to recover?" The light on my phone flashes. Shoot. Dunn on line two. The two people I cannot have speak to each other are one transferred call away.

"And once he's done in Detroit," Corrine says, "he'll come to me, is that what you're thinking?"

No. "Yes, Miss Ross."

"That's a really good idea, Shari. That's why you're on my team. Thank you for caring."

I'm just caring about my own tail right now, Corrine. "Call me when you're settled, Miss Ross."

"I will. You have so many good ideas, Shari dear."

That you steal from me, you wench! "Rest, Miss Ross. Get some sun."

"Thank you for everything, Shari. Oh, and cancel my appointment with Dr. Fine."

Done before I even did it. "Take care, Miss Ross."

"Oh, I will."

I click over to line two. "Sorry to keep you waiting, Mr. Dunn. Corrine and I were just comparing notes over the phone." Hey, that sounded almost honest.

"How's she doing?" Mr. Dunn asks.

"I think she's going to be doing a lot of resting. I'll be in your office in a minute."

I take three deep, cleansing breaths. This is it. This is the first time I get to pitch my ideas to the real boss around here. I hope he likes them all, but even if he likes half of them or only parts of them, I'll be happy.

Mr. Dunn's administrative assistant, Sheila, a taciturn black woman older than God, tells me to go right in. I've never been in his office, and although he has an outstanding view of Brooklyn, he hasn't done a thing to his space. A few framed awards hang from the wall over a black leather couch. Two black leather chairs face his desk . . . and that's it.

Mr. Dunn doesn't get up, merely reaching out his hand. I put my notes in that hand, and he lines up the pages before scanning the first ad.

"It's kind of a hodgepodge of ideas there, Mr. Dunn," I say, "but we're confident Mr. Peterson will like them."

He's looking at the billboard/web banner! I must have mixed them up.

"Female rider?" he asks.

"Yes sir."

He grumbles, or at least I think he's grumbling. Maybe it was his stomach rumbling. "Might work. Do a male rider, too. We can parse them out to gender-specific periodicals and websites."

"Yes sir." Not exactly a ringing endorsement, but he didn't say no. Who can I get? Tom? I can't ask him to do that, though he'd look so virile on that bike.

Mr. Dunn is now looking at the T-shirt idea. "My grandkids would like those. Make some extras. I'll need eight."

Cool! "Yes sir."

"Earth tones like green, rust, brown, tan. The whole environmental jazz."

"Good idea."

Oh no! Tom's drawing of me! Oh, I am so glad he put clothes on me!

Mr. Dunn holds it up. "Did you do this, Miss Nance?"

"Um, no sir," I say. "My, um, boyfriend did it."

"This is some excellent work," Mr. Dunn says. "If we ever have an opening in production, have him give us a call."

Tom working here? Not a chance.

He sets my picture aside and squints while reading the radio spot. "This is weak. The sounds of the city . . ."

Say something! "Um, whenever I hear static or nothing on

the radio, I listen more closely. Same with TV commercials. If I don't hear anything, I look at the screen."

"It might work," he says. "Ends well. No matter where you ride, you're home. Good stuff. Tell Corrine to tell production to make sure the sounds are clear, no sirens, lots of birds."

Whitman Park, here I come. "Yes sir."

He looks at my print ad, a collage of famous American places. "All-American stuff here. National parks are played out, though. Let's use landmarks from the city. Buildings, bridges, Radio City, Wall Street. The usual."

"I like that idea." Because I hate using Photoshop. There are too many buttons to play with on that program. Man, I'm going to be getting my exercise. Good thing I love to walk.

"I'm just working off Corrine's ideas, Miss Nance," Mr. Dunn says, blinking. "I'm sure she'll agree with me."

Oh man, I've forgotten my place again. Stupid, ignorant me. Good MultiCorp soldiers stay in their ranks. But Corrine has never had an idea of her own for you to work off of, Mr. Dunn.

Now I'm nervous. He's looking over the commercials. "Still sticking with the silence. Consistent. Come home to America. Point-of-view camera. Brooklyn Bridge. She and I think a lot alike. Good."

You and I think alike, Mr. Dunn.

"What do these numbers mean?" he asks.

"At fifteen miles per hour," I say, "a bike travels six hundred and sixty feet in thirty seconds."

Mr. Dunn blinks. "You walk across the Brooklyn Bridge every day, don't you?"

"Yes. I'm sure we'll be able to get some great shots of lower Manhattan from either the helmet or handlebars."

He nods slightly. "You might want to bring some tape of that to the meeting."

"Yes sir." Yep. I'm going to be extremely busy getting "tape." Mr. Dunn is such a dinosaur. Only that "tape" will *be* the actual commercial.

He swats at the page. "Now this is good. I like this. Yankee Stadium. Safe! Drive one home. We'll have to blur out the

Canon and MasterCard signs on the left field wall, but what an idea!"

And it was inspired by someone who marked up a picnic table in Macon, Georgia.

"I know a guy who can get us in there and let us run some tape," he says. "Let me know when you two have some time, and I'll make the call."

Very cool, but I'm trying to do this without you, Mr. Dunn. I suppose I could just . . . break in. No one will be in Yankee Stadium in November, right? "Um, do you have any other ideas that would help us, Mr. Dunn?"

"This is strong stuff," he says.

Thank You, Jesus!

"American made. Focused. Memorable taglines. You have a bike?"

The . . . bike.

Oh no!

I walked out of JFK without it! I stood there making calls all that time and completely forgot about it! How am I going to get it? I hear it costs a mint to get the airlines to deliver it to you. Tom! Tom has two bikes!

"Miss Nance, I asked if you had a bike."

Time for me to lie. "Oh, yes sir. Sorry. I was admiring your view."

He swivels slightly. "I never get tired of it." He swivels back. "Now, is the bike worth two grand?"

"Yes sir. Best made bike on Planet Earth." And I wouldn't have said that a few days ago.

"Where is it? I want to see it."

Oh, it's probably at JFK riding around and around on the luggage return. "I own one." Technically true. "I got it as a gift." True. "I have it back at my apartment." Okay, so I had to "hide" it somewhere. "I've been testing it out for Corrine."

"I thought you were sick."

Oops. "Um, well, that's kind of why I'm sick, Mr. Dunn. I've been riding it for the last few days. Not the best weather to go riding."

"I thought you were a walker."

I still am. "I'm expanding my transportation horizons, Mr. Dunn. I might even start riding it to work." Not.

He gathers up my notes and drawings and hands them to me. "You have enough background on Peterson Bicycles?"

And this is where I *really* shine. I take a deep breath. "Yes sir. Private company, grossed forty-seven million last year despite spending only seven percent of gross on advertising, mostly regional print and web, sells an average of twenty-five thousand bikes yearly despite never entering the national TV or radio markets, sold one millionth bicycle last year, accessories they create themselves make up fifteen percent of gross revenue, ships worldwide through UPS, foreign sales up eight percent each year for last four years, contract with U.S. Olympic team through 2016 and working on an extension, though it depends on the medal count, I'm sure, catalog and web sales consistent year-round, best months are in the spring and early summer, custom fits bikes on site, has several known cyclists as spokespeople, never had a recall in over forty years of business, hires thirty-five percent minority, no labor disputes in over forty years, excellent benefits packages for all employees, even parttimers, takes returns no matter how old the bike is, guarantees frame for life, all American components, every bike made on site, each bike made by hand." Ta-da! I want to bow.

Mr. Dunn sits back. "You have all that memorized?"

"Yes sir. I have fully immersed myself in this company."

"Well, I guess you have." He turns away from me. "Has Corrine met with Peterson?"

Twice. Oh, and once on a walkie-talkie. "Yes sir."

"Has she told you what he's like?"

I get to shine again. "Salt-of-the-earth, family man, father of three, grandfather of eight, likes to eat steak, rib eyes mainly, medium rare, works directly on the production line most days, does quality control and fixes machines himself, answers his own phone, a stickler for details, would rather wear work boots than dress shoes, hands-on manager, outstanding rapport with workers, drives American-made trucks, married over forty years, wife keeps the books."

He spins back. "You have an outstanding memory, Miss Nance."

"Thank you." It's easy to remember what you just lived yesterday.

"So we have an old-fashioned American family company with an all-American product. But Peterson Bicycles is not a huge company. What do they want with HHB?"

And once more, with feeling. "We feel that Mr. Peterson is hedging his bets. He spends so little on advertising and is still doing very well and bucking the trend of downward or stagnant bicycle sales. He wants to see what *could* happen if he spends more on advertising. We believe he'd rather have MultiCorp than Harrison Hersey and Boulder since we are the more cost-effective alternative. He's not afraid to spend money to make money but would prefer to get a lot of bang for his buck."

"Are these Corrine's or your assessments?" he asks.

All mine. "Mine, sir, um, but they're based on Corrine's assessments." Know thy place, Shari.

"I hope she's right."

Geez. Every assessment she's had for the last five years has been mine, and I was right every time.

"I wish I knew what HHB was planning," Mr. Dunn says. "Does Corrine have any idea? Her counterpart is, after all, her boyfriend."

I wish people would stop saying that. "Um, Tom Sexton isn't talking." To anyone but me.

"I suppose he wouldn't. How is Corrine holding up?"

She's *holing* up in Hawaii. "Fine, sir. A little sore, but she's managing."

"It must be tough to be in competition with your boyfriend," Mr. Dunn says.

It is. But it also has some nice, warm, juicy fringe benefits.

"Corrine is a tough cookie," he says. "She'll get through this."

No, she actually crumbles pretty easily, Mr. Dunn, and I've

been the one holding her together. I'm cookie glue. "Yes sir. I'll make sure she does."

He nods. "Corrine believes in business before pleasure. Remember that, Shari. Business always comes first."

I am so glad I'm wearing these boots with all this crap flowing in here. "Yes sir."

"You're lucky to have her for your boss."

Yes, I'm so lucky today. "Will there be anything else, sir?"

"No, no. Just keep me in the loop."

"Will do."

Once I leave his office, I resist the urge to scream in triumph because I pulled it off. I smile at Sheila, I wave at Ted, and I nod at Tia as I head through the heavy fire doors to the stairwell. I skip down several flights and stop, listening to make sure no one is moving up or down. And *then* I scream.

"*Yes!*"

Old Walt would say, "If you done it, it ain't bragging."

I ain't bragging.

I done it.

I regain my composure, return to the office, give an okay sign to Tia, and sit at my desk.

Yeah buddy, I'm good.

Chapter 21

Now if I could only remember little things, like the *freaking* bicycle that's the centerpiece of this *freaking* campaign!

I use my cell phone to call Tom, and he answers immediately. "You miss me already?" he says.

"Yes." I do. "Tom, I need to borrow one of your bikes. I left the one Mr. Peterson gave me at JFK."

He has the nerve to laugh. "Now *this* is a definite conflict of interest. I don't know if I should assist you."

"C'mon, Tom."

"It might require something of you in return."

I like the sound of that. "Like what?"

"I have two hands that like to give massages."

My back actually tingles. "I think we could arrange something."

"Don't worry about it, Shari. I had a feeling you'd forget it, so I picked it up for you."

He . . . did? "How did you know I'd forget it?"

"Shari, my dear, you tend to be a bit flighty."

"I am not!"

"Today you were."

True. "But how could you get it? You didn't have the baggage claim tag."

"I did have a twenty dollar bill."

No one's luggage is safe. I spin around in my chair. "So . . . how will I get this bicycle?"

"Well . . . I could ride it over to you now."

While I'd like to see him and get the bike, I already told Mr. Dunn it was back at my apartment, and Tom and I are not supposed to be seen together. "Not a good idea."

"Or . . . I can drop it by your place."

And see him again? Yes. "I'd like that." Very much. I am so glad I am flighty today.

"But how will I get home to Great Neck?" he asks.

Ah-ha. Interesting. He keeps bringing up Great Neck, but I am not going to his little bungalow. We may have known each other for five years now, but I do not just up and go to a man's crib after—oh yeah. He's already seen most of me, and we both seem to want what comes next . . . "How, indeed, would you get home? I know. I could fly you there. I'm flighty enough."

"I'll have to watch what I say from now on. Hmm. This is quite a riddle. How would I get to Great Neck from Brooklyn if I only have this bike, which you obviously need so badly?"

"I have a great neck *in* Brooklyn," I say. "This neck doesn't stray too far from Brooklyn, you know."

"Tempting. But I have so much work to do, and so do you." He laughs. "But you can't do *your* work without this bike. Man, this is a real puzzler."

"Sure is."

I hear him sigh. It's kind of sexy. "We are at an impasse. You see, my first instinct is to ride this bike back to Great Neck and make you come get it."

"So I can see your little bungalow," I say.

"Maybe," he says.

Maybe nothing. "My apartment is much closer."

"True. But then there's the principle of the thing. I rescued the bike, so I should get the reward, and riding over to Brooklyn is not my idea of a reward."

He *really* wants me to see his place and, um, do other things.

"I haven't been home in so long," he says. "I want to see if it's still there. It's a nice place. And it might be our office after I kick your butt."

I'd rather he did other things to my— Wow. Where'd that

thought come from? And wait—how'd he get the bike to Harrison Hersey and Boulder? "Did you ride the bike from JFK to Madison Avenue or what? And with your suitcase?"

"I didn't go to work."

Lucky him. Wait—is he down on William Street right now? I get out of my chair and drift to the window. I look down and only see cars. "So where are you now?"

"Yankee Stadium."

Huh? No! He can't be. "What are you doing at Yankee Stadium?"

"Safe!" he yells. "Sure is quiet here."

He's not . . . No. He *wouldn't* have. Would he? I look around and see several pairs of nosy eyes staring at me. I go out into the hallway, go in the bathroom, check each stall, and stand by the window. "Tom Sexton, what are you doing at Yankee Stadium?"

"Riding this beautiful red and black bike."

He stole my idea! "You . . . you read my notes!"

"They were right beside your plane ticket in your nice little bag."

I am too angry to speak!

"I'm having the hardest time getting to home plate in under fifteen seconds, Shari. I checked your numbers, and they're absolutely right. I stare at the speedometer while I'm riding, but I can't maintain fifteen miles per hour all the way through. I am, after all, pretty worn out because of you."

It's happened again! First Corrine, and now Tom! "You're . . . you're stealing my idea, and you know how that makes me feel!"

"I'm trying to steal home! Hey, that's not bad. Steal home with a Peterson bicycle? No. Sends the wrong message. Wrong connotation. Your idea is better."

"But you're stealing my idea, Tom!"

"No, Shari, I'm not. Okay, yes, I borrowed your notes for a minute, but I didn't steal your idea. I'm *using,* not stealing your idea for *our* presentation. I'm putting your idea to work."

And I thought that I took initiative. "It isn't right, Tom, and you know it!"

"Shari, please calm down."

"No!"

"C'mon, I've been thinking about this for a long time. Not sitting next to you on the plane gave me time to think. You would have distracted me. I would have been thinking about your smooth, silky skin, I would have asked for a blanket, my hands would have wandered to your nice warm legs. . . ."

He's trying to distract me and it's working. "Did you read through *all* my ideas?"

"Okay, so I borrowed your notes for *five* minutes while you were sleeping, but you proved what I've known for five years. Shari Nance, you are a genius. My ideas, while serviceable, aren't inspired. At all. Your ideas work on so many levels and will actually inspire people to buy a bicycle."

Now he's trying to distract me with a compliment. That's working, too. "I can't believe you did that, Tom. It's like working with Corrine all over again."

"You're missing the point."

A perky administrative assistant who can't be older than ten bounces into the bathroom. I wash my hands, dry them, and leave the bathroom. I head to the stairs. "*You're* the one missing the point, Tom. It's the principle of the thing. You ripped me off. I'm pissed at you."

"And I'm sorry, but hear me out."

I don't respond.

"We have to work this thing together as Methuselah's Breezy Hiccup. We have a golden opportunity to sell your ideas to Mr. Peterson and stick it to our employers at the same time."

I walk up several flights of stairs and flop down in the corner of the landing. "But Mr. Peterson expects either MultiCorp or Harrison Hersey and Boulder to represent him. There are contracts waiting to be signed!"

"Mr. Peterson will have no choice but to accept the brilliant presentation of Methuselah's Breezy Hiccup. He'll sign with us, I guarantee it."

All my plans are turning to crap!

"Oh, I'm sure we'll both be fired on the spot," he says.

"*What?*"

"You have a good digital camera? I bought the one I'm using a few years ago. It does the job, but I'm worried that it doesn't have enough clarity."

I slump against the wall. "We'll be fired on the spot?"

"We have to be fired if we're going to get the account," he says. "What kind of camera do you have?"

I close my eyes. "I don't have a camera like that, Tom, and I *cannot* get fired!"

"Maybe if I start on the warning track in center field and make a hard left . . ."

"Tom, this can't work!" My voice echoes a little. I stand and climb another flight.

"Yeah, I'll probably wipe out and slam into the bleachers. It would look so cool on YouTube, though."

He's out of his mind! "Tom, pay attention!"

"You worry too much, Shari. I have been praying for some way to leave Hairy Ads. You have been praying for some way to leave Cringe and MultiCorpse. This is the time for us to do it, and this is how we can do it."

It sounds . . . like the beginnings of a plan, but . . . "What if Mr. Peterson doesn't hire us?"

"With your ideas and my technical expertise, he will hire us. Trust me."

This is insane! "Tom, we really need to talk this through in more detail." I am not going to get fired on the day I'm supposed to shine! This is madness!

"You like my concept, right?" he asks.

I'd like nothing better than to rub MultiCorp's nose in my success. "It's, um, it's edgy, but I'm standing too close to the edge, you understand?"

"Just don't look down. Everything is looking up."

I wish I could be sure of that.

"So . . . your place or mine?"

I am so flustered right now. I need to be on my home turf. "My place." I give him the address. "Be there by six."

"I'll be the guy with the bike."

I don't know whether to be angry or happy! I hate this feeling. "Um, what are you wearing while you're riding?"

"What I wore on the plane. Why?"

Jeans, boots, sweatshirt. He's rugged, manly, and sexy. "Are you, um, smiling while you're riding?"

"Yes, well, when I'm not staring at the speedometer."

"Because it's important for you to be smiling and looking at the camera. And you're wearing a helmet, right? I don't want any family safety groups after us."

"Yes, dear. I never ride without one. I bought one on my way to the stadium."

What else was *I* planning for *my* commercial? "Um, make sure you end it with a shot of the plate, and try to get some dirt to fly."

"I already have."

"You have to do the voice-over." He has to. Baseball is a man's game.

"Your voice is sexier."

"We're selling a bike, not sex, Tom."

"Say 'drive one home' in your sexiest voice."

I look around. "Drive one home," I say in my *normal* voice.

"I am so excited right now," he says.

Oh right. Tell me anything. "Just . . . just be at my apartment by six."

"I'll be powerful hungry."

Of all the . . . "You want me to *cook* for you, too?"

"You owe me twenty bucks for rescuing the bike."

"Well, you stole my ideas!"

"Well," he says softly, "you stole my heart."

That's a heart stopper. "When?"

"You've actually been stealing my heart for a few years, Shari, a little at a time."

I want to believe him, I really do. But he has me climbing stairs and going crazy!

"Think about it," he says. "How many times did I call your office when Corrine wasn't there?"

And now he expects me to add them up? "I don't know, a lot."

"Just about every time," he says. "Almost all the time for the last two years."

He's right. He has been calling just to talk to me for a long time. "So what?"

"So . . . maybe I called her cell phone first to make sure she *wasn't* there so that you and I could talk without her interrupting us."

I don't know whether to be flattered or scared. He's been stalking me for two years! And instead of pouncing on me, he's only been calling me and trying to run me over with a bike. "Tom, I have been so lonely for the last two years. Why didn't you do something more than just talk to me? I would have turned twenty-five with a smile on my face."

"I didn't want to cost you your job."

What?

"If I dumped Corrine and started seeing you immediately, who would you be looking at five days a week just a few feet from you?"

Cringe. The woman scorned. Her fury in my face every moment. A worse wench goddess than she already is.

"Corrine would take her rejection out on you, wouldn't she?"

In a big way, hell on earth, the end of days, but . . . "She takes everything out on me anyway! And you're trying to cost me my job right now!"

"Ah, but I'm offering you a better job."

I am losing my mind. "But . . . but we just talked, Tom. We weren't romantic or anything. We never talked about anything even remotely, um, sexual, or long-term." Why am I mentioning these things? It must be on my mind. "I thought we were just chatting."

"I have always liked the sound of your voice. You actually

take an interest in *me,* not in what I do. I never felt as if I were some trophy to show off. We were equals."

"But two years, Tom."

"I've actually been hoping you'd move on, leave MultiCorp, at least switch to another account executive. I've even been hoping that Corrine imploded and was fired or just up and quit. Then you'd be free for me to pursue full-time."

"But you're pursuing me now."

"Because the time is right," he says.

The time is right. I want to believe it.

"Corrine blew LA, didn't she?" he says. "And don't ask me how I know."

I wasn't going to ask him.

"You gave me the hint when I called you, and it was correct. Corrine is not nor will ever be Mae West. Guess who's representing Carlo Pietro now?"

This makes sense. "Harrison Hersey and Boulder." I am still confused. "So you figured. . . . I wish you'd just get to the point!"

"Look, Shari. The light is fading, and I don't have enough pull for someone to turn on the stadium lights. Let me do a few more takes, and I'll see you in about ninety minutes."

My heart is so cluttered right now, and my mind is closing in on itself. "Just . . . just don't wreck."

"I won't. You be careful on your walk home. Bye."

I look around the stairwell. Wasn't this the place I shouted in triumph a half hour ago?

"Crap!" I yell this time.

The echo escorts me all the way down to my floor.

Chapter 22

My phone quiet, my thoughts loud, I spend the rest of the day adding Mr. Dunn's ideas to my own. I go to Ink Imprints' website and design my T-shirt online. Corrine and I have used them before, they promise a five-day turnaround, and best of all, we still have an account with them. I select chocolate, city green, and yellow haze, a Splash font, and put "No matter where you ride, you're home" on the front, "Get lost in America" on the back. I find and upload a simple black-and-white Peterson bicycle graphic for the pocket and order one in each size in each color from youth to adult. I debate whether to send them to my apartment or here and decide on here. No one will bat an eye when they arrive, and Tia signs for all the packages. I don't want to make any waves. I fill out and send a PO electronically to Ted, and in only half an hour, my T-shirts are on order.

I leave exactly at five—a rarity—and power walk home. I know I've set a record. Since it's only 5:45, I have time for a quick shower before starting dinner.

And I have no food.

Okay, I have no fancy food. I have a pound of ground beef, a one-pound box of elbow macaroni, and two eight-ounce blocks of sharp cheddar. The tomato on the counter is overly ripe, but it will at least add some color. I boil the macaroni in my largest pot while frying the ground beef, adding my whole arsenal of spices to the meat: seasoned salt and pepper. I am a simple person. As soon as the macaroni is *al dente*—I know a little about cooking—I dump it in a colander to drain. I return the drained macaroni to the pot, add a stick of real butter, grate the cheese over the macaroni, and add the tomato and ground beef. I turn the heat to medium-low, slap on a lid—done.

Now all I need is a man to eat it.

And said man better give me a better explanation for what he's done.

And an apology.

There's not much to tidy up in my mostly secondhand apartment. I found most of what I own—coffee table, lamp stand, couch, secretary table, TV stand, multicolored bamboo rug, bed, nightstand, kitchen table and two chairs, and framed pictures of old Brooklyn sprinkled throughout my four-hundred square feet—by browsing used furniture at open air markets and KJR Collectibles over on Dekalb Avenue. Other than the IKEA addition and a massive bookcase holding several hundred paperback books, I don't think there's anything new anywhere in this apartment.

Other than my new attitude.

Which I'm about to give to a man who stole my idea and my bike.

Tom arrives a half an hour late and stands in my doorway wearing a black helmet and holding his suitcase in one hand, the bike with the other, a camera bag slung over his right shoulder. Dirt speckles the wheels, his pant legs, and even his sweatshirt. He does not smell like oranges and lemons. Musk and funk, yes.

Two white neighbors from a few doors down, whom I have nicknamed "Trixie and Bubbles" because they often entertain three and four men at a time, walk by checking out Tom's booty. I give them a squinty smile, they roll their eyes, and Tom steps inside.

He hands me a camera bag, I take it, and I step aside.

"Where do I put it?" he asks.

I do not respond. I am the queen of the silent treatment. No man has ever beaten me at this. I hang the camera bag on a hook by the door.

"The bike?"

I shift my eyes to the left.

He shifts his eyes to the right. "The bathroom?"

I nod.

In a moment, I hear the helmet rattling around in the tub.

Tom steps into the kitchen. His hair is a mess, and I just know his hands are dirty. "What smells so good?"

Not you. I go to my skinny couch and sit.

He starts to speak and stops. He looks at his hands. "I'm a mess."

I do not disagree.

He washes his hands and uses a paper towel to dry them. "I did thirty-five takes, Shari."

Do not say my name.

"Um. I need a shower, huh?"

I do not disagree.

He steps over to the pot on the stove, lifting the lid. "My favorite foods. Beef, pasta, and cheese." He replaces the lid. He smiles at me. "Um, when will it be ready?"

I curl my legs under me on my skinny couch. I do not tell him it will be edible in half an hour, and I do not tell him that I will not be edible or even touchable until he fully explains himself.

He sits a few feet from me on the couch. "Hi."

I nod.

He looks around at my stuff. It takes him five seconds. "You have . . . an interesting place. What's that?" He points at my IKEA purchase.

My bonus from last year.

"It's boxy," he says. "It looks like wooden steps."

I sigh. It is the first sound I have made.

He nods. "You're pissed."

I nod.

"Oh." He stands and browses my books, pulling several out and reading the back covers. He puts them back haphazardly.

I am not amused. I had those books in a semblance of order. I like order. I like things to go the way *I* plan them, and here he is, ruining my books and everything else in my life!

He leans against my kitchen table. "Okay. Um. Let's talk."

I still have not heard "I'm sorry" or "I was a fool" or "What I did was wrong." I have not seen him get on his knees and grovel. Tom will be talking to himself.

He hops up on the kitchen table, and I am so glad it's solid oak. "I know I should have consulted you before using your idea. I know it was the wrong thing to do."

I may actually speak to this man tonight. But he's still not groveling.

"I called a guy who knew a guy, and I got into Yankee Stadium, so I went for it. It won't happen again."

I nod. It's time for me to talk. I have so much to say. How best to phrase my anger? I wish I had a pillow to throw. "So, Tom, are you going to explain your master plan to me and include *me* in it, or are you just going to go for it from here on out?"

He wrinkles up his lips. "I'm sorry. I should have included you. It won't happen again, Shari."

That's right. It won't. "I want you to put it all out there, right now, from start to finish, and don't leave anything out."

He has the nerve to smile. "You're the smartest person I know. I thought you would have figured it all out by now."

What the—! "But the plan keeps changing!"

He swallows that smile. "And you keep adapting, Shari," he says softly.

"I'm tired of having to adapt, Tom!" I want to punch him, but I'm afraid I'll break something important, like all of my knuckles. "This is my *life* we're talking about, man. I have everything riding on this."

"So do I, Shari." He joins me on the couch.

I look away. "Just . . . explain everything to me, okay? I don't want to get burned anymore."

He nods. "From the beginning then." He leans back and rests his arms on the back of the couch. "Corrine really messed up in LA. I figured, finally, she's finished, but this Peterson thing drops into both our laps right after." He looks at me. "Hairy Ads chose me because I ride a Peterson bike to work."

Figures. At least Harrison Hersey and Boulder has some sense. If MultiCorp ever represented a hiking boot company, they'd go to Corrine, who has never worn hiking boots in her life.

"So, I'm about to go head-to-head with her," Tom continues, "and it would be the perfect time to humiliate her."

Say what? "We would have done just fine, Mr. Sexton. Remember, I would have been working with her."

He shakes his head. "No, you wouldn't have."

"You're not making sense." Again!

"You would have been working with me."

He's still not making sense. "How?"

"I have been a senior account exec at Hairy Ads for eight years, and I have been entitled to have an administrative assistant working for me, but I've never used one."

"Because you like flying solo. Like today."

He reaches out and rubs my shoulder. "I think I've landed."

That's so nice to hear, but I'm still angry. Okay, I'm not as angry as I was. He's landed. Does that make me an airport? A runway? Okay, I'm angry again. I roll my shoulder away from his hand.

"Shari, I was about to hire you away from her, just when Corrine needed you most."

He would have hired me? "I thought you wanted to ask me out."

"I did, but I had to get you away from Corrine first."

I am still so lost! "But you could have done that two years ago!"

"I know, I know, and it's the biggest mistake I've ever made." He pulls an envelope from his pocket. "I even wrote up a contract." He hands me the envelope.

I open it up and see . . . Whoa. I would have been making double my salary! I check the date on the contract. "You had this ready to go last *Friday?*" The day I decided to become Corrine! Man, I jumped the freaking gun! Wait—no! *He* was slow on the draw!

"Yes. I was going to give this to you on Friday."

Wow. I would have jumped ship so fast that MultiCorp would have burn marks on their carpet. "But why didn't you give this to me on Friday? If you did, none of this would be happening right now."

"Australia happened."

"*What?*"

"Corrine called me from Delmonico's and invited me to Australia. While I assumed that you'd be working your butt off for her on the Peterson thing, I also figured that she wouldn't be doing anything but waiting for me, and I had never had any intention of seeing her."

Man, that's cold. "You . . . played her into thinking you'd come out there?"

"I wanted you and our future that badly, Shari. Can you blame me?"

Of course not. I'm worth having. But it's still right cold. "But you certainly have gone to a lot of trouble, Tom. Whatever happened to the direct approach? You know, like in the old movies. Just walk in and sweep me off my feet."

"I have thought so much about doing that. I even saw myself doing it and Cringe going ballistic. But then I decided doing that would only make her suffer for a day, she'd find a new assistant, the show would go on—and I'd still be working for Harrison Hersey and Boulder."

"But with me as your assistant, right?"

He turns to me. "I have never looked at you as an assistant, Shari, only as an equal. My dream was to begin my own agency, with you by my side, but I didn't know exactly how until Corrine went to Australia."

My mind is so cluttered right now. "But she's not in Australia anymore. She's in Hawaii now, still hoping you'll come visit."

Tom smiles. "Hawaii?"

"Yes." And this is cold of me. "I convinced her to stay in Hawaii so she can rest up for *you.*"

He nods. "She should probably get some sun in Hawaii to fade some of those jellyfish scars. At any rate, I wanted to turn Corrine into a hot mess. No matter how well you prepared her, and no matter how decent your production was, she would have been basically clueless when she returned."

And she would have sucked up the Q&A for sure.

"And after winning Peterson," Tom continues, "then I would steal you away in the fallout."

"What fallout?"

"Corrine would have blown two easy accounts in a row. Once is usually enough at Harrison Hersey and Boulder. And even if MultiCorp kept her, though I don't know why, she might have fired you for not making her shine."

What a . . . Machiavellian plan. "You really thought all that would happen?" My plan actually makes more sense than his plan does!

"Yeah. It was a simple plan, too. But then . . ." He shakes his head at me. "You happened."

Oh yeah. I messed it up. I became my own boss.

He massages my neck. "I didn't figure in a million years that you would impersonate Corrine. People don't generally impersonate people they despise." He slides closer and massages my right thigh. "You screwed up my somewhat complicated, thoroughly diabolical, but ultimately rewarding plans."

"I had plans of my own, Tom."

"If you had waited only a few more hours . . ."

"I . . . I had to do something." I remove his hand from my thigh, stand, and walk to the window. "I had to, Tom. I mean, I was just stuck. Peterson was calling, and Corrine wasn't available, and anyway, I've been wasting my time taking these stupid MBA classes that haven't taught me a single thing, I've been making someone else the star and getting no credit—I *had* to act." Wow, that was some performance. I should be in a soap opera.

"I know, I know," Tom says, "and I know how you feel, right? I was in the same position. I had to act, too." He sighs. "At first, I was so upset with you. Why couldn't you have waited two more hours? But then, I was glad you did."

Huh?

"When I saw you through that window down in Macon, it

was like kismet, fate, luck, serendipity, whatever you want to call it. There you were. It was destiny."

I rest my head against the window, the cold seeping through the pane cooling off my brain. At least I'm *somebody's* destiny. "You could have busted me out, cost me my job, and *then* handed me this contract."

He joins me at the window, sliding his big old paws around to my stomach. "You wouldn't have accepted."

I bump him with my booty. "I would have been pissed at you. And humiliated in front of some really nice people. And word would have gotten out, and no one would have hired me in this city ever again." I turn into him and bang my head against his chest. "So why did you let me play the role? Why did you let me play Corrine?"

"I wanted to see you in action, and I'm not disappointed at all. Shari, you would run rings around ninety-nine percent of the account execs at Hairy Ads."

I stop banging. "And the other one percent?"

"That would be me."

Ah. Of course.

He holds me out from him, his hands on my shoulders. "And now I have the *ultimate* diabolical plan."

"I have a plan, too." If I tried to punch him, I'd swing and miss. His arms are almost as long as my body!

"There are far too many holes in your plan," he says.

I know I have holes in my plan, but they are little holes, and they have been sealing themselves. "Such as?"

"Mr. Dunn will be at the meeting, right?"

"Yeah? So?"

"And Corrine *won't* be at the meeting. Isn't that your plan?"

I turn away and look out the window. "Right. I was going to run the show by myself. I was going to show Mr. Dunn I had what it takes."

"Mr. Dunn used to work for Harrison Hersey and Boulder."

I whirl around. "No, he didn't."

He nods. "He doesn't talk about it or even have it on his bio. Your Mr. Dunn was in the junior exec program at Hairy Ads about thirty-five years ago, only he didn't make the cut. They let him go."

Which is probably why he wants to stick it to "HHB" so badly.

"And if Corrine, Dunn's 'star,' isn't there to give him a chance at victory . . ."

I step around him and go to the kitchen. "I know I could pull this off without her, Tom." I open the pot and see a sticky, cheesy mess that actually smells kind of good. I stir it a few times. "I know I could."

He sits on the table again. "You probably would if you got the chance, but there are no guarantees that Mr. Dunn will even give you a chance."

"He'd have no other choice but to use me, Tom," I say. "What else could he do?"

Tom sighs. "I'll be blunt then. The CEO of an advertising agency can't let a lowly administrative assistant take on Harrison Hersey and Boulder by herself."

"I'm not lowly, Tom." Just short.

"I know you aren't, Shari, but that's not the point. No matter how fantastic you are, word will get around that MultiCorp has lost faith in its senior account executives. Current and potential clients don't like to hear that. Mr. Dunn would have to cut you off to save face."

"He'd cut me off to *spite* his face," I say. Shoot. Tom makes too much sense sometimes.

"And what about Mr. Peterson? He thinks you're Corrine Ross. While a lot of advertising is built around carefully constructed lies, you cannot legally misrepresent who you are when contracts are in the balance."

"I'll just explain to Mr. Peterson why I did it," I say. "He'll understand."

"Will he?" Tom asks. "This is a churchgoing man, a straight shooter. You weren't straight with him. You might have the better ideas, but he'll dismiss them because you lied to him."

He's right, but I don't want to give up just yet. I open a cupboard and take out two bowls, slamming them onto the counter. "But I *want* to do this, Tom!"

"And you will. Just hear me out."

I get two somewhat shiny spoons from a drawer. "First you say I will, then you say I won't. I am not a yo-yo!" I fill both bowls and spin one in front of him. I sit in a chair, while he picks up his bowl and starts to eat.

"That's a nice image," he says between bites. "You're not a yo-yo."

"I'm under a lot of stress, Tom."

He smiles. "It's good to know you can think on your feet."

"I'm sitting down now." I take a bite. Not terrible. Pretty bland. Needs salt. I add some. Better.

"You'll be on your feet in a second," he says.

What?

"Shari, um, you see, for my new ultimate plan to work, we first have to get, um, we have to get Corrine to come back."

I don't jump up. "No," I say calmly, wanting so badly to jump up! Wow! What's Tom smoking?

"Yes," he says, finishing his last bite. "We need her back in the office on Monday morning." He goes to the pot and spoons out another bowlful.

"And why do we need her?" I ask.

He smiles. "To do what she does best. We need her to mess things up."

Now I jump up. I wave my spoon at him. "That's what I've been trying to avoid!"

He slides into my seat and pulls me to his lap. I go willingly because I like his lap a lot. "Picture this: Corrine comes in after ten days away from the office, and you dump everything on her. Peterson, the deadline, the meeting. Everything. Can you picture it?"

I close my eyes. "Let's see, she'll be left-breasted, she'll be darker, she'll still be pining for you, she'll probably be wearing Jason Wu, poor man, and then I'll say, 'By the way, we have a finished product presentation to give tomorrow at two o'clock.

Just came up. Didn't want to bother you while you were in recovery. You ready to do some storming?'" Hey now. That might be fun.

"And how will Corrine most likely react?"

I open my eyes. "If she doesn't immediately escape to an expensive restaurant for lobster Newburg, she'll . . . she'll freak." Oh my! I am beginning to *love* this plan. I take a huge bite and chew it loudly. "Then she'll accuse me of withholding information. She'll scream at me for ruining her. She'll throw the ultimate wench fit, and everyone will finally see the wench she is." I smile. "She'll . . . go . . . off."

"And what will *you* do? I'm sure you've had this fantasy."

"Well, first of all, I will smile in her face the entire time. I'll also do happy dances under my desk. And then, I'll, um, I'll tear up my notes into confetti. No. I'll already have them shredded into confetti and just hand her a plastic bag. Then I'll . . . I'll put fingerprints all over her Plexiglas shield." I kiss his lips even though they're cheesy. "Then I'll tell her I've stolen you away from her, and then I'll quit."

"Precisely."

That sounds . . . wonderful, but . . . there's this problem called rent, utilities, food. "So . . . I'm suddenly unemployed. That can't be good."

Tom finishes his second helping, dropping his spoon into the bowl. "What's the first thing Corrine will do after you leave?"

Get something to eat? No. "She'll panic."

"Okay. She panics. Then what will she do?"

She'll call the client. "She'll call Mr. Peterson and ask for an extension." That he'll *never* give. Oh, man, this plan is the *junk!*

"And when Mr. Peterson says something like, 'No, Miss Ross, I guess I'll just have to go with Hairy Ads if you can't swing it . . .' "

"She'll . . . she'll go to Mr. Dunn."

"Would she *really* go to Mr. Dunn?" he asks.

No, she wouldn't. She'd have so much to explain to him that she couldn't possibly explain. "No. She avoids him all the time, especially when she has screwed up." I'm beginning to see where he's going with all this. "Then Corrine will call me. She'd try to get me to come back." This plan is getting more and more delicious.

"And what will you do?"

"I get to tell her off again!" Joy! Sheer bliss!

"One problem, Shari."

No joy? No sheer bliss?

"How else are you going to get into the meeting with Mr. Peterson? You don't work for MultiCorp anymore."

Oh yeah. Shoot. "So I'd *have* to go back to work for that wench?"

He turns me around so that I'm straddling him. "Yes." He starts massaging my lower back.

"But . . ." Oh, that's nice. "But I'll go back with what? My notes are confetti, though I'm sure I could remember everything. Corrine and I would have to do rush jobs on designs, some footage, but nothing finished or polished. We'd only have Monday afternoon, we'd have to do an all-nighter. . . . We'd get crushed." Squashed. Flattened. Pancakes for everyone. "But I have more pride than that, Tom. I'd try to come up with something decent."

He pulls me even closer, working my shoulders. "I know you would, Shari. And your pride is what I like about you most. Okay, your booty is fine, too, but . . . oh, and your thighs. Like vise-grips."

"Don't change the subject." But keep rubbing my shoulders while my legs wrap around your booty. "And while all this is going on, what will you be doing?"

"*Our* stuff."

"But what Corrine and I would piece together would essentially *be* our stuff."

He pulls up my shirt and works his fingers into my lower back. "Would it?"

Mmm. I have hot hands on my back. He's pressing all the right buttons now. "It would have to be. That would be all we had."

He works me just under my shoulder blades. "Unless . . ."

I can't think when he's doing that. "Unless . . ." Hey now. That's certainly sneaky. "Unless I feed her the worst possible ideas and all the wrong facts and figures, the wrong demographics . . ." More lies. Man. "We could literally fill that conference room with poop."

"You're so colorful." He works his fingers lower.

I start to squirm. "And then you would show them our stuff, win the account . . ."

He lifts me into the air and sets me on the table. "No."

"No?"

He rubs on my thighs. "I would add more poop to your poop."

This table is cold! "Why? And why did you put me up here?"

He looks away. "I was, um, I was . . . you know."

I nod. So was I. I felt him getting excited. I slide back onto his lap. "It's okay. It's actually a compliment." I lift up my shirt, he returns his hot hands to my back, and all is well with the world again. "So why are you adding more poop to our poop?"

He digs his fingers dangerously close to my booty. Whoo. "It's the best kind of payback. I've actually been working on my last presentation for Harrison Hersey and Boulder for a long time. It's already in the can and ready to go." His fingers sneak below my panty line, and my booty quivers. "It has nothing to do with bicycles, I assure you. It has everything to do with everything that's wrong with Harrison Hersey and Boulder. It will be a masterpiece of nonsense."

"But they'll fire you." And though he's only teasing me, he's about to light my booty on fire.

"It's what I'm counting on."

"That's . . . that's crazy." I pull myself back up onto the table to cool off. "But Mr. Peterson will be so angry and confused. He's such a nice man."

He reaches for me, but I scoot farther away. "We'll get to Mr. Peterson in a minute," he says. "Once I'm fired, you'll probably get fired. If you don't, you have to quit again."

My booty is getting cold, but I'm still not following him. "So in this scenario, we're not one but *two* unemployed people who have an ad campaign that no one will ever see."

"Only Mr. Peterson will see it," Tom says, "and then Methuselah's Breezy Hiccup will have its first client."

"How can we guarantee that?" I ask. "What if Mr. Peterson won't listen to us after the horror show we've put him through?"

He stands. "I like this table. Just the right height."

I'm glad I bought it.

He takes off his sweatshirt, the tightest T-shirt barely on him underneath. "He'll listen to you, Shari. He likes you. He gave you a bike. And once he sees what we have for him, he will love it, sign the papers, and take us out for rib-eye sandwiches."

Don't stop with the sweatshirt, though that T-shirt leaves nothing to my imagination. "I don't know, I mean, what about the legal ramifications?" That has to be the first time in my life that I have said the word *ramifications*. I must be nervous. "Technically and legally, the campaign we're creating belongs to our agencies, not to us. It's proprietary information, and we're using company time to collect it."

He steps closer and puts my legs around his hips. "Are we? We haven't actually done anything yet. I mean, Corrine went down to Georgia, right?"

And there's plenty of paper and some receipts to prove it.

"And I've been on unpaid leave since leaving Detroit," he says. "I'm using my own personal camera and equipment. I'm doing all of this on my own time. All you have to do is take some unpaid sick days, and we're technically doing all of this on our own time."

I frown. I'll have to deal with Piper the spitter again. "This sounds so shady."

He slides me closer. "So is advertising. We're just using shadiness against itself and to our advantage."

I hook two fingers into his belt loops. "So let me see if I can get this straight. Corrine returns, I quit, I come back when she throws a fit. . . ."

He slides me even closer to him, and I have no choice but to lock my vise-gripping legs around him. "Um, then I feed her crappy information, watch her give a crappy presentation, watch your career go up in flames with your poop, and hope Mr. Peterson will still hear us out when the, um, poop clears."

"Right. It's the crap." He slides me even closer, my jeans making squeaking sounds on the table.

"It will never work."

"It will." He slides his hands under my booty. "It will."

Can two pairs of jeans rubbing together down there start a fire? I think I'm about to find out.

"I really like this table, Shari. Solid oak."

And then we lose our minds for the rest of the evening. I can't get enough of him. I am like Velcro on that man, and as much as I want to tear off my clothes and his clothes and get down to business, I am having too much fun. On the couch, back to the table, on the floor—everywhere but my bed, even though I steer him there several times.

When we are both exhausted and barely have the strength to kiss and grope, I become his second skin. He turns, I turn. He stands up, I hold on. We become one pair of jeans and one T-shirt, and I can't let go. Even when we watch him skidding in to home plate thirty-five times, the dust flying just right, his smile infectious, his shoulders blocking out the sun, I don't let go of him. He cradles me in his arms and rocks me gently on my skinny little couch.

This is bliss.

But we both decide that the couch isn't comfortable for both of us. He's so big that he's half on and half off, his foot planted on the floor.

"You're not comfortable, are you?" I ask.

"Not really."

"My bed is big enough, but I'm a little scared." I'm a lot scared. My jaw starts to shake, and I can't make myself say it.

"What's wrong, Shari?" he asks.

"Um, Tom." I pull my hands off his chest. I'll have to explore it some more later. "Do you promise to answer any question I ask you?"

"Sure."

"And do you promise to answer truthfully?"

"Yes."

I squint. Hmm. He answered pretty quickly both times, so I guess I believe him. "Do you expect to have . . ." Why can't I say the stupid word? "I know you want to have . . . sex." I finally said it. "With me. Right?"

"Yes."

C'mon, jaw, stop wiggling. "I want to have sex with you, too, but . . . but I'm a little nervous about . . . it." I am so articulate.

"I thought you were going to ask me some questions."

Oh yeah. "Did you and Corrine have a lot of sex?"

He blinks. "Define 'a lot.'"

"Um, did you . . . have sex . . . every time you were . . . together?"

"For the first three years, yes. Every time. After that, only on special occasions like her birthday or the anniversaries that only she celebrated."

Every time. For three years. Hmm. "Um, would you say that your relationship with Corrine was based on sex?"

"Yes."

That was clear enough. "And was the sex . . ." I can't ask that.

"Was it good?"

"It's none of my business." But tell me anyway. I'm not that experienced. It's only been Bryan.

"Define 'good,'" he says.

When was it ever "good" with Bryan? "Um, fulfilling, um . . . meaningful."

"For three years, it was good."

"How good?" escapes my lips before I can stop it.

He laughs. "Do you want the play-by-play?"

I shake my head quickly. "No, um. That won't be necessary." I slide off him to the other end of the couch, slipping my legs under me. "Tom, I've only been with Bryan. I'm worried that . . . I want to satisfy you." Every time.

"I am so satisfied right now," he says. "These last few days have been more meaningful to me, and without sex, than all those years with Corrine. Perhaps I should tell you more about Corrine and me."

"Just not the play-by-play." Although I might learn a few pointers.

"I'll describe a typical date, okay?"

I nod.

"I pick her up in a rental car, something European. She wears something, um, revealing."

This is nothing that I didn't know.

"Um, *very* revealing."

Okay, easy access. No draws, bra. That would explain her stretch marks.

"We'd go to some function or other, she'd flirt, network, flaunt her body, and when it was over, we'd go back to her place." He shakes his head. "Um, just use your imagination for the rest."

My imagination is running wild right now. There's so much I don't know! "Just . . . tell me . . . a few . . . things."

"Um, how . . ." He winces. "She has some . . . tastes."

I'm almost relaxing. He's having as much trouble telling me as I'm having asking him to tell me. "She was . . . into things?"

He nods. "Yeah. Um . . ." He shakes his head again. "She had certain . . . needs."

Now I have to know. "Needs such as . . ."

"I am so embarrassed to tell you this," he says. "Um, she needed to wear interesting undergarments."

He's so cute! "Like sexy lingerie?"

"Um, well . . . she'd put them on, and I'd have to tear them off."

Only used once. What a waste of money! Flannel! Get flannel! "What else?"

He looks away. "Um, rope. On her, not me."

Corrine liked to be dominated? I can't believe it! "You tied her up?"

He shakes his head. "She tied herself up."

No danger in that. She knew what knots she used. "What

else?" This is actually pretty educational. "Did she use any . . . toys?"

He nods.

Okay. Single woman. Lonely. What's the fuss?

"And . . . um . . ." He slaps the couch.

I blink. "Spanking?"

He nods.

Okay, I think I've heard enough. Corrine likes risky sex. She likes to be dominated. She likes to be hit.

"Not hard," Tom says. "Once or twice would usually, um, do the trick."

I crawl across the couch and rest my head in his lap. "And which excited you the most?"

He winces. "The last one." He blinks at me, and I blink at him.

"And that turned her on?" I ask.

He looks down. "It usually, um, turned her off, um, finished her, if you know what I mean."

So Corrine "finishes" because of booty slaps. Interesting.

"And, um, smacking her booty excited you, too?"

He nods.

I hold out my hand. "C'mon."

He doesn't move. "Where are we going?"

"Just stand up."

He stands, and I hug him. "Thank you for your honesty."

"You're welcome."

I look up into his eyes. "Correct me if I'm wrong, but you haven't had much sex in two years."

"Um, about five times."

That's so sad. "And I, um, really haven't had anyone, um, make love to me." It was just the act to Bryan. I want to know what it *should* feel like. "But . . ."

He nods. "But."

"I want it to be special."

He smiles. "So do I." He exhales. "Wow. You had me worried."

I widen my eyes. "I had you worried?"

"Yeah. I was so worried that I wouldn't satisfy you."

Him not satisfy me? Is he kidding? He has to be kidding.

"Shari, I don't want sex to ever come between us," he says. "I don't want sex to ruin what we've got going."

Oh. Hmm. "You don't want to have a sexual relationship?"

"No, I mean, yes, I mean . . . I want something that is going to last."

I hug him tighter. "But you do want me . . . sexually."

"Yes, but mostly emotionally, spiritually, and intellectually. I want to be your best friend first."

I can't hug him any tighter. "You're, um, if I had to pick a best friend right now at this moment, it would have to be you."

"Thank you."

We both look at the couch. "Well, you can't sleep out on this couch."

"I can try."

I take his hand. "We'll figure something out." I lead him into my bedroom and push him onto the bed. "I have an idea." I go to my closet and pull out a white bedsheet. "I like watching old movies, old romantic comedies to be specific. Ever see *It Happened One Night?*"

He smiles. "Yes. Clark Gable and Claudette Colbert."

He's seen it? And he remembers their names. I thought I was good at remembering names. "Remember the motel scene?"

He nods. "A classic."

"Let's do it."

For several minutes, I feed Tom thumbtacks and he attaches the sheet to the ceiling and leaves a foot wide "smile" at the top. The sheet divides my bed in two with only a foot or so of fabric resting on the bed. I run around and take the lamp shades off the lamps on both nightstands.

"But I'll be able to see you, Shari," he says.

"And I'll be able to see you," I say, "but there's a wall between us."

"The wall of Jericho," he says. "Can you sleep with the lights on?"

I shrug. "I've never tried it."

"There's a first time for everything," he says.

I like this man very much.

We position ourselves on our sides of the room. I remove my bra under my shirt and drape it over the top of the curtain. He takes off his shirt and tosses it through the gap. I take off my pants and put on some flannel pajama bottoms. He takes off his pants. Shoot. Why did I have to buy four-hundred-count sheets? I mean, I can see most of him just fine, but . . . I like details.

We count to three and pull back the top cover together, slide into our respective sides, and just lie there.

"Shari?"

Oh yeah. Gable and Colbert talked through the "wall." I giggle. "Yes, Tom?"

"You have a very nice body."

"So do you." What I've seen of it.

"Um, I like it best when you turn sideways."

I blush. "Hey now."

"Um, if I reach across—"

"Not allowed," I interrupt. "You can't put your hand through a wall."

He's silent for a moment. "But what if there's a little hole in the wall, just big enough for my hand to go through, and I just happen to, I don't know, reach my hand through to hold your hand?"

My heart, my heart. "I think I see a hole, Tom."

I feel the bed shift slightly and then feel a hand on my thigh. "Oops," he says.

He's so cute. "Higher."

His hand crawls up my leg and I grab it before he can do any more damage. "You have a soft hand, Shari."

"You have a very big hand, Tom." Oh man. "Are you an active sleeper, Tom?"

"I don't know. I guess."

I hope you are, man. I pull his hand up to my lips and kiss it. "Good night, Tom."

"Good night, Shari."

I have to use both hands to hold his big hand, mainly because it seems to have a mind of its own. Oh, I move it around a little, too, but I will never get any sleep if I keep this up. I push his hand away. "I have repaired the hole in the wall."

"You're quite an engineer," he says.

I sit up and pull the "wall" tight against my body. "Give me a good night kiss."

He sits up and moves his body next to mine. How thick is this sheet, a couple of millimeters? And yet I feel every inch of him against me. I put my lips against the sheet, he puts his lips on mine, and we both fall back to our pillows.

I last maybe another minute before I slide my hand across to his side. "My hand is cold, Tom."

He takes it.

"Don't let go."

"I won't."

It is the first time I have ever held hands all night.

Bliss, pure bliss.

Chapter 23

I wake, strangely enough, at my regular time—7:30 a.m.—and slide my hand out of Tom's hand. I'm surprised he didn't crush it. I swivel to the edge of my side of the bed. I stretch and yawn. That, too, is part of my routine. I look back at Tom, his feet almost hanging over the edge of my bed, his hair plastered to a pillow, the sheets completely untucked, one pillow resting on the floor, the lamp shades on the floor—

It's only then I notice that the "wall" has fallen into a heap between us.

I frame the scene in my mind. I like this picture.

I'd have to call last night a success.

I slip into my closet, throw on an oversized sweatshirt, and go into the bathroom. After brushing my teeth, I stand in front of the mirror on the back of the door and survey the damage from our groping session. Hmm. No marks or scratches. I'll bet his back has a few. Not even any chafing. Ha! Another bent fingernail. My hair is a spider's nest. I check my eyes. Eww. Red streaks.

After a quick shower and lots of lotion, I wrap a towel around me and call the office to leave a message for Tia: "I'm taking an unpaid sick day today. Can you go back and make Monday and Tuesday unpaid sick days? Thanks."

I look in my cupboards for anything breakfast-like. I rattle a few cereal boxes. Nothing but expired dust in my Trail Mix

Crunch cereal boxes. No bacon. One egg. No muffins. Two heels of bread.

I am so unprepared to feed a man.

I weigh the pot of my concoction from dinner. Hmm. I hope he likes leftovers. I put the pot on to warm and fill up the kettle. I put the kettle on an eye and set up two mugs, both with herbal tea bags. I'm about to turn to clean up last night's mess on the kitchen table when I feel warm hands on my stomach and a man's lips on my shoulder.

"Morning," I whisper.

"Morning," he says.

This has to become part of my routine, too.

"We have a lot of work to do today," I say. I turn slowly and see him in only his boxers in all his hugeness. Is *hugeness* even a word? "You have to get dressed."

He tugs at my towel. "I'm wearing more clothes than you are." He looks me up and down, and I start to blush. "I could get used to this."

So could I.

While Tom takes a long shower because he has much more body to wash than I do, I put on jeans and a hoody over a green and yellow flannel shirt. I find some rag wool socks, slide them on, and skate to the couch. I watch Tom riding home at Yankee Stadium for a few minutes when my cell phone buzzes.

Tia's in the office early. "Hi, Tia. You get my message?"

"Yes, but I do not understand."

"I'll explain later."

"But Piper is a pain in my rear. She has you marked absent Tuesday."

Oh yeah. "Um, give me unpaid sick days for Monday and Wednesday then." I hear Tom singing something, but I'm not sure what it is. "And probably tomorrow and Friday, too."

"That is no good. That will give you three unpaid sick days in a row. You will need a doctor's excuse."

Shoot. It's sometimes harder *not* to work there than it is to work there. "Okay, um, wait. Don't I have some float days?" To work at home, make my own hours, pop in and out when I feel like it—what Corrine does every day. "I've never taken any."

"But you have to have many *paid* days, Shari. Why not use them instead?"

The water stops, but Tom keeps singing. It sounds like . . . Boyz II Men's "On Bended Knee." That's nice.

"I'll explain later, Tia," I say. "Um, let's get my week straight. Unpaid sick day Monday. Sick but I worked Tuesday. Float day today. Unpaid sick days Thursday and Friday. No three in a row."

"You should be an executive to keep all that straight."

I should be. "If Corrine calls, tell her I'm sick, that my cell doesn't work, that my apartment building lost phone service, and that Mr. Dunn wants to speak to her."

Tom emerges from the bathroom with narrowed eyes. I am so glad I have such small towels. "Huh?" he whispers.

I hold up a finger.

He clamps his lips shut.

I have Tom trained already.

"But as far as I know, Mr. Dunn does *not* want to speak to her," Tia says.

"Just tell Corrine that Mr. Dunn *wants* to speak to her," I say, pointing beside me on the couch, "and then Corrine *won't* call him. Understand?"

Tom nods and sits next to me. I take his hand, my eyes straying to that poor towel.

"I do not understand, Shari, but I will do it," Tia says. "Okay, what if Mr. Dunn calls?"

Yeah. What if he calls? Hmm. "Tell Mr. Dunn that I'm sick, but also tell him that Corrine is sicker and needs more rest." Hey, I told the complete truth that time. She's the sickest person I know. "Tell him he can call me anytime, though."

"Okay, if Corrine calls, your phone is broken. If Mr. Dunn calls, tell him to call you. What if Tom calls?"

I squeeze Tom's hand. "Tom won't call me, Tia." I kiss the back of his hand. "He's, um, Tom's here with me. I'll be working with him all day." If we ever get out of this apartment fully clothed. That towel has to be crying.

"You are working *with* him?" Tia asks.

"It's complicated, Tia."

Tom pouts.

"I'll explain later," I say.

"You have a lot of explaining to do later. I am so glad I am retiring next month."

And this gives me an idea. "One sec, Tia." I cover the phone. "Will Methuselah's Breezy Hiccup need a receptionist?"

"I guess," Tom says. "Sure."

I uncover the phone. "Tia, I may have a job for you, and soon."

"And I am not working for you now?" she says.

So true. "Well, yes, and thank you for everything you're doing for me."

"I am not sure I am doing anything," she says. "Now this job. Where will I work and can I work there until I am eighty?"

I cover the phone. "Where will she work?" I skip the "eighty" part. Tia barely looks forty-five.

Tom rubs at his beard stubble with his free hand. "She can work from home. We won't really need an office because we'll be traveling so much."

Yes!

"We'll be the first ad agency to go to the client and produce everything right there in front of them," he says. "We may never be home."

I love that idea. I uncover the phone. "You can work from home."

"I would like that very much," Tia says. "And when would I start this dream job?"

"A week from today," I say quickly.

Tia doesn't respond for a long time.

"Tia? Did you hear me?"

"Yes. A week from . . . I know, I know. You will explain later. It is complicated."

"Thanks again, Tia. Bye."

I set the phone on the coffee table and prop up my feet.

Tom props up his feet, too, and he wins by a foot. "I knew you had an accomplice."

I rake his hairy leg with my free hand while I tell him about Tia, and he agrees that I need her. "Before we do anything today, Mr. Man-in-a-tiny-towel, I need to know how we're going to get Corrine to come back by Monday."

"I'll just call her Saturday afternoon."

That's . . . too easy. "And say what?"

He puts an imaginary phone to his ear. "Hi, Corrine. Are you ready for the Peterson Bicycle presentation Tuesday?"

That would certainly do it.

"Play her," he says. "You seem to like to. So, Corrine, are you ready for the Peterson Bicycle presentation Tuesday?"

"What presentation?" I screech.

"I'm cringing," Tom says, and he tries to cross his legs, but the little towel won't let him. "Shari didn't tell you? You and I are pitching full, finished campaigns for Mr. Peterson of Peterson Bicycles on Tuesday."

"This is a joke, right?" I moan. "My happy spot is so sad!"

"I'm still cringing," Tom says. "And it's why I haven't been calling you, sweetie—"

"You call her 'sweetie'?" I interrupt. "She's the sourest person I know."

He sighs and frowns. "Will you let me finish talking to her?"

I roll my eyes.

"Um, Corrine, I thought you knew about the Peterson project. That Shari. She's something. No wonder she's been calling me so often, trying to steal ideas from me."

"What?" I shout. I also giggle. This is going to be so much fun!

"You're very good," he says.

"Thank you."

"Um, yeah, I think Shari's trying to pull this one off all by herself, can you believe it? I think she's after your job. She even followed me down to the bicycle plant in Georgia to spy on me."

"She didn't!" I shout.

Tom moves away from me. "This is spooky, Shari. You have her down."

"I've had five years of practice behind her back. Go on, Tom."

He slides back and rubs my thigh. "Shari is awfully cute, Corrine, but she needs to buy bigger towels."

No way. I will put only washcloths in there from now on.

"Why didn't you tell me Shari was so cute before?" He blinks at me.

"Oh. My turn. Um, how do you know she's cute?"

He nods. "I saw her in Georgia. And well, one thing led to another, and that thing led to another thing, and um, well, things quickly got out of hand, and well . . ."

The rat! "Well what?" I shout.

"I don't want to go into this over the phone."

"Into what?" I whine.

"Something kind of happened, but I really should tell you in person."

And now I'm feeling slightly guilty about Bryan. Why haven't I told Tom that Bryan won't be coming up? Geez, I've forgotten Bryan already!

Tom blinks at me. "It's your turn."

What did he say? "Um, what happened between you and Shari, Tom Terrific?"

He shudders. "You're *very* good."

I rest my head on his shoulder. "And you're evil."

He nods. "I just can't believe you didn't get any hints that Shari would try to ruin you like this, Corrine."

I stick out my chest. "Imagine the left one's bigger."

Tom raises his eyebrows.

"Shari dear *has* been telling me to take next week off. The wench! I am coming home immediately!"

Tom sighs. "It's a very good thing your phone's busted. She'd be yakking at you all day Saturday and Sunday. Does she know where you live?"

I pat his thigh and stand. "She doesn't care where I live. Or how I live." I offer my hand to him, which is stupid because I couldn't possibly pull him up.

He takes my hand and pulls me to his lap. "You'll be rid of her in a week."

And that feels so good to know. "She could always call Mr. Dunn."

He shakes his head. "Not gonna happen, sweetie."

I don't mind if he calls me that. "Nah. She wouldn't. But what if she did?" I shake my head. "Nope. No matter what she says to Mr. Dunn, she'll sound like a fool. She wouldn't want him to know a thing." I kiss his stubble. "I like this look. Rugged. Bristly." I squint at his ears. "No sideburns or a moustache, though." I snuggle into his chest. "You should write for the movies."

He kisses me on the nose. "Are you ready to become famous?"

"Yes."

"We have to find a pothole."

"In Brooklyn? Please. It would be harder to find a fully paved street."

He nods. "You're right. Ready to fly?"

"Hey, you get to jump the pothole, too."

He squeezes my booty, and I nearly cry out for joy. "If I have to. I'm going to be filming your booty a lot today."

I blush. This man, this man.

"Just make sure you also film the bike."

Chapter 24

Before we do anything with the bicycle, we go to Modell's Sporting Goods on Fulton Street to buy me my first bike helmet. I pick out a black Giro Phase adult mountain bike helmet, not just because it looks cooler than his plain "turtle shell," but it has the flattest top.

"It has to hold up the camera, right?" I say. I look at the price. Eighty bucks! Well, my head is worth it. "You pay."

Tom pays.

I like Tom.

We probably look strange to anyone watching us. Two people, both *carrying* bike helmets, push *one* bicycle from Fulton Street to Columbus, Whitman, and Cadman Plaza parks to get some sound. With the camera lens on, I hit the Record button, and Tom uses his fancy Nike watch to time out thirty-second intervals of sound. The birds are pretty cooperative. I wish it were windier. We get plenty of car horns, buses changing gears, and several sirens. I kick a few leaves. I even giggle a few times to break the silence. Tom turns the bike upside-down and cranks the wheels, hits the brakes, and cranks again. It doesn't simulate the actual sound of bike tires on pavement, so I make him run alongside me as I ride.

I like Tom. He can almost keep up with me.

Yes, quite a few people think we're nuts. A few nod at us, a bunch of folks stare wide-eyed, and others shrug as if to say,

"Hey, it's Brooklyn—to each his own." I try riding and holding the camera at the same time and nearly run into a tree.

Tom pops out the little mini-DVD and pops in another.

"This is my last one," he says.

"I know a guy," I say, and we go over to Gristedes on Clark Street to get five rolls of duct tape and all the mini-DVDs they have in stock. At the checkout, I stare at the cashier. Yeah, we're into that. Whatchagonnado about it?

We sit on the curb outside Gristedes. I watch Tom attaching the camera to my helmet, and he nearly uses two rolls of duct tape just to keep the camera level.

"What are we going to do with the other three rolls?" I whisper.

"You into that?" he asks.

"No. You?"

"No. Besides, it would take more than three rolls to hold me down."

Interesting. "Maybe we could use them to hold up the 'wall.'" I smile. "Someone pulled it down last night."

He raises his hand. "It was me." He sets the helmet on my head and tightens the straps. "Wiggle your head."

I do.

"It seems to be holding."

"The camera or my head?"

He winks. "Both." He stands behind me and looks through the viewfinder. "I guess we're ready."

"As long as the battery holds out."

"I have a spare."

I like Tom. He thinks of everything.

And he also tore down the "wall" last night. I don't need to know why.

I might tear it down myself tonight.

We roll the bike to the Brooklyn Bridge until we get to a less crowded section about a third of the way across. "I'll run along behind you until we get to thirty seconds," Tom says. He points at a splash of pigeon poo on the ground. "That's your starting point."

Lovely.

"And I . . . just . . . go?" I ask.

He kisses my cheek. "Just . . . go."

He turns on the camera, and I zip left of the solid yellow line, swerving around pedestrians who don't know their right from their left. I try to look up as often as I can to capture the Woolworth Building, the Transportation Building, the Manhattan Bridge, and the buildings around Wall Street. I look down to focus on the handlebars, the front tire, my hands—my brown hands! There's an unspoken sales message there. I look right and left to catch the East River, and I might have gotten a barge or ferry. I look up at the clouds, the sun, and an eternity of blue sky.

After the first run, Tom stands at the thirty-second mark, I roll the bike back to the pigeon poo, and I take off.

Thirty times.

Such is the glamorous life of the wannabe advertising executive.

I take off the helmet, sweat trickling down my cheeks to my ears. "Your turn."

After readjusting the chin strap, we find that our new helmet just barely fits his big head. The first time he rolls by my thirty-second spot, only twenty seconds have elapsed. Show-off. I have to run to where he stops.

"Try to keep up with me," he says.

"Try not to show off then," I say.

He kisses me.

I like Tom. He kisses me at the right moment every time.

For *each* of the next twenty-nine runs, I take ten more steps backward while he rides the bike back to the starting point, and somehow this man gets to me in thirty seconds each time, though he's laboring and huffing on the last couple of runs.

While Tom does a quick check of what we've filmed, I check in with Tia.

"All quiet," she tells me. "No calls. It is as if the phone gods are smiling on me."

And me.

"Please let me know what you are doing, Shari," Tia says.

My stomach gurgles. "Right now, I'm about to go to lunch with Tom."

"You are on a date?" she asks.

"Something like that. Call me if anything happens. Bye." I smile at Tom. "How's it look?"

"Tiring, especially the last couple," he says. "I am so out of shape."

That would be a no.

"So where am I taking you to eat?" he asks.

I take his hand. "Someplace I've never been able to afford. You're buying, right?"

He nods. "Wherever you want to go."

Have I mentioned that I like Tom? I'll bet I have. I'm already going places with him I've never been.

We go to the River Café, which sits in the shadow of the Brooklyn Bridge. So we don't leave the bike unguarded—we didn't think to buy a chain lock—we eat out on the deck, the bridge hovering above us. We share oysters and crab soup while watching seagulls, boats, and, well, *life* breaking out all around us.

"How are we going to do the voice-overs?" I ask.

"I have a studio at my house."

La-dee-da. Doesn't everyone? "You are bound and deter-mined to get me to your house."

"Because you'll love it."

I'm sure I will. A single room in his bungalow probably has more square footage than my entire apartment. "We still need 'wheel shots' all around town. And a decent digital camera."

"And," he adds, "a nice deep, long pothole to leap."

"It shouldn't be too hard to find." My feet dance under me.

"Are you nervous, Shari?"

Anything but! I'm excited. I'm doing real work here! "Just happy."

He looks into my eyes, and I look right back. "You, um, wanna go look at our footage?"

Footage. Hmm. Where's he going with this? The man is insatiable. Of course, so am I.

"It'll look better on your TV than on this little screen," he says.

My poor couch! My poor table! Do we have enough duct tape to keep the "wall" from falling? Will I even want the "wall" between us anymore?

Yes, Lord. I'll put up the "wall." They were hypothetical questions.

"As long as you keep your footage to yourself," I say.

He pouts. "I'm hurt."

"You remember why, right?"

"I agreed, didn't I?" he says. "But I'm still hurt, okay? It isn't easy not doing what I want to do, especially when you asked me to kiss you good night. That was so hard, Shari."

And it was hard for me, too. All the more reason for me to make you wait, man. Then it will be special. "Best friends first."

He sighs and nods. "Best friends first." He leans in and takes my hands. "The camera we'll buy can have other uses, too."

How absolutely naughty. "Let's go get us a camera."

Tom smiles. "I know a guy . . ."

Instead of walking and pushing the bike as before, Tom puts me up on the handlebars, my booty just barely hanging on, and we ride. I know there's an ad that has a picture of us, well, maybe not *us* exactly, doing this. For three miles to Flushing Avenue, we turn more heads than a hairdresser and a barber combined. And I feel scared, excited, proud, embarrassed, and powerful. *Alive.* I feel alive, maybe for the first time in my life. I want to let go of the handlebars and fly, but I ain't crazy.

I watch my short legs waving in the air, feel Tom's hands steadying me, hear him humming "I'm So Glad I Found You," a seriously old R & B song by the O'Jays. I counter by singing

Mariah Carey's "We Belong Together"—and I nearly fall off the bike when he sings the high parts along with me!

This, too, is bliss.

Okay, it's more than bliss. This is the absolute *junk*.

Tom talks to his "guy" at Supersonic and buys a Panasonic Lumix GH1 camera that has more bells and whistles than a train yard. He also buys four interchangeable lenses, another tripod, a high-end photo printer, two years' supply of printer ink, a couple hundred sheets of premium 8½ x 11 photo paper, and a huge photographer's bag to put all but the printer inside.

All to the tune of $3,900.

"Your credit card company must love you," I say.

"It's my debit card, Shari."

I have trouble processing that. I have a debit card, too, but the most I've ever had in my account after paying my bills wouldn't cover a third of what he's just spent!

I ain't no gold digger, but . . . that's the absolute junk, too.

"So expensive," I say.

"An investment," he says. "And you'll pay your half once we're incorporated."

He thinks of everything. "What if I'd rather pay you in other ways?"

He only smiles.

I think we'll be even by the end of the night. My fingers are itching to give this man a back rub. And a front rub. And a side rub . . .

When we leave Supersonic, we both look up. Where's the sun? We weren't in the store that long. And then it starts to rain.

"Call it a day?" I ask.

"It's a day," he says.

I like Tom. He listens to me.

When we get back to my apartment, I strip down to some old gym shorts and a T-shirt with holes and rips in all the right places, yet Tom keeps his distance and his sweatshirt on. He sits at the other end of the couch while I pout.

"I thought we were done working," I say.

"This is the fun part," he says.

We then watch every Brooklyn Bridge video. We number each one and take notes as we go. Some of Tom's rides give me motion sickness, and mine come out better because it was sunnier when I rode and I was a whole lot steadier. I can hear myself breathing heavily on the last few runs.

We compare notes.

I look at my list. "Numbers four, eight, and fifteen."

He looks at his list. "I had four and eight, too. Why not thirty-seven?"

I flip through my notes. "Your knuckles were especially hairy in that one. I don't want to bite off of Geico and the cavemen."

He flips a few pages back in his notebook. "Fifteen? You were huffing and puffing."

"It adds realism."

He sighs. "Well, we agree on four and eight. We'll make the final decision once I get time to play with it at the studio." He pops in the Yankee Stadium DVD. "Let's look at these the same way."

After watching them and taking rapid notes—fifteen seconds goes by in a flash!—I star only one of the segments. "To be honest, only twenty-four is worth using," I say.

"Same here," he says, but he's studying a blank page!

"You didn't take any notes, man."

He shakes his head. "It's no use, Shari. You were right about the others. So I says to myself, I says, 'What's the point in arguing with Shari? She's always right.'" Tom could never be a gangster. "That's what I says to myself."

"And I want you to keep that in mind at all times."

"I will." He stands and stretches. "Let's go to the bedroom and listen to the sounds we collected."

"Um, that might affect your focus, Mr. Sexton." And mine. And then we'll have to put up the "wall" again.

I hear his back crack.

Oh. "My couch is pretty uncomfortable, huh?"

He nods. "It was built for small people."

"Whatever."

He smiles. "Small sexy people."

That's better.

We go into my bedroom, and he somehow hooks the camera to my little shelf stereo. I lift up the "wall," and he sighs.

Yeah, big boy, you and me both.

After he uses thumbtacks and some duct tape, we lie on the bed, and for half an hour, we listen, booty-to-booty, the "wall" between us, to thirty-second bursts of sound.

"You first," he says.

"Nah," I say. "You first."

"Um, eleven, nineteen, and forty-nine."

I look at my list. Did I number wrong? "There wasn't a forty-nine."

"There will be." He reaches under the curtain and pulls up the back of my shirt. "I need to touch you, Shari, and you need a back rub. Number forty-nine will capture the sounds you're about to make."

I try to stay focused and slide away from his hands. "Eleven is on my list, too. Eleven it is."

He reaches even farther and somehow latches on to the elastic on the back of my gym shorts. "When did you first wear these?"

Let's see. Sophomore year. "Twelve years ago." I try to pull away, but it's a feeble attempt. I wave his hand away, but he holds on.

"I can't see very well," he says, "but did you have that booty twelve years ago?"

So fresh! "No."

I see a sweatshirt fly over my head, feel my shirt rising up my back, and soon feel one seriously smoking hot hand working me to distraction.

I, um, I have to put my glasses on the nightstand. I don't want them to, um, get damaged should I lose my mind.

I wrap my arms around a pillow. "Does *this* mean we're done for the day, boss?"

"We're only just beginning, and don't call me boss."

"You're the boss, boss," I say.

He taps my booty.

"Careful," I say. "I bite."

"So do I."

I like Tom. He says the nicest things.

"Um, Shari?"

"Yes, Tom?"

His hand disappears, the bed bounces, and in a moment Tom is on my side of the bed. "I promise to behave," he says. "I can't give you a proper back rub with one hand. Shari, you need some lotion. I could play tic-tac-toe on that back."

I point to my dresser. Whoo. I'm about to get waxed. "But only if you behave." Not so sure about me.

He stands beside the bed and warms up the lotion first. He starts at the back of my neck, that little small space that has to be one of the best yet most neglected erogenous zones on my body. Even though I pant quietly, I know my nipples are puncturing my pillowcase. He shapes and digs into my shoulders. That earns a groan. He makes big circles, little circles, in-between circles, and lots of straight lines on my back, working his way down to my booty. And when he gets to the small of my back and really cranks it up, I cry out, but not in pain.

"You okay?" he asks.

I nod. The things he's doing to the parts of my body that he has yet to touch is driving me crazy. I shouldn't have worn such tight shorts! I might actually chafe!

He pops up my waistband again, and he is silent for several delicious moments.

I turn slightly and see him staring hard at my booty. "What are you doing?"

"Worshiping. Having a moment of silence. Taking a mental picture I hope never fades."

"How long do you need?" I ask. *Please* take a long time.

"A lifetime."

I like Tom. He always gives me more than I ask for.

"Um, does your booty need massaging?" he asks.

Does Peaches need Herb? Does Ashford need Simpson? Does Kid need Play? I answer by wiggling my booty.

Don't worry, Lord. I'm keeping my drawers on.

Instead of massaging my booty through my shorts, he worms his hands up my thighs and under my panties until all I feel is tight drawers in front and man hands in back. He does some serious damage to my booty, and in less than two minutes, I make this sound.

It's a sound I've never made before.

It's not in any language I've ever heard, nor can I even spell it.

It emanates from my toes, travels up to my booty, and explodes out of my mouth at about a hundred and fifty decibels.

I just know it had lots of Z's and S's in it, ending in a series of O's and a delightful mmm. . . .

Chapter 25

That was intense.

I haven't had an orgasm in . . . I can't remember. And we haven't even gotten busy yet!

After he removes his hands from my grateful booty, I sweep my shirt back down, sit up, and scoot against the headboard, catching my breath. I quickly yank the covers up to my stomach.

"You're, um, we're . . ." I stop. "Tom, that was . . . that was completely unexpected."

He nods. "Can I say what I'm thinking?"

"No."

He drops his eyes. "It isn't anything bad."

"Okay. What are you thinking?"

"That never happened to me before either." He frowns at his crotch. "I may have to do some laundry soon."

I widen my eyes. "You, too?"

He nods. "It's like I'm in high school or something." He blushes. "I feel pretty stupid."

Well, well, well. I turned him on without turning over. And he—*wow!*—he did the same to me. I stretch my neck side to side. "That was definitely a tension breaker."

"Yeah."

I lock eyes with him, and he doesn't look away. I will never find another man like him. I need to make all this permanent somehow, and although we're both kind of embarrassed, this might be the best time.

"What exactly are we doing here, Tom?" I ask.

He starts to move closer, but I shake my head.

He stops. "We're enjoying each other's company, Shari. Very much, I might add. We're becoming friends."

"You know what I mean. Are we . . ." I have to be out of my mind to ask this so soon! "Is this a lifetime thing, Tom?"

"What do you want it to be?" he asks.

That's *not* how that question is supposed to work. "You don't want to answer till I do, is that it?"

"I want what you want."

That's still not an answer. I must test him. "So if I say . . . ring, wedding, marriage, child . . ."

He smiles, his shoulders relaxing. "I'd say *rings*—I want one, too. Um, rings, elope to Jamaica, passionate marriage, and children."

Elope? Children? "No wedding?"

"I have no one to invite. Come to de islands, mon."

I burned so many bridges at home that I might not have anyone show up either. "What if I want a wedding?"

"Do you?"

Not really. I shrug. "I suppose it's negotiable." Hmm. He said children, as in more than one. "How many kids?"

"Two."

Reasonable. "A boy and a girl?"

"Two girls," he says. "I want to be outnumbered, outvoted, and controlled by women for the rest of my natural life."

I must *possess* this man. "You are a very wise man." I open my arms to him, and he slides in behind me instead. I rest my head on his chest, and he wraps his arms around me.

"Well, Mr. Sexton," I say as coyly as I can. "This is sounding right serious, I mean, I hardly even know you, sweetie."

"There were some times these last few days when I thought I had known you all my life," he says.

Wow. I don't know what to say to that.

"You're the mystery girl I've had in my dreams since I was sixteen, only I could never see your face," he says. "And now that I've seen you up close, I know I won't ever have to dream about my mystery girl again." He squeezes my hands. "Because she's here."

That is so sweet, maybe the sweetest thing I've ever heard.

"And, Shari Nance, I am seriously, helplessly, head-over-heels, shamelessly, and endlessly in love with you."

Oh . . . man. I heard "Shari Nance." I should have known something like this was coming. But maybe he's only saying it because he's in my bed and just had some, um, release. I have to make him repeat it. "You're what?"

He picks me off his lap and turns me around, wrapping my legs around him. He looks me in the eye. "I am ridiculously, passionately, fully, wildly, and out of my mind in love with you, Shari Nance."

Maybe he's not just saying it. "So soon?"

"What do you mean, so soon?" He smiles. "I have known you for years. You've been my friend for years. I can talk to you like I can talk to no one else on this earth, and we've been talking for years. But this morning when you yawned and stretched on the edge of the bed. That little sigh you made. That sly smile. I knew at that moment I wanted *that* for the rest of my life."

He took down the "wall" so he could watch me wake up? That's so odd. He could have torn down that "wall" and had his way with me. "You wanted to see me at my worst? Hair a mess, breath humming, crust in my eyes?"

"You were the most beautiful person, place, or thing I have ever seen in my life at that moment."

It's nice to be wanted, and everything he said *was* true, but . . . I was at my worst.

"I've, um, I've never spent the night anywhere with anyone, Shari," he continues. "And you've had me staying with you three nights in a row. This is a big deal for me."

Never? Well, I can see why. He barely fits in any bed. "You never stayed the night with Corrine?"

"No. She always kicked me out." He sighs. "She didn't want

me to see her in the morning, and for that, I am eternally grateful. But you . . . I want to wake up with you."

This is so . . . sudden. He skipped the "best friend" part and
went to the "love" part. "You never stayed the night with anyone else?"

"No."

"So because you spent the night and saw me yawning, you
know you love me."

"That's not all, Shari," he says. "It's how I *felt* about staying,
how I *felt* when I held your hand all night, how I *felt* when I got
to see you wake up. I was here to see it. I saw you when you
thought I was asleep, and I saw *you*. I saw *you*. Just you. I didn't
see the room anymore, didn't see the window, didn't see the bed,
the ceiling, the floor, the bedspread, or the 'wall.' Just you. I saw
you, Shari Nance."

He's saying such wonderful things. Why isn't my heart aching
or something? "Was I floating in the air?"

He stops smiling and drops his eyes. "You weren't floating in
the air, Shari. It's hard to explain."

Man, he's serious. *This* is serious. I can't play this off. And I
certainly can't tackle this man. I'd bounce off.

"It was like . . ." He looks up for a moment then back into
my eyes. "You know those photographs where the subject of the
picture is in crystal-clear focus while the rest of the picture is
fuzzed out? That's how you looked. You were in focus while the
rest of the world disappeared."

"Maybe you just had sleep in your eyes." What an insensitive
thing to say, Shari! Why'd you say that?

He looks away. "I saw what I saw. And I feel what I feel." He
slides closer to the headboard, and I have no choice but to come
with him. He looks toward the window. "Sun's setting."

I look at the window. It looks pretty. "I'm rarely here to see it
on a weekday."

Tom is silent.

Shoot.

"So, what's on the agenda for tomorrow?" I ask.

Tom is still silent.

"Tom?" I don't ask what's wrong. I know what's wrong. He loves me, and he now knows that A, I don't believe that he loves me, and B, I don't love him in return.

He sighs. "Shari, I've just told you that I love you."

"I know." And it scares me.

"Doesn't it affect you in any way?" he asks softly.

"Um, it's still sinking in. I feel . . ." What a time for Chaka Khan's "I Feel for You" to play in my mind. "I . . . I feel good about it, Tom." Thank you, James Brown. "I feel bliss. My heart is uncluttered, and my mind is open." Is that what love truly is?

"No . . . comets, shooting stars, rainbows, fireworks?"

No. Well, I did have those a few moments ago, and from a booty rub! "I just had quite a few of those during my, um, back rub." But that's not what love is. Comets fly by, shooting stars burn out, rainbows fade and go away, and fireworks blow up and leave lots of smoke. "I feel . . . calm. Content. In the right place." I feel . . . tears? I'm crying? "I feel home."

"Do you think that it might be love?" he asks.

What is happening? And why am I crying? "Yes. Yes, it might be. I'm where I should be, and it's with you. I don't have a care in the world."

He wipes a tear from my cheek.

"This is so familiar, Tom," I say, and it is. "You there. Me resting on you. Us talking, making plans. I want this." I watch my tears dot his T-shirt. "Yes, Tom. Yes. This must be love."

That night, after tearing down that silly "wall," I sleep with a real man for the first time in my life *without* having sex with him. It is the most intimate thing I have ever done in my life. I touch him, hold on to his arms, feel his breath on my hair, hear him purring in my ear, and it is glorious. Bliss, sheer bliss.

It has to be love.

Love is here.

Love is home.

I'm finally, *really* home.

Chapter 26

We're much quieter on Thursday.

I didn't think it would ever be possible.

We're actually kind of shy, trying to be all business. We wander with the bike and two helmets, my tote bag clipped to the rack in back, me in boots, my North Face jacket, and brown corduroys (about as dressy as I want to be for this shot), Tom in jeans and a sweatshirt. Tom carries the photography bag over his shoulder and holds my little hand with his big hand. To anyone watching, they'd think we were two young (hey, twenty-seven and thirty-four *aren't* old) lovers out on a stroll on a cool but sunny fall day.

We are actually looking for the largest pothole in Brooklyn.

We find a nice fat canyon on Dean Street in Boerum Hill in front of an immaculate row of redbrick brownstones. The pothole seems so out of place for such a nice block, but it's November, and I read somewhere that there are 73,000 unfilled potholes in Brooklyn. Who goes around and counts them all? Your tax dollars at work. It's obvious that even Boerum Hill isn't immune to bad roads. The problem is a red Honda Element parked dangerously close to where we'd have to land after our leaps. I set up the tripod on the sidewalk near a metal railing and take a few quick shots as some cars go by.

"You're thinking Photoshop, aren't you?" Tom asks.

I snap away, even though I know very little about this camera. Auto-focus is the bomb. "I don't want either of us eating a bumper today."

"We could find another pothole," he says.

I look at the pothole. "This is by far the deepest one I've ever seen. Sound echoes in that thing. We may even find Jimmy Hoffa and Amelia Earhart down there. We will use this one somehow."

I swing the tripod a few feet into the street and take several more shots with the black railing and a door framed in the background.

"I could try," Tom says.

"I like your teeth."

Tom places the bike in the pothole and swings up onto it. "What if I make it fly?"

I knew he was Superman. "Go for it." I ready the camera.

Tom bends his legs, hunches down, then yanks up on the handlebars, and the bike jumps about a foot off the ground.

Very cool. "Do that again, and look straight ahead with a smile on your face." I snap away, reminding him to smile, reminding him to look ahead, encouraging him to be Superman. I lower the tripod after about twenty "jumps" to make it seem that he's leaping higher.

"Your turn." He takes over camera duties as I get on. "Remember to smile, look ahead, and be cute, Superwoman."

I have trouble keeping the bike balanced, and my first few attempts only raise up the front wheel.

"Wheelies are so cool," he says, clicking away.

The first time I completely get my balance, I drop down, bend my legs, and jerk up.

"Three inches," he says. "Didn't even clear the top of the pothole."

Shoot. "This bike is heavy, Tom."

He lies on the sidewalk beside the pothole and points the camera up at me. "Try again."

"I'll land on you," I say.

"Just . . . go."

I make several more attempts until my arms and legs start burning. "No more."

He turns the camera around. "Take a look."

I don't know what settings he used, but it looks as if I'm much higher above the pothole than I really was. I'm even smiling. "How'd you do that?"

"I read the manual."

"When?" We fell asleep together and woke up together.

"While you were dreaming. I couldn't sleep."

I don't even remember dreaming. Weird. I always remember my dreams. I smile at Tom. Yeah, he's the reason I'm forgetting them now. I was in the arms of my dream all night.

An elderly white woman wearing pink slippers, plain white tube socks, and a parka over a pale yellow housedress covered with flowers comes out of her brownstone. "You from DOT?"

The Department of Transportation? Is she kidding? Tom and I are actually *visible*.

Tom smiles. "Good morning, and no, ma'am."

She stands next to the bike and stares at the pothole. "I've been calling about this eyesore for weeks."

"It's a dandy," Tom says.

"Tell me about it." She looks at Tom, shielding her eyes from the sun. "Then what are you doing?"

Hmm. Camera. Tripod. We must be taking pictures. "We're doing an ad campaign for this Peterson bicycle," he says. "Do you know who owns the red Honda?"

"You're selling a bike by taking a picture of a pothole?" she asks.

"Well, we actually want to jump the pothole," I explain, "and the red Honda is in the way."

She looks at me. "What for?"

"To show the bike's capabilities," I say. "You know, this bicycle is able to leap deep Brooklyn potholes in a single bound. You know, Superwoman, Superman."

She blinks at me. "That's crazy. The best place for a bicycle is on the ground."

I can't argue with that. "Yeah, it is. How would you sell this bike?"

She looks the bike over from back to front. "Oh, I don't know much about advertising. I ran a market with my husband for fifty years, but food sells itself." She slides her wrinkled hand over the seat. "This bicycle reminds me of my first Schwinn. Mine had fenders. Chrome. A basket on the front. A little bell."

"Did it have tassels?" I ask.

Her face erupts into the sweetest smile. "Oh yes. Pink and white ones. And whitewall tires. I used to ride it all the way to Coney Island and back when I was a young lady."

"You still have it?" Tom asks.

"Oh no," she says, a trace of sadness in her voice. "It's long gone."

Tom takes her picture.

"You just took my picture," she says. "Did you get my good side?" The woman is a born flirt.

Tom takes out a little notepad. "What's your name?"

Her eyes widen. "Anne Collier. Is this really for an ad, like on a billboard?"

"That's what we're hoping for, ma'am," Tom says. "Why don't you move it to the sidewalk. By the railing." He takes several shots in succession. "You want to ride it?"

"Oh, oh my," she says. "I haven't ridden a bicycle in sixty years."

I know she wants to ride it, even after sixty years. "Would you like to try?" I ask. "It's a very safe bicycle." I offer her my helmet.

"Well, I suppose I could try," she says.

I help her with the helmet, and Tom helps her up onto the bike, steadying the handlebars while I hold the back tire in place.

"Well, I'm up here," she says.

"I'm going to let go," Tom says, "and you can just coast if you want to."

"Okay," she says, "but don't let me fall."

"I won't," Tom says.

Her face is shining! This is so beautiful.

Tom lets go, Mrs. Collier pushes down on the pedal, and as she coasts down the sidewalk, Tom runs backward and shoots away, Mrs. Collier's housedress fluttering behind her.

She even shouts, "Whee!"

She squeezes the brakes too hard and nearly falls, but Tom catches and steadies her. He helps her off, and they walk back to me.

He turns the camera around to her. "Look."

"Ha! That's me!" She beckons me over. "Oh, would you look at my face! Ooh, my hair is flying every which way! And I'm wearing slippers and white socks! I look a sight! Ha!"

I get a look. *That* is a picture of pure joy. That is a picture of pure abandon.

"It's like I'm riding my first bike all over again," she says.

Goose bumps race up my legs to my chin.

Tom blinks at me and mouths, "Wow."

I quickly write that one down. I note her address. "Mrs. Collier, thank you for being such a good sport."

"Um, it's Mrs. Harland Collier. Harland is . . . no longer with us, but I still keep his name. He's why I rode all the way down to Coney Island so often."

That's so sweet and sad.

She looks from Tom to me. "Are you two . . . an item?"

"Yes ma'am," I say quickly. "Yes, we are."

"I knew it." She folds her arms in front of her. "I could see it in your eyes when I was watching from the window. Harland and I ran our market for fifty years together over in Carroll Gardens. Isn't it wonderful to work with the man you love?"

"Yes." I smile at Tom. "Yes, it is."

"When will I be up on a billboard?" she asks.

"We have to win the account first," I say. "But if we win, very soon."

"Wonderful," she says. "You'll let me know where?"

"I have your address," I say. "We'll even send you a copy."

"Thank you, thank you," she says. "Just think. If they had filled in that pothole, I wouldn't have ridden a bicycle today."

We leave her beaming, just beaming.

Tom and I practically skip away. "We need to get to a park," he says, "and we need to get more people riding this thing, the older the better, every possible ethnicity."

Now there's a plan! "It's like I'm riding my first bike all over again. Why didn't we think of that?"

Tom shrugs. "Maybe we're too young."

Chapter 27

Our first few attempts at coaxing people to ride the bicycle are unsuccessful.

"You must be joking!"

"Are you crazy? You want I should break my *other* hip?"

"Is this some TV show where you pull a prank on someone? Where are the hidden cameras? Is that one over there up in that tree?"

"I never learned to ride."

"Is it safe? Anything you have to wear a helmet to ride *cannot* be safe."

But then we meet Arnie, a bowlegged black man who has to be at least eighty, in Cadman Plaza Park. He jumps right onto the bike and takes it for a five-minute spin. He circles Tom several times, and Tom keeps on snapping away. After Arnie, we have a line of people waiting to try. Some even ride with no hands! Their faces shine. They literally glow with joy. No model could re-create that joy, even if they were paid to do so. I keep track of names and addresses, promise to send all of them copies, even if we didn't use them, and three even ask where they could buy the bike!

"It's better built than my car. Of course, just about everything is built better than my car these days."

"Just look at that craftsmanship. Handmade, you say? I believe it."

"So smooth I thought I was riding on air."

"I didn't know they made bikes like these anymore."

Fifteen elderly people ride the bike. Seven men, eight women, none under fifty-five. Hispanic, black, Asian, white, Jewish, Italian, even the cutest Russian woman who didn't want to give the bike back!

"We have to use the word *home* somehow, too," I say as we rest under a tree, my back against his chest, my legs splayed out in the leaves. "I feel it."

"You sure?"

I'm sure. "That word ties everything else together."

Tom throws some leaves into the air. "Home of the brave?"

I bite my lower lip. "How about . . .'A memory of home—it's like I'm riding my first bike all over again.' What do you think?"

He sniffs a little sigh and shakes his head. "You don't need me at all, Shari. That's brilliant. I'll just take the pictures from now on. You do all the thinking, okay? I'll just nod my head."

That's one of the best compliments I've ever gotten. "Keep thinking, Tom. Brilliance is not always perfection."

He tickles me. "Stop quoting Cringe."

"I'm her, remember?"

He turns me to him. "Never." He kisses me softly. "We can't stay here all day doing this."

"Why not?"

He looks up. "Beautiful day for taking pictures. Didn't Mr. Dunn want a New York landmark spread, too?"

I nod. "Do we still need to do it?"

"It's up to you."

I like that phrase very much. It's up to me. I can't remember the last time I heard anyone say that to me. I don't think anyone has actually said that to me my entire life. "I think we should still do it. The light is so magical today."

He takes my picture. "The light, um, was especially magical just then."

I blush. "We have to get down to Coney Island, then back to the Brooklyn Bridge, over to Times Square. Tom, we need to get

a move on." And now I'm sounding like him! This man has already rubbed off on me.

"I wish we had a car so we could go take pictures of this
bike," he says.

I roll my eyes at the irony. "Ha-ha."

"No, I wish we had my car. It's in Great Neck crying out to
me. Can't you hear it crying, Shari?" He pulls out his cell phone,
hits a few buttons, scrolls down . . .

"What are you doing?" I ask. "Calling your car?" Maybe
he's Batman.

"I'm getting us a taxi," he says.

"Right," I say. "We're going to have a taxi driver take us to
all these places so we can take pictures of a bicycle."

"As long as he gets paid, why should he care?" He punches in
a number. "Yes. I need a taxi for the rest of the day . . . Don't
worry about the expense, I'll pay it. And if you can, send your
oldest, most experienced driver, the one who knows the city
best. . . . I'm at Cadman Plaza Park with my girlfriend and a red
and black bicycle. You can't miss us." He closes his phone.

"Your girlfriend," I say.

"Should I have said something else?"

I nod. "I am not a girl."

"Well, hot, sexy friend who makes interesting noises during
booty rubs wouldn't have—"

I don't let him finish. Leaves are very effective for stuffing
into a nasty man's pants. I'm sure I'll be finding leaves in my bed
this evening.

"You also said, 'You can't miss us,' " I say. "What'd you
mean by that?"

He smiles. "We're the two happiest people here."

Uh-huh. We are, but I think he meant something else.

When the taxi driver shows up, I immediately think I'm talking to George Burns, only he wears Mr. Magoo's glasses, Speed
Racer's racing gloves, and a World War II bomber jacket. I'm
actually a little taller than he is.

I immediately like this driver very much.

Tom asks him to open the trunk.

"You're putting the bike in the trunk?" he asks in a typical Brooklyn accent. "Are you hurt?"

"No sir," Tom says.

The driver opens the trunk, Tom sets the bike inside, but the trunk lid won't close.

"Has to close," the driver says. "Regulations."

Tom maneuvers the bike out of the trunk and fits it into the backseat.

"Now where are you two gonna sit?" the driver asks.

I smile. "Up front with you. I'm Shari, and this is Tom."

He looks at each of us for a moment and sighs. "Carl."

I put my hand on his shoulder. "I don't bite, Carl. Tom and I are taking pictures of this bike at various New York landmarks for an ad campaign."

"Yeah?" Carl says. "Who do you represent?"

"Methuselah's Breezy Hiccup," Tom says.

"Never heard of 'em," Carl says. "You out of Jersey?"

"No," I say. "We're straight out of Brooklyn."

"With an office in Great Neck," Tom adds.

Carl squints at me. "Brooklyn *and* Great Neck? Is he kidding?"

"Yes," I say, sticking out my tongue at Tom. "So is it all right if we ride in the front with you, Carl?"

"Long as you pay," Carl says, "you can sit anywhere you like."

When we get in, Carl just lets the taxi idle.

Oh yeah. Where to? "Where are we going first, Tom?" I ask.

"Um, Carl," Tom says, "we want you to give us suggestions for where to take pictures, and maybe you can even pose on the bike."

"Suggestions?" Carl says. "For places to take pictures? In *this* city?"

"I know, stupid question," Tom says.

"Well, you have to go to the Garden, Yankee Stadium, and the Empire State for starters," Carl says.

"And Coney Island," I add.

Carl nods. "Definitely. Gotta take a picture of that bike on the boardwalk. And Central Park, Radio City, Sylvia's . . ."

Carl knows about Sylvia's home cooking in Harlem? "Why Sylvia's?"

"You got me all day, right?" he asks.

We nod.

He straightens up his gloves. "I gotta eat, don't I?"

And then . . . we see the city from a Peterson bicycle's perspective. We hit the Brooklyn Bridge again, the Cathedral of St. John the Divine, Central Park, the Chrysler Building, the Empire State Building, the Federal Reserve Bank, the Flatiron Building, the Grand Central Terminal, Madison Square Garden, the New York Public Library, the New York Stock Exchange, St. Patrick's Cathedral, Temple Emanu-El, Times Square, the United Nations, the World Trade Center site, and Coney Island. We don't spend a great deal of time at each spot, and Carl never turns off his Sinatra music, giving anyone watching us something to sing or hum. I impress Tom with my ability to play dashboard drums along with Buddy Rich, and Tom blows me away with his flawless rendition of Perry Como's "Catch a Falling Star."

This job is a blast!

As the sun starts to set, Carl heads toward Harlem, and I smile because I'm hungry, too. After taking photographs of the bicycle at the Apollo Theater, Abyssinian Baptist Church, Hotel Theresa, the Lenox Lounge, and Strivers' Row, we get to Sylvia's, the world-renowned soul food restaurant on Lenox Avenue and 127th Street. Bill Clinton, Nelson Mandela, Jesse Jackson, Al Sharpton, Magic Johnson—stars, movers and shakers have eaten there.

Carl gets the chicken livers sautéed with onions and peppers and covered with gravy. Tom and I do not. We eat smothered pork chops and barbecue ribs off each other's plates, and I am much faster with my fork than Tom is. We try to get Sylvia herself to get on the bike after we finish.

"Child, that ain't for me," she says. "I got my feet, and they've been carrying me just fine so far."

Carl, however, proudly gets on the bike in front of the restaurant with Sylvia standing nearby.

It is easily our best shot of the day.

After a quick stop at an ATM to get more cash, Carl drops us off at the Brooklyner, and Tom pays him.

You don't want to know the final tally. Carl can probably retire now and move to Jamaica.

I walk around to Carl's window. "I'm gonna miss you, Carl." I kiss his cheek.

Carl doesn't speak, but the glimmer of a smile lights on his lips. He nods at Tom, and he rolls off.

Once inside the apartment, we load all the pictures into my computer, and they all look fantastic. Because of that last picture of Carl, we have sixteen billboards (or web banners and magazine ads) that speak of joy, freedom, America, and old-fashioned values. The fifty landmark shots are decent, but they pale in comparison to our real New Yorkers.

"These are incredible," Tom says. "Just incredible."

"All thanks to a Brooklyn pothole and Mrs. Harland Collier," I say, starting work on the web banners. "What should we do with the landmark shots?"

He massages my neck. "Not sure. Mr. Peterson could run them in the New York market. Newspaper, magazine."

I lean back and he kisses me. I lean forward. "If you keep massaging me, I won't get these done."

He stands at the window. "I wish I could start on the videos . . ."

"Okay, okay," I say. "Tomorrow we'll go to your studio. It's late, I ate too much, and I just want to make these perfect." Click and drag, shrink. Adjust contrast, brightness.

"What about Bryan?" Tom asks. "Isn't he coming tomorrow night?"

Oh yeah. Bryan. Why do I keep forgetting to tell Tom about this? "I should have told you this earlier," I say with a sigh. I should have told him the day I did it. "I, um, called him when we got back to JFK. Bryan won't be coming. We are officially finished." I watch Tom's reaction in the reflection of the window, and he looks . . . puzzled? That's not the relief I expected to see.

"You gave him a 'Dear John' over the phone," Tom says.

I nod. Yep. Heartless me.

"How'd he take it?" Tom asks.

"He was sad," I say. So was I. "But he'll get over it."

He turns my chair away from the computer and faces me. "I'll bet he was devastated. If I were in his position, I'd come storming up here after you."

"He won't, now let me finish these." I try to turn my chair back to the computer, but he holds my chair in place. "What?"

"What if he *does* come up here?" he asks.

I sigh. "But I won't be here, right? I'll be at your little bungalow in Great Neck. I am staying the weekend, right?"

He searches my eyes. "But you knew him for twelve years."

And you didn't answer my question. "More like eighteen years. What's your point?"

He shakes his head. "Eighteen years, and you can just . . . call him up and dump him."

Oh. That's his point. "It wasn't easy, Tom. He was . . . he was my first. My first real date, my first boyfriend, my first lover." The first man who almost asked me to marry him not ten steps from here. "Why are you so concerned anyway? I thought you'd be happy that I'm completely free."

He lets go of my chair and returns to the window. "I'm putting myself in his place. I'm trying to feel how it would feel if you gave up on me. I don't think I would ever get over losing you."

"You won me, Tom, so there's nothing to lose, right?"

He doesn't answer.

"What's wrong?" I ask.

"I have the strangest feeling that Bryan is going to be here tomorrow, that's all. He has known you for eighteen years. He grew up with you. He was your first. Don't you think he'll fight for you?"

Why are we even having this conversation? "He may have

grown up with me, but he didn't grow with me. I changed, and he stayed the same."

He kneels in front of me. "But isn't there something comforting about that? Bryan was someone you could count on."

"I can count on you, too," I say. "I'm relying on you more and more by the second. Why are you sticking up for him?"

He frowns. "I don't know. Maybe I'm just sticking up for myself, or my future self. You could just as easily brush me aside once I stopped 'growing with you.'"

I'd need a bulldozer to brush this man aside, and I need to grow another foot just to see eye-to-eye with him. I look into my full-grown man's brown eyes. "And you could do the same to me, right?"

"I won't do that, Shari," he says. "I don't think you'll ever finish growing. I have so much trouble keeping up with you already. Your mind works so much faster than mine. I just hope you will do me the courtesy of telling me face-to-face should you ever want to dump me."

"Oh Tom, I won't dump you."

He doesn't speak.

Okay, here's another point. "So I should have said, 'Sure, Bryan. C'mon up here to Brooklyn so I can dump you'?"

Tom wrinkles up his lips. "No."

"Bryan was planning to stay with me through Thanksgiving Day." I blink several times. "Would it have been better that Bryan and I shacked up for the weekend, without the 'wall' because he would have expected to get him some, and then I could have dumped him Thanksgiving Day?"

Tom looks away. "Of course not. Geez." He stands and goes to the window. "I'm just saying, if I were him, I'd be knocking down your door tomorrow night."

"But I won't be here, right? I'll be in Great Neck."

He sighs. "I think you should be here tomorrow night, just in case he does show up. You owe him that much."

"Didn't you just hear me? He was planning to stay with me—here—through Thanksgiving."

"I heard you."

What's going on? "You *want* me to spend the weekend and then some with my ex-boyfriend?"

"Of course not, Shari." He shakes his head. "I was just saying that Bryan would have to be a complete fool not to come up here, okay? That's all I'm saying."

Is this our first fight? I think it is. I need to calm Tom down. "Well, as long as you're here with me, it won't be a problem."

"Isn't this something you have to do on your own?" he asks.

"I don't know what the problem is!" I pick up a pencil and throw it at the window. Yeah, this is our first fight. I throw things. "You sweep me off my feet, do things to my body without even . . ." I have to say this now. "You made me have an orgasm without even having sex with me, Tom. That has never happened to me before, and it scared me. You hold me like I've never been held, and you say the sweetest, most heart-stirring things to me. I have made my decision, Tom Sexton. I have chosen you. End of story."

He picks up the pencil. "I didn't mean to upset you, Shari."

"I'm not upset. I'm just a little pissed."

He smiles. "So fiery."

I try not to laugh. "I'm content. I want you, just you. Bryan was holding me back in so many ways. You want me to take off."

"Your clothes."

"What?"

"I want you to take off your clothes."

Now? While I'm pissed off? "I have to finish these banners, Tom. I'm not as technologically gifted as you are. I actually have to *think* about every button I click."

"I just want to take some pictures while you work." He picks up the camera. "It will give my hands something to do, and I promise I won't interrupt you."

Why don't I believe that? I want him to interrupt me. I look out the window. "And you want me to take off my clothes in front of this window?"

He shakes his head. "No." He squints. "But you could show me a little more skin."

I'd love to. "Tom, I make it a point to be fully clothed whenever I walk around in here."

"You were only wearing a towel yesterday morning."

I roll my eyes. "That's different, and it's not as if anyone can see me. They'd have to be on a line with me." And there isn't anyone on a line with me. I've checked.

He looks out the window. "I'll bet there are people with telescopes out there, and I'll even bet that they've seen you in that towel." He turns. "You may already be on the Internet."

Despite my anger, I am strangely intrigued by this. I'm already beginning to sweat. Why do I feel so alive with this man? "You'll, um, you'll have to, um, give me some directions." He gives very good directions.

He walks over and turns my chair to face the window. He rubs my shoulders before sliding his hands down my sides to my pants. I watch him pull my shirttail from my pants. He kisses my neck. Oh man. He unbuttons the bottom button, pressing my shirt against my thigh. He kisses my ear while he unbuttons the next two. I wish this shirt had more buttons. He frees the last button between my breasts and pulls my shirt apart. I am so glad I'm wearing a nice white bra today.

He steps back and takes a picture from behind me. "Sexy," he says.

I giggle. Now where was I? Oh. Adjust contrast, bump up the color—

He returns to the back of my chair. I watch his hands travel down my sides again. He pulls my shirt apart wider and slides the shirt off my shoulders. He takes several more pictures, and I'm beginning to get hot and bothered.

I can't possibly finish the web banners now.

"Throw your head back and close your eyes, Shari."

I close my eyes. It's like I'm his puppet or something. I hear the clicks, see the flashes, and hear him humming.

"I'm going to move you closer to the window now," he says.

I feel the chair sliding effortlessly, I feel his hands on my ankles, I feel him placing my feet on the window ledge. More pictures. Sweat beads. I don't dare open my eyes. I am so glad I'm wearing my jeans.

I feel his breath in my ear. "Think nice thoughts," he says.

I am.

He rolls up my pants legs. Flash. He unbuttons but doesn't unzip my jeans. Flash. He repositions my arms across my chest. Flash. He closes my shirt, buttoning one button in the middle. Flash. He crosses my legs. Flash.

"You should be a jeans model," he says.

"Right," I say.

He gently puts my feet on the floor. Flash. "Should I use the telephoto lens to see if anyone is looking at you?"

I open my eyes. "There's no one out there, Tom."

He shows me my last picture. Hey, that's nice. The lighting is perfect, and I do look sexy.

"You'll never know that for sure, Shari," he says. "I was out there, and you didn't see me."

"I wasn't looking for you." Then. I jump off my chair and approach him. "Give me the camera, man."

He does.

"Sit."

He sits.

"Close your eyes."

He does, but he won't stop smiling.

"No smiles."

He tightens his lips, but I can still see a smile.

I size him up in the viewfinder. There's so much here to work with. "Take off your sweatshirt."

He does.

I will need a wide-angle lens for his chest. I get a chair from the kitchen, stand on it, and begin snapping away.

"Am I allowed to talk?" he asks.

"No."

I wish he had some buttons on his shirt to play with. What could I do with that T-shirt? I don't want to tear it up. Yet. "Take off your T-shirt."

He does.

I take lots of pics of his pecs. "Put your hands in your pockets."

Man, he can barely get them into his pockets. And that is so sexy. I take more pictures. "You could model jeans, too."

He smiles.

"No smiling."

He frowns.

I focus and take pictures of his shoulders, his neck, his hairline, his ears, and his face. If I print these out right, I can make a Tom puzzle.

"You can open your eyes and talk now," I say. I hand him the camera. "Take a look."

He makes no sounds at all as he scrolls through the pictures until he gets to his body parts. "Man, I need to shave," he says. "That is a very big ear." He widens his eyes.

Oh yeah. I took a picture of his package. Bad Shari, bad, bad Shari.

I hand him his T-shirt, but he doesn't put it on. He sets the camera on my computer table and holds out his arms.

That's my cue.

I straddle him, unbuttoning the only button holding my shirt together. "I want to, um, get some skin-to-skin contact."

He sighs. "And I want to hold you. Funny how we both want the same things at the same time."

I take off my glasses and put them on the computer table. "Then let's kill two birds with one stone." I remember we're in front of the window. "Um, someone could see us."

"I want them to," he says. "And I hope they have a very good telescope."

And then we, well, try to rub the skin off each other. Kisses, sighs, nibbles, my front wearing out his front, his hands wearing out my booty.

He takes a breath. "I'm beginning to like your apartment very much, Shari. There are so many possibilities here. We will live here five days a week, weekends if you want. We don't even have to travel. We can stay here twenty-four hours a day." He pulls me close and rubs my back.

"Are you as excited as I am?" I ask.

"Yes." He buttons up my shirt in a flash. "I don't want you to catch cold."

That will never happen as long as he's around, but my skin was just getting its happy on. "Why'd you do that?"

"I just got an idea, and if I keep feeling your skin, I'll forget my idea."

Okay. My skin scrambles his brain. That's good. "What's your idea?"

"While I was taking pictures of you and while I was, um, putting my hands all over you, I got an idea. I looked at your skin, and I looked at my skin while I was touching your skin, and well . . ." He locks my eyes with his baby browns. "Why don't we do everything in black and white?"

I blink. I practically do a lap dance on the man, and this is the idea he comes up with?

"We can do the entire campaign in black and white," he says. "Old school all the way. Nostalgia. I'll show you what I mean." He scoots the chair closer to my computer and loads up the picture of Carl. He tinkers with the shading until . . . "What do you think?"

Fantastic. Oh. Look at all those shadows! "Do another one."

The next picture looks just as crisp, just as sharp. The Internet hardly has any black-and-white banners, so they're sure to stand out.

I can't stop smiling. "If during the Q&A Mr. Peterson asks me why we went with black-and-white, what will I tell him?"

"The truth?" Tom says.

That I was massaging my man with my front in plain view in a window overlooking downtown Brooklyn? "Mr. Peterson will have a heart attack. All those rib eyes."

"We can just say we were inspired by the night sky of downtown Brooklyn."

Better. "But you know I'll be thinking of what we just did

when you say it." I put my hand in his. Those are some sweet contrasts, too. I turn into him, grinding my booty on his package. "I'll repeat the question. Are we going to pull an all-nighter?"

"Shari Nance?"

Is this . . . no. This is just horny talk. "Yes?"

"Shari Nance, would you care to watch the sunrise with me?"

That was sweet and sexy. "I'd love to watch the sunrise with you." I focus on his eyes, so soft, so open, so uncluttered. "I love you, Tom. I really, really love you."

"Thank you, Shari." He holds me close. "I love you, too."

He carries me to the bedroom and lays me on my side of the bed. "I think we're going to need the 'wall' back up tonight," he says.

I shake my head. "No." My heart is about to escape my body and go bouncing through the window into downtown Brooklyn. "I don't want a wall to come between me and my best friend."

He blinks. "Are you sure, Shari?"

I sit up and remove my shirt and bra. "I've never been more sure of anything in my life." I slide out of my pants, my underwear going along for the ride.

He wriggles out of his jeans and boxers. "You're so beautiful," he whispers.

I start to tear up. "I've never felt so beautiful, man. Come here."

And then we . . . make . . . love. It's quiet, slow, controlled, and even peaceful. Our lovemaking has a rhythm, slow, steady, and passionate. And when he hums in my ear, I whisper in his. When he nibbles on my ears, I chew on his shoulders. When he sighs, I giggle and groan. But when he drives deeply into me, I have to hold his hips from going too far. But eventually, I can't stop him anymore, and I don't want to stop him. I have to possess his entire body.

That's when we stop making love and commence to knocking some serious boots, we start some furious banging, and we rattle the headboard. Trixie and Bubbles have nothing on us. This man, this beautiful, muscular, intense man drives me home again, and again, and again till I dig my heels into his booty and let him completely become one with me as I shout so loud I swear the windowpane wobbles.

"Best friends for life," he whispers as I curl up on his chest afterward.

"For life," I whisper, watching my hand disappear into his.

And we're still one when the sun rises.

This, too, *all* of this, will be part of my morning routine until the day I die.

Chapter 28

Although it's only twenty-one miles to Great Neck, we are not in a place to get there quickly if we want to use public transit. I go online and find that it would take two *hours* to get to Great Neck if we used the subway, buses, and the Long Island Railroad.

Tom shrugs it off. "Carl will be here in a few minutes."

"How does Carl know to be here this morning?" I ask.

"I told him yesterday to be here this morning."

I tug on his belt loops. "So I was going to Great Neck no matter what today."

He nods. "Yep."

When Carl arrives, we exchange pleasantries, though Carl still doesn't smile at me. We load the bike into the backseat and take off.

And I fall completely asleep on Tom's shoulder until we get to Shorecliff Place and Tom's little bungalow that isn't a bungalow at all. It's a two-story white *house* with black shutters and a nice view of Little Neck Bay. Old, tall oak trees, colorful leaves everywhere, lots of privacy, a somewhat flat yard.

A house.

Carl offers his cheek to me this time, and he half-smiles. "See you soon," he says.

I stand with Tom looking up the sidewalk to the front porch. "You said it was a bungalow."

"It's a pretty small house for around here," he says. "Only four bedrooms and two baths."

Only. I'll bet the kitchen is as big as my entire apartment.

He opens the two-car garage first, and I see a golden '65 Mustang without a speck of rust on it.

"And you have a sixty-five Mustang coupe," I say. "What color is that?"

"Prairie bronze," he says. "How'd you know it was a sixty-five?"

Bryan kept me well-informed about cars. "I know cars, all right?" I run my hand over the roof, nodding and smiling. A muscle car for a muscular man. "A classic."

"And a gas guzzler," he adds.

I look inside. "All original?"

He nods. "And it's how we'll travel from now on."

Except for two Peterson bikes up on racks and various yard equipment including a weed eater and a lawn mower, the garage is spotless. Tom's no gear head.

He pauses at a door. "Don't, um, go crazy about what I've done with the place, and remember that I'm rarely here."

"So it's a work in progress," I say.

"Something like that."

He opens the door to a kitchen bigger than my apartment, a circular oak table surrounded by six matching oak chairs, tile flooring, all the appliances, at least fifty cabinets, and a refrigerator the size of a Volkswagen. Very nice.

We step into what should be a living room, but it's completely empty. "I won't ask," I say.

"Thanks," he says.

We enter another huge room—I'm guessing it's the family room—and find more empty space. Except for one chocolate sectional sofa in front of the fireplace, there's nothing but carpet, and I have yet to see anything on the walls except paint.

I can't resist. "Um, don't you live here?"

"Not much," he says.

"It's so unfinished," I say.

"Basement, too. Nothing but boxes down there."

Hmm. This place is a blank canvas. It just needs an artist like me to fill it in. I sit on the couch, and it's nice and comfy—and wide. Yeah, this is a Tom-size couch. But there isn't a speck of dust or ash in the fireplace. "Don't you ever have a fire?"

"I think we will have a fire soon."

I like the sound of that.

He takes my hand and leads me up some shiny wooden stairs to the second floor. He opens the first door we come to—a serviceable bathroom. Blue and white tile. Nothing fancy. It, too, doesn't look used. No towels on the racks, no toiletries, no goo or hair in the sink.

"I never use this one," he says. "There's another bathroom connected to the master bedroom."

I nod.

He opens the next door, and I see his studio. *This* is where he spends his money. The average Radio Shack has less stuff. Some people buy furniture. Tom buys electronics.

I recognize four large flat-screen monitors and four computers and a server, but there are other machines I cannot identify. In one section, he has an entire recording studio complete with hanging, shielded microphones and a soundboard. I sit in one of the two circular rolling chairs and slide across the hardwood floor.

"Welcome to Methuselah's Breezy Hiccup," he says.

I spin in a circle. "I won't touch anything."

He sits in the other chair. "I expect you to touch everything." He looks at his setup. "We have just about everything we need to produce just about anything."

What could be missing? It looks like the cockpit of a really wide airplane.

And I'm going to be his copilot.

We leave the studio, and he opens another door. Ah, the workout room, a single Bowflex machine in the middle of the floor, a fancy treadmill facing the only window, which looks out at Little Neck Bay. That's how he maintains his abs, shoulders, biceps, legs, and booty. If I spend any time in here, I will weigh ninety-five pounds in no time. I may have to work out just to keep up with him.

He skips another door—"Empty room," he says—and we enter the master bedroom. I only see a king-sized bed without a headboard, a nightstand without a lamp, and a dresser without a mirror.

This is a bachelor house.

He shows me the view from the huge bedroom window. "You can sometimes see Queens on a clear day."

"Why would I want to see Queens?" I ask.

He stares at me. "Why, indeed?" He squeezes my booty. "Unless someone out there has a telescope, and we're getting, um, involved."

He thinks he can out-nasty me. "We'll need a mirror somewhere." I look up at the ceiling over the bed.

"I'll get us one."

He earns a kiss for that.

"And when will all this be paid for?" I ask.

He squints at the ceiling. "In about fifteen, sixteen years."

That's not too bad. "You mind my asking how much you paid?"

He flops onto the bed. I like how this man thinks. "When the housing market tanked, I got it for a little over eight hundred thousand."

I crawl onto the bed and hold on to one of his legs. "You have that kind of money?"

"Hairy Ads pays well when you win. They give out ridiculous bonuses for 'winners.' I haven't always gotten them. But thanks to you and 'just . . . go,' my bonus this year should cover the yearly taxes on this place."

"Where's my half of the bonus?" I ask.

He shakes his head. "Haven't gotten it yet, but when I do, I'll have to deduct your half of the camera costs."

I push his leg away. "Uh-uh. I get it. In cash. I need new clothes." I crawl onto him. I would make a seriously bad blanket for this man. I prop my chin up on my hands and stare into his eyes. "Tom, why haven't you done more with this place?"

"I'm never here."

"No, really."

He smiles. "I was afraid that I would put the wrong furniture in it."

Huh? Furniture is furniture. "You better explain that one."

He rubs my back. "Well, up until two years ago, this place was even emptier. I only had the furniture in this room, the kitchen set, the Bowflex, and some of the studio equipment."

I shake my head. "So why'd you buy a four-bedroom house?"

"An investment for the future mainly." He frowns. "I was also trying to impress, um, Corrine."

"You poor, deluded man," I say. "Don't you know that is impossible?" Wait. He said up until two years ago. Hmm. "Corrine didn't like it, huh?"

"No. I can even safely say she hated it. She said, 'This is not what I expected of a man who works at Harrison Hersey and Boulder.'"

It's not what I expected either, but an almost half paid-for, secluded house with so much space? "I love it, especially the couch."

He kisses me. "Thank you."

"For loving the house or liking the couch?"

"Both." He plays with my hair. "I bought the couch for you last year."

He is continually losing me. "What?"

"I bought it for you."

I'm still lost. "How could you buy a couch for me last year?"

"Well, I, um . . . Hmm. Remember when I told you I was sort of following you?"

I nod. "You weren't sort of doing anything."

"Yeah, well, I, um, I memorized your skin color, and, well, that couch is your color."

He bought a couch based on the color of my skin? That is a *dark* couch. "It was summer, wasn't it?"

He nods. "And now that I know that you're really made up of a million shades of brown, I was afraid you wouldn't like it."

I smile. "We'll break it in soon in front of the fire."

He hugs me. "You were the first person ever to sit on it."

"Just now?"

He nods. "What else does this house need?"

Me! "Some new carpet." I feel a draft. "And some new windows. It's drafty in here."

He holds me. "I'll keep you warm."

I look at the bare walls. "And something on the walls. You need some art. You're an artist, aren't you? And more furniture, lots of that."

He smiles broadly.

"What?"

"Are you saying that this place needs a woman's touch?" he asks.

"No, I'm saying it needs *my* touch." I stare at the wall. "It needs major touch-ups, too. Look at the paint! I'll bet it's full of lead. And everything is so bland. What is that, off-off-off-white?"

He smiles. "So you like it."

"I just said I love it." I jump up and bounce on the bed, trying to touch the ceiling and missing by at least six inches. "I mean, I can jump up and down on a bed and not bother the people downstairs." I leap off the bed, take off my boots, and run down the hallway, sliding all the way to the top of the stairs. "I can also go skating."

Tom catches up to me, but I slip away and fly down the stairs to the kitchen.

"Where's the basement door?" I ask.

He points at a door in the kitchen, I open the door, and I go down to . . . wow. He wasn't kidding. There has to be a thousand square feet of nothing down here, boxes stacked neatly in a far corner. We could have a bowling alley down here. We could ride bikes in the winter down here. Our *kids* could ride bikes and go skating and play down here. This place is so uncluttered. There's that word again.

I go back upstairs to open spaces, light, room, and warmth. I drag Tom back to the bedroom and throw myself onto the bed. "I'll get lost in all this bed."

"I'll find you."

I lie on my back, imagining what I'll see when Tom puts up that mirror, deciding that I'd have to be on top if I'm to be seen at all. "How come there's no TV in here?"

"There are several in the studio."

"I know that," I say. "We'll need to put one in here. I like to surf commercials."

He chuckles. "So do I. I thought I was the only person on earth who liked to do that."

"They should have an all-commercial channel," I say, "but not like those infomercial stations. Just twenty-four hours of commercials from around the world. Man, you'd never get me out of bed." And he wouldn't.

"I will have to put a TV in this room immediately."

I kiss him. "This place has possibilities." We are so not living at the apartment, not with all this space to play with. "You know what else it needs?"

"What?"

"Children." I turn my head to look out the window. "You have such a nice yard. You'll have to move that Bowflex to the basement, though. We'll need two bedrooms, right?" I roll off him and pull him on top of me, looking up at the ceiling. If I keep my head to the side of his head and peek over his shoulder, I'll be able to see everything. "I could move my entire apartment into this room alone."

"So you're rethinking your apartment and whether we should keep it."

I roll my eyes. "I'm rethinking it, yes." I don't think I ever want to go there again. Hmm. Maybe we'll keep it till my lease runs out for some more fun in the window. "It does have its uses, doesn't it? We may even get a telescope."

"Indeed."

"Yes!" I shout, and Tom snaps his eyes shut.

"What was that for?" he asks, carefully opening his eyes.

I smile. "I just wanted to hear the echo. Can the neighbors hear us?"

"I doubt it," he says.

"Yes!" I shout again.

He rolls off me and the bed in a flash. "You know I like it when you shout, but we have some work to do."

Oh yeah. Work. "Go on. I'll be there in a minute."

This place is amazing. Oh, it's not quite ready for me to live in it yet. There's so much to do. It isn't easy turning a house into a home, darling. I'll have to paint everything first. Vivid colors. Nothing drab. Tia can help me choosing all the right colors. I'll really enjoy tearing up all the carpet and replacing it with something from this century. The floors are okay, but I'm sure they could use some refinishing. The windows have to be replaced. Aluminum frames? Please.

I go into the master bathroom expecting a garden tub, separate shower, and a double sink. All I see is puke green tile, a puke green toilet, and a puke green bathtub. Who decided puke green would be a good color for a bathroom? This bathroom has to be destroyed and rebuilt with . . . mirrors. Yes. Lots of mirrors.

I leave the bathroom and open the sliding closet door. Whoa. There must be fifty suits, all of them blue, gray, or black. Expensive but hideous. Tom will have to donate these to charity. Five pairs of very nice black dress shoes, though, and a few more pairs of boots, all Chippewa boots. Oh, look at the jeans! There must be twenty pairs. Ha! Flannel shirts, too!

My best friend is me, and I am my best friend.

Um, thank You, God.

I wince. Yeah, about last night, God. I sigh. Sorry, but we had to, okay? Don't be mad. We'll make it right, I promise. We're meant to be, right? We just, um, jumped the gun a little. Um, amen.

I fling myself onto the bed again. It's so quiet here. I won't be able to sleep. Where are the airplanes? Maybe they pay extra to live in Great Neck so the planes don't roar overhead. Where are the sirens? Where are the horns, the bus brakes screeching, the people screaming at each other? I listen for a minute.

I may go crazy here. It's too quiet. I'll just have to scream a lot.

I slide off the bed and root around in his dresser drawers. Lots of silky black dress socks. They could make nice blindfolds. Hmm. Him or me? Or both of us? Later maybe. I pull out an XXL Cal sweatshirt and hold it up to my body. It hits me at the thighs. Might be sexy. I strip off my shirt and bra and put it on. I'm wearing a sweatshirt dress. It's all the rage. I drop my jeans, feel the cold hit my thighs, and slide my jeans back on. I'd rather be warm and sexy than freezing and sexy any day.

When I return to the studio, I look up at two of the flat screens. I see frozen, black-and-white, antique-y views of lower Manhattan.

"Good timing," Tom says, his hand on a mouse. "The one on the left is number four. The one on the right is number eight." He turns and looks at me. "Nice dress."

I model it for him. "It's what every future ad executive is wearing these days." And if you would turn up the freaking heat, you'd see a lot more of me sprouting from this dress.

"We could wear it together," he says.

I like Tom. He has so many interesting ideas.

I rest in his lap as he runs both commercials simultaneously, rewinds, runs again, rewinds . . . It makes me dizzy.

"They're both great," I say.

"I like eight better," he says. "I get to see your sexy hands more."

I put my sexy hands on his face and kiss him. "You are a genius."

"I know what I like." He kisses my nose. "You're so easy to work with. Now for Yankee Stadium." He double-clicks on an icon. "This is number twenty-four."

At first Tom is just a speck, and then he's a full-grown man racing toward me, hitting the brakes, and skidding, dust flying in the air.

"That dust is fabulous, darling," I say. "Can you have the graphics appear out of the dust?"

"Good idea."

"And airbrush out the signs on the left field wall," I say. "I

don't think Canon and MasterCard would like us too much because we used a Panasonic camera and your Visa card."

"Kid stuff. I'll do it later. Now we need the voices." He tickles my stomach. "You ready to do some yelling?"

"I thought you were the one yelling 'safe,' and I was the one
saying 'drive one home.'"

He rolls us to a microphone and shouts "safe" twenty times
with pauses in between.

And despite the noise, it's how I feel. I feel so safe that I'm
weightless.

When it's my turn, I say "drive one home" twenty times. At
first, I whisper it, showing Tom a little stomach. Then I say it as
sexily as I can, showing Tom my bare sexy back. Eventually,
though, I get silly and sound more like a cartoon character than
a grown woman.

He cues each up, and we choose a manly "Safe!" and a sexy
"Drive one home."

I start chewing on his ear.

"Not yet."

I pout.

He offers me his other ear.

I chew on it a while, and he gives my neck several trillion
goose bumps with his tongue.

"Okay," I say. "Quit wasting time, Tom. Let's get to work."

We listen to thirty seconds of sound with all the speakers in
the room cranked up. I hear birds, leaves, my giggle, and wheels
flying in the wind.

"I like the giggle the best," he says.

"It's incredible," I say. "You have to do the voice-over. You
have more of a radio voice than I do."

"Okay." We slide back to the microphone, and he starts
recording, saying, "No matter where you ride, you're home. Peterson Bicycles. Made in America since 1969."

"You added the date."

He nods. "Hits up the nostalgia angle. 'Made in America for
over forty years' doesn't have the right punch."

"What's next?" I ask. I am so eager today.

"Let's see, we need to fine-tune the spots to the millisecond, lay down the voice-over tracks, tinker with and add the graphics . . . make copies. We will always have backups."

"Always." I love it when he's serious.

He rolls his neck in circles. "It might take a few hours." He kisses my cheeks just under my eyes. "You need a nap."

I could use one. "Because you kept me up all night, man. Aren't you tired?"

"Some. I'll manage."

The man never sleeps. "I could be working on the actual presentation."

"Or you could be working on a nap," he says. "I think these sell themselves. Just cue 'em up and let 'em go. If Mr. Peterson has any questions for why we did it this way, I'm sure you'll nail it."

So am I. "I'll write one up just in case. Always have a backup."

He rolls his eyes. "You could also be creating the false information for Corrine."

"I could, but . . ." I look at all the cool machines. "I want you to teach me everything you're about to do. I'll have to learn eventually, right?"

He smiles. "I like you."

"I'm likable."

Because I am a slow learner, for the next *four* hours we make those spots sing, shout, and do lap dances while I do a sultry lap dance on Tom. The final products are everything as professional and slick as what you'd see on TV. Tom is so patient with me, especially when I keep asking the same stupid question: "What's that button for again?"

I rub his shoulders, he rubs mine, and we drink tea. I have to brew a family-sized tea bag in a saucepan because the man doesn't even have a teakettle. We eat a few stale barbecue potato chips, a few bites of some frozen turkey dinners that taste like fish and freezer burn, and a pint of slightly crystallized mint chocolate-chip ice cream.

After taking a long walk outside to wake up, we use his empty living room floor to lay out the sixteen billboards, re-arranging them until we like the order. We organize the fifty landmark photos in the same way. And then I use the computer images of the photographs to make two PowerPoint presenta-tions—one for our friends on the bike, the other for the land-marks.

"You're good at this," he says.

"Corrine never complained," I say. "And we'll use the land-mark PowerPoint as a backup."

Tom grudgingly agrees. He's just mad he had to pay Carl a mint for something we might never use.

Then Tom suggests we add some country instrumentals while our friends ride the bike. "A little 'Dueling Banjos.'"

Um, no. "Isn't that the song from *Deliverance?*"

"Yeah. So?"

"Not the message we want to send." He's so slow sometimes. "Tom, these are all shots of New York! Sinatra, baby. 'New York, New York.' We were just singing it with Carl." Duh.

"But what if Mr. Peterson doesn't like Sinatra?"

Tom is tripping. "Who doesn't like Sinatra?"

"Mr. Peterson is from Georgia. He's not a New York boy."

True. Hmm. "Well, Ray Charles and 'Georgia' wouldn't match the pictures. Why not something from Broadway?"

He nods. "A little Gershwin. 'Summertime.'"

I think the song will work until I run the lyrics in my head. "No fish jumping. Cotton? Also not the right message. And we took all the pictures in the fall, not the summertime."

He stares at the ceiling. "'Rhapsody in Blue,'" he says.

I stare at the ceiling. So that's where he gets some of his ideas. I look him in the eye. "Woody Allen used that song already for *Manhattan.*"

"It's a signature New York song, Shari."

"I don't want to bite off anyone, especially Woody Allen. Why not something by the Allman Brothers?" And I don't know any of their songs.

He looks at the floor this time. "'Ramblin' Man' might work. You ever hear it before?"

I shake my head. I was never into music made by guys who borrowed food from soul food restaurants in Macon, Georgia.

Tom goes to another computer, finds the song after scrolling through his iTunes list, and cues it up.

I won't ask him why he has that particular song in his library.

As we listen, I wince. It's a bit too rowdy, though the instrumentals are excellent. "Tom, I don't think the being born in the backseat of a bus part is going to help us here. It also references several other *southern* states. Can you see Carl's picture while that song is playing?"

"No." He scrolls to another song, and we listen to Otis Redding's "(Sittin' on) The Dock of the Bay." We decide that, while the song is an all-time classic, it's too moody and mentions San Francisco, not New York.

"This is so silly," I say, wishing I had left on my bra. Is there no insulation in this house? "I mean, we're stressing over music that won't be part of the campaign."

"Details, my dear, are very important," Tom says too seriously. "How food is presented often makes it taste better."

I want to mock him so badly, but he's right. The presentation is the key.

"How about . . . I don't know." He sighs and scratches his head. "We need something that lasts about three minutes and twelve seconds, roughly twelve seconds per slide."

I won't ask him how he arrived at twelve seconds. It's probably a Harrison Hersey and Boulder thing I wouldn't understand.

"Let's just run the show silently until something pops in our heads," I suggest.

He agrees. And it's not just because he likes me. I saw the suggestion on the ceiling. He must have seen it, too.

I watch our sixteen new friends, and I see them as survivors, every last one of them. Some of them survived World War II as children, and all of them lived through Vietnam, disco, bell-bottoms, hippies, the Reagan years, and 9-11. They deserve the greatest respect. And despite their struggles, they can smile while riding a bike on a fall day in Brooklyn. I always get goose bumps when I see the last slide of Carl. And he just wanted to stand beside the bike. "No," he said. "I will just stand here, and you will take the picture."

Taking a stand.

" 'Stand Tall,' by Burton Cummings?" Tom says. "No. That song has something about falling."

Hush. I'm thinking. And stop thinking along the same lines as me!

" 'Can You Stand the Rain,' by Boyz II Men?" he says.

"It wasn't raining, Tom." Now, hush!

"I got it! 'I'm Still Standing' by Elton John."

He waits for my approval.

He doesn't get it.

And then it hits me. Night. Darkness. No fear. " 'Stand by Me' by Ben E. King," I say. "Please say you have that."

"That's it!" He hugs me. "And I do."

He finds the song and plays it "live" while the PowerPoint runs. I sing along, Tom joins in, and when the last slide of Carl fades, the song fades out.

I swallow. "That's perfect." That nice slow, uplifting song, those happy old people on bikes, every one of them someone's "darlin'," the black-and-white pictures—it's freaking perfect.

Tom looks at me, and I look at him.

"Wow," he says. "If that isn't sonic branding, I don't know what is. Mr. Peterson needs to get exclusive rights to that song."

And that would cost a mint! "We do good work here at Methuselah's Breezy Hiccup." I stretch, yearning for a pillow. "We're the junk."

"And that can be our slogan. Methuselah's Breezy Hiccup— We're the junk."

I laugh, resting my head on Tom's shoulder. "Man, it's getting dark out." We've been working for nearly eight hours, and I never even considered it to be work at all. Mrs. Collier was right. Working with the one you love is the absolute best. "What time is it?"

He looks at his watch. "A little after six." He sighs. "I'll bet Bryan's standing outside your door by now."

Not this again. "No, he isn't."

"You don't sound too sure."

And I don't. "He isn't coming."

"Why don't you call him and find out for sure?" He picks me up, stands, turns, and sets me gently into the chair. "I'll want your undivided attention later." He kisses me. "I'll give you your privacy."

And then he leaves the room! The nerve!

"I don't want to call him, Tom!" I call out.

Tom comes into the room with my cell phone, turns it on, hands it to me, and leaves again, shutting the door behind him.

"I'm not calling him," I whisper.

But he could be out there right now looking for you, Shari.

All right, all right.

I dial Bryan's cell.

Chapter 29

"Hello?"

Now I'm nervous. He answered on the first ring. "Hi, Bryan. How are you?"

"How do you think I am?"

I don't want to ask the next question. "Where are you?"

Silence.

Oh no. "You didn't come up to Brooklyn, did you?"

More silence.

"Bryan, are you in New York? Are you at the airport?"

Silence.

"Bryan, answer me. Are you at my apartment?"

Even more silence.

"Bryan, I'm . . . I'm at his place right now, and it's twenty miles from my apartment. Where exactly are you?"

"Where I'm supposed to be, Share. Back home in Virginia, where we drink lots of beer before going to high school football games and, how'd you say it? Oh yeah. Reliving our glory days."

"Oh." Where's the relief I should be feeling? "Why didn't you answer me?"

"I was finishing my beer. State semifinals tonight. We're gonna win state again."

At least he's going on with his normal routine. "What did you do with the plane ticket?"

"I gave it to my sister. She'll be shopping tomorrow up there or something. Maybe you'll see her."

Not a chance.

"So you're at his place," he says.

I just want this phone call to end. "Yes."

"What's it like?"

"Um, Bryan, I'm sure you have to be getting ready to go to the game, so I won't keep you any longer." And I don't want to torture him anymore.

"What's it like? I'm your friend. You're supposed to tell friends stuff."

He's pretty drunk already. Geez. "How drunk are you, Bryan?"

"Pretty stinking drunk. So what, does he live in a mansion?"

Not drunk enough to forget his question. "No. It's a house."

"Big?"

The man, his package, his potential, or his house? "Not particularly." For Great Neck.

"What's he drive?"

Bryan is a car jock's jock. He fixed my car for free so many times. "A Mustang. A sixty-five. A classic."

"Good car, great car."

I have to steer him back to something safe. "Are you at home?"

"Yeah."

"Who's driving you to the game?" This is crucial. Salem cops don't play.

"Nobody."

Oh man. "Bryan, please don't drive. Call Tony or Rich to come get you."

"Who said I was driving? Might not even make it out the door. Think it's in that direction."

He always was a funny drunk. "Just promise me you won't drive."

"All right, I promise."

Silence.

"Bryan?"

Silence.

"Bryan?"

"Yep. Just killed another one."

He was always a thirsty drunk, too. "Please go on with your life."

"I plan to. Gonna find me a honey tonight."

I blame rap music for his transformation from a quiet, ordinary white kid to a tattooed homeboy with an earring. "I hope you do. I know you will. You . . . you deserve someone special."

"Thought I had someone special."

Here we go again. "I'm not that special, Bryan. You deserve someone better than me."

"What's he got that I don't got, Share? Huh?"

A future . . . and I'm an integral part of that future.

"Money? He got money?"

When drunk Bryan gets going, there's no stopping him. I've learned it's best just to let him rant.

"House, great ass car, money. He as good-looking as me?"

I have to step in here. "No one is as good-looking as you are, Bryan." And he was pretty cute, especially when he grew his moustache.

"That's right. I'm a certified honey heartbreaker. You said so yourself."

Once. "You're right. I bet you find a hot, horny honey tonight." I'm hoping he'll laugh.

He doesn't laugh. "Won't be you."

Ouch. "I know."

"Won't be the same."

More ouch. "I know that, too."

"Well, I gotta go." He sighs heavily. "Sorry, Share."

Most ouch. "You have nothing to be sorry about, Bryan."

"Yeah, I do. I'm just . . . sorry. I should have followed your dreams."

Click.

I turn off my phone.

I feel like crap.

But what if Bryan had followed me up here five years ago? Would I be as happy as I am now? Would I even be trying to do what I'm trying to do? I guess I'll never know.

And that's kind of what hurts.

I wander to the bedroom. No Tom. I check the workout room. I go downstairs and don't find him anywhere. I hear a car start up. He's leaving?

I run into the garage and see him revving the engine with the hood up, and for an instant, I see Bryan doing the same thing with my car. I was just a passenger in Bryan's car.

I know I will be driving this car.

Tom drops the hood and turns off the car. "Still works," he says. "Everything okay?"

I nod. "He's not in New York. He gave the plane ticket to his sister."

He wipes his hands on a paper towel. "You okay?"

"Yeah. A little . . . sad."

"Want to talk about it?"

I take his hand. "No."

"Well," he says, "we have a few more things to do upstairs."

He says the right thing every time.

But when we get upstairs, he leads me into the studio.

"I thought we were done," I say.

"We need to make backups of everything," he says.

I slump into a chair. "You're so thorough."

He kneels in front of me. "I can do it some other time."

Yes. Some other time. "Tom, I'm cold."

"Then I'll just have to warm you up."

I look at my hands in his. "I . . . I just need to be held."

"I can do that."

He carries me to the bed, pulls back the covers, and sets me down. He slides in next to me and begins rubbing my back and massaging my neck and shoulders. I pull his arm around me, and we just snuggle for a while.

"We both still have our clothes on," I say.

"I know."

"Seems like old times," I say.

"It's nice."

"But it's not a first anymore. Like our little photography session yesterday. That was a first. We need to make a list of things neither of us has ever done. A list of firsts. I want to share a lot of firsts with you." I put his hand over my heart. "I want to share the *rest* of my firsts with you."

"Me, too, but it's going to be a long list. We're both small-town kids."

"But you've gotten to travel all over the world. You've been places that are only names on a map to me."

He hugs me tight. "There are still plenty of places I'd like to go. Like Alaska."

I shiver.

"Wild, untamed, rugged. I want to give my boots a real workout. And keeping you warm will be my biggest priority."

That might be fun. "I guess I'd go, as long as keeping me *hot* would be your biggest priority. How about some place warm like . . . Tahiti. For after I freeze my booty off in Alaska."

"Agreed. I'd have to keep you cool there."

"I like to sweat." I turn to him and drink in his eyes. "I've never . . . been married."

"That will be at the top of our list." He kisses me.

This feels so right. Hear that, God? "And I've . . . I've never been . . . somebody's mama."

"Second on our list."

This *has* to be love. "In that order."

"Yes."

This *is* love. "And I've never . . ." There are so many things I've never done! "I've never gotten a tattoo." I know, from becoming a parent to getting a tattoo. I am wasted tired. "I've always wanted a tattoo. And maybe a piercing somewhere dangerous. I've just been too chicken."

"What and where?" he asks.

I feel his warmth envelope me. "Nothing crazy and no place too kinky. Just a . . . heart . . . somewhere." I am drifting off so smoothly, so peacefully.

"We'll do that tomorrow. Get some sleep, Shari."

"Good night, Tom."

And the last thing I remember is a single kiss on my lips.

Chapter 30

On Saturday, three days to go before the big meeting, Tom serves me breakfast in bed, a first for both of us.

We eat frosted brown sugar cinnamon Pop-Tarts and split an apple, and the two of us decide to stay in bed and work, mainly because this bed is the warmest place in the house. Tom brings in several legal pads, and we get hard to work on the false information we're going to feed to Corrine. We try not to make it too ridiculous, but it is so much fun! We list incorrect sales numbers and revenues. We rewrite Mr. Peterson's bio to include several marriages and make him sound like an aristocratic playboy who lives in a mansion. Tom creates a carefully constructed demographics analysis that focuses solely on single men between fifty and fifty-five. I throw in a few recalls. We suggest that Peterson leave the under-thirty crowd entirely and focus only on the wealthy 1 percent in this country. We even make a final suggestion, based allegedly on Mrs. Peterson's demands, that Peterson *raise* the price of their bicycles and take the company public.

After showering together in the puke green tub, we dress and take the Mustang—such power!—a few miles to Flushing and Murder Ink. While I get a simple, tiny red heart on my right shoulder, Tom hands the tattoo artist a picture of my face to put on his right arm!

"When did you draw that?" I ask, wincing a little as the heart takes shape. I am such a lightweight when it comes to pain.

"Last night," he says.

"But my eyes are closed," I say. Ouch . . . ouch.

"Because you're peacefully dreaming," he says.

And I don't remember my dream again. Oh. There he is. "But you won't be able to see me on your arm."

"I'll be able to see it in a mirror," he says. "But that's really not the point, is it?"

I smile—and wince. Yeah, other women will see me. Ow! That tattoo is more proof of permanence. Yeah. That's me on my man's arm. Back off, wenches! I will have to buy him some wife-beaters.

Even though I have a smallish face, his tattoo takes such a long time to do! Once I'm done, I am so bored. I look at some pictures of where other women have gotten tattoos. I'm pretty adventurous and I am actively looking for more firsts in my life, but I don't want tattoos down there.

Or do I?

I pull my tattoo artist back into action, and she and I create a road map of where I like to be kissed most. We go into a little booth to do them. She puts another tiny red heart on the back of my neck under my hair, another just above my left breast, and one just above my panty line in front. I turn over and she adds one just above my right hip. I turn over again so she can put one on the inside of my right thigh about three inches from my stuff. Including the one on my shoulder, that's six hearts for Tom to kiss.

And his tattoo still isn't done!

I go back to the booth. "One more makes seven."

My ankle? Not very erogenous. Below my belly button? Ouch. I shrug and drop my drawers, roll over, and point to my right cheek. My booty doesn't like me very much, but I'm hoping Tom will kiss it and make it better.

I take a look at Tom's tattoo before they cover it up, and I can't believe what I see! My eyes are open behind my sexy glasses. That has to be a first for Planet Earth. Who puts librarian glasses on the face of a hot female on a man's arm? That tattoo can only be me.

Only me. Yeah, this is permanent.

Walking afterward is a bit of a chore, but I manage, especially when Tom opens the door to Alicia's Jewelers.

At first I don't want to go in. "Tom?" I say in the tiniest voice.

"C'mon," he says.

He didn't have to twist my arm at all.

We browse the engagement rings and bridal sets. So many beautiful rings, and such ridiculously high prices!

"Do you believe in long engagements, Shari?" he whispers.

My legs become jelly. "No." Where is this small voice coming from? And why can't I stand still?

"So we can skip the engagement ring and go straight to the wedding band," he says.

If it weren't for the glass case I'm leaning on, I'd be on the ground. "Sounds . . . sounds like a plan," I whisper.

Tom walks past the gold wedding bands and looks down on the platinum rings. Platinum? Oh man. The only tag I can see says "$18,000"! Even with 50 percent off, that's still nine grand!

He points at a ring. "That's the one." He looks around the store. "I need some help here."

So do I. All Bryan and I ever did was *look*. I never even tried one on.

A sales associate takes the ring from the case and hands it to Tom.

Give it to me.

He analyzes it carefully.

My finger. *Now.*

He turns to me and slides it on my left ring finger, but he doesn't let go!

Let go. *Mine.*

He holds it there, squinting. "A little loose. Hmm."

Let go of the ring, Tom. It's not yours.

He slides it off my finger! "I like it," he says. Only then does he check the tag. "Reasonable."

What's reasonable about $13,000? At half off, that's still . . . four months' rent and the entire cost of what's in my closet!

He smiles at me. "Did you ever try on a wedding band before?"

I shake my head. "But technically, I didn't actually try it on. You didn't let go of it."

"I know." He nods to the associate. "We'll take this one." He hands her *my* ring, and she boxes it up.

I grab his right arm, and he winces a little. "Oh, sorry." I grab his other arm and whisper, "Um, Tom, you haven't even asked me to marry you yet."

He shrugs. "So you'll get the ring before the proposal. Another first. Not exactly the best spot to propose." He looks down. "Floor's clean, but . . ."

"But Tom," I whisper with more authority, because I *know* these things, "it is customary to ask *before* you buy, especially if it's a wedding band."

He starts to put his hands on my shoulders and ends up holding my hands instead. "This is no ordinary love, Shari. There is nothing customary about it at all. And when I do propose, aren't I supposed to have a ring to put on your finger?"

"Well, yes, but . . ."

"Isn't that the custom?"

"Sure, but . . ."

"You said we could skip the engagement ring. So this will have to suffice."

He hands the associate his debit card, they complete the transaction, and she hands him a little bag, a bag full of my dreams. He pulls the fuzzy box out of the bag and hands the bag to the associate. "I won't need this." He holds the box out to me, my eyes get as big as Jupiter, and then he tucks the box into his back pocket! "Come on," he says.

I don't move. "Where are we going now?" And it had better be a place where he can propose to me immediately!

He rubs his stomach. "I'm hungry. Pop-Tarts and half an apple aren't enough to satisfy a growing boy. Aren't you hungry?"

"Yes, but not for food, Tom."

He smiles. "You'll need your strength. Let's go eat."

We stop at the Terrace Diner a block away, and I decide this, too, is part of Tom's diabolical plan. He's going to squirrel the ring away in something I'm eating. Or maybe he'll drop it in my drink when I'm not looking.

"You ever have a buffalo burger?" he asks.

"No." But for him to do that, I have to be away from the table or totally oblivious. My ring is being crushed against his booty right now!

"Me neither," he says.

We order two buffalo burgers, and Tom makes a Dagwood Bumstead sandwich out of his, adding cheddar cheese, lettuce, tomato, sautéed onions, mushrooms, bacon, and even a fried egg. I just get cheddar cheese and bacon. After his first bite, he can't let go of his sandwich, and he goes through half a dozen napkins.

"How about here?" he asks.

"Huh?"

"No, no, you're right," he says. "Not while we're eating. That's been played out. I'm supposed to put the ring in something you're eating or drinking. So overdone. Besides, you never left the table for me to do that. Let's go."

"Where?"

"First we have to get the car."

We walk back to Murder Ink, get in the Mustang, and drive over to the Long Island City Marina. Okay. Water. A view. Few people. An isolated, sort of natural spot. We walk out onto the pier and look at boats in Little Neck Bay, most of the boats moored, some sailboats zipping by, lots of seagulls hovering and swooping.

He pulls me to him. "Look straight across . . . there." He points to a spot on the opposite shore.

I look and don't see anything worthy of my looking.

"You see it?" he asks.

I don't.

"Our house."

Oh. I'd need binoculars. I turn to him. I guess here is as good as anyplace else. I mean, except for the guy fishing over there, the rainbow of gas films around the pier, the seagull poo on the railing, it's, um, perfect.

"So . . . how about here?" he asks.

I cannot speak!

"You're right," he says, shaking his head. "A guy gives his girl a ring by the water. Something organic and universal about that. But it's too trendy in this environmental age. Let's go."

I take his left arm and squeeze it. "Tom, you're . . . you're going to entirely too much trouble here."

He smiles. "I know. I want it to be perfect."

"But I just want it," I whine.

"Hmm. That was a first."

"What was?"

"That little whine," he says. "Kinda sexy."

We go to the car again, and before he can pull out of the lot, I reach over and keep his hand from shifting into reverse.

"Tom, really. You could give it to me now." In a '65 Mustang? Well, it is a classic. "That's a first for both of us, right?"

"In a car?" he says. "I'm sure it's been done a million times. I want this to be so original that no one can top it ever. A *world* first."

I let go of his hand. "How can you be sure of that?"

He backs us out. "Let's go to . . . an arcade. No. How about . . . oh, I know."

We drive a while this time, and my feet can't stay still. Because the Mustang only has an AM radio, we listen to Caribbean music on WPAT, and my feet are practically running by the time we get to Bedford Avenue in Brooklyn.

"Where are we going?" I ask.

"You'll see," he says.

He parks near Spoonbill & Sugartown, Booksellers. "You know this place?"

Wow. I only told him *once* that this was my favorite bookstore. And I thought that *I* had a good memory. This man, this man. He's been hanging on my every word for five years! "This is my favorite bookstore."

"Yeah," he says. "You mentioned it a few years ago during one of our little meaningless chats."

Chats will never be meaningless for me again. "You're going to propose to me inside a bookstore? I'm sure it's been done." But right now, I don't care if a billion people have done it. I want that ring.

"Ah, but *where* in the bookstore?" he asks. "In what section? Mmm?"

Sometimes this man and his details drive me crazy!

We go in, my heart pounding like a *djembe* drum. He pauses in front of the new books on the tables. I hold my breath. New books for a new life. A new beginning. It makes sense. Gimme!

He moves on.

He pauses in front of the lighted glass cases containing rarer books. I hold my breath. Rare books for a rare relationship. We are so rare we're practically raw! Yes. I'll take that ring now.

He moves on.

He comes to a complete stop next to an old radiator beneath a stack of Asian art books. I hold my breath. Art books for our artistic future. I am the yin to his yang. I get it. Give me the ring.

He shakes his head . . . and then continues right on out the door! He stands in front of a table full of used paperbacks and smiles while browsing. Here? Okay, I mean, these are used books, heavily thumbed, ripped, worn out. We're not any of those things!

"Look at the title of this one," he says, pointing to a book with a black cover.

Will Happiness Find Me? Happiness is sure taking her freaking time!

"I might get this one," he says. "I want to know how it ends."

I see the bulge in his back pocket. That bulge belongs to me. While he's reaching for that book, I just snatch it up out of his pocket, open the box, and put the ring on. "There. I'm wearing it." I snap the box shut and hand it back to him.

He takes the box. "You ever going to take it off?"

"Never."

He pockets the box and looks to the sky. "Thank you!" He turns to me. "Finally." He drops to one knee.

Here? On a sidewalk on Bedford Avenue in Brooklyn? "What do you mean, finally?"

He holds my left hand. "A man giving an engagement ring is ordinary. A man giving a wedding ring is different, but it's still not too crazy."

A few people walking by slow down, and a few even smile and stop. Tom and I are definitely a show wherever we go. Oh, my heart!

"But a man *annoying* the woman he loves so much that she *steals* the ring from his back pocket *before* he can propose to her in front of her favorite bookstore on Bedford Avenue in Brooklyn—that's got to be a world first." He squeezes my hand. "So, Shari Nance, will you—"

"Yes."

He laughs. "You didn't let me finish the question."

Someone in the crowd says, "Yeah."

I pull him to his feet. "You don't have to." And then I lay the smooch of a lifetime on him while an even larger crowd gives us some applause. I'm still tongue-tied with him when the crowd fades away.

"What if I didn't take the ring?" I ask.

He pulls me to him. "You would have stolen my idea eventually."

"Hey man, it's the other way around, right?"

He kisses me again. "You get what you want, Shari Nance," he whispers. "You go for yours. You just . . . go." He laughs. "You are so predictable."

"I am not!"

He holds up my hand. "Ring looks nice."

Yeah, it does. "But hey, I'm not predictable."

"I can read you like a book." He picks up *Will Happiness Find Me?* and goes inside to pay for it. When he returns, he says, "We'll both read it."

"At the same time." Another first. "We'll be *sharing* a book for the first time. You hold it, and I'll turn the pages." While we get intimate. Yes. But where? I want a world first, too. "Um, take me to a park."

"A park?"

"Yes. A park, the more secluded the better."

"Why?" he asks.

"You'll see."

I have to prove to this man that I am as unpredictable as he is.

Chapter 31

He takes us to Great Neck Estates Park on the other side of Little Neck Bay and not too far from our, I mean, his house. I'm so acquisitive. The park has lots of red mulch, tall trees, and gentle wavy water. We walk on the beach to a rickety-looking pier. Yeah. This is the place. We go up some stairs, cross the pier, and go down some stairs to a floating dock.

"Sit," I say.

He sits. "Sittin' on the dock of the bay," he sings.

I look all around us. We're alone. I sit until my booty is all up on him. "I'm going to let the waves give you a lap dance while we read, you predictable man."

He takes off his jacket and puts it on me backward, the bottom of the jacket covering us up perfectly. "A nautical lap dance with a good book," he says, squeezing my thighs. "Definitely unpredictable."

I grind a little. "I should have worn a skirt."

"You wear those?"

"No," I say. "Let's read . . ." And do a little grinding.

When Will I Find Happiness? is the strangest book. It's full of random questions, two per page, written in white script on shiny black pages. Sometimes words and phrases are crossed out making two or more questions. So while the waves rock us and I try to rock his world, we answer the questions. We both agree that hunger is an emotion. I get right emotional when I'm hungry, while Tom says he only hungers for me. I hunger for him, too, but I have to have quesadillas at least once a week. We both agree that we can't leave reality in peace, though he says sometimes reality can be peaceful. Like now. I think something *can* be unbelievable, but Tom thinks there's really nothing left to be unbelievable. He's jaded. He is a little older than me. I'll have to fix that. When it comes to the freedom of birds, we both agree that birds have it made, especially if there's a McDonald's nearby. All those spilled fries. We both agree that life is made up of caves. We hibernate in some, hide in others, and sometimes get lost and need rescuing from others. I guess we're both coming out of hibernation now. Look out, world!

But there is one question that we answer simultaneously: No, there can *never* be too much of a good thing. Never. We prove it.

As soon as Tom turns the last page and closes the book, he says, "A day of firsts."

"Yes." I look at the ring. "Um, I don't mean to press you, but . . ."

He presses me down, wiggling my booty just right. "I like it when you press me."

I like it when he presses me, too. "When are we going to make us legal?"

He marches his fingers down my back. "Let's see . . . Monday morning is out."

Oh yeah. "But after I leave MultiCorp, we could go straight to the courthouse till Corrine begs me to come back. I plan to wear the ring no matter what. I want to wave it in front of her face."

"Of course."

And I can blind *her* for a change. "We could wait till after the meeting Tuesday. We might be cutting it close. I think we have to get there by five."

"You've researched this."

"It's what I do." And I'm a woman who should be married by now. Of course I know all the procedures. "I like this place."

"I do, too." He puts maybe two fingers into my back pockets. I have to get jeans with bigger pockets. "You know, we *could* wait for Wednesday, Shari."

I shake my head. "Not when we're unemployed."

"We won't be." He wraps me in his arms. "But we'll be hustling to get those spots and ads out to the world, so . . ."

I wish I could marry him right now! "Well, no matter when, I'd like Tia to be my maid of honor."

He kisses my cheek. "I could get Carl to be my best man."

We are so weird. "We could celebrate at Sylvia's . . ."

"Carl sure likes those chicken livers." He chews on my earlobe. "Honeymoon?"

I shiver. "Definitely Tahiti."

"It's a long plane ride," he whispers.

"They have blankets . . ." I will be worn out by the time we get there.

"And very small bathrooms . . ." He removes his fingers and pulls out his cell phone.

"Who are you calling?" And at a time like this!

"Cringe."

I grind into him. "That is so wrong on so many levels." And I like it very much. "Don't put her on speaker. I don't want her to hear me laughing."

"Corrine! How are you?"

Then there is an *extremely* long pause. What's the wench saying?

I turn and mouth, "Turn it on."

He hits the speaker button.

". . . and it was *so* horrible, Tom," Corrine moans, "and I'm scarred for life, and I needed you, and they poured vinegar all over me . . ."

"Corrine—" Tom says.

". . . and I've been calling and calling," Corrine interrupts. "Where have you *been?* Where are you *now?* Why aren't you here with *me?*"

Give the man a chance to answer!

"Where are *you* now?" Tom asks.

"I'm in Hawaii," Corrine whines. Ooh, I have not missed that sound.

"Oh, that's right," Tom says. "Shari told me a few days ago. It must have slipped my mind."

The devil.

"Shari told you?" Corrine says. "How could Shari tell you? Her phone isn't working."

"It's been working fine for the last few days," Tom says, "but she didn't call to tell me." He winks at me. "What are you doing in Hawaii anyway?"

"But she told me . . ." Corrine's voice trails off. "I'm in Hawaii waiting for you to come comfort me in my hour of need, Tom."

Tom squeezes my entire booty with his free hand. "I know you, Corrine. You're somewhere in the city working on the Peterson Bicycle account."

"The what?" Corrine yells.

Now we're cooking.

"The Peterson Bicycle account," Tom says. "You know, the competition between you and me. We're presenting finished campaigns to Mr. Peterson on Tuesday, but, of course, you already know this."

Oh, this is delicious!

"What competition?" Corrine whines.

"Quit kidding around, Corrine. It's MultiCorp versus Harrison Hersey and Boulder, a historic first. You're going up against me on Tuesday."

And I'm grinding hard on this man. Whoo. She's bound to hear me panting.

"I have *no* idea what you're talking about, Tom!" she screeches.

"You don't?" Tom asks.

"No," Corrine says. "Shari has told me *nothing* about this."

Tom tries to control his breathing, too, but he's doing a bad job of it. "That means I must be going up against Shari."

I do not ever want to leave this position. We may stay here all day.

"No wonder she was trying to *pump* me for information down in Georgia," Tom says. "She's quite an amazing woman."

Yeah, that's right. I'm an amazing pumper. Is that even a word?

"Quite an . . ." Corrine starts to say. "What was Shari doing in Georgia?"

Stealing your man.

"She was touring the bicycle plant with me, you know, gathering facts, seeing the product firsthand. I just assumed she was down there on your behalf."

"She was . . . This is . . ."

Corrine is officially flummoxed. Yes!

"What *exactly* was she doing down in Georgia, Tom?" Corrine asks.

"Your job, it sounds like," Tom says.

Hallelujah!

"I guess old man Dunn didn't think you were up to it after LA," Tom continues, "but don't sweat it. Shari has it all under control."

And I do, though if I keep rubbing my booty on him, I may lose control.

"She's doing . . ." Corrine says, her voice trailing off to a whisper. "No, she . . . Shari is just my stupid administrative assistant. She would never even think about doing something like this to me."

Wanna bet? And who's stupid, wench?

"And Mr. Dunn would not assign her to any account, I assure you, not even to work on an account we already manage," Corrine says. "She isn't qualified, Tom. She doesn't even have her MBA!"

"She sure seems qualified to me," Tom says. "She let me look over her ideas, and they are outstanding. Man, you've been lucky to have her for five years. I have my work cut out for me."

"She *let* you look at her ideas?" Corrine yells.

Well, actually, he kind of peeked on his own. He also peeked at my booty. He was worshiping it in silence.

Tom pulls me closer. "Well, um, Corrine, that's the . . . How do I break this to you gently?"

Tom should be an actor. He is so convincing!

"You're scaring me, Tom," Corrine cries. "Break what to me?"

He looks me in the eyes. "Well, she was trying to use all her feminine charms on me, and I wanted to see her stuff, so . . ."

I love what he does to my stuff.

"I, um, spent the night with her. I've, um, spent several nights with her as a matter of fact."

"Oh . . . You . . . This . . . Tom, why?"

I want to laugh so badly!

"Yeah, I feel kind of bad about it now," Tom says, shaking his head slowly, "but it gave me the opportunity to steal some of her other ideas while she was sleeping."

"Oh no, Tom!" Corrine cries. "Tell me you didn't sleep with my assistant!"

Tom sighs. "I did. I know. Bad form. But I only did what you've been doing to her for years, right?" He raises his eyebrows.

"She has so many ideas, Tom. She's a gold mine for me, Tom. She's the reason I'll make partner before I'm forty, Tom. And she's so stupid she doesn't even realize how badly I'm using her, Tom. That's what you've been telling me for the last five years."

The wench said all that? She better not wear an afghan or whatever that scarf-thing was on Monday, or I'll strangle her with it.

"I am . . ." Corrine doesn't speak for a long time. "I am completely at a loss right now. I just . . . I just can't . . . believe this is happening."

"Well," Tom says. "I gotta go, Corrine. I have some things to do."

"Don't hang up!" Corrine shouts.

He kisses my nose. "It's something pretty intense, Corrine."

Yes, this is intense. This is the reason I'm alive.

"What am I going to do, Tom?" Corrine asks.

"If I were you," Tom says, "I'd get back here as soon as I could. Gotta run. Bye." He snaps his phone shut and kisses me tenderly. "And *that* is how we get Corrine to come back."

Very slick. "She really said all that about me?"

"That and more," Tom says. "I spared you some of the crueler things she said."

I have to know. "Such as?"

"Promise you won't hurt me?"

I look down. "I could never hurt you." Not in a million years. "So what else did she say about her gold mine?" I turn and wrap my arms around his neck.

"Shari, please don't ask me to tell you. Just accept that it's some cruel mess, okay?"

"I want to know. It will help me get into character on Monday." I kiss his chin. "You promised to be honest with me."

He nods. "Okay. Um, she said that even if you got your MBA, she would write a scathingly bad recommendation to keep you out of the JAE program. She said that you had to be the most naïve person she'd ever met and that it was easy to keep you in your place. She called you a field slave. She said that you looked like a geek in your glasses and were probably in love with her because you were a lesbian."

"Wow!" I shout. I stand and dust myself off. "Just . . . wow!" I knew she was hateful, but . . . wow! Man, if I weren't so pissed, I'd start crying!

I run up the stairs, across the pier, down the other stairs, and onto the beach, Tom trailing behind me. I turn to him. "I *made* that wench," I say, balling up my fists. "She is successful because of *me*. And she had the nerve . . . ooh, she is going to get it so bad on Monday. A field slave? A lesbian? Oh, man, it's *on*."

"Shari?" Tom asks from a few feet away.

"What?" I am scalding hot right now.

"This anger, this raw emotion I'm seeing from you."

"What about it?" Corrine must be put in *her* place, and I'm the one to do it.

"Shari, it's making me, um, excited."

Are his jeans crying? They are! "Let's go back to our house where you'll have more room." I grab his hand.

"Yes," he says. "I have this incredible urge to fill you in on a few things."

We sprint down that beach to the car, he breaks speed records getting to the house, and he won't even let me get up the stairs before, well, filling me in, right there on the hardwood stairs.

And at the moment when I think he's going to split me in two, I look at my ring, shining like a beacon and have some seriously evil thoughts. The wench didn't get this, did she? Oh, she got her shiny hair, but I got this to blind her with on Monday! Oh, I'm gonna destroy her, and she'll wish she had never been born!

"Shari?"

Huh? Oh yeah. Tom is making love to me on the stairs. "What?"

"Your nails."

I extricate my nails from his booty. "Sorry. Just had some things to work out."

He looks behind him. "I think I'm bleeding."

"Sorry. Can you maybe . . . Upstairs. Now."

He carries me to the empty bedroom, puts me up against the wall, and we rattle the plaster for half an hour. It's like I'm riding a pogo stick that will never fall over, and just by holding my hips, he balances me so well we even spin around in a circle before banging to the floor and creaking the floorboards.

And the only thought going through my head is: Corrine is going to get *banged*.

Chapter 32

For the rest of Saturday, we "christen" every room in that house, even the cold basement. I will never look at the Bowflex bench the same way again since it gave Tom the perfect angle of entry. We end up in front of a roaring fire on *my* couch, and I know I lose at least five pounds from getting busy there. And just when I think we can't possibly get frisky again, he says something or turns a certain way or I make a sound, and we're back at it.

"Why are we so insatiable, Tom?" I ask.

"I think it's because we talked for five years without doing this," he says. "We're just making up for lost time."

I do not disagree. I wipe some sweat from his chest. "Got any baby oil?"

"No."

"Whipped cream?"

He shakes his head.

"Um, pudding?"

He laughs. "Are you hungry?"

I'm not hungry for anything but this man. "I just want to end this night with another first."

He picks me up off the couch. "I know just the thing."

He takes me up to the empty bedroom, but instead of slamming me against the wall again, he tells me to wait there. He comes back a few minutes later wearing a pair of jeans and carrying a roll of masking tape and that overgrown Cal sweatshirt.

"Ooh, kinky," I say.

"Um, no," he says. He hands me the sweatshirt. "I thought we could . . ." He pulls out a length of tape. "I thought we could design our baby's room."

Oh man! I cry immediately this time. I put on the sweatshirt.

"This room has been empty long enough," he says.

I let the tears fall.

"Where, um, where do you want her to sleep?" he asks.

I step into him and bawl. The sex is beyond wonderful, the future we have so bright. But this man just *knows* my every button, and he also knows the perfect moment to push it. After I recover, I kiss him tenderly.

"At first," I say, "she'll have to sleep in the room with us."

He nods.

"But after that . . ." I survey the room. "I want her desk, a drafting desk, not one of those school desks, a drafting desk to face the window."

He hands me the other end of the tape. "About four feet by three feet, I'd think."

We tape out a rectangle. I look out the window at all the lights. Oh, the things she'll draw, and if she has half the talent of her father, she'll be quite an artist.

We mark out her crib and changing table, her dresser, and even an entertainment center, but there is still so much space!

"Books! She has to have lots of books!" I turn to Tom. "Two bookcases."

Tom has tears in his eyes. "Yeah," he says. "Lots of books."

Books. All those recommendations that led to this.

And then we just stand there in that empty room, holding each other until we start to move in a little circle. "Are we dancing, Tom?"

"Yes," he whispers. "We're dancing in our daughter's room."

Another first for both of us.

We spend the rest of that night in bed and actually sleep for a change. We wake together at six, I take a hot bath alone, he takes a long hot shower alone, and then he gets ready for church. He puts on a sharp blue suit and those fancy black shoes and I almost don't want him to leave the house! He takes me to my apartment where I put on some black dress slacks and a white blouse, my only "fashionable" clothing, and then we walk hand-in-hand to Brooklyn Tabernacle.

It's all so romantically ordinary!

We attend the 9 a.m. service, and for the first time in my life, I have a man beside me. I could never get Bryan to attend church, even on Christmas, but here's Tom standing, clapping, singing, praying, and praising beside me. During the sermon, he holds my hand with his left hand and holds the Bible with his right, and during the altar call, he puts his arm around me.

This is better than bliss.

And when we hold hands and lift them high in the air during the benediction, I realize something powerful.

I've already won.

No matter what happens on Tuesday, I have already won.

After eating a few slices of pepperoni and bacon pizza from Tony's Famous Pizzeria on Fulton, we go back to the apartment. I change clothes and pack a little suitcase, and then we're off to Great Neck to prepare for battle.

It's like the calm before the storm, and I feel more confident than I've ever felt in my life. We finalize the false information, and if Corrine accepts it all as fact, she will easily sound like the most ignorant advertising executive ever born. We then run our own presentation several times, and when that slide of Carl hits the screen, I still get goose bumps.

"Now we'll run a Q and A, your first, right?" Tom asks.

I nod. Let's do this.

"First question. Why black and white, Mrs. Sexton?"

I hesitate. What did he call me?

"You can never hesitate, Shari," he says. "You know this question is coming."

It's just that the name he called me . . . threw me. "Ask me again."

"Why did you choose black and white for this campaign, Mrs. Sexton?"

"Peterson Bicycling is an old-school company with a tradition of excellence. Their bicycles are timeless, and we felt—"

"Keep it all in the present tense," Tom interrupts. "Makes it immediate."

I take a deep breath. "We *feel* that black-and-white photography best captures the timeless quality of their product. Those bicycles are built to last. These images will last a long time in the mind of the consumer as well."

"You're good."

Because I'm Mrs. Sexton. Almost.

"Next question. Why old people, Mrs. Sexton? Why not younger people in a more conventional target demographic for outdoor activities?"

"Old-school company, old-school values," I say, imagining myself in front of the Petersons. "The people in these photographs are full of joy. They've survived into their advanced years, and yet they still know the value of an American-made product and the joy it can bring."

"I'm getting goose bumps," he says.

I rub my arms. Me, too.

"This product is sold worldwide," he says. "Why did you choose New York as a backdrop for this ad campaign, Mrs. Sexton?"

"New York *is* America," I say without hesitation. "It's where many of our ancestors first arrived." Just not mine. "New York is a survivor, too. It's as undefeated as the people who live here. Peterson bicycles reflect that ideal. Solid. Sturdy. Rugged. Tough. Fast. Vibrant. Peterson bicycles make riders of all ages, races, colors, and creeds feel alive."

"Just one more question, Mrs. Sexton."

"Yes, Mr. Sexton?" I smile at my future husband.

"How did you come up with all these ideas? I mean, you don't even have an MBA and have never done anything like this before in your life."

"To be honest, I told myself, 'I would never buy this product.'" And that *is* honest. "And then I rode it, felt like a kid again, felt free, and felt home. It's just a bike, I told myself, but the emotions I felt were intense. I won't stand by this product, Mr. Peterson. I'd rather ride it."

"I wish I had written all that down," Tom says.

"It's all up here." I tap my head. "And here." I put my hand on my heart. "This simple bicycle brought me love. I could never forget any of this." I kiss him. "I just hope I can sleep tonight."

He looks outside. "And it's already night."

We've worked all day on a Sunday, and we've only left this bed to go to church and to eat. "I should be exhausted."

"And if you aren't," he says, "I'm going to make sure of it."

He leaves the room and comes back with five mismatched candles. "It's all I could find."

I smile.

He lights them all and even lights several sticks of incense. "Aroma therapy," he says.

It does smell heavenly.

He leaves again, and in a moment I hear soft music coming through the walls. He returns and lies beside me. "I'll have to route some speakers in here."

It's just loud enough. India Arie, Keyshia Cole, Alicia Keyes. Nice choices.

"Now," he says, "I can either talk you to sleep, or . . ."

I am so comfortable right now. "Or . . ."

"Or I can try to fulfill one of your fantasies."

He's already fulfilled so many! "Tom, you *are* a fantasy. Just having you here beside me is enough." I close my eyes. "Just you, man. You're the only fantasy I'll ever need."

And as we drift to sleep, I no longer hear two sets of breathing or feel the vibration of two hearts. I only hear one person breathing, one heart beating.

Bliss.

"Just you," I whisper. "Always, only, just you."

Chapter 33

We wake before the birds have stirred and before the sun has even started to glow.

Today will be a *huge* day.

I collect all that I brought to Great Neck, and Tom drives me to my apartment so we can shower together, I can change my clothes, and we can eat some frozen waffles with tons of butter and syrup. After I turn on my phone, we listen to a few of Corrine's *thirty* voice mails to me, each shriller than the one before, the last the most civil: "I know why you're not answering your phone, Shari. We will talk about this on Monday morning, oh yes, we will."

I am so not scared.

I should be amped and hyper, but I'm not, mainly because Tom communicates with touches and smiles, a hug or two, and several kisses.

We're not all talked out. We're just resting our gums for what's to come.

Tom drives me to work, kisses me, and I get out carrying my tote bag, my original notes shredded and packed into a freezer bag. It's so ordinary, so domestic, this scene. A man dropping off his woman at work.

Okay, the confetti in the freezer bag is kind of strange.

"Where will you be?" I ask.

"I might just circle the wagons for a bit," he says.

"I wish you could be there." I do. I'm about to make a scene.

"It'll be just as fun to hear you tell it secondhand," he says. "I like your voice, remember?"

Yeah. "Bye." Another kiss. "Keep your phone handy."

"I will." He nods and merges into traffic.

To conserve my energy, I decide to take the elevator. I smile the entire time. I'm actually happy to go to work today.

When I leave the elevator, I go straight to Tia. "Morning, sexy," I say.

"She is already here," Tia whispers.

I feel a tinge of queasiness in my stomach, nothing to worry about. "Did she say anything to you?"

"No." She fidgets with her hands. "What is going to happen, Shari?"

Fireworks in November, maybe some rockets' red glare and some bombs bursting in air. "You may want to get a better seat." I show her my ring.

"Tom?" she says.

I nod.

"Oh, to have your life for one day."

I squeeze her hand. "You have to be my maid of honor."

She smiles. "I will accept this honor." She looks to her right. "Will it be loud, Shari?"

Fireworks, rockets, and bombs are always loud. "Yes."

Tia smiles and claps her hands. "I will move closer then. I do not wish to miss anything."

I take a quick breath and exhale. "Wish me luck."

Tia shakes her head. "You have the most luck of anyone I know. I will wish you a louder voice."

I strut to my desk and sit, shooting a quick glance at Corrine, who wears an almost normal navy business pantsuit and a white blouse. She's even wearing sensible shoes, a pair of black flats. She has her elbows up on her desk, her chin resting in her hands.

She almost looks like a normal boss. Almost.

Instead of removing my jacket and booting up my computer

as I normally do, I just sit there spinning idly in my chair. Hmm. Maybe I should start this show.

"Good morning, Miss *Cross*." Oh, that felt *so* good. "How are you feeling this morning?" I spin to face her. "You look no worse for wear."

Corrine grits her teeth, which is not a pretty sight. "Get over here. *Now*."

"I prefer to stay at my desk if it's all right with you," I say, not whispering at all. This isn't a day for whispering. This is a day for shouting. I want everyone at MultiCorp to hear this today.

"Shari, I *said*, get—"

"I'm staying here." I squint. "Your breast seems almost back to normal, Miss Cross. I'm so happy for you. Or did you just add stuffing to the other one? I'll bet that's what you did. And I don't smell any vinegar. You clean up nice."

She rolls *her* chair around to me for the very first time. Hey, another first. She works her jaw and lips, but I hear no sounds.

"What's up, Miss Cross?" I ask brightly.

"I don't know what you're trying to pull here, Shari," she whispers tersely, "but I will—"

"I've been working, Miss Cross," I interrupt. "You know, developing an idea, researching, coming up with a plan, immersing myself in a product, following through, taking a business trip that's strictly business." Except for the part at the hotel. That was pleasure. "You know, other than the traveling part, everything *I* have normally done for the last five years that *you* have taken full credit for. I'd say you have won ten, no eleven of your fifteen accounts solely because of me."

"Lower your voice," she whispers.

I shake my head. "It's too quiet in here. Mondays should be loud, don't you think? I think folks need it louder on Mondays so they can wake up from their weekends."

Corrine looks around. "You think you're something, don't you?"

I lean closer and widen my eyes. "Yes. I do."

She leans closer. "And you think you can just go into that meeting tomorrow all by your little self and win that account?"

I feel a twinge of doubt, but only a twinge. "Oh, I'm pretty confident I'll win. Tom is a tough nut to crack, but I'll be all over him." I stare a hole in her nose. "Tom, um, likes me to be all over him." I lean closer. "And I really like him to be all over me."

She does the chin twitch and mouth quiver trick again. She is so entertaining. Oh, here come the hands. They flutter so beautifully in the air. Today she may achieve liftoff. "What have you done, Shari?"

I smile. "Your job, Miss Cross. And a whole lot better than you ever could do it on your best day. Now, do you want in on what I'm doing, or do I go to Mr. Dunn and tell him how much help you've *not* given me? I mean, Miss Cross, why, taking vacations to Australia and Hawaii when you should be working on winning another account after screwing up LA, why, that is tantamount to treason." Oh, it's so much cooler to *say* that line to someone else. I blink several times. "It's also tantamount to termination, don't you think?"

"You . . . you . . ."

"Me . . . me . . ." I say. I finally get to mock and echo her out loud today. Bliss, pure bliss.

"You will *never* get into that meeting tomorrow, Shari. You know that, don't you? Mr. Dunn won't let you anywhere near that meeting. Understand? You're not at all qualified."

There's that twinge again. I roll my eyes. "But, if they don't let me into that meeting, you'll never work here again, Miss Cross. You may never even work in advertising again, not that you ever worked in it in the first place." I wave my ring under her nose. "Like my ring?" I admire it. "It's platinum. Tom gave it to me."

Corrine blinks. "What?"

"You know, Tom. Magic tongue. Large package. Such soft, soft brown eyes. *That* Tom. We're skipping the engagement and

going straight to the wedding. Long-term relationships with superficial people just don't suit us." Well, shut my mouth! Corrine's mouth is shut! Another first. I wish I had brought the
camera.

"You . . . you . . ."

"Me . . . me . . ." I say again.

"You are so fired," she says. "Give me your notes and get
out."

I could just toss my freezer bag onto the table and leave, but
I'm not budging yet. "You want all my carefully made, detailed,
deeply thought-out notes that you first dismiss and then claim as
your own brilliant ideas?"

She sucks in her breath. "They belong to MultiCorp, not
you."

A tiny twinge. "You know, I took a lot of unpaid time last
week. Four out of five days, actually." The Tuesday when I was
here but wasn't is causing me yet another twinge of doubt.
"That's when I made all these notes, so technically I was working on my own time, so technically, they don't belong to anyone
but me."

She sucks in her breath again. There must not be enough oxygen in here today. "G–give them to me, Shari."

She actually stuttered. Wow. "Or what?"

"Or . . . or . . . I'll have you prosecuted."

Though this scares me, I'm ready for this. I shrug. "Fine with
me. Then I'll get to tell the world all about you. And the entire
story will be in court documents. They keep those around for a
long time, and sometimes the whole mess makes the newspapers, the radio, and TV. Oh, and the Internet. Can't forget the
Internet! Miss Cross, your name will be all over those documents, the newspapers, talk shows. You'll be famous." I sigh.
"However, you may never even *work* again. But, if you want to
take that risk"—I put my face an inch from hers—"you go right
on ahead."

Corrine jerks back, and several of her tresses fall out of place.

Is that sweat on her upper lip and nose? Eww. "Please, Shari, just . . . give me what you have."

She just said "please." Another first. And she's relenting already. I am playing this woman like a drum. "For old time's sake, Miss Cross?"

"Fine. Yes. Whatever. Give them to me."

I shrug, reach into my tote bag, and pull out the freezer bag. I place it on my desk. "Here they are."

She won't even touch the bag, as if it's a freezer bag full of poop. "What's this?"

Your lentils, Cinderella. Hey, I get that part of the original Cinderella story now. "You asked for my notes, and these are my notes. I shredded them so they wouldn't fall into the wrong hands. Tom's been snooping around."

Her mouth drops open. C'mon, where's a fly? I'd settle for a stray dust particle. "What do you expect me to do with these?" she asks.

"I don't know." I stand. "Get a magnifying glass and put them back together, I guess." I smile. "It will be like putting together a great big puzzle."

She reaches for my arm. "I need to know what you know, Shari."

I look down on her. Man, whoever did her weave left some big gaps of scalp. "Didn't you just fire me, Miss Cross?"

"You're . . . you're unfired. Please, Shari, I'm begging. I'll convince Mr. Dunn to get you into the JAE program."

This conversation is going in a wonderful new direction. I could just sit down and start feeding her the lies, or . . . No. Tom's circling the wagons. He's waiting for me. But I have so much else to say! "You know that Tom and I talk, right?"

"What's he got to do with anything?"

I bend down. "He has told me everything evil that you've ever said about me for the past five years. You think I'm stupid? Who's stupid now? You think I'm a lesbian? I'm marrying *your* man. You think I'm naïve? You're the one who thinks I'm in love with you. You think I'm a field slave. Well, you know what,

I'm proud to be a field slave. I'm no house slave like you." Did I leave anything out? Oh yeah. "You also thought I was easy to keep in my place." I stand tall. "I ain't in my place no more, Missy Ross." I laugh loudly. "You have to be the dumbest Harvard graduate who ever lived." I whip out my phone and hit the speed dial. "Tom?"

Corrine's mouth is wide open again. Here, fly. Come here, fly.

"Yes, Tom. I'll be right down." I snap my phone closed, and Corrine jumps. "Good-bye, Corrin-cula."

"What did you call me?" she asks.

I step around her. "You know, Dracula. Corrin-cula. You have this little fang. You ought to get that fixed." I look around the office. Everyone is listening. I see Ted nodding and Tia dancing. Even Mr. Dunn is visible? He's out of his cave. Nice. "Bye, Miss Cross. Doing business with you has *not* been a pleasure."

I walk over to Tia, who's doing some salsa moves. "High five?"

She slaps my hand. She picks a piece of paper from her desk. "This is my resignation!" she yells, and I jump. I didn't know Tia could yell. "I am out of here!"

"You sure?" I whisper. "You only have a month to go till retirement."

"Ah, I was going to call in and use all my vacation days in December anyway," she says. "You still have a job for me, right?"

There's that twinge again. "Um, right." I hope.

I look back and see a grown woman, a Harvard graduate, sifting through the confetti on my desk. Why isn't anyone clapping? Why isn't anyone else celebrating with me? I know Ted has alimony and child support to pay, but he could at least stand up for me. I sigh. They're all scared. Poor little rabbits. I used to be like you, but today, I am no longer a rabbit. I am a lion, and I am invincible.

Tia stands in front of me, her coat already on. "I am ready."

"You already cleaned out your desk?"

"I boxed up everything last week and have already taken it home. Let us go."

Should I go box up the meager pickings in my desk, too? "I forgot to clean out my desk."

Tia shakes her head. "There is nothing there for you." She pushes me toward the hallway. "Just . . . go." She laughs.

I move into the hallway. How'd she know that slogan? "Tia, have you been talking to Tom?"

She laughs even louder.

Chapter 34

The second Tia and I step out of the elevator, my phone buzzes. Corrine already? I knew she'd be desperate, but whoa! I check the screen. Yep, it's her. I let it buzz. I don't want her to mess with the buzz I have right now.

I burst through the double doors to the outside and see Tom waiting beside the passenger door of that beautiful Mustang. I run to him and give him a hug. But who's in the backseat? Carl? What's a taxi driver doing in the *backseat* of my man's car? I turn to say good-bye to Tia, but Tia opens the back door of Tom's car and gets in.

"What's going on, Tom?" I ask.

He kisses me. "Your steed is ready, milady."

"What?" Oh yeah. A Mustang is a horse. "I mean, where are we taking Tia and Carl? Are we going out to eat?"

He puts his hand on my booty, and in public! "Get in the car, Mrs. Sexton."

I get in, and my phone buzzes again.

"She's already calling?" Tom asks.

I nod. Desperation can sure make a person persistent. "Now what's going on, Tom?"

He gets in and rolls away from the curb. "You can't answer your phone yet."

I know. Duh. "I don't intend to," I say, my voice rising, "now *tell* me what's going on!"

Tia chuckles. "I was the same way."

"My wife, too," Carl says. "Had the jitters. Yelled all day. Made everyone crazy."

"I had to take a Valium," Tia says.

Carl looks at Tia. "Me, too."

What are they talking about? Are they . . .

No.

I look straight ahead.

Oh . . . my . . . goodness.

"Tom?" I whisper.

"Yes, Shari?"

Oh, now *my* jaw and lips get to twitching. It must be catching. "Am I . . . Are we getting married today, Tom?"

"Yes."

I don't ask how.

I don't ask where.

I don't ask when.

I cannot speak.

"That's why you can't answer your phone for a while," Tom says. "You have to make your own day before you can make hers."

I'm getting married.

Today.

I look at my jeans and boots. "But I'm wearing—"

"The right clothes," Tom interrupts.

"You look ravishing, my dear," *Carl* says.

I turn slowly and look at him. Carl is smiling. I didn't know he could.

Carl turns to Tia. "I always wanted to say that to someone."

Tia beams at Carl. "A woman always likes to hear it."

"I hear you like to dance, Mrs. Fernandez," Carl says. "I can still trip the light fantastic."

She beams at me. "I love to dance." She smiles at Carl. "But please call me Tia."

Carl nods. "And you can call me Carl."

I look at Tom, and he shrugs. Them? A taxicab driver and a currently unemployed salsa dancer? Them? I look back and see them cutting their eyes at each other. I grip Tom's hand fiercely.

Absolutely *anything* can happen in New York City.

And then, we ride the whirlwind . . .

Our first stop is the Office of the City Clerk on Worth Street, where Tom and I fill out forms while my phone buzzes a hole in my pocket. Then we fill out a judicial waiver so we can get married within twenty-four hours because Tia says that I *have* to be married today. By whom? Where? Exactly when?

All Tom says is "I know a guy."

I know a guy, too. His name is Tom, I'm about to marry him, and he won't give me *any* information about my *own* wedding!

We drive around seemingly aimlessly for twenty minutes until he pulls into a parking spot on Avenue of the Finest. I look ahead and see the Brooklyn Bridge.

No . . . way. "I'm marrying you on the bridge," I say.

He nods, checking his watch. "In about half an hour."

How can he be so freaking calm? I even ask him, "Tom, how can you be so freaking calm?"

He squeezes my hand. "I'm feeling kind of breezy today."

Grr.

Tia and Carl get out, and I open my door, too.

"Not yet," Tom says. "Close your door, Shari."

I close my door. "Why?"

Tia takes Carl's arm, and I watch them walking away, both of them smiling.

"Why aren't we going with them, Tom?" I ask.

"The bride always comes in last."

Oh yeah. "But it's going to take us a while to get there, isn't it?"

He shakes his head at me. "We will be arriving in style, Miss Nance. Hey, that may be the last time you ever hear that name."

How much style can it be? You can only walk or . . . ride—

"We're riding bikes?"

"Just one."

I sit back. Wow. And I once thought I'd never buy a Peterson bicycle. "With me on the handlebars."

He nods. "And if I can keep us at ten miles per hour, we should hit the center of the bridge in five minutes."

He did the freaking math! So in twenty-five minutes, I'll be married. I may always like Mondays now. "But I don't have a ring for you!"

"Carl got it for me," he says, "and Tia is holding it for you."

A taxi driver picked out my man's ring? "But I didn't pick it out," I say. "I'm supposed to pick it out."

He smiles. "Another first!"

I can't help but laugh. "You're taking this first thing too far now, Tom."

"I know."

"Did you pick out your own ring?" I ask.

He shakes his head. "My best man did. His father did jewelry repair for Tiffany's back in the forties, so he knows a thing or two."

"This is crazy." I kiss his cheek and watch my feet running on the floor mat. "And you've known Carl for how long?"

"A few days." He smiles. "Another—"

"Don't say it," I interrupt.

"Yep. Um, I'm going to need your ring now."

I cover it with my right hand. "You'll have to fight me for it."

"I'm only borrowing it, Shari."

I give him the ring. "Can't I be just a little early?" I have to get out of this car!

He opens his door, and I fly out of mine. He opens the trunk. "I had to take the wheel off so it would fit." He pulls out the tire, handing it to me. "Tired?"

Boo.

He pulls the rest of the bike out and attaches the wheel while I slap his helmet on his head. "Ready?"

Am I? Am I ready to ride across the Brooklyn Bridge on the handlebars of a Peterson bicycle? Isn't that what marriage is like anyway? Riding across together, bridging lives where the rubber meets the road . . .

This is no time to get philosophical.

I don't want to be late for my own wedding.

"Ready," I say.

Tom has to carry the bike up a bunch of stairs, and then I put on my helmet, which isn't exactly a veil, but it will have to do. I'm not wearing a gown. I'm not wearing flowers in my hair. I'm not wearing a garter. I'm not even wearing any makeup. What kind of a bride am I?

A happy one because I am wearing a smile.

I look at my boots waving in the air. My boots are old. I will be sporting a scintillating ring. The ring is new. I feel the warmth of the sun seeping through my jeans. My jeans are blue. Borrowed? Shoot. I left my tote bag in the car.

"I need something borrowed!" I shout to Tom as he weaves us around pedestrians and other bicyclists. "You borrowed the ring, now give it back."

He shakes his head. "Take my watch."

A borrowed watch? Hmm. I unclip the watch from his wrist and slip it into my back pocket.

I'm set.

The crowd thickens, and Tom has to slow to a crawl. "We're here."

He helps me off the handlebars. "But we can't be halfway yet," I say.

He puts his arm around me. "We will be. This is the aisle of the sanctuary."

We walk with the bike, and the crowd parts like the proverbial Red Sea. I guess word got around about the crazy couple getting married on the Brooklyn Bridge. An amazing assortment of people shake our hands and hug us, many taking our pictures. We break through the crowd into a clearing, and there's Carl and Tia and a huge black man holding a Bible. My goodness, he's Reverend Wilder, one of the many ministers at Brooklyn Tabernacle.

Tom reaches out and takes the minister's hand. "Reverend Wilder."

"Tom," Reverend Wilder says. "Right on time."

I'll say. Oh, my stomach is rocking!

"Reverend," Tom says, "this is my bride, Shari Nance."

Reverend Wilder gives me a big old bear hug. "I've heard a lot about you, Shari. I think I've even seen you getting your praise on, too. It's about time Tom found the right woman, don't you think?"

"Yes." I take Tom's hand. So many people are here! "Um, don't we need a permit or something?"

Reverend Wilder shakes his head. "God is everywhere, child. Now hush up and let's do this thing."

Yes, let's do this thing.

"Turn and face your betrothed," Reverend Wilder says.

As the crowd tightens around us, I face Tom, holding both of his hands tightly. Just you, man. Just you. I start to cry, but I'm laughing, too, and it makes me want to shout!

"Dearly beloved, we are gathered here in the sight of God, Manhattan, and Brooklyn on this old bridge . . ."

Yeah, now folks are clapping. *This* is worthy of applause. I wonder if anyone up at MultiCorp is watching. Oh, goofy me. I didn't send out any invitations.

"And today, we are here to form a bridge between this man and this woman." Reverend Wilder closes his Bible. "I'll dispense with the other stuff." He straightens and looks around. "I think a song will say it all." Reverend Wilder nods to a quartet of young black men, who all wear old Brooklyn Dodgers jerseys. "Gentlemen, you're on."

And then they sing "Bridge over Troubled Water" in four-part, on the corner in Brooklyn, doo-wop harmony that has me crying my guts out. I like the song, but now the words make sense to me. I've felt weary and small, and I know Tom will dry all of my tears. He will definitely be by my side, especially when life gets rough, and he will comfort me. I'm weeping by the time they sing about the "Silver Girl." Yeah, that's me. My time has come to shine, and all my dreams are on their way. I look into Tom's eyes, seeing how they shine.

Yeah, I have me a best friend who will stand behind me and beside me for the rest of my life.

"Do you, Shari Nance, take Tom Sexton, to be—"

"I do," I interrupt.

The crowd laughs. A few folks even shout, "Brooklyn!"

"I have to say the whole thing," Reverend Wilder says.

"No, you don't," I say.

Reverend Wilder shakes his head. "Tom, where'd you find this one?"

"She's been in my heart my entire life," Tom says.

The crowd says "aw," and Reverend Wilder nods. "So do you, Tom—"

"Yes," Tom interrupts.

The crowd laughs again, Reverend Wilder smiling and laughing. He addresses the crowd. "I don't know why they asked me to come here to do this. They seem to have it all under control."

More laughter. I am having a chuckle of a wedding.

Reverend Wilder focuses in on me. "You love him, Shari?"

"Yes," I say.

He turns to Tom. "You love her?"

"Yes," Tom says.

"Good enough for me, and good enough for God," Reverend Wilder says. "Like my nana used to say, 'You two jes' keep on keepin' on, hear?'"

We both nod.

"Where are the rings?" Reverend Wilder asks.

Tom pulls out my ring, and Tia hands me Tom's. I compare Tom's huge platinum ring to mine, and I know my ring could fit inside his. We both look at Reverend Wilder.

"Whatcha lookin' at me, for?" he says. "Let's do this thing."

Tom slides on my ring. "Shari Nance . . ." He smiles.

Go on . . .

"I'll tell you later tonight," Tom says, and he's blushing.

A Brooklyn "whoo" sounds out.

And I'm blushing! I'm a blushing bride!

Tom shakes his head. "No, I need to say something more than that in front of all these witnesses, don't I?"

I nod. Almost every woman in the crowd nods, too.

"Shari Nance . . ." He laughs. "Man, I'd *really* rather tell you later tonight." He steps in and whispers, "We have a deadline here, right?"

"Say your piece then, man," I whisper.

Tom steps back. "Ladies and gentlemen," he calls out in a

loud voice, and I even jump a little. Big man, big voice. "I have before me the sweetest, kindest, smartest, most sensual, and definitely most stubborn woman I have ever met in my life. And as God is my witness, I want her more than anything I have ever wanted in my life. I want you, Shari Nance. Just you."

Wow. And he's supposed to be so shy. My goose bumps don't go away as the applause gets louder and louder. I stare at my boots. I have to top that?

A woman a few feet from me says, "Go on, girl. Do your thing."

I slide on his ring, and I have to twist it to get it over his knuckle. "All right," I say loudly. "Ladies and gentlemen, I have before me the sweetest . . . No. I don't want to bite off him. This has to be original."

Some laughter.

"Tom, I can't say that I've been waiting for you all my life." I can't. Fantasies like this hardly ever come true. "I have been waiting on your butt for five years, though, and that's a very long time to keep a Brooklyn girl waiting. Am I right?"

The cheers tell me I'm right. I'll bet some of these men watching are going to get badgered to death by their Brooklyn girlfriends tonight.

"But now that we're here on the greatest bridge in the world, and now that we're about to become man and wife, I have a few things I'd like to tell you." On a whim, I pull out Tom's watch and check the time.

More laughter.

I put the watch back in my pocket. "I promise to listen only to you. I promise to fuss only with you. I promise to . . ." I thought I was out of tears, and here they come. "I promise to love only you for the rest of my life." I turn to Reverend Wilder. "I'm done."

Reverend Wilder blinks. "You sure?"

"I've said all that needs to be said," I say.

Reverend Wilder raises his hands over us. "By the power vested in me by the state of New York, almighty God, and the great city of Brooklyn, I now pronounce you man and wife."

And then we kiss to thunderous applause.

I know we'll be on YouTube.

Why?

Because we're setting the world's record for the longest kiss ever given and received on the Brooklyn Bridge, and on a Monday, no less, and there must be a hundred cell phones held in the air around us.

Tom pulls back first. "Hi, Shari."

"Hi, Tom." I hug him. "And that's how we began."

"Yeah."

I look up at my *husband* for the first time. "Now what?"

He winks. "Answer your phone the next time it buzzes."

Right. "Details, right?"

He nods. "Always."

Chapter 35

As if on cue, my phone buzzes while we get even more hugs and handshakes and even a few high fives from our "invitees." Our wedding guest book would contain at least two hundred names. I hug Carl and Tia, and then I answer the phone.

"Hello?"

"Shari!" Corrine yells. "Thank goodness!"

I kiss my man loudly. I'm sure Corrine heard it. "What's up, Corrine?" No more of that "Miss Cross" business. I am more than her equal now.

"Why haven't you answered your phone, Shari? I've been calling for hours."

She sounds hopelessly desperate. I smile. "Are you in the office, Corrine?"

"Yes."

"Well, I've been getting married. If you look out the window, you'll see our wedding party on the Brooklyn Bridge. I'm the one waving. I don't know if you can see me."

When I start waving, everyone around me starts waving. Corrine *has* to see us now.

"You . . . you just *married* Tom?"

"Yep. What do you want, Corinne? I have a honeymoon to go on." Just not today. Sigh.

"Shari, I really need you."

It's my turn, wench. "Go on . . ."

"And I'm . . . I'm sorry for using you the way I have. It's this business. You understand. It's just business."

I roll my eyes. "No, I don't understand, and I never will. And it isn't the business, Corrine. It's you. I'll never understand you."

"Well, um, I'm sorry, okay?"

Tom and I start pushing the bike back to Manhattan, several bouncing Coke and Sprite cans tied to the rear fork. I need a picture of this! "Okay, Corrine. What do you want?"

"Look," she says. "I know you have everything memorized, and I haven't filed the paperwork for your firing."

How nice. But she's never done any paperwork before! I probably would have had to fill out my own termination notice!

"So could you . . . could you come back?" she pleads. "Please, Shari. I can't do this without you."

Tom's plan is running according to schedule, but I have to tweak it a little. "I'm going on my honeymoon, Corrine, but . . ."

"But what?"

"But we're not leaving until Thursday."

I hear Corrine sigh. "Well, that's good."

For you. "But I refuse to do an all-nighter."

"Oh, I wouldn't ask you to do that, Shari," Corrine says. "I just need the information."

I wink at Tom.

Tom smiles.

I smile.

We have an all-nighter of our own to do.

"Um, Corrine, there's just one more stipulation," I say.

"Name it."

I'm about to, wench. "I must be allowed to go to the meeting with Mr. Peterson."

"But you can't," she says way too quickly.

I shrug. "Oh well. Enjoy unemployment, Corrine. I hear the lines can get long for unemployment benefits, so get there when they open and bring some bottled water. I wouldn't want you to dehydrate."

"Wait."

I don't. I keep pushing the bike and listening to the little tumbling cans.

"Administrative assistants have never been allowed in those meetings since I've been at MultiCorp," she says.

"There's always a first time," I say. "Let's set a precedent."

"It's just not done, Shari. Mr. Dunn only wants qualified people he believes in and trusts in those meetings."

I got your qualifications, wench. "From all the times you texted me and called me, you weren't all that qualified to be in there either."

Ah. Now she's breathing heavily. "It gets very intense in there, and I just needed confirmation from you for what I already knew."

"That is some serious bullshit right there." Please forgive me, God. I should have only said "BS." But abbreviations don't have the same effect as the actual word.

"What did you just say, Shari?"

The BS queen doesn't recognize BS when she hears it, probably because she hears it coming out of her mouth so often. "Qualified or not, you didn't want me in those meetings because you didn't want your assistant to sound more intelligent than you are. After all, I'm LIU, Brooklyn, not Harvard. You were afraid I would show you up."

"I was never afraid that you would *ever* show me up, Shari."

Pride goeth before a fall, wench. "Prove it. Let me into that meeting."

"It's not the proper protocol, Shari."

I sigh. "Okay, I'll just call Mr. Dunn and ask him for permission."

"No!" she yells. "Um, perhaps we can make an exception for this meeting."

Gotcha, wench. "I knew you'd see it my way. You know, you see just about everything my way, don't you?" We're almost to the end of the bridge. "If you weren't such a bad boss, we wouldn't be in this position, Corrine."

"I haven't been a bad boss, Shari," she says quickly. "I could have fired you on numerous occasions."

And she wants me to come back today? "Name *one*."

"When you . . . when you let me fly out to LA unprepared."

I mimic her stance and voice and say, "It's a line of designer clothes. What could be more perfect for me?"

Tom cringes. Yeah, I should have warned him.

"You should have warned me," she says. "It's your job to take care of me."

Yeah. I'll take care of you good tomorrow. "And now it's your turn to take care of me. If I don't get a guarantee that I'll be part of that meeting tomorrow, you don't get any information today."

"Is that all you want?" she asks.

It's all I need. "Oh, your respect would be nice, too, but actually—no. Getting your respect would diminish me. I just want to be in the mix for the first time, maybe even share some of the credit that is rightfully mine."

"I see," she says.

She doesn't.

"I'm beginning to understand," she says.

No you aren't, and you never will.

"You just want some of the glory. I understand that perfectly, Shari. It is an *awesome* feeling when you win an account. Oh, you poor dear girl. You probably haven't had many triumphs in your life because of your upbringing."

Lord, is there a special place in hell for her? And if so, can she go there now and can I watch her in torment? Just asking.

"Please get back here as soon as you can, Shari," she says. "I have a production team on standby."

On standby to produce what? "I have to ask my husband." I cover the phone. "I don't want to go." I pout.

He rubs my back. "Go for it."

I sigh. "Oh, all right." I uncover my phone. "Tom says I have to be home by six o'clock and not a second later."

"Okay. Fine. Just . . . get here."

Click.

The nerve! She needs me, and she hangs up on me.

I kiss Tom. "I'll miss you." I pull him to me. "Where will you be?"

"I'll be at Hairy Ads stealthily cleaning out the office I never use," he says. "It shouldn't take Carl, Tia, and me very long."

I look at Tia. "You're going to Hairy Ads with them?"

She hooks her arm into Carl's. "Carl promised to take me to Sylvia's, and Tom is our ride back to Carl's taxi."

I like the way this is working out. Just like the movies.

Tom drops me off once more, but I don't want to get out of the car. "I really don't want to go back in there. They all saw me leave in a blaze of glory, and now they'll see me coming back in."

"The sooner you get in there," he whispers in my ear, "the sooner we can get back to—"

I don't let him finish, opening my door, jumping out, and closing the door. I even run inside and push my way into the elevator. And when I enter the office, I already have my jacket off by the time I hit my chair.

"I'm going to talk, and you're going to take notes," I say to Corrine, who is, strangely, sitting at *my* desk, my notes mysteriously absent. "Agreed?"

"It might be easier if you—"

"No negotiations," I interrupt. "I talk, you take notes. Agreed?"

She nods.

And then for the next three hours, I sit on the edge of Corrine's desk laying it on so thick that I almost start laughing, especially when she asks me to repeat my last lie. I tell her the goofiest ideas, and she drinks them in and even agrees with me, nodding her head and saying, "Oh, that's good, that's very good." I keep talking right up to 4 p.m., and she has filled an entire legal pad with notes.

"Your insights into this company are insightful," Corrine says.

How freaking redundant. "Now we're going to talk about Tom," I say with a smile. I just need a little more insurance for tomorrow. "Tom has been using your tail for years just to get to *my* ideas."

"No, he hasn't."

Time to bust her out. "Corrine, he's been using your booty. Sex." I let that sink in. "Let's see, how did he say it? Oh. He just listed your *needs*."

She doesn't speak. I have her complete attention.

"Let's see if I remember them all, um . . . rope, was it?"

Her lips are so tight I can see veins!

"Um, one-use drawers. Toys?" I nod and smile, slapping my desk hard. Ow, my hand. "Does that sound familiar?"

Corrine's eyes drop. "He told you all that?"

"Hey, don't sweat it," I say. "It almost makes you human. So because of your needs, you revealed a few of my ideas to Tom."

She still doesn't look up. "I may have let a few things slip."

Time to seal the deal. "And what you let slip was privileged, proprietary information, wasn't it? Those ideas were Multi-Corp's ideas, right?" I put my nose a millimeter from hers. "If you try to screw me out of going to that meeting tomorrow now that you have all this information, I will have my husband, a *very* well-respected ad executive from Harrison Hersey and Boulder, come talk to Mr. Dunn about your indiscretions and improprieties." I'll bet she didn't know I knew those words. "You hearing me, wench?"

"I hear you," she whispers, looking around. "I'll get you into that meeting."

I stand. "Well, I gotta go."

Corrine stands. "Um, just make sure you leave your cell on."

I shake my head. "Uh-uh." On my wedding night? Is she serious? "No way. Go with what you have. I am a married woman now. I have to tend to my man."

"Well, uh, be here at your regular time so we can go over the presentation."

I wouldn't miss it. "I'll try, but I'm going to have a *very* busy night. You understand. See you tomorrow." I turn to leave then remember my graduation pen. I snap it out of its holder and put it in my tote bag.

That's right. I've graduated.

I give Tom a call, he meets me at the curb on William Street, and he whisks me off to the apartment. I'm just about to throw *him* up on my kitchen table, when he hands me my phone.

"Who am I supposed to call now?" I ask.

"Your parents," he says. "After we win tomorrow, I want to meet them." He sits on the couch and picks up the remote control, clicking and turning on the TV. He won't even look at me. Hey, yo, over here. Look at your blushing bride!

He flips through a few channels.

I stare at my phone. "I can tell them some other time, can't I? This is our wedding night."

He turns down the volume. "And we'll have one, but you have to let them know you're married, and soon. We may be all over the Internet by now. Did you see all the cell phones in the air?"

I did. Wow. I'll have to collect all the footage so I can see my own wedding sometime.

"You wouldn't want your parents to find out that way, would you?" he asks.

He has a point. I shake my head. "I'll, um, I'll be in the bedroom. Where *we* should be."

He smiles. "We'll be in there in a moment."

I go into the bedroom and slump onto my bed. I know this is necessary. I know I owe them this vital information. I know I owe them much more than I've given to them. Man, I feel so prodigal all of a sudden. I dial a number I haven't dialed in years.

"Hello?" Mama says.

"Hey, Mama. It's me, Shari."

"Charles!" Mama yells. She never covers the receiver. "Shari's on!"

"How are y'all doing?" I ask.

I hear some static. "Your father's getting on the other line."

"Okay," I say.

"Hey, Shari," Daddy says. "How's my baby?"

I have so much to tell them. "Um, are you both sitting down?"

Two yeses.

"Mama, Daddy, I'm married." I wait for the onslaught.

It doesn't come.

"I'm so happy for you, Shari," Mama says.

"So am I, baby," Daddy says.

Who are these *nice* people? Who has replaced my parents? Why aren't they quoting the Bible at me? "Um, you don't seem too surprised."

"Why would we be?" Mama says. "Tom already called us."

Tom already . . . called. I nod. Yeah. That's something Tom would have done. Wow. He's building bridges that I burned long ago.

"He talked my ear off for most of the morning, baby," Daddy says.

Circling the wagons, he said. He was talking to them the whole time I was destroying Corrine.

"He even asked me for your hand in marriage," Daddy says. "How old-fashioned is that?"

"It's the right thing to do, Charles," Mama says.

"I know that, I know that," Daddy says. "He sounds like a really fine young man, baby."

"He is, Daddy." I look up and see Tom standing in the doorway. I mouth, "Thank you." He shrugs.

"And so polite," Mama says. "He told us he's been attending church with you for two years. Is this true?"

It's sort of true. "Yes, Mama."

"I wish we could have been there," Mama says.

"Yeah," I say. "It was beautiful."

"Oh, I know it was, baby," Daddy says. "I've watched it a couple times already. On that YouTube thing."

It's already out there! That is so cool!

"Are you eating enough, honey?" Mama asks. "You sure looked skinny in that video."

"She looked just fine to me," Daddy says. "And what have

you done with your hair, baby? Why is it flying around so much?"

For the next two hours, on my wedding night, I rest against the chest of my husband on my bed and talk to my parents. Well, they talk to each other a lot while we talk, too, but it's just like being at home. Tom takes the phone several times to tell them how nervous I was, how stubborn I am, how many children we're going to have, and how much he's been trying to get me to eat. Neither of us tell them about tomorrow. I don't want them to worry.

"Mama, Daddy, I'm really exhausted," I say.

"You should be, all the work you've been doing," Daddy says. "You're doing me proud, baby, and I—"

"Charles," Mama interrupts. "It's their wedding night."

"I know it is, woman," Daddy says.

"She's not really exhausted, man," Mama says.

Oh my goodness! "No really, Mama, I am so tired right now, more tired than I've ever been."

Tom rubs my shoulders. "Tell them we're coming to visit this weekend."

So soon? "Really?" I whisper.

He nods. "And then it's on to Tahiti."

"Okay," I whisper. "Um, Mama, Daddy, Tom says we're visiting this weekend."

I hear silence.

"Mama?"

I check my phone. It's working. My battery meter's half full.

"Baby," Daddy says softly, "we can't wait."

"Mama?"

I hear a click.

"Daddy?"

"It's okay, baby," he says. "Your mama's just a little emotional right now. She'll be happy to see you, too."

Mama's . . . crying. I guess that's good. "Is she okay?"

"Woman, you had your *own* phone," Daddy starts to say, and then I hear Mama say, "Drive safely, child. See you soon. I'll have your room ready. Good night."

Another click.

I lean back into Tom. "My mama never cries."

"Another first," he says.

Yeah. I didn't know my mama *could* cry. And now she's crying . . . because I'm coming home.

"Tom?"

"Yes, baby?"

I pinch his thigh. "You ain't my daddy."

He growls.

"Tom, I am really tired." I am more than exhausted.

"Me, too, and we have a huge day tomorrow."

I look up at him. "You don't mind if we don't . . . consummate our marriage?"

"We'll have time," he says. "Shh, Shari. Just rest."

And then I sleep for what seems like forever.

Until I wake up in the middle of the night, run to the bathroom, and have the worst vomit burp I have ever had.

Tom's awake when I return. I don't know if he ever sleeps. "You okay?"

I snuggle up to him. "I'm fine. Just excited, I guess."

"I can't sleep either," he says. "I usually don't sleep a wink before a presentation."

I turn and put my booty on him. "Then let's not sleep together."

"Have I told you how much I like the way you talk?"

What did I say? Oh. "I meant, let's just . . . watch the sunrise. . . ."

I don't make it to the sunrise, and Tom has to shake me several times to wake me in the morning. I look up and see him fully dressed. "Morning," I say, trying to kick out of my covers.

"Don't get up," he says.

Fine with me. I return to my pillow. "What time is it?"

"Three thirty," he says.

I do not like what 3:30 a.m. looks like. "Why are you dressed? Aren't we supposed to do one more run-through at your house?"

"At *our* house," he says.

Oh yeah. I'm a home owner now.

"I think you need more sleep, Shari," he says.

"But I want to practice," I say. Oh, that was convincing.

"You'll be fine," he says. "You're a natural."

I grab his leg. "Are you going to look all corporate on me today?"

He grimaces. "Just for one more day."

I push his leg away. "I probably won't recognize my own husband." I sit up. "Um, what if people at the meeting know we're married?"

He shrugs. "So they know. I doubt it, but we'll just have to cross that bridge when we come to it."

I bury my head under the covers. "You're so funny at three thirty in the morning."

He pulls back the covers and plants a hot, juicy kiss on my cheek. "And this time tomorrow, we'll still be going at it."

Yep. "Kiss me again."

He kisses my stomach, his tongue lingering a *long* time.

Now I'm awake.

I sit up. "I'm going to be so nervous, Tom."

"You'll be fine," he says. "And I'll be there with you."

Beside me all the way. "Drive safely. I love you."

He kisses my lips. "I love you, too, Shari. Get some sleep."

And I don't sleep well at all until the alarm clock jolts me awake at 7:30 a.m. because this is the first day of the rest of my life. So many things have come into place so quickly and with such good timing. There are so many "what-ifs" that went in my favor, and there are still more possible what-ifs today. What if I had waited two more hours for Tom to hand me my contract? Would we be on our way from Great Neck to Harrison Hersey and Boulder for work right now instead? Would we even have fallen in love, or would he just be my boss? Would Bryan still be in the picture? What if the jellyfish hadn't stung Corrine? What if Corrine hadn't stayed in Hawaii and had come back to the city sooner? Would I have backed down and shared my information with her and let life go on its less-than-blissful way? What if Harrison Hersey and Boulder chose someone other than Tom for this competition? Would I have ever met Tom? I suppose Tom would have eventually approached me at Brooklyn Tabernacle, but would we have—

This is too much to think about. And even though I haven't been very godly and won't be very godly today, I have no other explanation than God. The Lord works in mysterious ways all right.

And this beautiful mess is the proof.

I put on my rugged outfit, the one I wore down in Georgia, try to eat a waffle but can't finish it, and take one last walk past Whitman Park and across the Brooklyn Bridge. I don't walk nearly as fast as I usually do, drinking in everything and everybody, and thinking very little for a change. Oh sure, I'm still curious about Tom's presentation. "A trade secret," he told me. Hmm. He just wants to surprise and impress me. He's already surprised me in so many ways. He followed me on a bike on this very bridge. He called me just to talk. He drew me. He drew me in, too. He made me steal my own ring. Okay, he didn't *make* me steal it, but . . . And he called my parents. Man, I don't know if I could stand a lifetime of surprises like that.

I am seriously tripping. Of *course* I could put up with all those wonderful surprises.

I drift into my building and stand in the elevator, no smile today. I'm a little sad because this is the last day I'll ever work here. It's been a chore, don't get me wrong, but it's the place I've been going to for five years. It has many memories. Hmm. Most of them are bad memories.

Yeah, I am still seriously tripping.

I pass Tia's spot, now staffed by a young Hispanic woman. I wave at her, and she waves back. I'll bet we would have been friends. I arrive at my desk ten minutes late, and this is yet another first. I have never been late before. I sit at my desk, idly looking in drawers for anything I might want to take with me. I find nothing that interests me, not even a pack of Post-its.

My phone lights up. Ted. "Hi, Ted."

"Hi, Shari Sexton," he says.

I feel a twinge. I don't need to feel any twinges today. "You know?"

"Your video went viral," he says. "A million hits as of midnight."

The twinge intensifies into a pang. "What can I do for you, Ted?"

"I, um, I just wanted to wish you and your husband well. That's all."

Ah. "Thank you, Ted. And thank you for putting up with me all these years." I look over at Ted. Yep, he's blushing.

"You've been easy to deal with, Shari," he says. "Unlike everyone else."

I'm going to miss Ted. "You take care of yourself, okay?"

"Okay."

"And maybe the Mets will do better next year, huh?"

"Yeah. Bye, Shari."

"Bye, Ted."

Corrine sweeps in looking immaculate as always in a dazzling black Who Cares Who Made It dress, but the circles under her eyes tell a different story. She's been up all night.

Unlike me.

"Are you ready to see what we're presenting?" she asks.

I nod. "Sure."

We go over to production, sit in uncomfortable plastic chairs, and watch some of the most *ridiculous*, jacked-up commercials and view the most *offensive* ads I've ever seen. They are all very well produced, but they suck so bad.

"What do you think?" she asks as the last crappy slide fades, no music in the background. I would have used "Something Foul" by Nas for this PowerPoint's background music.

"It's edgy, Miss Ross," I say. "Really cutting edge." Really cutting your own throat! The guillotine will be falling later. Heads, mine included, must roll!

And that's when I have another vomit burp, run to the nearest ladies' room, and spew my half-eaten waffle. Man, I'm falling apart. I have to get myself together.

When I get back to my desk, my phone lights up again. "Shari Sexton, Miss Ross's office." That's right. I know my own name. It's the last name I'll ever have.

"Piper in personnel. I noticed you're here today."

Okay, wench. I need to put you in your place today. "Yes. I'm here, Piper in personnel. Did the system notice I was here today, too?"

"No. You have failed to log on to the system at your appointed time."

I roll my eyes. "So I'm not here until I log on."

"Correct."

"So if I work on a presentation all day, and, oh, help make this company millions, I'm not here unless I log on."

"Yes."

"Miss Ross never logs on," I say.

"She doesn't have to," Piper says.

I sigh. "Piper in personnel, do you call every MultiCorp employee to inform them that they are here or not here?"

"No."

No hesitation. "So what's the problem?"

"Please log on."

I log on. "Happy?"

"Yes. There is another problem. You are now married and have incorrect information in the system."

Wow. News is certainly traveling fast. Go away, twinges. "How is it a problem? It's only been one day."

"The system has you listed as a single woman when you are obviously not a single woman anymore."

"Like I said, it's only been one day," I say. "I just got married yesterday."

"Yes, and you showed up afterward to work with Miss Ross, again without logging on to the system."

I blink. "So I wasn't here yesterday when I *was* here yesterday?"

"Correct. You should have also come immediately to my office to revise several important forms."

"But I wasn't here, right?" I say. "How could I have come to your office yesterday if the system said I wasn't here?" I have this wench now.

She doesn't respond.

"Piper in personnel? Are you there?"

I hear her clear her throat. "You must revise tax forms, beneficiary change forms, and spousal information forms."

"Wow, that's so formal," I say.

Piper in personnel does not laugh.

"Um, what do you need spousal information for?" I ask.

"To see if you plan to go on his health plan," she says. "Payroll needs to know immediately."

But I don't intend to work here after today. Hmm. "I will call them." Not.

"You must come to my office this afternoon to fill out these important forms, or your paycheck will not reflect your new status."

"Oh, I will," I say. "Thanks for calling. Bye." Not gonna happen, Piper. I log off. Wow, I was "here" for five whole minutes today.

I look up at Corrine staring at me. "Yes?"

"I'm just concerned about what you're wearing today," Corrine says. "This is a very important meeting, Shari."

"I know that." And I know my outfit is much more appropriate than yours for this meeting.

She shakes her head slightly, and her hair doesn't move. She must have had that weave tightened. "If you ever want to get into the JAE program, Shari dear, you must learn to dress more professionally."

"I'd rather eat," I say.

"What's that?"

"I'd rather eat," I say. "You spend, what, ten, fifteen, maybe twenty thousand a year on clothes?"

She squints. "About that, maybe more. Why do you ask?"

She may never get it. "Miss Ross, I spend that much on rent for a year."

"That little? Is your building rent controlled?"

Okay. She'll *never* get it. "Never mind."

She sits on the edge of my desk. "No, I'm interested."

Now she gets interested in "the help." I don't want to get into this right now. I just want all this to be over. "Do you mind if I go to lunch early today? I'm really hungry."

She puts her hand on mine. "I was going to take us out to Delmonico's for a pre-battle meal."

I remove my hand from under her hoof. "It's okay," I say. I only want quesadillas right now. "I'd rather eat something simple. My stomach's been bothering me."

"Oh, you just have some butterflies," she says. "I get them all the time, and trust me, the more often you do this, the fewer butterflies you'll have."

So that's what she has in her head instead of brains. Whatever, wench. "Um, so may I go to lunch early?"

"Sure," she says, showing me all of her teeth, including the little vampire tooth. "In fact, why don't you meet me in the lobby at the Millennium at, say, one thirty. That will give you a two-hour lunch."

Which would be a fairly short lunch for her. "Fine." I stand. "See you at one thirty."

"I'll be there waiting," she says. "Go team!"

I get my usual at John Street Bar & Grill, eat like a horse, and leave an extra-big tip. I'm going to miss this place. Maybe I can get Tom to bring me here every now and then.

I walk over to the World Trade Center rebuild in front of the Millennium and marvel at the progress. From ashes to beauty. Story of my life. Sort of. I'm not Cinderella, though I did have an evil step-monster for a boss. And today, I get to ride off with the prince.

What are those quesadillas doing down there? The Twist? Geez. Chill out.

I go into the Millennium, find a bathroom, and barf up my meal. Am I that nervous? Geez. I know what's going to happen. Sort of. I know what I have to do. For the most part. Our campaign is sound. Of that I'm sure. Tom will be there. Of that I'm surest. So why am I so nauseous? Maybe the waffle was bad. I hope that's it.

I'm sitting in the lobby when Corrine walks in carrying her

"lucky" briefcase, one that cost at least a thousand dollars. I look at my tote bag and shrug. It ain't the package—it's what's inside.

"Let's go get us a win," she says, leading me to the elevator.

Yes, let's go get us a win.

"I'll show you how it's done," she says.

No, no, you won't.

I'm gonna show you how it's done, Mr. Dunn will can you, and you'll be done in this town, Corrine dear.

It's showtime.

Stomach, please take a nap or something. Mama's got to go to work now.

Chapter 36

The view from the meeting room on the fifty-fifth floor of the Millennium Hotel is breathtaking, incredible, and inspiring. I stand at the window soaking up all that energy, all that industry, all that resilience. I don't think I'd ever get tired of just . . . looking.

And I'm about to become part of all I see.

I hope.

And I hope I keep breathing! Geez, there is a definite lack of oxygen at this altitude.

When the bigwigs from Harrison Hersey and Boulder enter, I smile at my man. Yep, Tom cuts quite a corporate figure in that black suit, but I think Tom could wear a garbage bag and still turn heads. Mmm. *That* is going home with me. *That* will be in my bed holding me for the rest of my natural life. I want so much to give him a kiss, but everyone looks so serious, even Tom, though he does give me a quick wink.

And that takes my breath away. C'mon, man. I'm trying to breathe over here.

Mr. Dunn arrives next, and he and Corrine do a quick pow-wow at our table, beads of sweat dotting his forehead. Eww. He used too much cologne, which reminds me of the subway, which reminds me how far away I was from this moment five years ago.

I hope I don't start to hyperventilate.

I sip a bottled water and kind of drift from window to window. I don't mind that Mr. Dunn is completely ignoring me. I mean, after today, he'll have to explain *why* he completely ignored me and my potential for five years. Yeah. I'm the "star" he let get away.

Mr. and Mrs. Peterson are the last through the doors, Mr. Peterson in what might be his only suit. Mrs. Peterson, wearing a stylish white dress that actually slims her, leaves him and comes over to me.

"Shari, is it?" she whispers.

The twinge jumps past the pang to a convulsion. I look at my boots. "Yes ma'am." Oh man. Your sins will find you out, all right.

"I just love YouTube," she whispers. She smiles at Tom. "I am so glad I was able to help you two in some way."

I nod. "Yes ma'am. And I am so very sorry—"

"Shh," she whispers. "You were just goin' after your man. No shame in that. I did a few iffy things to get my man, too, and I've never regretted a single one of them for forty years."

I turn to her. "But I lied to you and Mr. Peterson."

She hugs me. "All is fair in love and war," she whispers. "And it looks as if the war is about to begin." We turn toward the U-shaped table. Everyone is seated but us.

I take a seat between Corrine and Mr. Dunn and look directly across at Tom. Mr. Dunn's eyes scrunch up at me, and I smile. I know I'm not supposed to be here, Mr. Dunn, but my boss invited me. After all the introductions, I learn the men surrounding Tom are Mr. Harrison, Mr. Hersey, and Mr. Boulder. Geez. They sent all their guns.

Good thing they're all dressed for their own funeral.

Wait a minute. If Mrs. Peterson already knows the truth, does Mr. Peterson? I am so afraid I'll puke all over this table!

At some cue I don't notice, both Tom and Corrine stand simultaneously. "Ladies first," Tom says, and he sits.

"Thank you, Mr. Sexton," she says, smiling at no one in particular. I suppose this is how you smear a smile on a crowd. It's so fake. She walks into the space between the tables, a widescreen TV set up behind her.

"Mr. Peterson, it's so good to finally meet you," she says, her hair sending out its usual moonbeams.

Mr. Peterson looks from Corrine to me and back. "And who are you?"

"I'm Corrine Ross." She nods at me. "I think you've already met my assistant, Shari."

"But that's—" Mr. Peterson starts to say, but Mrs. Peterson is fast in his ear whispering.

Please don't bust me out, *please* don't bust me out . . .

"Okay, okay, Freda," Mr. Peterson says to Mrs. Peterson. "Um, what was your assistant's name again?"

"Shari," Corrine says.

"Shari what?" Mr. Peterson asks.

Corrine hesitates. "Shari . . . Sexton."

Mr. Peterson nods once at me, sighs, and shakes his head. "Go on."

It is not the greatest moment in my life.

"Thank you, Mr. Peterson," Corrine says.

Thank you, *Mrs.* Peterson! I owe you a thousand Monday lunches at H&H. And thank you, Mr. Peterson, for listening to your wife. I owe you a bloody rib eye or two. I look across at Tom. He is so cool. Why isn't he at least fidgeting? My feet won't stop running in place.

"Mr. Peterson," Corrine continues, "I think what we have for you today speaks for itself. I hope you enjoy it." She nods to a technician, the lights dim, she takes her seat, and the worst ad campaign ever made for a bicycle begins.

A snarling, barking, slobbering mass of hounds in search of a fox precedes eight bicycle-helmeted, upper-crust, *ancient* white men wearing red coats, white pants, and black boots, who burst out of a forest on Peterson bicycles. The lead rider blows a trumpet then beeps the horn on the bike. Wow, they used a lot of blue screens for this one. It all looks so fake! It looked so much better on the little monitor in the production room. More bicycle horns sound, we hear gunshots that make everyone jump, we see close-ups of the bike and lots of dirt, and the scene fades to the words "Peterson Bicycles: The Rolls-Royce of Bicy-cles."

I glance at Mr. Peterson. Yep, his mouth is open.

The fifteen-second spot is a shortened version of the fox hunt.

Mr. Peterson's mouth is still open. I hope there are no flies in here.

Then the billboards flash up on the screen, and I mean, they really flash because there's some serious nudity going on. Each billboard has several scantily clad models frolicking on and around a bicycle. One bicycle is missing its seat, and a model seems to be caressing the seat post, her lips dangerously close the top of the post. The last picture is so nasty—the woman is obviously nude, her naughty bits barely hidden by the seat and the handlebars, her legs spread very wide—that Mrs. Peterson gasps.

Mr. Peterson's mouth is closed now. Yep, that's a good ol' Georgia boy frowning and scowling.

The radio spot is the real kick in the tail, a rip-off of the Oscar Mayer song:

My bicycle has a first name, it's P-E-T-E-R.
My bicycle has a second name, it's S-O-N by far.
Oh, I love to ride it every day and if you ask me why I'll say . . .
that Peterson Bikes have got a way with A-M-E-R-I-C-A.

Corrine squeezes my leg, and I almost laugh out loud.

I had nothing to do with the radio ad. That was all her.

"Lights please," she says.

The lights come up. Mr. Dunn coughs. The HHB upty-ups snicker. Corrine is completely oblivious. Ouch. It's going to hurt her even worse now that she thinks she just blew Mr. Peterson away.

"Do you have any questions for me, Mr. Peterson?" Corrine asks.

Mr. Peterson shoots the most evil look at *me*. "No," he says.

It's also not one of my best moments.

Corrine's hands shake. "Uh, I can go into more detail about our concept, Mr. Peterson."

Mr. Peterson simply shakes his head.

"Well, um," Corrine stammers, "thank you for the opportunity to, um, thank you for the opportunity."

I look to my right. Mr. Dunn has his forehead pressing into the table, and if he presses any harder, he'll go through the table. It would be hard to hide in here, Mr. Dunn. Is that some drool coming from his lips? Eww. I look at the Harrison Hersey and Boulder bigwigs, and they all look so smug, so superior, so freaking Republican.

Tom stands, nods at me, and turns to Mr. Peterson.

Nail 'em, Tom! Hit 'em hard! Go team! That's *my* man.

"Mr. Peterson, it's good to see you again, sir," Tom says. I just love his voice. I might just ask that man to make a few babies with me.

Mr. Peterson nods.

"And you, too, Mrs. Peterson," Tom says, flirting his butt off. "I like that dress."

Mrs. Peterson smiles.

My man can work a room.

"After visiting with you kind folks, I learned a great deal about . . . craftsmanship and integrity." He moves over to the TV. "I was impressed by the amount of craftsmanship it takes to make a single Peterson bicycle. I was also impressed by your integrity, Mr. Peterson. At this time, I'd like to show you what we at Harrison Hersey and Boulder think about craftsmanship and integrity." He nods at the technician, and the show begins.

We look at a split screen on the TV. On the left screen are ads made by Harrison Hersey and Boulder for an expensive European sports car while the right screen is dark—at first. After several slick ads run on the left, the right side of the screen fills with pictures of the same expensive cars wrecked, smoking, and falling apart, with uncountable recall notices and headlines announcing lawsuits scrolling through the carnage!

HHB is going *down!* Yes!

The left screen then shows an ad for a building while the right screen shows the same building collapsing. A cruise ship sails boldly on the left and sinks on the right. Cute "moms" sell products on the left that are linked to sickness and obesity on the right. A restaurant chain with a catchy jingle rolls on the left while fat percentages balloon out of nowhere on the right. An ad for a Las Vegas casino runs while a red line showing rising crime rates in Las Vegas climbs off the screen.

The kicker, though, is a hidden camera video on the full screen of Hairy Ads execs talking to someone who sounds exactly like Tom!

> Tom's Voice
> This vehicle is overpriced, under-tested, and flat-out dangerous to the public, Mr. Harrison. It failed every crash test, and it barely gets eleven miles to the gallon on the highway. It's a lemon, Mr. Harrison. This is a lawsuit waiting to happen.

> Exec #1
> Why do you care, Tom?

> Tom's Voice
> Because it's overpriced, under-tested, and dangerous to the public.

> Exec #2
> When will you ever understand what we do here at Harrison Hersey and Boulder, Tom? We turn shit like this into gold all the time. . . .

Tom smiles. "Lights please."

I want to give him a standing ovation! Whoo! My butterflies are freaking gone now. Whoo! Encore! Author! Author!

The silence in that conference room is so loud, that if I screamed, no one would hear me. One of the Hairy Ads men, Mr. Harrison himself, approaches Tom and says something.

Tom doesn't react. "What was that again, Mr. Harrison?" he asks.

"I said," Mr. Harrison says loudly, "you are fired, Mr. Sexton."

Tom exhales and loosens his tie. "Thank you, Mr. Harrison. Nice toupee, by the way. Does your mistress in Milan like it better than your mistress in Paris does? Or are you bald for one and hairy for the other?"

Mr. Harrison's mouth drops open.

So does mine. Two mistresses *and* a wife? With that hair? The man needs a body lift, too. Eww, he has hairy ears.

"You . . . you will *never* work in this town again!" Mr. Harrison says.

That tired old cliché? Man, Mr. Harrison is whack. I was hoping for something more original than that from the head of a powerful advertising agency. I mean, he could have said, "You are dismissed, sir!" or "I'm giving you the sack, Jack!" or "You are terminated!"

Tom winks at me. "I don't plan to work in this town again, Herb."

That's right. We're going on the road, y'all. I'm going to see the world!

Mr. Harrison points at Tom. "You will hear from our lawyers, Mr. Sexton."

Tom removes his tie and tosses it on the table. "Can't wait, Herb. Um, now that I'm fired, does that mean the confidentiality clause doesn't apply? *Good Morning America* is always looking for whistle-blowers with video to back up their claims. I have twenty hours of meetings for them to use, Mr. Harrison. Might even make a good *Dateline*, don't you think?" Tom removes his jacket and throws it onto the table. "Or *Sixty Minutes*."

I wonder how far my man will go. Mmm. The shirt! Take off the shirt!

Mr. Harrison's mouth drops open again. Eww. Look at all those filled cavities and beige teeth. His mistresses must be blind.

I sense movement near me. Oh, it's Corrine. She's staring at me with evil eyes.

"Yes, Miss Ross?" I should have been an actress.

"You're fired, Shari," she whispers.

But no one heard that! I want to go out in style, too. "What?" I say as innocently as I know how to.

"I said that you are *fired!*" Corrine says loudly, the word *fired* coming out in a kind of screech, like fingernails on a chalkboard.

I push back in my chair and prop up my boots on the table, but I don't take any clothes off like Tom. I am already properly attired. I look directly at Tom. "Thank you, *Cringe*. That's the nicest thing you've ever said to me."

"You . . . you . . . *bitch!*" Corrine yells.

This is a very big conference room. I distinctly hear an echo. I didn't even know Corrine knew that word. I shrug. I guess you just never truly know people.

Mr. Dunn stands, his mouth open, too, but no drool escaping this time. "Miss Ross, *you're* fired."

This has to be some sort of record. Three firings in about thirty seconds. This will make the front page of *Advertising Age* for sure.

"It wasn't my fault!" Corrine shouts. "*Shari* fed me the wrong information."

"And it's your job to double- and triple-check your facts!" Mr. Dunn shouts. He stares me down. "You never would have gotten through the JAE program, Miss Nance. Never. Not in a million years."

"It's Mrs. Sexton," I say. I point at Tom. "I'm married to him. Isn't he gorgeous?"

Well, at least we know who doesn't watch YouTube. The HHB nerds look at each other with the most quizzical expressions, all of them bobbing for flies. Mr. Dunn looks as if he's about to expire.

"And as for your little junior executive program, I know I would have aced it," I say, "unlike *you*, Mr. Dunn."

"What?" he yells.

Geez, all this yelling. You'd think Brooklyn had just broken out in the room. "Didn't you fail a similar junior executive program . . ." I point across the table at the HHB drones. "With them?" I smile at Mr. Harrison. "I'm right, aren't I, Herb?"

Mr. Hersey approaches Mr. Peterson. I wouldn't do that if I were you. That good ol' Georgia boy is *pissed.*

"Mr. Peterson, I'm Jim Hersey, and I want you to know that what you saw here today in *no* way reflects the vision—"

"Y'all can leave now," Mr. Peterson interrupts.

"Um," Mr. Boulder says, "I'm Bob Boulder. What we're trying to say is that this man—"

"I've heard enough," Mr. Peterson interrupts. "Y'all can leave. Now."

Mr. Harrison strides over to Mr. Peterson. "Look, Tom Sexton is obviously a disgruntled employee who—"

"Who told the damn truth!" Mr. Peterson shouts. "What part of 'y'all leave' don't y'all understand?"

The Hairy Ads fools sweep out first, Dunn and Corrine fussing right behind them. I distinctly hear her say, "But it's *not* my fault! It's *hers!* How can you fire *me* for something I didn't do?"

Lifetime memories. I will never forget these moments. Oh, for a video camera.

Once the doors close, Tom motions to me, and I kick my legs off the table and swing into action. I stand, and my legs feel pretty sturdy.

"Mr. Peterson, Mrs. Peterson," I say softly, "I know you probably don't like me very much right now."

Only Mrs. Peterson smiles. Mr. Peterson's face is so red! No more rib eyes for you, mister.

"But I have very good reasons for all the foolishness you've seen today. The fact is, I *love* your bicycle." Wow. I'm about to cry. "Your bicycle brought me the man of my dreams." I fight the urge to run over and hug Tom. This is business, and I am currently unemployed, so I have to be all business to get some business. Or something like that.

"Y'all are really married?" Mr. Peterson asks.

I show him my ring, and Tom shows him his. "We were married yesterday on the Brooklyn Bridge," Tom says.

Mr. Peterson starts to speak and stops. Then he squints.

"What was that little show you two put on at H and H all about then?"

I move closer to the Peterson's table. "As you've probably already figured out, I, um, I was impersonating my boss, who just got fired and who used to be Tom's girlfriend, and Tom, strangely, didn't bust me out at H and H because . . ." I turn to Tom.

"Because, Mr. Peterson," Tom says, "I've been in love with Shari for a long time."

Mr. Peterson looks at Mrs. Peterson. "That was the craziest conversation I think I have ever heard in my life." He looks at me. "I thought the two of you were out of your minds."

Mrs. Peterson pats his hand. "They were, dear. They were crazy in love. Go on, Shari."

I move to the edge of their table. "After meeting you two and touring your plant, Tom and I decided to join forces. Neither of us were happy with the agencies we were working for, and as you've seen here today, neither of us really belong, you know?"

Mr. Peterson nods.

"But in order for us to have you take us seriously, we had to put on that sorry little show you just saw." I almost tongue-tied myself. "I saw how disappointed you were, Mr. Peterson, and it broke my heart. I am so sorry. I know I have no right to ask you for anything. I lied to you. And you gave me a gift, and I returned the favor with this nonsense. But after you see the ad campaign Tom and I have come up with, I *guarantee* that you'll be glad you're not having MultiCorp or Harrison Hersey and Boulder take your hard-earned money. Again, I know I have no right to ask this, but will you give us a chance to prove our worth?"

Mr. Peterson loosens his tie and throws it onto the table. "You promise it won't be like any of that other shit?"

"Mr. Peterson!" Mrs. Peterson yells. "Language."

"Well, dear," Mr. Peterson says, "that's what it was."

Mrs. Peterson sighs. "You could say manure."

Mr. Peterson rolls his eyes. "Sorry, dear." He looks us over. "Y'all ain't originally from New York, right?"

"No sir," Tom says. "I'm from Oregon, and Shari's from Virginia."

Mr. Peterson frowns. "And you think I'm gonna like what I'm about to see?"

"Yes sir," I say.

"Well," Mr. Peterson says, looking at Mrs. Peterson, "it couldn't be any worse than the *manure* we've just seen. Show me what you got."

Yes! Thank You, Lord!

I nod at Tom, Tom nods at the laughing technician, and our commercials begin. The fifteen-second spot gets a nod from Mr. Peterson. The thirty-second spot gets another nod. The radio spot earns two nods and a half smile. During the PowerPoint of all our new friends, Mr. Peterson actually smiles while Mrs. Peterson points at the screen and whispers in his ear. I look under the table and see four feet tapping in tune to "Stand by Me."

When the music ends, Tom pulls my T-shirts out of his briefcase! Where'd he get them? He hands several to Mr. Peterson. "For your grandkids."

"How did you get them, Tom?" I had completely forgotten that I had ordered them.

"Our *secretary,* Tia," he says. "Remember?"

Duh. Tia will get a lifetime supply of quesadillas for this.

Mr. Peterson holds up a shirt. "I *really* like this slogan."

"Shari designed them," Tom says. "And she came up with just about everything you've seen."

Yeah, buddy. I'm getting me some credit today.

"Get lost in America," Mr. Peterson says. "No matter where you ride, you're home." He starts to smile, the smile becomes a laugh, and the laugh turns into a hand slapping the table. "By *God,* you two!"

I hold my breath.

Mr. Peterson stands and offers his hand to me. "I knew there was something I liked about you, Miss Ross, or whatever your name is now."

"I'm Mrs. Sexton now." I take Mr. Peterson's hand, and he shakes it once. "Does this mean, um, that we're, um . . ."

Mr. Peterson nods. "You're hired."

Although I know it's completely unprofessional, I jump up onto the table in front of Tom, scoot across, and hug the skin off him.

"How soon can all this run?" Mr. Peterson asks.

Tom turns me around but leaves his hands on my hips. "It will take us most of the day, the night, and part of tomorrow morning, but we can have it all out there by five o'clock tomorrow evening."

We can? I never even thought how we'd do that. Just leave it to Tom. The man knows his details.

"How much are you asking?" Mr. Peterson asks.

Oh, it's my turn. "We're a brand-new company, Mr. Peterson, so we're only asking for the *right* to do your campaign. You've already paid us with a bicycle and your infinite patience here today."

Mr. Peterson blinks at us. "You have to be compensated somehow. With commercials like those, I might even start watching TV again. What'd it cost you to produce all that?"

"About five thousand dollars," I say. "We did all the production ourselves to keep costs down."

"There's still airtime and ad placement to pay for, Mr. Peterson," Tom says. "And that can get pretty expensive."

"You just get me on the air," he says. "Five thousand dollars. Amazing." He confers with Mrs. Peterson. "My secretary here says a hundred grand is fair. What do you say?"

I say my future baby's room is now furnished! What am I saying? My whole house is now furnished! I may even get a car out of this . . . and another pair of boots . . .

Tom nods. "It's more than fair, Mr. Peterson, and it will be our pleasure to grow with your company."

"Well, what do you call yourselves?" Mr. Peterson asks. "I want to brag on y'all down my way."

Tom winces. "Um, we've been calling our company Methuselah's Breezy Hiccup."

Mr. Peterson blinks. "That's a mouthful."

Oh no! Not again. We just won! I shouldn't have to do this!

"Excuse me, y'all." I run out of the room, find a bathroom, and spew again. There can't be anything left inside me. Why am I falling apart?

"You okay, dear?" Mrs. Peterson asks.

I didn't even hear her come in. I flush, leave the stall, and stagger to the sink, cupping the water with my hands and taking several gulps. "I don't know why I keep puking, Mrs. Peterson."

She smiles. "When did it start?"

I tell her I'm puking and she smiles? "Last night." I drink some more water. "I got out of bed just in time, and today I can't keep down anything I've eaten for more than maybe an hour."

"How many times have you puked, Shari?" she asks.

I love southern women. They get right to the point. "Three times today, four total since last night." I shake my head. "I wish I knew what it was. I am never sick. Never. I thought it was all the excitement, but I may be coming down with something."

She feels my forehead. "Sounds like morning sickness to me."

I blink at her. "But we've only . . . I mean, we've just gotten started!" Well, we did make up for a lot of lost time over the weekend.

Oh my goodness!

"You feel perfectly fine after you've puked?" she asks.

"Yeah. I do," I say. "Why is that?"

She hugs me. "I think you're pregnant, Shari."

"I can't be." Can I?

She steps back and holds my shoulders. "Most women don't have morning sickness till the fourth month or so if they even have it at all," she says, "but folks like us are the rare exceptions. I had it real bad just a day or two after conceiving all three of my kids."

I blink at myself in the mirror.

Wow.

Well.

Hmm.

I suppose I ought to be.

I mean, it's about time I was . . . somebody's mama.

I start to cry. I turn to her. "I need to tell Tom."

She nods.

I return to the conference room, wiping at tears that don't want to stop. "Sorry about that, Mr. Peterson." I step into Tom and look up.

"Are you all right?" Tom asks.

I nod, letting the tears fall. "Um, Tom, I've been rethinking our agency's name. I think we should just stick to Breezy from now on."

"Okay," he says. "Are you sure you're all right?"

"I have never been better." I look into his eyes. "And we're going to name our daughter Breezy, okay?"

He nods. "I like that name. Breezy Sexton. Very cool."

He's still not understanding me. "Um, we're going to be naming her pretty soon, Tom, like in August."

Tom's mouth drops open. He has such nice teeth. Ooh, just look at that tongue!

"And after Breezy," I continue, "we'll have a little girl named Bliss."

Tom closes his mouth, nods, and lifts me high into the air, and his shouting rattles the windows on the fifty-fifth floor of the Millennium Hotel.

I'll out-yell him later tonight at our house. The neighbors won't hear us. The city of Queens might, though.

He sets me down. "Really?"

I nod. "I think so. I've been puking all day."

He shouts again.

Pitiful. He doesn't use his diaphragm at all. I'll teach him.

After shaking hands with Mr. Peterson and filling out a contract, Tom and I stand looking out that window at all the lights of Manhattan.

"Ready to go home, Shari?" he asks.

I smile at Tom. "Man, I am already home."